RISE FROM THE ASHES

A BÁNALFAR NOVEL

C.S. HALE

RISE FROM THE ASHES

By C.S. Hale

Edited by Jody Wallace at www.jodywallace.com
And Jessica Nelson at Indie Books Gone Wild www.ibgw.net
Interior design by Gaynor Smith also of Indie Books Gone Wild
Cover design and line of kings by Melissa Stevens at theillustratedauthor.net
Map by Maria Gandolfo at Renflowergrapx

Published in the United States of America

ACKNOWLEDGEMENTS

Many different pieces go into fueling an author while he or she is working on a book. Or even the idea of a book. My thanks go out to the following who helped make Rise a reality:

Chris Carrico — Thank you for making London my city. She wouldn't have become my muse without you.

Bethany Adams — I don't know how I would have kept writing without you all these years. Well, I would have kept writing, but it wouldn't have been as much fun.

The staff at Cafè Tropea — Thank you for providing me with endless lattes while I wrote much of Rise. You provided me with a home away from home.

The guys and gals from ChapterCon — Thank you for welcoming me into your community. I am still completely gobsmacked that you awarded *Fall From the Moon* Best Book Opening.

Heather Palmquist-Lindahl and the rest of the Nashville tribe — Thank you for all of your support and encouragement over the years. And laughs. Your cat photos and Nerf fights help keep me going when I'm overwhelmed.

To the gals at Eastside RWA — Thank you for providing me with a circle of fellow writers. You are a much needed refuge from reality. I mean real life. Nah. Reality.

Ashlin — You've become my biggest fan. I count myself blessed.

P & D — You took over setting up my website while I was drowning with real life and writer life responsibilities. I can't believe I get to be your mom. This one is for you. (Seriously. Look at the next page.)

For P and D

Who always inspire me

ORBAC CARBREY - Miray
DÖNAL - Cirane   CARWYN   TOREN   YAREENA
ÖTTEN - Edinna   LAREEN - Adzil Jaharan
CAPAREN - Richeza
ENARTIN - Reina
VALEMAR - Astrid

BÁNALFAR
N
Vanerife
Lendurig
THE ARCHJARN MTS
Taspar's Bridge
Rock Dorach
CORDAIT LANDS
Torfin
Aedenfal
Gladama
THE FAIRFADA STEPPE
Verlun
Snow Reach
THE SKARGORN MOUNTAINS
Darland

CHAPTER 1

The tablet's cursor flashed, pulsing like a heartbeat, mocking me. *Recommendation…*

I shoved the tablet away. The book-sized piece of black glass skittered across the table, saved from a plunge to the floor by my correspondence box. The archaic desk instrument contrasted the sleek modernity of the tablet and illustrated the dilemma I found myself in—allow the Astrun Federation to trade for the chalcopyrite on this planet or protect the people and their medieval Earth level of development by saying "no." Either answer put me in a lose-lose situation.

Ancient enemies of my husband's people, the Cordair mined the chalcopyrite in their lands to Bánalfar's east. A "yes" would enrich their coffers, potentially funding their greatest desire—take back the lands of Bánalfar. A "no" would allow the Cordair to save the resource and fund their ambitions in the future.

I flung myself out of my chair, the harsh scratching of wood-on-wood filling my ears as the chair's legs scraped against the floor. I threw open the door and stalked back to my bedroom. The training tunic and leggings were in my hands before I consciously registered what I had reached for. They were a tight fit now around my belly, but running in the woods would lower my blood pressure and keep the once longed-for tablet intact.

Slipping down the passageways of the High, I headed to the castle's watergate. The boatman's eyes widened as he took in what I was wearing. I hadn't trained in two months, not since I had alerted the galaxy's law enforcers—the Shororato—to the presence of Hormani black market traders on the planet, but the boatman ferried me to the other side of the Leisna river without comment.

"I'm going for a run," I told him.

"Yes, my queen."

As the craft bumped into the bank, I stepped to the board in the bow and attempted to leap from the boat. The tight waistband of my leggings dug into my surprisingly tender belly, and the muscles of my core clenched, throwing off my balance. The dank, smelly water at the river's edge loomed beneath me. I grabbed handfuls of weeds, attempting to slow my progress. The long grass cut into my hands but held firm. I hauled myself up the bank, my sides heaving with the effort.

"I believe you're forgetting your shadow, my queen." Erris's youthful voice carried from across the river. The young King's Guard stood, hands on his hips, on the watergate's steps. An amused smile lit his face. Whether from my clumsy exit or from his joke, I couldn't tell.

"Am I needing a shadow?" I called back.

"If that's the way you get out of a boat, then yes."

The boatman looked at me in question. I sighed. "I guess I could do with a shadow." Erris would follow me, unseen, anyway. He'd been picked for the King's Guard for his stealth, not his fighting

prowess, and no one would let Bánalfar's pregnant queen go far without an escort.

The boatman dipped the oars, making for the landing at the watergate, an open tooth in the High's otherwise imposing walls. I crossed my arms against the chill carried on the fall breeze. I would be warm enough once I was running in the wood.

Erris sprang from the boat as it bumped back into the bank and landed lightly in the grass, hardly leaving a footprint. "Where to?" he asked with puppy-like exuberance.

"Anywhere," I said. "Just anywhere."

Valemar was waiting for me when I returned. My husband's jaw clenched as he took in my training leathers. "I thought you were done with that when the Hormani left."

"I am…I was…" I crossed to the wardrobe to strip off the sweaty clothes and avoid the scowl that twisted his face. "But it was run or destroy the tablet so I chose to run."

Valemar growled. "You still haven't decided? I thought that should have been an easy one. You risked your life to stop that trade. Why let it continue?"

My fingers fumbled on the edge of my tunic. I tightened my grip and pulled it over my head. "Because I was supposed to have been gone, too. There would have been no Outsider presence on Crenfor." I dropped the tunic to the floor. My hands strayed to my belly. My voice lowered. "Now off-worlders will always be here. The damage is done. Bánalfar and Crenfor are changed forever." Valemar stepped behind me and placed his hands over the bulge that housed the child he had longed for. "So many paths. So many futures. How can I know which one to take?"

Valemar's hands snapped back. "I would have thought the path was clear." His heavy footfall shook the floor as he walked from the room, leaving me alone, half-dressed.

Iree laced me into a gown and put my hair up but I couldn't make myself leave the dressing room. My heart hammered at the thought of facing another dinner, on display like an animal at the zoo. A hated animal.

Since the day I had arrived on the planet eight months before, I had been treated to disapproving glances and grudging acceptance by the citizens of Aedenfal. It followed me everywhere, whether I was in the castle (the High) or the town (the Low). With my dark mahogany hair, I looked too much like the Cordair, Bánalfar's enemies to the east. However, at five foot four inches tall, I was considerably shorter than the other inhabitants of the planet, and my flat, rounded ears were nothing like their erect, wolf-like ones. But a thousand years of conflict had taken its toll and covered me like a stain.

I wandered the halls of the High, hoping my feet would find the banqueting room of their own accord. But the handle my fingers closed around belonged to a different room. My breath rattled in my chest as I recognized it. I hadn't managed to go anywhere near my old quarters since my return from the capital city of Vanerife three months before. Ghosts lingered in the room and I hadn't found the courage to face them.

Somehow the knob turned and the door opened, creaking on hinges stiff with disuse. I lit a rushlight from the hall sconce and peered into the dark. Holding the small candle like a talisman, I stepped in.

The bed was still there. The table with its bottles and decanters. I ran my fingers down the bottle of üsgeh. The whiskey-like alcohol had once provided me with the courage to get through the night of my unexpected wedding.

I swallowed hard and bit my lips as my gaze fell on the door to my former dressing room. Placing the rushlight in a holder, I searched for the strength to open the door. While its hinges moved freely, it scraped across my heart.

The racks were vacant, the shelves bare. Everything had been moved to my current dressing room upon my return from Vanerife. The space was empty but somehow still filled with Daria's calming presence.

My knees gave way and slammed into the floor. "I miss you." I closed my eyes and pulled up the memory of the soft strokes of the brush as she dressed my hair. I could see her face right behind me, smiling at me in the mirror that now lay thick with dust and neglect.

Daria had been more than my dresser. She had been the first true friend I had made in Bánalfar. Daria would have walked me through the trade scenarios, helped me to see which was the correct path. Or simply held my hand and told me that everything would be okay.

I clutched the edge of the chair; afraid I would sink even further onto the ground. "Oh, Daria," I whispered. "What have I done? How can I choose?"

The rushlight had long gone out. Darkness covered me like a blanket as I lay on the floor. My hands had eventually become too weary to hold me up. The floorboard by the bedroom door squeaked. Light flickered in the hall and soon filled the room.

"Thank the Mother," Valemar whispered as he spied my prostrate form. In an instant, he was at my side. He brushed the hair from my face and pulled me into his lap. "Oh, Astrid."

I stared at the chair legs. I couldn't bear to see pity etched onto his face. "I miss her."

"I know." Valemar's hand swept down my hair, a painful imitation of Daria's brushstrokes.

I forced my cramped legs to unfold and struggled to my feet, leaning on Valemar's arm for support. "I should go…we should go." It was too hard to feel Daria's presence with Valemar looming over me.

He laced his fingers through mine. I gave them a squeeze, mainly to stop the questions I didn't feel like answering. I swallowed down the lump in my throat and offered up a prayer, my eyes tracing the once familiar walls, and led Valemar from the room.

I didn't bother getting out the tablet and staring at the message the next day. "Yes." "No." Both would result in catastrophe for Bánalfar and Crenfor, despite Valemar's insistence that the answer was easy.

After breakfast, I put on the leather training tunic and leggings and stood in the side doorway of the courtyard until Erris noticed me. He motioned to the King's Guard opposite him and melted into the shadows. Another guard soon took up the vacated place.

There was no boyish bounce to Erris's step when he joined me. I left my questions alone and hoped the run would put the spring back into his stride. We took the boat to the far bank of the Leisna and ran through the woods and fields that surrounded Aedenfal.

The run quickly became the hide-and-seek game that Erris loved so much—the two of us creeping along, spying on others.

When I began to get winded, we sat in the cover of a grove and watched a farmer harvesting some kind of root vegetable. It was well into autumn, and though Aedenfal would have been warmed by the Coriolis Effect on a coast, the mountains to the south and east trapped the chill, promising a freeze in the days to come.

"What is he harvesting?" I asked Erris, still unfamiliar with much of the flora and fauna of Bánalfar.

"Torna," Erris said. "They'll keep until the spring vegetables begin to grow." He snapped off a blade of grass and twisted it between his fingers, eyes still focused on the farmer and his work. "What are you running from, my queen?" His voice was hardly louder than the breeze winding its way through the barren branches.

I plucked a longer blade of grass and wound it around my index finger. I opened my mouth to answer but the words wouldn't come, only a soft sigh as I exhaled.

The farmer kept at his task, stabbing the pronged spade into the ground, pushing on the handle until it raised the soil-covered vegetables, knocking the earth from the white and purple globes before throwing them into the waiting cart.

Erris was right, I was running. Just a month ago my most fervent wish had been to stay on the planet, and now here I was—running away.

I dropped the grass and got to my feet, leaving Erris's question unanswered. In my former life, I'd always been on the move, and it felt good to have at least the ground traveling beneath my feet if not the vastness of space passing outside my window.

Erris pushed himself up, his eyes focused on the ground. A flush crept across his face.

"You are very observant," I said. "But I have no answers for you as I have none for myself." I attempted a lopsided grin.

The red receded from his face and his usual boyish grin grew. *Knave indeed.*

Erris's eyes twinkled. "Then I suppose we should run."

I chuckled. He was right. If I was running away then I should at least be running.

I returned from my run with Erris and went to bathe and dress for dinner. Though the two hundred people assembled in the hall rose when Valemar and I entered, there were few friendly faces to greet me. Cadalin had moved back to her lodgings in the Low with the departure of the Hormani, and Bréick, her son was too young to leave behind. I saw little of Vienne, the weaver's wife, and Niah, her daughter-in-law, except from across the room. Other duties had taken up my time since my return from Vanerife, and with Laera, the steward's wife, still in exile in Lendurig, they only came to the High for dinner.

My hand strayed to my belly as Valemar and I sat, and the quiet thunder of four hundred feet filled the hall. I had first met the women when they were sewing clothes for Bréick. At some point, my child would need a layette. Before long, I would need to set aside my other roles and take up that one—a woman who invited other women to sew with her. But Daria would not be among them like she had before. I would have no shield, no true friend.

Valemar squeezed my hand under the table but I didn't meet his eyes. If I did, all of Aedenfal would see the tears I barely held back fall. I forced a smile and turned my attention to Padrid, Aedenfal's librarian. He, too, smiled, but it didn't reach his eyes.

I wondered what was bothering him and realized that Valemar had leaned away from me, caught up in whispered conversation with Garris, the steward. The mental gears in my head began to turn

with a nearly audible click. Something was wrong. My smile curled up even further as my inner protocol specialist took over. *Mask the truth.* Rule twenty-one. I needed to be more merry so that the others watching wouldn't take alarm.

My heart beat out a tempo, striking against my ribs. "Tell me," I whispered toward Padrid, and hoped that my forced amusement had reached my eyes.

His cup came to his mouth, blocking his lips from view and any who could read them. "Just rumors from Snow Reach."

I laughed though the wine in my stomach turned to stone. Adan, the steward of Snow Reach, had died mysteriously not long before I arrived on Crenfor. Adan's karawack, Sari, had since bonded to me. Sometimes an echo of her shriek at his passing traced along our link, raising goosebumps on my skin.

I waited until we'd returned to our rooms to ask Valemar what he had heard. Waited until he was intent on unlacing the ribbon that bound me into the silk-like gown of anapali wool.

"What's the news from Snow Reach?"

Valemar's fingers fumbled with the lace. Tremors shot down the ribbon, coursing through the stiff fabric that held the eyelets. "Nothing for you to worry about."

I turned to face him. "But you are worried."

Valemar's fingers traced my jaw. A sad light filled his eyes, and he pulled me into his arms. Valemar's head brushed against mine as he peered down my back, and his fingers returned to their task. The ribbon finally came free. He eased the gown from my shoulders.

My breasts had swelled with pregnancy though my stomach showed only a pooch that previously would have signaled an overindulgent meal. Valemar's gaze traveled from my breasts to my stomach, a tangle of emotions filling his eyes. Anger. Hunger. Loss.

It should have been easy. The Shororato had allowed me to stay, something Valemar and I had thought impossible just a month before. But he had never had an easy time matching his expectations of me with reality. I stood before him, still here and miraculously pregnant, but unable to give him what he wanted—the Cordair hamstrung, stuck in their mountains, and no threat to the Alfari. At least, that was what he thought denying Federation trade with the Cordair would bring. And looking at my belly, where his child grew, only reminded him of all the uncertainty.

I reached up and cradled his face. "Tell me."

Valemar's eyes flashed with hurt. He reached up, grasped my hands, and removed them. A muscle ticked in his jaw.

Then he dropped my hands and strode from the room.

CHAPTER 2

I wolfed down my breakfast and put on my training leathers the next morning. Alone, I ran all the way back to the farm to watch the farmer continue his harvest. The bark bit into my spine as I leaned against the tree, and I welcomed the pain for it distracted my body from the ache in my heart.

Stab…push…thump…stab…push…thump.

It could have been the blood coursing through my heart instead of the pitchfork.

I leaned my head against the tree. The farmer had a task to do. He was gathering the fruits of the year's labor, preparing for the scarcity of winter. I lifted my head as the revelation hit me. I had spent all my time on Crenfor preparing for a confrontation with the Hormani and the Cordair, but my harvest had not been what I had expected. Or what Valemar had expected. I had expected to be removed from the planet and spend the rest of my days in prison. Valemar had expected that the Hormani traders would be forced to leave and that the Shororato would keep the Cordair on a tight leash. It had nearly killed him when I'd told him the truth—that I wasn't supposed to be on the planet either and the Shororato would remove me, too.

And then Shale had revealed that I was pregnant. I got to stay, and Valemar had thought that our lives would finally be simple. Simple like the farmer still at his task—*stab...push... thump*. But it was so much more complicated for me.

A branch cracked behind me. My head whipped around.

Erris stepped through the brush, and I laughed. He had made the noise so that he wouldn't startle me.

I turned my gaze back to the farmer as Erris came to stand next to me.

"We could ask him if he'd like some help," Erris said.

I snorted. "Sure, and probably give the guy heart failure, making him wrestle with whether or not he should allow Bánalfar's queen to dig in his garden."

Erris shrugged. "They all know you want to be a servant queen."

I arched an eyebrow. "And you really think he'd put a pregnant woman to work?"

"Oh, yeah." The rest of Erris's air rushed out. "I keep forgetting you're pregnant."

But Erris was right. I was a servant queen. I couldn't serve by harvesting crops, but I could serve in other ways. I just needed to figure out what to do.

It had been weeks since I had visited the Cair. Weeks since I had donned the long red veil and walked the twisting streets of the Low to the city's cathedral, though I hadn't been veiled the last time, the day that Valemar had gathered the inhabitants to tell them that the Shororato were coming. And somehow, I hadn't seen Shale—

Bánalfar's seer, their Mödatal—since she'd broken the news of my pregnancy and saved me from being sent to the Shororato prison on Karjiny Five.

I mulled that over on the mile or so walk through town, hidden by the lace that marked me as a worshipper and flanked by my King's Guard escort. Shale had saved my life over and over. And here I was, hoping she'd rescue me again.

Galwin took up position in the hall of the Cair's dormer. Segur waited in the nave. I lifted my hand to knock on Shale's door.

"It's open, Astrid," she called before my hand could touch the wood. *Show off.*

Shale sat curled up in her chair, her bare feet tucked next to her. Her long, red hair spilled past her pointed ears and onto her shoulders. "Tea?" she asked as she gestured for me to take the seat across from her.

The flames flickering in the open grate of the fireplace filled the darkness of her rooms with a warmth that didn't quite dispel the chill that had settled into my soul. I huffed lightly before I said, "Yes, please."

Shale arched an eyebrow as she poured me a cup. "It's good for your growing baby and not just conception."

The stream of amber liquid stopped, and I picked up the cup. "Are you still trying or are you expecting as well?"

"Still trying." A serene smile lit her face. Shale picked her cup up and curled back into her chair. "Ask."

I ran a finger along the rim of my cup. "How can I serve?"

"You are serving."

"As a brood mare." The harshness in my voice surprised me. "As…" I squeezed my eyes shut. How could I explain the impossible position the Shororato had put me in?

Shale sighed. "You are already doing what you can. You will be called upon to do more —"

"More?" I whispered.

She sighed again. "You are feeling more alone than you expected to. You *are* more alone than you expected." My eyes stung as I lifted them to hers. A gentle sadness filled her green eyes before they closed. "You are still the Moon Princess. You have fulfilled the prophecy but your role continues." A small shudder twitched her face.

My breath caught. She had "seen" something unexpected and was now trying to hide it from me. Several heartbeats passed. Tension gathered in the room.

Shale's face finally relaxed. Her eyes reopened. "I know it's hard," she continued. "I know Valemar is angry with you. He is stuck in his vision of what the world should be like—again—and is punishing you for not meeting it. But you are the Moon Princess. What you needed to do was revealed to you when you were ready. And it will be again."

My heart clenched. The last task had nearly killed me in so many ways. "I don't know how to begin," I whispered.

"You will," she said. As she had said so many times before. "Just follow your heart."

Shale's words were of little comfort but I knew she wouldn't tell me more. Lost in my thoughts, I wandered back to the High, searching for a pattern, some thread to follow to anchor me as I moved toward the future. I shut out the street noise—the rumble of carts and the tangle of voices in conversation that swirled around me. Galwin's bulk parted the crowd with ease and Segur's watchful eyes never missed a cue, which made the icy sensation that pierced my veil and lifted the hairs on my neck all the more startling.

Shivers ran down my spine, causing me to stumble. Galwin's hand shot out to steady me. "What is it, my queen?" he asked. His other hand gripped the hilt of his sword, ready to pull it out. Segur closed in, placing me securely between them, as he scanned the road.

"Nothing," I said, lifting a smile they would never see beneath my veil. I had a sense of curtains falling back into place somewhere behind me, a change of light perhaps. I often noticed tiny things others didn't, one of the reasons I always trusted my instincts. In fact, I had even made *Trust your instincts* number twenty-three on the list of rules I'd created as when I worked as a protocol specialist.

Goosebumps rose along my arms, but there was no concrete threat to alert my guards to. Just a feeling that something wasn't as it should be. "I wasn't paying attention to my footing. I'm sorry if I alarmed you."

I forced one foot in front of the other as Galwin placed his bear-like bulk more distinctly between me and the people lining the streets who pressed themselves against the stuccoed walls to keep from being trod on.

The cold patch remained on the back of my neck, setting my nerves on high alert. God, I hated this town.

Window boxes that had been so cheery in summer were now empty, framing windows dark and hollow like a crowd of lidless eyes, observing my every step. I lifted my head higher, even though it tightened my throat and made it difficult to draw a deep breath. Just a half mile to go. I could do that.

I had never been so relieved to pass beneath the portcullis of the High's gate. "Thank you," I told Galwin and Segur. I kept the veil in place instead of pulling it off, the better to hide the panic no doubt etched on my face.

"Our pleasure, my queen."

The cold confines of the High added its own barrier between me and whomever had been watching me. Safely in my room, I stripped off the veil and tossed it across the bed. My mouth opened and closed as I fought back the urge to gulp air into my constricted lungs. Hyperventilating wouldn't help. A soft whine wormed its way up my throat and filled my ears. I paced the room, waving my hands to dispel the feeling and silence the noise.

I knew someone had been watching me. Just as they had on my wedding day.

I stopped short as the memory surfaced. The eerie feeling that someone wished me harm. I had walked many times to the Cair and to the shops in the Low and hadn't had a repeat of that odd sensation. Until today.

I left the room and headed for the stairs that led to the High's ramparts.

A rabbit warren of twisting passageways, Aedenfal's High had been constructed with confusion in mind. But after nine months of exploration, I had learned my way around. Better than I wanted to in some cases.

I pushed open the heavy wooden door. The crenellations rose higher than my head then lowered to chest height. The pathway between them was wide enough for a man to swing a sword. I walked about halfway down to where the path widened out on the roof of the High's round tower, nodded to the guard I passed, and paused along the wall where I could see both the Leisna and the Low.

I shivered as I looked back upon the route I'd taken to the Cair and then swung my gaze over to the woods that lined the far bank of the river. Even the trees felt like they reached for me. My breath became a weight, slowly suffocating me.

My hands gripped the rough stone. I closed my eyes and leaned forward, mentally pushing at the tightness that gripped my chest.

Air was never this hard to come by in Torfin, Glábac, or Vanerife. Aedenfal always seemed to press it from my lungs.

I opened my eyes at the sound of footsteps and straightened up. Concern etched the guard's face. I flashed him a warm smile and held it in place until he retreated back to his post.

Town. Trees. Stuff, everywhere I looked. I turned my gaze upward. The sky was a blotchy, steel gray. Clouds hid the blue that had been visible all summer, but the air didn't carry the distinct smell of rain. Yet another blanket to cover me.

A breeze lifted the hair from my shoulders and pushed the darker splotches across the sky.

Open sky. Stars.

I wanted to see the stars…all around me.

But that was never going to happen again.

I stayed on the rampart, watching the clouds race by, hoping for a break in the gloomy veil. The guards changed and still I stood, even when I could hear people entering the courtyard, gathering for dinner.

I sat when I saw the first pinprick appear in the darkening sky, curled my back up against the stone and let the tiny light work its way into my soul. At first, it played hide and seek with the clouds. When the clouds grew fewer, other stars came out to join it. My breath began to condense as the chill of the autumn night air settled in.

The weather was a clue as to the season but I had no idea how long their year was or how many months they counted. *Something I really should rectify.*

Most likely, they would have something similar to an Earth year. Planets need a special set of circumstances to support life. The blood-red moon rising somewhere behind me was one. Or any moon to pull the seas and keep things from stagnating. Planets must also be a certain distance from their sun—not too warm, not too cold. And they need a quick enough rotation so that one side didn't boil while the other side froze.

The sky darkened and more stars appeared in the deep blue curtain overhead. I leaned my head back and soaked them in, blinked as moisture grew in my eyes. I missed the quiet darkness and vastness of space. I had been able to breathe there.

I sat there long enough that I had to tuck my toes under my skirt and ball up my hands under my arms to keep them warm. I might have sat there all night if Valemar hadn't come looking for me. I sensed his presence as soon as he entered the rampart, but kept my gaze on the heavens.

The guttering torches threw his face into a jumble of light and shadow. A sight I caught in my periphery, afraid to see the expression on his face.

"Astrid."

He took the cloak from his shoulders and covered me with it. I shivered in the sudden warmth as his transferred body heat leached into my chilled frame. Valemar lowered himself to sit beside me.

"You've never taught me the constellations," I said, as my eyes traced the stars again, searching for something familiar in their pattern.

Valemar rested his arms on his knees. "Something I've neglected."

"You're going to have to go to Snow Reach," I said as the fear that had been lingering around me all day finally took form. That was what I was afraid of, wasn't it? That he would leave me alone in this place that sucked the very essence from my soul.

"I hope not."

It wouldn't be the wisest thing to do—move an army to a mountainous stronghold this close to winter. *Just how close* was *winter?*

I leaned my head against him, eyes still fixed on the one thing that allowed me to breathe. "I'd ask you again, what the possibility is, but I have a feeling I'd get the same answer."

Steam swirled around us as Valemar exhaled and his breath condensed. His hand snaked under the cloak and found mine. I shivered anew as my body realized just how cold I'd let it get. Valemar drew me to him.

I relaxed in the warmth and security his arms offered. Safe. Protected. For the moment, understood. But his silence told me he had given me as much information as he would. *Fine.* I had my own secrets. Like the strange sense I'd had of being watched on the way back from the Cair. There were enough shadows in Snow Reach without adding others to Valemar's list. I would just have to trust that Shale would warn me if any serious threat developed.

Valemar rested his chin on my head. "Have you had enough stargazing for the evening?"

"No," I said, and sighed. "But I suppose you're going to tell me it's time to go in."

Valemar gave me a squeeze and then pointed at the sky. "See the box those four stars form there? Then the curve?" His hand traced the air in front of me. "That's Gairgé, the hunter."

A hunter in the sky. "Orion," I whispered, and bit my lip, fighting back the pain that washed over me. I hadn't realized how much I missed the familiar pattern.

"Orion?"

I blinked. "We have a hunter constellation on Earth, too. Different shape, though. What else is out there?" I asked. I needed to make this my sky.

Valemar's hand crossed over me to point into the sky at my left. "See those two bright stars? And then, if you follow it over—" His hand moved to the right. "—there are three that rise and fall with those other three little stars trailing off like a tail."

They did look like a tail. "Uh huh."

Valemar nuzzled my ear. "That's Gregar, the sky bohar. He's the herald of autumn."

My eyes began to sting. This was what my life was supposed to be like now. This was my reward for having sacrificed myself to rid Crenfor of the Hormani. Not more politics to drive a wedge between me and my husband.

"I love you," I whispered to Valemar.

"I love you, too," Valemar said, and my breath hitched in my chest.

"Show me some others," I said, wanting to stay the way we were for as long as possible, for I knew the hours would be few before the stupid trade agreement would turn my usually tender husband back into an angry king.

CHAPTER 3

I found Padrid in the library in the morning. There was much about Crenfor I had neglected to learn. At first, when everything had been new, I had focused on the things necessary for my survival and then, when I thought I'd be leaving, I had switched to the those that would enable me to call the Shororato. It was time to fill the gaps.

Aedenfal hierarchy, my brain supplied. I would need to study it sometime, but today I needed to learn to mark time. Oh, I knew the hours in a day and that Blood Moons—full moons—came every thirty days, but what about the rest of it? Pircyon Six had yearlong seasons. A three-year-old child might have never experienced snow or summer. Anaterris Three's orbit gave them year-round summer, a condition that created alternating rings of rainforest and desert around the planet.

The seasons on Crenfor were longer than those on Earth. I had been on Crenfor nine months, arriving when spring was just shifting into summer. Now we were into autumn.

"How many months are there in a year?" I asked Padrid.

His shaggy gray eyebrows rose. "Sixteen."

"Oh." I pulled out a chair and dropped into it. That made their years…a third longer than Earth's. And raised so many more questions.

I had just begun to consider what that meant for life expectancy when Padrid closed the book he had been reading. "I take from your reaction that things are different on…Earth."

"We have twelve months that average thirty days each."

"Ah—" he began before a puzzled frown grew, pulling his brow into heavy creases. "Average?"

"Most months have thirty or thirty-one. One month has twenty-eight but every four years they add in an additional day to catch the calendar back up to the actual orbit."

"Your calendar must have been losing time at some point."

"Yes, it became a holiday for fools when they corrected it. If you didn't know when it was actually April first then you were a fool who could be tricked by anything." Padrid laughed. I looked down. "And I feel like fool for not having asked about the months of the year before."

You didn't know you were staying, his eyes said. "And you'd like to know now."

I shrugged. "I seems important now. Summer seemed to last forever, and now…" My eyes were drawn to my belly.

Padrid leaned forward and patted my arm. "Of course."

He stood up and went to one of the bookcases, bringing back a book that, though large in size, was thin. Gold letters spelled out *Tre Ata Léirth do na Sasira*.

"*An Illustrated Guide to the Seasons,*" Padrid said, though his was not the only voice I heard. The language chip I'd had implanted in my brain when I first started working for Agçay Enterprises spoke with him, translating what I assumed was old Alfari.

Padrid opened the book and turned the protective cover page. I gasped. The depth of the colors and gloss of the image after what had to be hundreds or even thousands of years was incredible.

"Are there crushed gems in the paint?" I asked.

Padrid chuckled. "You know a bit about everything, don't you, my queen?"

I smiled. "You're right. I often do." It was a side effect of the years I had spent as a protocol specialist, researching information for not only the business deals I was involved in but the things needed to sweeten the deal for Agçay's many clients. "Just not when it comes to Crenfor."

A large yellow sun sparkled on the page, glittering with an iridescence that I attributed to topaz. Sixteen red objects circled it. Each glowed with the scarlet hue of Crenfor's blood red moon and were labeled with what I took to be the names of the months. The page was quartered and showed scenes from the four seasons—the state of the plants and trees, glimpses of the weather, people at work.

"Where are we now?" I asked Padrid.

"Redhar—End of Harvest." His lips quirked up. "Do you know the day?"

From the illustration, I assumed that the full Blood Moon counted as the first day but I'd never kept track of the time between the moons, partly because I wasn't overcome with the urge to mate on the nights of the full moon, unlike the rest of the people on Crenfor, and partly because life here didn't seem to be divided into weeks, something my Earth-born body still expected, despite the amount of time I had spent traveling the stars.

"No," I said. "My people divide their months into periods of seven days. The ancient peoples used to mark the days of rest and worship—six days of work and a day of rest. You have only the

Blood Moon and the Resting Moon." I observed the first because of the changes it wrought in my husband and the second not at all. The Resting Moon, their new moon, was a time when people went to the Cair to pray that the Blood Moon had brought a child.

My fingers lightly touched my belly where my impossible child grew.

"Seven days?" Padrid said. "They marked out days of rest and worship?"

"Well, God only worked for six making all of creation and then rested on the seventh, so how could we lowly humans be expected to work for more days than God?"

"So Father Sea rested after he worked?" Padrid asked.

"Bigger than Father Sea," I told Padrid. "The god that shaped many of the cultures on my planet is said to have created everything in the universe."

Padrid's lips moved in a silent "*but…but…*" His eyes widened, and he nodded. "I guess you would need to rest after that much work."

"And the Alfari don't?" None of us had ever taken "time off." Not Valemar or Iree, my dresser, or any of the other Alfari I knew. We just moved through life from one day to the next.

"What would you need to rest from?" Padrid asked.

"Work," I answered.

Padrid's eyebrows lifted. "Why would you need to rest from work?"

"Because, without rest, a person's energy burns out, much like a candle," I said.

Padrid looked at me askance. "People on Earth need their rest mandated? They can't manage their energy on their own?"

"They…" I drifted off. Retired people did. They often didn't know what day of the week it was, yet they still did the work of

running their lives. "They are easily caught up in their striving to accomplish more," I said. "The day of rest was a reminder that there is more to life than work. That your workers have lives to lead and families to cherish, as well."

"Greedy," Padrid said under his breath.

"True."

Padrid's face grew serious and he leaned closer. "You can tell Valemar, if you want, but I wouldn't go talking about your 'weeks' to anyone else." His eyes rose, taking in my dark hair. "Might give others the wrong idea about your people."

My cheeks colored. I shivered, remembering the feeling of being watched the day before.

Padrid placed his hand on mine. "It will be our secret." He pointed back to the illustrations. "Today is the twenty-third day of Redhar. The next moon marks the beginning of the month of Dureth and the beginning of the winter season."

"Do you get snow here at Aedenfal?" I asked. The winter quarter of the illustration had been done in blues, greens, browns, and white.

"Yes, though not usually until Eanir and Lardreth," Padrid said, naming off the next two months.

Summer here had been longer than I usually experienced. Actually, it had been nine years since I had experienced a full season anywhere. With all my traveling, a few days, sometimes as many as fourteen, were all I had planet-side. This would be followed by a couple of weeks on a starship as we returned to Earth. I would have a few days on my home planet and then I'd be off again.

I stretched my back, hoping to dispel the buzz that coursed through my veins. Maybe my hatred of Aedenfal was just frustration at not getting to travel any more.

"So there are sixteen months, four to each season," I said, forcing my focus back to the illumination. "Is there a song that teaches children the months of the year?"

Padrid chuckled and then began to sing in a deep baritone voice,

"Luthrach, Breán, Earlar, Dérach
Seeds are planted, sprouts then spring up.
Amduil, Fásmil, Lúil, Dresam
These will greet the summer's bright sun.
Anform, Gihru, Dorchma, Redhar
Harvest soon we all will gather.
Dureth, Eanir, Lardreth, Gheistor
Winter's chill spent by the fire.
Spring and summer, autumn, winter
Now a year has passed us over."

The tune was catchy and definitely something I could learn. I sang it softly, reading the months written under the red moons that glowed from the gems embedded in the paint, Padrid joining in when I lost the tune.

"Does your year start with Luthrach?" I asked.

"It does."

"Any holidays or festivals?" The only one I had experienced thus far was the pilgrimage to Glábac. The King's Wine was an important event but I had missed it when Valemar had banished me to Vanerife.

"Gellirhird is held on the first day of Lardreth. We give thanks for the bright light of the moon in the depths of winter."

Bright light. I held back a snort. A full, red moon was still dark compared to the near daylight glow of Earth's full moon.

"Altbain, the New Year, is celebrated on the first day of Luthrach. The first crops are sown and, despite the chill in the night air, Blood Moon couplings are usually done outside. Comrach—High Summer—is often celebrated by picnics under the sun in the late evening, but it is not as widely observed here in Bánalfar compared to Darland where the light lingers until almost midnight.

"The Alfari tend to view every day as a gift from the Mother and the Father. Just as people go to the Cair when they want, we feel no need to slow down as your people do. The moon brings us all together once a month and gives us rest once a month. The trees, the animals, feel no need to 'take a day of rest.' Why should we?"

Why indeed?

We broke for lunch when I received a note from General Creskin. The head of the Shororato garrison on Crenfor had written to request an audience this afternoon since I wasn't *"using the tablet."* More than two days had passed since I had last been able to bring myself to turn it on. My lips twitched as I refolded the paper and tucked it back in the envelope. The poor man was going to have to make the four-hour ride from the Shororato encampment out by the Fairfada. I wondered how he would fare, being used to the near instantaneous travel starships afforded.

The calculations danced in my head. He was already on his way. The note in my hand was his way of telling me not to go anywhere.

I went up to my room to have Iree help me change. Though I was officially the Astrun Federation ambassador, General Creskin had a tendency to view me as Protocol Specialist Carr. I wanted to ensure that it was Queen Astrid Carbrev that he met with.

Iree laced me into a blue gown that represented the Lian Isles of Bánalfar and I had her place the gold and silver crown studded with peridot on my head. I frowned at the image of it in the mirror. Valemar's long, white blond hair blended with the gold and silver and became part of the crown, almost like a halo. My dark hair created no such illusion. I preferred the crown with the cabochon rubies but the Moon Princess reference would be lost on the general.

I also decided to meet with him in the throne room. Valemar poked his head in while I waited for General Creskin.

"Receiving by yourself?" he asked.

"Astrun business," I said, hoping he wouldn't linger. Valemar had still not forgiven the general for nearly taking me away and I feared they would become two bulls, locking horns.

"As king—"

"You are not needed," I said, cutting him off. I went to him. "I don't require your protection."

Valemar opened his mouth and then closed it. A scowl lifted into place. "Very well," he said in terse reply and turned to go.

"Valemar—"

But my husband just raised a hand in farewell as I stared at the back of his retreating form. The door to the council chambers closed behind him.

"Great," I muttered. About ten minutes later Tovan alerted me that the general was approaching. I placed myself on the green velvet cushion that lined my throne as four King's Guard came in a side entrance and took up positions by the main door.

It opened moments later. The general was alone and without the helmet that matched the rest of his white armor. "Ambassador Carbrev," he said in acknowledgement.

"General."

The general eyes scanned the four guards flanking the door. "Perhaps somewhere a little more private."

Shit. I lifted a smile into place. "Of course."

I rose from the throne like the queen I was and gestured toward the door Valemar had disappeared through. "This way."

The general mounted the steps to follow me, the King's Guard watching him all the way.

I said a little prayer as I opened the door and held back a sigh of relief when I found the room empty. I crossed to the head of the table and sat in the elaborately carved chair. The general did not sit.

"We still don't have your assessment," he said.

I tapped my fingers against the table. "It's not an easy 'yes' or 'no.' There are many factors to take into consideration."

"Then I should tell you that limited trade has begun with the Cordair."

"What?" I snapped. "According to Astrun Federation rules, nothing can go off-planet without its citizens' consent."

"And the Cordair do consent, Ambassador Carr."

"Carbrev," I corrected. I clenched my fists. "Do you want me to say 'no' right now? You would not have engaged in this trade if I was not still on this planet."

"But you are on this planet. You are changing this world. Your every day here does that, and though you are carrying a child of this world, he or she will make an even bigger impact on this planet—an alien child that may one day rule this country." My heart skipped a beat. I fought to make sure it didn't show on my face. "You have made no recommendation, and so the Astrun Federation is willing to listen to other of Teridun's—"

"Crenfor's," I corrected.

"—inhabitants."

I nearly gave him a "no" right then. "So the Astrun Federation has decided to become Hormani traders?" The general turned scarlet. I sat back in the chair. "Why did I call you?"

"Because the Hormani would have eventually succeeded in killing you."

The blood drained from my face and then rushed right back in. Loss and anger wrestled for control of my emotions. I drew a deep breath through my nose. "War between the Alfari and the Cordair is but a knife edge away. The Hormani made it so. Trade in that ore made it so. You would be assisting the Cordair in their efforts."

"And doing nothing will ensure the Cordair move against you anyway," General Creskin said.

I took another deep breath as I collected my thoughts. "How much ore are we talking?"

"Half a ton to start."

My breath came out in a rush. It was an utter fortune at fair market value. Chalcopyrite olivine was the most valuable substance I had come across in the galaxy. "And what are you paying them?" I lifted an eyebrow, emphasizing the question. General Creskin knew I was aware of the mineral's true value.

"Gold." But he didn't say how much.

I sat up and massaged my forehead. "Miners were willing to take gold?"

"Well they're not getting alien technology."

It was robbery, even if they were handing over the same weight as the chalcopyrite, which I didn't think they were. It was robbery. And yet...

There was no way to balance the scales. Compensation at the ore's true value would give the Cordair the resources to buy anything—arms...armies—to enable them to take back Bánalfar.

Gold was valuable but wouldn't make that large of an impact on Cordair coffers.

The general had made clear this was happening with or without my consent. "*One* shipment," I said. "You can delay the others. Tell them you need to check its purity or something." A pounding started right behind my eyes.

General Creskin dipped his head in agreement. "One shipment." He turned for the door. "You've bought yourself some time, Ambassador," he said over his shoulder. "Use it well."

CHAPTER 4

I toyed with how I was going to tell Valemar. Or if. The one thing—no, the only thing—he had wanted from me as the Moon Princess was the Cordair's ambitions stopped for good.

You always keep him in the dark, an insidious little voice whispered in my head.

That was true. Especially when the stakes were high. I pushed myself out of the chair. Maybe a bath would soak away the worry.

I brushed my hands through the water, creating waves that splashed against the sides and reminded me of the waves that broke against the shore in Vanerife. Would Valemar send me into exile again when I told him about the trade? He couldn't wait to be rid of me when I had finally confessed that I wasn't actually from their moon. Had Daria not died in an attempt on my life, I might still be in Vanerife.

I let my mind drift, watching the ripples my hands created. Vanerife had felt more like home than Aedenfal ever had, even though Valemar had not been there. And now, even though Daria would not be there, even though she had died there, I missed it.

All too soon, Iree opened the towel, warmed by the fire to dispel the autumn chill seeping into the room, and dried me off.

"Which dress would you like to wear tonight, my queen?" she asked.

"The gold one, I think." I hardly ever wore it for it cast a sallow pallor on my skin but I longed for the warmth of at least the color.

Gold. I squeezed my eyes shut, trying to block out the image of the Cordair payment.

The color still felt right. *Trust your instincts*. Rule twenty-three. So I did.

Valemar could tell something was wrong as soon as I joined him outside the doors to the banqueting hall. A frown creased his brow. But I merely placed my hand atop his and faced the doors. At least they opened without fanfare, though the sound of the crowd rising to their feet was loud enough to beat against my skin.

"You'll have to tell me sometime why meals have this tradition," I said to Valemar, raising a smile that felt more cheeks than lips.

Valemar inclined his head to the assembly and so did I before we made our way to the table.

"How did your meeting go with General Creskin?" Valemar asked as we washed our hands.

I dried mine and handed the towel back to the server. "Not now," I whispered.

Valemar gave me a sharp glance.

Padrid was seated at my right, something I normally enjoyed but I was in no mood for his enthusiasm. I scanned the room. I still didn't know the vast majority of the inhabitants, something PS Carr would never have been guilty of.

Fine. I pushed Astrid—me—away and searched my soul for PS Carr. She was tucked up in a corner, hiding. A wave of sympathy broke over me. This had been the place of her death. She'd stepped into the escape pod onboard the dying *Palmas Cove*, crashed to earth on the Fairfada, and invented me to survive. I was not the wisecracking smartass she had been.

She's still part of you and you are who she is, a voice whispered in my head.

I straightened my spine and leaned toward Padrid. "Just who are all these people?"

"They are mainly inhabitants from the first few blocks around the High. You see, they were once the last line of defense between us and invading armies," he explained. My eyes widened. "They came when needed, and so the tradition has been to welcome them back every evening. We feed them and thank them so that should they ever be needed again—"

"They'll feel beholden," I said.

"Not exactly the intention," he said. His brow pinched in thought. "Though that would be the result."

I scanned the room again. Two hundred people gathered here every evening to protect their king.

From me.

Yes, that certainly explained my reception. "Why haven't you told me this before?"

Padrid shrugged. "You never asked."

My gaze roamed over the crowd again. A man seated three tables away stared at me. I lifted a smile but he ignored my greeting. Instead, he bent his head and whispered in the ear of the man on his left.

I closed my eyes and drew up the mental armor of PS Carr. One table at a time. I could learn them one table at a time.

Valemar brushed the hair from my still flushed face and kissed me again. "How did your meeting go with General Creskin, my *grabeg*?"

I pulled back, pushing myself deeper into the mattress. "You want to know now?" I asked, staring up at him.

Valemar caressed my lips with his. "Well, I did ask you earlier and you deferred your answer to later. This is later."

I gathered my resolve and pressed him firmly against me. My neck arched as blood rushed to my groin. "Remember this—" I said, and curled my legs around his. Valemar gave a contented groan. "—and not the anger."

Valemar reared back. "Anger?" His eyes flashed, the warrior awakening.

The sight stopped my words. He had thrown furniture in Glábac when I told him I wasn't from the moon.

Fear must have shown on my face for the fire in his eyes dimmed. Valemar toyed with my hair. "Why would there be anger?"

I swallowed. "Because…" The deal with the Cordair hadn't been of my doing but Valemar wouldn't see it that way. He'd been wanting me to tell the Federation "no" for weeks. And I could have said "no" today, but I hadn't. "Because something came up." Valemar pushed away, pressing his forearms against the mattress. I shivered as his warm chest lifted away from mine. I increased my grip on his legs. "And you're not going to be happy about it."

"As-trid." Valemar drew my name out in warning.

Don't send me away. The words rose on my lips but I didn't speak them. "I agreed to one exchange of the chalcopyrite."

Every muscle on his chiseled body stood out as Valemar tensed. Slowly, he reached back and unwrapped one of my legs from his. "I never should have left the two of you alone."

I unhooked my other leg and let him climb off me. "You would have just insisted that I tell him 'no.'"

"Exactly!" Valemar snarled.

I sat up and wrapped my arms around my legs. "And I keep telling you it's not that easy." Valemar gave a disbelieving bark of a laugh. "It's not!" I insisted.

Valemar marched over to the cupboard and drew out a night tunic. He yanked it over his head and reached for the trousers. My heart clenched. He was clothing himself so he could leave me.

"If I say 'no' then Raislos has renewed reason to get rid of me." The trousers slowed their ascent. "And he and General Creskin have been talking anyway."

"What?" Valemar turned to face me.

"Yes." I laughed and shook my head. "That was the news he'd brought. They'd done a deal. The general was just here to inform me."

"But you're the ambassador."

I shrugged. "I warned you there was the possibility that trade could continue even without the Hormani."

Valemar took a moment to process this. Confusion began to fill his eyes. "Then you couldn't have said 'no'? They would have done it anyway?"

I bowed my head. "Probably not. But that would have created other problems."

The fire reignited in Valemar's eyes. "Really, Astrid? What could be worse than a well-armed Cordair army headed our way? Would your Shororato even deign to stop them?"

Probably not. Not with me here. "Fine. Do you want me to give the Shororato what they truly want? There's really only one thing standing between you and your desire to have all this end." I gulped back a sob that filled my throat. "Because the general pointed that out to me as well. I'm the reason for the Shororato to stay. Remove me and the trade ends. I'm sure I could negotiate the return of your child as soon as he or she is born."

With a resounding crack, the cupboard door split down the middle under the force of Valemar's fist. Yes, furniture did seem to break whenever I told this man the truth.

"Do you want me to make that the simplest answer?" I couldn't resist goading him. He'd made me pay the price of his disapproval too many times.

"By the Father, Astrid," Valemar said. His eyes closed. He took a deep breath through his nose, his jaw clenched.

"Not so easy now, is it?" I asked.

Valemar slowly turned from the cupboard and walked to the door. He opened it and left without another look.

I sat in the library the next morning with a map of the Low in front of me, writing the names of the people I remembered from last night's dinner. I chewed on the end of the pencil as I thought. "The woman who was at table three, wearing the blue dress embroidered with the branches, is Blanid…" My voice trailed off as I struggled to remember her last name.

"Pöbid," Padrid supplied. I wrote it down.

"And her husband is…" My brain wanted to say *Colin* but that wasn't right.

"Coran."

"And he's the wine merchant," I said, adding the information to the little rectangle that represented their house. It physically hurt, sitting there, calling up the names, doing something that PS Carr would have found so easy. I pressed my fingers to my heart and tried to keep from grimacing with the pain. My anxiety seemed to be increasing with the task rather than easing.

"My queen?"

I removed my hand.

Maybe it was because PS Carr had worked for someone else. Maybe my success in meeting with the ambassadors in Vanerife had been that I was doing those things as Reina's aide. I hadn't been doing them for me.

"I'm just having a hard time remembering," I said, the lie slipping off my tongue far too easily.

Padrid patted my hand. "Maybe we should take a break." I gave him a warm smile and nodded. Padrid rose from his chair. He laid a hand on my shoulder before disappearing into the maze of bookcases.

I traced the map, running my fingers over the names of the families. If Valemar had asked PS Carr to do this, she would have completed it the second—well, probably third—day. It was what the client needed.

My fingers came to rest on some of the names. Malfin Errig and his wife Döna lived right across from the High's main gate. I had to have been introduced to them at the formal dinner the night after my wedding, but they had been two in a sea of many. *Ösin Agos and his wife Brait. Henred Valla and Jarwyn.* My brain refused all efforts to match faces to the names.

I put down the pencil and closed my eyes. Move. I desperately needed to move.

You need to fly, whispered the little voice in my head.

Yes, I answered. I would have given nearly anything to be on a starship, out in the great star-spangled void of space. Maybe that was why I kept running in the woods and fields around Aedenfal.

Maybe that's why you should ride.

I hadn't been on a darana since I had returned from the Hormani camp, but that was mainly because I hadn't wanted to go anywhere.

I rose from the table and went to find Ferrick, the High's healer. It had been too many centuries since people on Earth had regularly ridden horses—the closest equivalent to a darana—and I didn't know much about pregnancy. Other than the cravings. And that eventually you got as big as a house and couldn't see your feet any more.

I knocked on the door that stood ajar to his second story workroom. Drying herbs hung from the rafters. Bottles and boxes lined the shelves, labeled in neat, tidy handwriting. *Silver purse. Blue duster. Moon's blood.*

Ferrick stood by the window crushing something with a mortar and pestle. "Ah, my queen," he said, glancing over his shoulder. "What can I do for you?"

"Is it safe to ride?" I asked, stepping into the room. "For the baby?"

Ferrick wiped his hands on a towel. "As long as you don't fall off. The sudden stop can tear the placenta away from the womb and then your body does what it is told, thinking that you have given birth." The blood drained from my face. "But at this stage, if you needed to travel, we'd be less likely to put you into a carriage. All the jostling would be much less comfortable than the slow, steady walk of Loenir."

"So I'd be fine?" I asked for clarification.

His face lit with a warm smile. "Yes. Feeling restless?" I nodded. "Ah, well, you're probably heading into your second trimester. Most women get a surge of energy. Lets them get things done, to prepare, before they become weighed down and tired during the third."

"You count trimesters?" I asked.

"Pregnancy here is generally about nine months. How is it with your people?"

"The same."

"Our women are usually sick for three, work hard for the next three, and then nest during the last three months."

I smiled. "It's about the same for us." At least, it had been for my sister-in-law, Amy, who had been the only pregnant human I had known.

"Well, then, if you want to go for a gentle ride, I don't see anything stopping you."

I found Calan, the darana master, and then stopped by to see Orin to arrange my guard.

"Does Valemar know what you're doing?" Aedenfal's seneschal asked me.

"No. I don't tell him when I go running. Erris just tags along." Erris was a shadow on foot but I had never seen him on the back of a darana.

Orin's eyes narrowed. Valemar was sure to know of my plans before Loenir was even saddled. I sighed.

"Look, the time is coming soon enough when I won't be able to do anything. I just want to ride Loenir while I can."

"I'll have Conmel and Segur meet you in the courtyard," Orin said.

"Um, on the bank opposite the watergate," I said. "I don't feel like riding through town."

Orin's eyes narrowed again but he didn't ask any questions and I didn't offer any information. I wasn't going to tell him I didn't want to ride through the streets, my every movement observed. If I hadn't already known that Shale wouldn't answer, I might have screwed up the courage to go ask her who was watching me. She'd probably *seen* who in town wished me ill.

Valemar met me in our rooms just as I was pulling on my riding gloves.

"You're going out on Loenir?" His tone spoke his disapproval in volumes.

"Yes, Ferrick assures me it's fine as long as I'm at a walk and don't fall off. Besides—" I turned from the dressing table. "—you'd have me on her in a heartbeat if you thought I needed to travel to Torfin or Lendurig."

Valemar's jaw clenched. The air in the room changed as his irritation practically took form between us.

I sighed and rubbed my brow. "Is it always going to be like this now between us? Me being a constant disappointment to you?" I didn't look at him. His words could lie. His eyes couldn't.

"By the Father, Astrid."

"Yes," I snapped. "You say that to me a lot these days." I raised my head. Sadness and anger swirled in his eyes. "So if you're not going to stop me from going," I said, heading for the door, "then I will see you at dinner."

I waited to hear his footfall behind me, but it never came. A thousand tiny needles stabbed at my heart. Only a month ago, he had been willing to fight the Shororato in order to keep me. Now I was half afraid he would have just let me go.

CHAPTER 5

My King's Guard escorts were waiting for me when I stepped out of the boat. Conmel offered me his hand to draw me up the bank. The daranas' breath steamed in the chilly air, making them look even more like a herd of deer on the forest's edge. Elk, to be more precise—a herd of elk with solid not cloven hooves, though common riding darana had their horns sawed off.

"Hello, my pretty girl." Loenir snuffled my outstretched hand. I had not seen Loenir since I had left her in Piltuir five months earlier when I'd boarded the royal barge that would take me to Vanerife to begin my exile. Loenir tossed her mane and stomped her feet as if to say, *Where have you been?*

"Busy," I answered, taking her bridle and pulling her closer. Her breath was warm and moist and the heat from her body drove away some of the autumn chill. "But I shouldn't have been too busy for you."

Conmel gave me a leg up. "Looking forward to having your own darana today, my queen?"

"More than you could possibly know."

Heymond and I had traveled in stealth to the Hormani camp, invisible after drinking heichdar blood. To keep our presence unknown, we had ridden doubled up—Heymond sharing Conmel's mount while I rode with Alill. Any observer would have thought the two visible riders were merely a regular border patrol.

I leaned forward along Loenir's neck and whispered in her ear. "You're going to have to go gently, my pretty girl. You're carrying two of us today." Her eye rolled back to catch mine, and she gave a small nicker.

I wrapped my arms around her, savoring the contact, as Conmel mounted his darana. Segur was already astride his mount and shook his head in disbelief as I snuggled further against Loenir. I breathed out, partially a sigh of relief that it was just the three of us and partially a release as a sense of bliss began to wash through me. The power I could feel between my thighs provided the sense of freedom I had been longing for.

"Where to, my queen?" Conmel asked.

"West," I answered as I gathered up the reins. I wanted to put space between me and the burdens that plagued me in the east. "Let's ride somewhere west."

At my command, Conmel turned his mount and set us along the path that followed the Leisna until it came to the Syfil bridge and the Western road, leaving Aedenfal far behind us.

I was sore when I lowered myself into the bath a couple of hours later. Sore, but satisfied. The autumn breeze had blown my unbound hair around and reddened my cheeks. I had felt alive. Loenir had picked up my mood and nearly danced down the road. But, as if she had understood the words I had whispered in her ear, she'd not asked for more. It had still been enough that my thighs burned from the exercise.

I slipped my head under the water before Iree added the oil that would help relax my muscles. "You look content, my queen," she said. "The ride must have done you good."

"It did," I said, resting my neck against the edge of the tub as she came around to shampoo my hair. I moaned as her fingers massaged my scalp, working away the last of my tension.

Iree dipped the ewer and rinsed the soap out of my hair. I leaned against the back of the tub, eyes closed.

"Which dress tonight?" she asked.

I debated. A part of me wanted to wear the green dress I'd arrived in, the one I'd had commissioned for my brother Finn and his wife Amy's traditional Highland wedding in Scotland. I had kept the gown in my traveling wardrobe as formal dress was still expected some places in the galaxy. With its long skirts and bell-shaped sleeves, it had saved me from setting foot on the planet with its medieval Earth level of development clad only in a skintight pair of pants and shirt.

The dress was thoroughly me but obviously foreign. The fabric and style were unlike anything on Crenfor. Wearing it would have been tantamount to walking into the banqueting room and announcing, *I'm different.* As if my smaller height, dark hair, and strange ears didn't already do that.

"Maybe the purple one," I said. The sunset sky had been the same color the night before, where the deep blue of night mixed with the red light from the nearly full moon. The dress showed off my curves, skimming the tops of my swelling breasts and framing my collar bone. A sight that Valemar took his time drinking in when I appeared downstairs for dinner.

"My king," I said, inclining my head.

He laughed. "As if you'd obey me as your king." That was certainly true. I rarely obeyed him. Alfari husbands and wives only promised to feed, shelter, and protect the other from harm.

"It was a formal greeting," I said. "We're evenly matched in rank." Valemar raised an eyebrow. It was the first time I had said it aloud.

"What?" I asked. "The ride 'brushed away the cobwebs' as they say on my world." Valemar frowned at the unfamiliar word. "Things spun in homes by a creature similar to a gresán," I said, naming the Crenfor equivalent of a spider.

Puzzlement furrowed Valemar's brow. "You have gresán in your homes?"

I held out a pinky and framed the nail. "They're that size. Well maybe not," I amended with a frown. I stuck out my thumb instead. "All right, about that size. They leave webs in unused or uncleaned areas."

Valemar smiled. "And the ride cleaned out areas you haven't used?"

"Maybe." I turned the blush that rose into a smolder. "Maybe you can help me clear out some other cobwebs later."

Valemar's eyes traveled hungrily over me again, and then the doors were opened and we both lifted smiles into place.

Padrid and I were ensconced in the library, still filling in the infernal map of residences that surrounded the High, when one of bird master Ean's assistants brought in a message for me—the tight, thumb-size roll of a karawack message. I put down my pencil. There were only two people who would send me a message via karawack—

my friend Brinna in Torfin and Valemar's mother, Reina. I didn't envision Brinna being the author.

Padrid turned his attention to some papers to give me some privacy as I broke the seal. *Ambassadors are asking permission to meet with the ambassador. Please advise. R*

I released the edge, and the messaged curled back up with a small *snap*.

"How far south does Bánalfar allow foreign ambassadors to travel?" I asked.

Padrid slid his distraction aside. "Raislos shows up here with infuriating frequency, but he's not exactly an ambassador and he's not exactly traveling south." Padrid flipped his long, graying braid over his shoulder. "Reina?"

I hummed my acknowledgement.

Padrid leaned back in his chair and folded his hands over his chest. "I don't see Valemar agreeing to it right now."

"Why?" I asked. "Because of Snow Reach?"

Padrid gave me a sidelong glance. His eyes met mine, and he gave a tight nod.

"What *is* going on at Snow Reach?"

Padrid looked surreptitiously around as he sat back up. As far as I knew, we were the only people in the library but the heavy bookcases blocked much from sight. Anyone could be around. Padrid placed an elbow on the table and curled a fist to his mouth. To the casual observer, he could have been picking his teeth. I leaned forward. "Reports have surfaced that Prince Ander has traveled into Bánalfar."

I tried to place the name. I knew I had heard it in the early lessons that Padrid and Valemar had given me.

"Second in line to Darland's throne," Padrid breathed, biting his thumbnail.

My eyebrows rose, and I sat back in my chair. Padrid laughed but I knew it was a mask for our conversation. "When?" I pulled the map I'd been working on toward me.

"Not long after Valemar came south to look for the Moon Princess."

To look for me.

The hair on the back of my neck rose. "So who do you think I *should* have sit next to me at dinner tomorrow?" I asked in a louder voice.

"Lesgé Cahnt," Padrid said, pointing at one of the rectangles near the High.

"Why's that?" I asked, genuinely interested.

Padrid smiled. "She's a right old gossip. You're bound to get all kinds of information off of her."

I smiled, even knowing that her loose tongue would cut both ways.

With Reina's message needing an answer, I went in search of Valemar. The door to his study stood open, ready to receive inquiries.

"Ah, Astrid." Valemar's eyebrows rose. I closed the door behind me and watched them fall. "What can I do for you?"

Reina had probably sent him a karawack as well. Hell, they were probably in constant communication about me. I rolled back my fingers to expose the karawack message curled in my palm. "I'm sure Reina sent you one as well, asking about the ambassadors' request to come see me."

Valemar looked back at the ledger in front of him and scanned an entry. His pen scritched as he made a mark next to it.

"So what do I tell her? I may be the Astrun Federation's ambassador but travel through your lands is still controlled by you."

"Is it?" Valemar lifted his eyes from the lined book.

"You are still the sovereign authority in your land."

"Only my authority is not absolute anymore, is it?"

I held back a sigh, tired of the sniping between us. "Do you want the Shororato housed elsewhere?" I knew their presence goaded him.

Valemar threw the pen down. "No."

"Do you want me to ask the Federation to appoint someone else as ambassador?"

Valemar sighed heavily and steepled his fingers. I let him think.

"No," he said. His hands lost their pose, and Valemar shook them, freeing his sleeves. He picked up the pen again.

"Your neighbors are going to want to find out how much things have changed—Capalnoc, Zagré, Tuljerd, and the others. Even Darland. Uncertainty breeds fear, and fear is a powerful force."

Valemar glowered up at me. "You don't need to tell me that."

"You're hoping that by doing nothing it will appear as if nothing has changed," I said with a dawning understanding. "And inviting them here to Aedenfal, so deep in the heart of Bánalfar—"

"*Will* signal that things have indeed changed."

I sat. "How about inviting just Aren Loör? He's your cousin." Valemar tapped a finger on the table, thinking. "You could have him accompany…" I searched for inspiration and smiled when I found it. "A delivery of darana you've purchased. He and I have met. It's a perfect excuse all the way around."

But Valemar didn't share my enthusiasm. Worry filled his eyes.

"Or not," I said. "It is your decision."

Valemar rubbed his brow. "No, you're right. It's a good idea. It's just…" He tried to lift a smile into place.

My arms prickled. *Prince Ander.* He was worried about Prince Ander.

"Never mind." Valemar sighed. "Send your reply to my mother. Have Aren come. I will follow up with one of my own." He gave me a tired smile. "Anything else, my love?"

My heart warmed with his words. "No, my husband. I will leave you to it."

It was still early when Iree and I ventured out the next morning. Shopkeepers were just beginning to set up their wares, and servants were still rushing home with bread for their households' breakfast. I had put aside my fear of intrigue lurking in the Low and decided to visit the dressmaker Daria had taken me to the first month I'd been here. Valemar had filled a dressing room full of clothes for me— for the Moon Princess—before I'd ever arrived but the weather was turning colder. I longed for things that were not only warmer but of my own choosing. And though my gowns all laced up the back, I also needed some clothes that could accommodate my growing baby bump.

The door jingled as I opened it, and Galwin took up his post outside the door.

"My queen!" the overeager proprietor squeaked, clapping his hands together and coming out from behind the cutting counter. "What can I do for your today?"

"Good day, Master Iru," I said, bracing myself for the man's enthusiasm. "I am going to require a winter wardrobe. One that will accommodate the growth of Bánalfar's heir." The tailor trembled with joy.

"Of course! Of course!" He began to tick off a list on his fingers. "Day gowns. Evening gowns. One for Gellirhird, of course. Fur lined cloak. Night dresses."

I tried to keep up with him in my head. What *was* I going to be doing the next five to six months?

"And that should bring us to Altbain, which we may as well get out of the way now," he said, flinging his arms wide as he finished.

Iree waited patiently beside me. Daria would have stepped forward and taken charge. "Do you have sketches or something for me to look at?" I asked. I'd never had custom clothes made before, other than the dress for Finn's wedding, and I wasn't really sure what was involved.

"Yes, yes! This way, my queen."

I followed him to the back of the shop. A headless mannequin displayed a dress that had been dip-dyed to create an ombré of light green at the bodice deepening to dark green at the hem. Master Iru pulled out a stack of illustrations.

"These are just a starting point," he said. "Something to get the ladies' imaginations going. We, of course, can add in details to reflect your status and your tastes."

I leaned over my shoulder and whispered to Iree. "How many day dresses do I have now?" Having helped negotiate thousands of business deals, I had learned that one should never tell a prospective vendor just how large an order could be. While there were times it sweetened the vendor's efforts, if things went pear-shaped, as my boss Hamit liked to say, it was better to walk away and find another source rather than yank the unfilled portion away.

Iree leaned down and spoke to the back of my head, hiding her lips. "Six."

"And evening dresses?"

She smiled at the tailor before dipping her head again. "Seven."

I held back a groan. *Wonderful.* I would have to pick out thirteen. No, fourteen. No, fifteen dresses today if I included both of the holiday dresses.

Master Iru snapped his fingers twice over his head. A curtain parted and a young woman appeared from another room. "A table and chairs for the queen," he said. "And some refreshments."

I gave Iru a thankful smile. At least I wouldn't have to make all the decisions while standing up.

I lasted through three day dresses and four evening gowns, including my dress for Gellirhird, before I ran out of steam and wanted nothing more than to lie down for a nap.

I was rather proud of the dress we designed for the winter holiday. Instead of the traditional red, I had selected a deep midnight blue *soien*—a Fairfada-grazed anapali wool that had the stiffness and shine of taffeta—that was to be embroidered with stars. The edge of the gown would be a reverse ombré with the color lighter at my toes, gradually darkening as it rose toward my hips, a representation of the sky as it heralded the dawn. Or, in this case, the signal that longer days were coming.

Master Iru had been enchanted with my ideas. "While everyone else is dressed as the moon, you will be dressed as the heavens."

I gave a small shrug. "Even the Moon Princess needs a night off."

I picked out fabric and trimmings for a new red dress as well. Both were unusual but Master Iru knew to keep the designs secret. Whatever I wore would set a trend. Dressmakers had been bribed throughout the ages and on most planets by clients wanting to be the first with a style or have the most spectacular creation so that everyone else could be viewed as having copied them.

Which was why I had purchased the entire bolt of a special gresánve the first time I'd had Master Iru make something for me—a bed gown. I still shuddered to think there could be other Moon Princess nightgowns out there, clinging to every curve, turning its wearer into a facsimile of me. Master Iru wouldn't risk me taking my trade elsewhere. Especially as he was sure to suspect that I still had half of my wardrobe to fill.

I returned to the High and lay down, my eyes closing as soon as my head hit the pillow. When I opened them, my mind filled with the coming dinner. I wasn't really up for having Aedenfal's greatest gossip supping on my right, but at least it would be a short dinner due to the Blood Moon.

"Astrid Carr," I said aloud to myself, "you were one lucky bastard." She had gotten to flit from assignment to assignment, putting on and taking off a new mask, a new role, every few days. I was stuck in the same one day after day. One that had been handed to me, not even chosen.

There was a soft knock at the door. It cracked open a few inches. "My queen," Iree's voice called softly. "It's time."

I sighed and sat up. Light from the hall streamed across the floor as Iree pushed the door open.

Collect allies. Rule number eight. Lesgé was an asset to be cultivated. I could do that. As much as I despised dinners at Aedenfal, I could still use them to gather allies.

CHAPTER
6

Lesgé was just the first of several of the wives I had join me at the high table. I hated the nighly performances, just as I had thought I would, though I was too practiced a protocol specialist to ever it let show. Artifice was a thrill when it was temporary. It was a murky web long term, something that could tangle you up and hold you until you were bitten in the ass.

After several nights of playing the gracious queen, I put Cadalin next to me to offer some relief. Bréick was now almost two months old and Cadalin had begun to long for adult company, finally returning to the High's dinners. I was thrilled for it gave me the opportunity to quiz her about pregnancy and babies.

"Have you started your layette yet?" she asked. Her light, wispy voice always reminded me of the summer breeze.

"No," I said. The ladies of Aedenfal had been working on hers when I arrived, led by Laera, wife of the steward. Valemar banished her to Lendurig when she had voiced her disapproval of me and her doubt that I was the Moon Princess in front of him. Garris, her husband, had stayed. I didn't know how they made that work though

I was sure both of them found it difficult. "I still have time, and you know I'm not much good with a needle."

"We'd love to help you," she said. "After all, you helped me. And then sheltered me and Bréick here in the High when things were uncertain."

"I was glad to do it," I said honestly. Cadalin's bright, innocent outlook had been the one point of light in Aedenfal's sea of disapproving women, and she was the closest thing to a friend—a female friend—that I had in this town.

"And I would be glad to return the favor." She smiled kindly.

"I don't know how much time I would have to help you sew," I told her. "There are many responsibilities that require my attention." Cadalin nodded. "But feel free to use the solar. That way I will be able to join you when I can."

Her eyes began to shine. "Of course, my queen."

"And remember, you can save me the diapers." The one thing I could sew was a hem. Laera had made sure that was where my talents had been put to use. I was well versed in making diapers.

Cadalin laughed. "We can do that."

Reina sent me a message that we could expect Kyvet Aren Loör by the resting moon. I had worked with the Capali ambassador and Reina on securing more darana for Bánalfar's army. I smiled, thinking of how good it had felt to exercise my protocol specialist talents that way in Vanerife. Then my breath hitched and I blinked hard, remembering what had followed. Daria had eaten the poisoned tarts and died the day after my meeting with the kyvet.

Valemar found me in my study, still staring at the curl of paper in my hands. "Ah." He came in and placed a kiss on my head. "I see

you have heard from Reina as well." I gave a shaky nod. Not only would the visit bring up the specter of what I had lost in Vanerife, but the need for the darana was part ruse and part reality.

"Raislos won't be happy that Capalnoc is traveling this far into Bánalfar. Or that Aren is bringing war darana with him," I said, finally setting the message aside.

Valemar took a seat across from me. "You gave Raislos plenty of reason to be happy just days ago."

I raised my eyebrows. "You never did ask me what he is getting in return." Valemar gave an irritated shrug. "One…" I waited for the chip to translate the weight for me. "Weyn of ore in return for equal weight in gold." I'd been pleased when General Creskin had sent me that detail though he didn't inform me of when the trade would actually take place.

Valemar's eyes widened. "So much!"

I shook my head. "Not really. In terms of its worth, the Cordair are being cheated."

"Mother and Father," Valemar breathed.

"My true dilemma," I told him. For the first time, Valemar actually seemed willing to listen. "I say 'no' now and the Cordair get to save that resource. The chalcopyrite is used to fuel the engines of starships and is the most valuable substance in the galaxy." Valemar's arms went slack, striking against the arms of the chair. "Do you want me to save that threat for your descendants?"

"Mother and Father, Astrid," Valemar said again, stunned.

"I could say 'no' today and my children's children's children could face a foe with nearly limitless wealth." Valemar closed his eyes. "I say 'yes' and I'm no better than the Hormani."

Valemar's eyes snapped back open. "But you suspected that the trade might continue."

"I did. But I didn't expect to have a voice in it. Raislos still does not know the ore's true value. If he did, he might be willing to bank its future worth and wait."

"Or demand better payment," Valemar said. "Would he get it?"

I sighed. "I'm having a hard enough time weighing potential futures without putting that into the mix."

Valemar gave me a cunning smile. "So your conscience does have limits."

I ran a hand through my hair, pinning it to my scalp, in the hopes of pulling the answer from my brain. I released my hair and shook my head. The Cordair had devastated the land, cutting down every tree in sight, including some of the sacred trees of Gladama, in order to fuel their smelters before Valemar's ancestors rode down from Vanerife and drove the Cordair out of Bánalfar. "I've been to planets where the environment was destroyed. It's still a balancing act on my—"

I stopped as I realized that Earth was no longer *my planet*. "—on Earth," I continued. "How much do you sacrifice for progress? From what I've heard of the Cordair and their ancestors, my heart tells me that they would sacrifice everything."

"It's what they've done before," Valemar said. "They still can't conserve what lives in the Archjarn and have to import much because of that."

"I don't want another Antilli Carbrev to have to rise if the Cordair can afford limitless resources. I don't want the Baraáda fighting to save the barat trees of Gladama now or a hundred years from now." I ran a hand over my mouth "But that's exactly what could happen if I don't do this right."

"Oh, Astrid." Valemar reached across the desk and took my hand.

"Forgiven?" I asked.

Valemar's hand tensed, tightening around mine. I had just about lost hope when he gave my hand a squeeze. "For now."

"What could the Cordair buy with a weyn of gold?" I asked.

"I'll check into it."

Valemar tried to release my hand but I caught his up again. "And don't use the heichdar," I said. A new look of irritation crossed his face. "The Shororato will be monitoring both sides. The heichdar blood will make your scouts invisible, but the Shororato are sure to be using thermal imaging."

Valemar frowned. "Thermal imaging?"

"A way to see living things by the heat they give off. A figure of a man that is not seen to the naked eye but shows up in perfect detail with a special lens—" Valemar groaned. "Yes," I said. "Something that would definitely be investigated by the Shororato."

This time it was Valemar who covered his mouth with his hand as he thought. "Should we dismantle the lab?"

"I've thought about that," I confessed. "Ever since I returned from the Hormani camp. I think it is safer right now where it is." I rubbed my forehead. "I don't know how long it will be before they inventory the flora and fauna." I feared for the heichdar when they did. Some would be transported off-planet while the Shororato tried to uncover the animals' near perfect cloaking ability. Such a technically advanced people wouldn't think of drinking the blood directly from the animal in order to gain its invisibility. Then again, the Shororato might be able to isolate the substance and develop injections instead.

"They could find the heichdar in the wild?" Valemar asked.

"Someone eventually will." I shook my head. This planet deserved protected status for several hundred more years. Yet with

my presence, and now the Shororato's, the "Do Not Contact" ordinance protecting Crenfor could be lifted.

With weary eyes, I looked at my husband. He gave me a grim smile.

"You did warn me that I wouldn't want the Shororato here," Valemar said.

Unfortunately, there really hadn't been any other choice.

Kyvet Aren Loör arrived in Aedenfal ten days later. He brought with him twelve magnificent fighting darana and one particularly stunning specimen that was somewhat smaller than Valemar's elephant-sized, moose-like warhorse.

"Who is this for?" I asked Valemar as he inspected the animal in the courtyard.

"You," the kyvet said with a chuckle. Aren stood next to me, arms crossed, watching Valemar.

"Me?" I was sure I had heard him wrong. The intimidating animal had to be for someone else. Heymond was a more likely candidate. "You expect me to ride to war?"

Aren laughed, a deep musical hum that danced against my skin. "No, my princess. We expect Slánta to save you from war."

Aren turned his astonishing blue-gray eyes on me. The golden blond hair about his shoulders danced in the light breeze. Valemar's eyes narrowed and he stared at his cousin but one side of the kyvet's mouth simply hooked up in a smile.

"You expect—" I glanced between the animal's legs, searching for its gender. "—him to save me from war? He's built like Muirbrook. He's the kind of animal meant to charge into the hordes and render absolute destruction." The Viking blood in me flamed to life. My

spine straightened. On that animal, I could be an avenging Valkyrie. I half-wished Aren would ask me to try him out.

"Exactly," Aren said with a smirk. "Nothing would stand in his way to carry you to safety."

"Aren," Valemar said in warning.

"Cousin, you have married the Moon Princess. She's already shown what she can do."

I looked back and forth between them. Valemar clucked to the animal as he ran his hands over him then lifted its feet and inspected the massive, un-shod hooves.

"Want a ride?" Aren asked.

I felt every eye on me. Most of the High had stopped their work and had gathered in the courtyard. I scanned the crowd. Something in my gut told me that the watchers needed to believe that Rákal's gift was for Valemar. "Not today," I said, despite my longing.

Aren frowned. He, too, gave the crowd a surreptitious once-over and then broke out in a deep, barking laugh. "Heymond," Aren called out to the captain of the King's Guard. "Let's have your spook try him out."

Erris melted into view from behind a pillar. Valemar gave a tight shake of his head. "Keyan, try out your back-up mount."

Aren's face was full of satisfaction as Segur gave Heymond's lieutenant a boost up the copper-brown animal. "Something you're not telling me, sister," he said quietly. His lips barely moved.

My heart filled with envy as Keyan settled himself behind Slánta's neck. It took me a moment to register the kyvet's words. "Sister?"

"Well…I already call Valemar 'cousin' and you are family. You carry not only an Alfari heir but a Capalian one as well. Should you need to, Slánta would carry you to us." He gave me a moment to soak that in.

Keyan moved Slánta through some tight maneuvers. Despite the animal's plate-sized feet, Slánta traveled as if he walked on air. Aren lifted his chin in approval.

"Why don't you want the eyes to know he's yours?" Aren asked while studying the performance. "Who do you think is watching?"

Keyan pulled back on the reins. Slánta reared up and then hopped forward, hooves flashing as they cut the air before him. *Courbette,* my chip supplied, answering my unspoken question. I had once entertained a Dsibian *bastig* broker at a performance of the Spanish Riding School in Vienna. The animals were poetry in motion, which was what had enabled the school to survive nearly a thousand years, long after the majority of Earth had given up riding. And Slánta's moves were beautiful; all the while his posture and flashing hooves communicated the message, *Don't fuck with me.*

I applauded as Slánta's feet returned to the ground and he tossed his mane. "Just a sense," I murmured. "Nothing truly worth mentioning. But since you asked…"

"Nicely done," Aren said, adding his voice to the others. It then lowered. "I take it you haven't told Valemar of your suspicions."

"No," I said. Keyan urged the great darana around the perimeter of the courtyard. Their brisk pace blurred the High's stones into a smear of gray. "He has enough to worry about without me adding fanciful imaginations to his plate." Aren stroked his chin.

Keyan brought the great animal back to the center of the yard. "Moon Princess's turn," Aren said, taking the reins. "Let's give the heir a taste of true power before he is even born."

"Capali tradition," Valemar said, coming to stand next to me.

My mouth rose in a smile. "Learning to ride before they are even born?"

"But, of course," Aren said. "In Capalnoc, we are practically born astride. A darana, not the earth, is our natural home."

"I guess if it's tradition," I said, sweeping away my earlier fears. Who could complain now if I tried the animal out?

Keyan dismounted, swinging his leg over the animal's neck and sliding down, his back against the darana's shoulder. Valemar boosted me up and over Slánta's wide neck. He was too massive for me to ride on his back. With his large, moose-like horns, it felt as if I had taken shelter in a tree. A deadly tree.

I ran a hand along his neck, letting him get used to the feel of me. His ears flicked and then rotated back, focusing on me. I leaned forward and buried my lips in his mane. "Hello, my honored gentleman."

"Would he carry you, wife?" Valemar asked.

I straightened up and gathered the reins. "Gently now," I murmured to Slánta. "There are two of us you are carrying."

Awareness traveled down the leather that connected us. Slánta held himself a little more erect. His eyes and ears became more alert to our surroundings.

It seemed silly for me to put him through his paces. Keyan had just done that better than I ever could.

Nothing would stand in his way to take you to safety. Aren's advice traveled through my mind.

I took a deep breath and closed my eyes. *Show me how you would save me.* My muscles tightened in tiny ways, communicating my thoughts to the great animal.

Slánta swung his head from side to side, scanning the courtyard. Then, with one burst of power, he jumped forward. Within two strides, I knew he was heading for the gate and the Low.

Not safe, I thought, molding myself against his neck.

Slánta's gait changed, and he curled to the right.

The stables will be fine, I said in my mind, giving Slánta a destination.

Those gathered in the courtyard parted like the sea as Slánta danced his way toward the stone buildings that housed the other darana. I had thought Loenir and I were well matched but I felt not a single bump as Slánta's feet covered the ground. I was no more than a necklace to the creature.

I drew him to a standstill at the entrance to the stable yard. Aren and Valemar came up to help me down. I took Aren's hand as I swung my leg over Slánta's neck the more traditional way, and Valemar caught me as I slid down.

"Reina should have seen that," Aren said to Valemar. He gave me an appreciative smile. "If you weren't so obviously foreign, I'd swear you were Capali."

Valemar snorted. "You should have seen her when she first learned to ride. She did well on Slánta but her performance was due more to the fine animal you brought me." Valemar caught up Slánta's reins. His words stung, and I wondered if Valemar had insulted me on purpose.

Aren's eyebrows rose a fraction. He stroked his chin and shot me a glance that was filled with compassion. And maybe a bit of longing. Then he brushed Valemar's words away with a gesture.

"You have Muirbrook, and your wife did such a good job negotiating the other animals —" Aren said with a sweep of his hand, "—that your uncle thought you should have another, should you have need of it."

The king of Capalnoc had taken me under his protection. Without even trying, I had managed to secure us an ally in whatever the future held.

We adjourned to the presence room. Warm, spiced wine was brought in to dispel the chill from the courtyard. The stones and the wooden structures had been covered with a dusting of frost that quickly melted with the sun's touch. There was no mistaking that we had crossed over the threshold to winter. Four months of winter.

I warmed my hands on my goblet as Aren drank deeply from his. Valemar simply sipped his wine.

"I take it that it's me you have come to see," I said to Aren.

He flashed me a smile that made my skin tingle. Aren set his cup on the small, circular table next to his chair. His mouth quirked up. "You know, I didn't really believe you were the Moon Princess when we met in Vanerife." I held myself still and silent as the memory of Daria's strangled gasps washed over me. "Though the attempt on your life the next day did make me wonder if I had underestimated you. I am sorry for your loss."

I blinked away the sting that rose. "Thank you."

"And now there are others from your world on the edge of the Fairfada."

My eyes met Valemar's, silently asking what I should tell the ambassador.

"They are here to observe," Valemar told Aren.

I raised my eyebrows. It wouldn't be long before word of the trade got out.

"Mainly," I said. "The outsiders found that the Cordair have resources that some find valuable. And while those outsiders are now gone, the wider…" I searched for a word that would hint at what was out there without frightening the kyvet. "Alliance of those

who travel the stars are now curious about what your planet holds."
Aren paled. "It's my job to keep things in balance."

"You're not from the moon?" Aren said.

"No."

He swallowed deeply and then drank from his wine, washing down his fear. I glanced at Valemar. Apparently, Rákal had not told his ambassador everything.

Aren held his now empty goblet between his hands.

"I say this not to frighten you," I explained, "but because it is the truth. A truth that should have been kept from you and the rest of Crenfor for many hundreds of years."

"*Toma*," Aren swore. "That's why you didn't tell me in Vanerife."

"No," I said. "Those were things for a king to hear first."

"And much shouldn't change from what has always been," Valemar said. "The armor that the outsiders supplied to the Cordair has been reclaimed."

"At what price?" Aren asked.

"Gold," I said. "Raislos wasn't happy but that armor wasn't supposed to be here."

Aren's head jerked up at my words. He frowned, silently repeating what I had said. "Then you...?"

"No," I said. Valemar reached out and took my hand, as if to keep me from leaving. "I'm not really supposed to be here either." *Still want to offer me your protection?*

Aren's gaze traced the pattern in the carpet. "Then wealth is still flowing to the Cordair."

"For the time being," I said. Valemar squeezed my hand again, this time in warning. "I think the Alliance representatives want to ascertain what impact our presence has made on Crenfor."

"Think?" Aren asked.

I smiled. "Oh come, kyvet. You know that no ambassador truly knows the intentions of those they serve."

"And your…?" Aren asked, searching for a name to go with the Outsiders.

"The ones that are here on the edge of the Fairfada are law enforcers. They will make as small an impact as possible on Crenfor. They would like to not be here at all." Again, Valemar squeezed my hand. "You have nothing to fear…Capalnoc has nothing to fear…as long as they are left alone."

Aren rose and paced the room. "Do they act as your protection detail?"

"No," Valemar answered. "Bánalfar does. Astrid is my wife."

"But if they've named you as 'ambassador,' as kyvet…"

"An ambassador works to establish cooperation and understanding. Come, *Kir* Aren. Take your seat." I gestured toward it. "My role has really changed since we last met." Aren glanced at my abdomen and laughed. "A queen is meant to produce heirs," I said.

Aren refilled his goblet and sat. Valemar released my hand.

"The Cordair are still bold," I said. "Their aspirations have not changed. The Shororato will watch them but most likely will not interfere. Bánalfar still needs the resources Capalnoc can provide."

"The Shororato? Those are the enforcers on your eastern border?" Aren asked.

"Yes. They will mostly observe. Raislos does not have the same advantage he did two months ago but his plans still spin." I reached out and placed my hand on his arm, able to feel the lean, sculpted muscles beneath his sleeve. "This delivery of darana will help." I turned my gaze to Valemar. "No matter where our army is needed."

CHAPTER 7

I went down to the stables after dinner to see Slánta. With the kyvet here, Valemar and I had dined alone with him in a smaller room rather than joining the communal dinner. After the tea had been poured, I had excused myself and left the two men to have their own conversation.

I grabbed a handful of grain from a nearby bin and offered it to the enormous darana. Slánta took it with a grateful snuffle, his nose hairs tickling my palm as he gathered it up. With deep chestnut eyes, he observed me as he chewed.

Muirbrook swung his massive head out of his stall and fixed me with a look that said, *Where's my grain?*

I gave Slánta's neck a pat, lost in thought. He was mine. Rákal had sent him to me. And told Aren to greet me as "sister." I absentmindedly ran my fingers through Slánta's coat.

I was carrying Bánalfar's heir. And somehow my child was also in line to the throne of Capalnoc. What had I missed? What hadn't they told me?

Slánta leaned into the pressure of my fingers. I glanced up. Instead of the half-closed eyes I expected, his eyes were watchful, scanning the aisle behind me. I looked over my shoulder as Muirbrook swung his head toward the stable door.

I lifted the latch and entered Slánta's stall. My God, he was huge, larger and bulkier than the Clydesdales once used on Earth to pull enormous loads. My head didn't even reach his shoulder.

Slánta took a step and placed himself between me and the door as I pulled it shut. My hackles rose as he pressed against me, sheltering me as if I were a foal or fawn or whatever young darana were called. Muirbrook nickered and stamped a hoof, causing a rumble that reverberated beneath the stones under my feet.

I ducked behind Slánta's powerful front legs as my heart took up the tempo of a frenzied blacksmith. He grunted and gave me a gentle shove. *Right.* There were two of us. I tried to slow my heart rate back down.

I don't know how long we stood there before Slánta tossed his head. He swung it around and nosed me. Whatever he had sensed was gone.

I stroked the velvet hairs on his nose. I had been half afraid of the shadows in the Low, and now I feared there might be some within the High.

Still unnerved from my experience in the stables, I huddled against Valemar after our lovemaking.

"What is it, my love?" he asked.

"Why would Rákal send me a warhorse?" The arm I was tucked under began to stroke my side.

"Technically, my uncle sent *me* a warhorse," Valemar replied.

"And yet—"

"Aren should not have said those things to you," Valemar said, cutting me off. "The Capali can be somewhat dramatic, as you've no doubt learned from my mother."

"So he's not mine?" I asked.

"He's mine, Astrid, and what is mine is yours."

I still didn't feel any better about it. "And how is our child an heir to the Capalnoc throne?"

"Rákal has only one child—Kasiel. And should anything happen to him then our child could possibly inherit."

"Possibly?"

"He—or she—would have to compete in a tournament to show they were worthy of taking up leadership."

The clans of Scotland had done something similar when determining a new chief. I rubbed my fingers along one of the barat leaves that made up the livery collar tattooed on Valemar's neck and chest.

"It all seems so much more real now," I said. "War. I didn't think we would still be preparing."

Valemar gave me a gentle squeeze. "Ah, Astrid, that's the way it goes. Neighbors always want something you have. You only get to keep it if you are willing to fight for it."

The truth in his words left me with little comfort.

The next morning, I went to the jaldun practice room as soon as I had finished my breakfast. The pants of my training leathers no longer fit. Iree had gone in search of a replacement, and the ones she returned with fit my belly but fanned around my ankles like sails. A style that, while fashionable some places, was distracting and somewhat dangerous. There was more fabric to catch a blade

on or trip me, but I moved through the various katas with the same intensity as when I had last trained, weeks before.

Valemar didn't join me. Whether closeted away in a meeting with Aren or attending to other matters, I didn't know.

The blades hissed as they cut the air. My feet shuffled quietly against the stones. The extra fabric of the larger pants flapped with every shift of my weight.

Valemar had once threatened to have me learn to defend myself clad only in my nightgown. When the extra fabric snapped against my ankle again, drawing my attention away from the position of the knives and resulting in me slicing my knee, I determined that I would need to train dressed in something other than the usual practice clothes. Many of the moves would cut a skirt to ribbons, something men didn't need to worry about with their long tunics, but it would be something I would have to deal with if I ever needed to pick up a knife and fight my way out of a situation in my usual dress. Iree would need to find me an old gown.

I finished the first set of fourteen forms and started in again, irritated when my breathing became rough. It had only been two months since I had last practiced jaldun, but I had already begun to slip into the unfit shape of a pampered diplomat.

A pregnant diplomat, the voice in my head said.

My belly responded with a flutter.

I froze. Slowly, I put the blades together in one hand and pressed the other to my stomach.

Nothing.

I waited a dozen or so heartbeats but the sensation didn't reappear. I returned the blades to the rack and made my way back to my room to change, focus gone. Shuffling papers around my desk would be a more productive way to spend my time.

Aren appeared in the open doorway of my study.

"Come to say goodbye?" I asked.

He leaned against the frame. "You'll have me for a couple more days. I want to make sure the darana are settled."

A smile twisted my lips. "You just want more time to see what's going on in Aedenfal."

Aren gave a lazy shrug, and my heart skipped a beat. He looked like a god standing there in my doorway. *You're married,* my brain hissed.

"That does tend to occur when you stay in a place for any length of time." Aren straightened. "May I?" he asked, gesturing toward the chairs in front of me.

"Of course," I said, and inclined my head.

Aren reclined in the chair. "Why did you come to Crenfor?"

I stiffened as screams echoed in my ears. Flickering lights took over my vision. I closed my eyes, trying to dislodge the memory of all the horror that had occurred after the plasma explosion took out the *Palmas Cove's* engines. I forced my jaw apart to answer. "I had no choice. Some say it's because I was meant to be here."

"And you?" Aren asked.

I sorted through the papers before me. "It took me a long time to even consider that I could be the Moon Princess. Eventually, I had to believe they were right. No one else could have driven away the Hormani."

"I thought your law enforcers did that."

"No one else could have called them. And Raislos would have been well prepared for war, maybe even have been able to march all the way to Gladama before the Shororato became aware that things on Crenfor were not as they should be."

"And what do you think now?" Aren asked.

"Small ripples in a larger sea that has always been there," I said. "And what has changed for Capalnoc?"

"Not much," Aren said with a smile. "But I wanted to see for myself." He rose to leave. A smile started then twitched away. Aren's mouth became a straight line. "Those things you sense, you fear, *Kira*…The moon whispers. While you are no Mödatal, I believe you can hear them. Do not let the Mother's warnings go to waste."

And with that, Aren bowed and left the room, leaving me to wonder what he knew.

I spent the afternoon in the solar. Cadalin, Niah, Vienne, and Féown, whose husband was head of the leather working guild, had gathered there. Bréick slept in a basket nearby.

"We are working on your layette," Cadalin told me when I entered.

"Did you save me the diapers?" I asked, keeping my voice low so I didn't wake the child.

Vienne colored, having been party to the intended insult to me. One I had chosen to ignore out of practicality. There really hadn't been anything else I could sew.

Féown colored as well and looked at the other women. Cadalin simply smiled and pulled an unfinished, white square from the basket beside her. "You do hem very nicely," she said to me.

Cadalin handed me the fabric and then a needle fitted with white thread. My fingers folded the edge easily, an action that still reminded me of the movements of origami, and I began to weave the needle in and out, tacking down the edge.

"What sorts of things is Bréick doing now?" I asked Cadalin.

"Trying to push up whenever I set him on his tummy," she said. "And always smiling."

"Will Erhard continue to travel now that winter has come?" I asked.

"Not as much as he has, but yes. Most of his trade is in the north and they don't get the chilly weather we do here."

"What do they do with the anapali during the winter?" I asked Niah. Her father kept flocks on the great grassland of the Fairfada.

"They've moved them further north," she said. "They'll shear them come spring and then bring the herds back down this way. Anapali like temperatures a bit warmer."

"Does cold weather give them a thicker coat?" I asked. Animals on Earth grew thicker, warmer fur as the temperatures dropped.

"The ones that aren't on the Fairfada do," Vienne said. "But it's the quality of the grass that makes the biggest difference." Vienne's husband was head of the weaving guild. "The Fairfada animals are taken where the grass grows lush. South in the summer and north in the winter."

I reached the end of the first edge and folded the corner in the special way the women had taught me. I held back a sigh. Sewing wasn't the same without Daria. Just as I had known it wouldn't be.

"So tell me the gossip," I said to get them talking so I wouldn't have to.

"Well," Cadalin said. "Sifan Mortif, the head of the cura guild—" Cura was a beer-like brew made from fermented grain. I had always preferred wine over it. To me, it somehow tasted of old socks, though it did distill down to a potent alcohol. "—has gotten himself engaged to a young woman from Asgill. A redhead."

Vienne gave a harrumph. "She should have gone to the Cair. I don't know how her parents managed to keep her."

"She was talfia—" Féown said, using the Alfari word for strawberry blond, "—until she was three years old. Then it turned dark."

"Still, touched by the Mother," Vienne said.

"I'm sure that's why he wants her," Cadalin said. "Bringing a daughter of the moon into his household is sure to bring him blessings."

"Or curses," Vienne muttered.

They eyed me surreptitiously. "I've been both," I said. "And I'm not even a redhead." The younger girls giggled.

Bréick stirred in the basket, grunting a whine before falling back asleep. His mouth moved as though he sucked, his lips closed. "He should be fine for a while," Cadalin said, and turned her attention from her son back to the barat leaves she was embroidering along the hem of the small, green gown in her hands.

"Some places tightly wrap their children in cloths," I said, thinking of my Earth history as well as the infants I had seen swaddled on Cadona Prime. "But that's not the practice here?"

"We do the first few days," Vienne said. "But they need to explore the world." She smiled. "If they weren't ready to do so, they wouldn't kick so much in the womb."

"When do they start to kick?" I asked.

"Any time after the fourth month." Vienne's gaze fell to my belly. "Have you felt your child kick?"

I wordlessly mouthed the names of the months and counted on my fingers. I wasn't quite sure when I had conceived. The scientific odds had been against it, so the pregnancy had come as a complete surprise.

"I thought I felt a flutter earlier today," I said. "But I must have imagined it."

"It may have been," Vienne said. "Sometimes women feel lausachtai early. Others, not until the child has grown large."

"And then it becomes not so fun, if reassuring," Cadalin said.

"How common are children?" I asked, thinking of Rákal's only child. Valemar's line had been cursed with low fertility for several generations. He had been an only child as had his father and grandfather before him.

"My great-grandmother was from a large family," Vienne said. "But now most couples only have two or three children."

"By choice?" I asked.

"Choice?" Vienne said.

"Some cultures know how to impede conception so that children can be spaced out and resources better managed. So that a woman is not worn out producing child after child while trying to manage a growing brood and the running of the household."

"We would not interfere in the work of the Mother and the Father," Vienne said. "Their gifts are too precious."

It sounded like the Carbrev men were not the only ones struggling to conceive. I wondered what had changed.

I still thought about it that night as I lay on Valemar's chest, absentmindedly running my lips over his tattoo. "What is it?" he asked.

"Birth rates have gone down," I said. "Not just for your line but others, too. Do you know why that is?"

"Have they?"

"That's what the women implied this afternoon. They said that families are smaller than they had once been."

"Hmm." Valemar rubbed my arm. "That may be true. My parents only ever worried about our family."

"But your uncle, Rákal, has only the one child."

"Yes, but he has moon children," Valemar said.

Despite the many months I had been on Crenfor, the idea of the offspring of unmarried people being given over to service was not one I had gotten used to. "It's still strange that they would have decreased," I said. People on Earth had sought birth control once children were no longer necessary to work the farms or apprentice into trades and send their earnings home. That didn't seem to be what was happening here.

Valemar leaned forward and kissed the top of my head. "Always so worried."

Maybe. But it seemed that there was a lot to worry about.

Aren left a few days later. He wanted to be back in Vanerife before the Blood Moon. "Better choice of partners," he told me. His eyes smoldered as they held mine. A blush rose on my cheeks.

"Do you still feel like you're being watched?" he asked quietly as we walked together to the courtyard where Valemar waited with the rest of the Capali contingency.

I hadn't been outside the High since visiting Master Iru's dress shop and nothing had given me a sense of unease since the episode in the stables, but the hairs on my arms lifted every time I thought of venturing back into town. I nodded once.

Aren frowned. "Don't ignore it," he said to me after a moment. "We sense the world with more than our eyes and our ears. Something is not as it should be." He clasped his hands behind his back. "And you still haven't told Valemar."

"And have him chasing ghosts?" I asked.

"He's chasing them anyway," Aren answered, making me wonder if he had been party to discussions regarding Snow Reach.

"Then he doesn't need to be chasing them two ways."

"Three."

"All the more reason," I said, and my mind began to race. *What could the third ghost be?*

Aren stopped and turned toward me. "Your husband may go on winter campaign." My heart dropped. Hearing Aren say it made the possibility more real. "If things aren't safe for you here in Aedenfal then you need to come to Vanerife."

The hairs on my arms told me that would be a bad idea. I threw Aren a glance and continued down the passageway. "I have a feeling that's exactly what someone wants me to do." I just wished I knew why.

CHAPTER 8

Almost overnight my stomach pooched out. No longer looking like I'd merely had a heavy meal, the bump visible under the fitted gowns I wore now proclaimed to everyone who saw me that I was pregnant. Having lived with Cadalin during her final weeks of pregnancy, I knew I wasn't huge, but the shape was still foreign on me. And though I sometimes spent hours with my hand on the bump, I never felt anything move inside.

"It's still early," Vienne told me, noticing how I now held my sewing there when I worked. "It's your first. It might still be several weeks before you feel the baby move."

I smiled at her but didn't tell her why I hoped it would be soon, that I was afraid Valemar would leave and miss out.

In the days that followed Aren's departure, Valemar had grown increasingly distracted and moody, shutting himself up in the council chamber for hours at a time as Heymond, Orin, and a host of other King's Guard came and went. Aren's warning ate at my heart, filling it with a fear my brain couldn't really justify.

I invited Shale up to the High for tea. My nerves wouldn't let me venture to the Cair but I hoped the seer's presence would calm me. If she behaved as usual, I would know that things were fine.

She smiled when I rose to greet her, the folds of my dress framing my swelling stomach. "My queen," she said, and inclined her head.

"Thank you for joining me." I gestured for her to take a seat on the sofa.

"You have grown more comfortable in your role," Shale observed. She arranged her robes around her as she sat. "How may I be of service to you today?"

"Tea?" I asked, more out of habit than anything else.

"That would nicely drive the chill away," Shale said. Her eyes went to the fire crackling in the grate as I poured. She murmured a thanks as I handed it to her.

"You saw something when I was last at the Cair." I picked up my own cup and took a small sip before I continued. "And—" I set the cup back down, afraid my hands would shake and spill it. "I felt someone watching me on the way back."

A serious expression settled over Shale's face.

I clasped my hands in my lap. "I've felt like I was being watched before—on the ride to the Cair when Valemar and I were married. At the time, I chalked it up to someone who didn't believe that I was the Moon Princess.

"Things have been better here in Aedenfal ever since Valemar sent Laera away and so many others left, too. And yet..." Shale stayed silent as I sorted through my emotions. "I've been gifted a warhorse and offered protection in Capalnoc." I lifted my eyes to hers. "Shale, what is going on?"

"The mistrust that always lies behind the acceptance of something new," she said gently.

"Do I need to be afraid?"

"Fear is useful as long as it does not control you."

"Who is here in Aedenfal that wishes me ill?" I asked even though I didn't expect an answer. I didn't get one. "Is it Prince Ander?" I didn't like the timing of his appearance in Bánalfar. Shale simply held my gaze.

I had to move. I got up and paced the room, finally stopping in front of the fire. I watched the yellow-orange flames dancing among the logs. As Shale had once remarked back in Vanerife when I had been surprised at her use of one even in the hot weather, fire calmed your thoughts and let you see what was beyond.

"Valemar is going to go to Snow Reach, isn't he?" I said more than asked. "And leave me behind, alone." I closed my eyes. If Valemar left, I would have no buffer, no protection against the attitudes that permeated the town.

"Whether he goes or not is for Valemar to tell you, not me."

My heart sank. "Of what use are you?" I whispered.

"Oh, my queen," Shale said. "I would never leave you alone. I've been here for you before you ever knew it."

I put a hand on the mantel and fought for control of my emotions, something I had found harder to do of late. But I needed to. If Valemar rode to war, I would be the one ruling Aedenfal.

Or Garris will rule it, the voice in my head whispered.

He had stayed when Laera had been banished, stayed to serve Valemar. I rubbed my brow. *But would he serve me?* Or would I be just a pregnant wife, shunted off to the solar?

"One thing at a time, my queen," Shale said.

I stared into the fire, assessing my options. It was my sixth sense I was listening to. Valemar still hadn't confided in me.

As much as I wanted a game plan, I had never worked with Garris. To do so now, before plans had been announced, would

upset the balance. As PS Carr, I had spent much of my time in my cabin studying. I walked into every meeting prepared, having run every scenario possible. But if Valemar wasn't going to confide in me, I would be working blind.

However, I did have a resource in Aedenfal, the medieval equivalent of a tablet—Aedenfal's historian and librarian. It all came back to Padrid. Padrid would help me prepare.

The sound of tea pouring broke through my thoughts. Shale wore a smile when I turned around.

"See," she said, her mouth curling up cat-like. "You always know what to do."

But Padrid wasn't in the library, and the halls of Aedenfal rarely gave up their secrets. There were too many twistings and turnings, too many back passageways for the knowledge of someone's whereabouts to easily spread through the ancient castle.

I shunned the solar and my study. Now that my fears had gone from vague imaginings to more solid suspicions, I was too nervous for jaldun. I ended up on the ramparts, presumably to take the late afternoon air.

The moon already hung low on the horizon, a red ball that would be full in four days' time. My breath came out in a rush, steaming in the chill air, as my mind flicked back into analysis mode. I couldn't see anything happening until after the Blood Moon. No one would begin a campaign with an army about to be hit by a sexual frenzy. But come the second day of Eanir, all bets were off.

I watched the activity at the stables for a while and then turned my attention to the wood on the other side of the Leisna. The trees had lost their leaves in the month since I had gone running with

Erris. A forest of brown-gray branches reached for the sky like bony fingers.

The weak winter sun began to set, the pale yellow light slowly changing to orange and then red as the moon rose higher and offered the coming night its glow instead.

I headed inside, debating which dress to wear, not for the sake of fashion, but wondering which would impart me with enough courage to face them all when I had so much fear in my heart. For I couldn't show it. I had to be the model of calm for the citizens of Aedenfal.

Iree laced me into the new red dress that had been delivered the day before. Master Iru had created gowns with wider panels between the lacings. As my waist and bust increased, longer ribbons would create a larger crisscross pattern along my back. The crown with the cabochon rubies completed the ensemble.

I met Valemar outside the doors to the banqueting room and placed a trembling hand on top of his without ever really looking at him. He curled his fingers around mine but I kept my gaze on the door. If our eyes met, I was afraid I would melt into a weeping puddle.

Then the doors opened and I lifted a smile into place. The small thunder greeted us as the diners rose. I stepped forward. The Moon Princess could get through another dinner.

I had invited Vienne to sit next to me. We could talk of babies and fashion. The older woman's more reserved energy was just what I needed tonight.

And still I didn't look at Valemar. Even on the way back up to our rooms, even after I stepped into my dressing chamber—empty of Iree since Valemar usually undressed me at night. I had lifted the crown from my head and was about to place it in its box when Valemar's hands closed over mine.

"Astrid."

I froze.

Valemar brushed my hair back and tucked it behind my ear, ran his finger along its curve. I placed the crown on its velvet and shut the lid. My gaze followed the gold swoops and swirls embossed on the leather.

"What is it, my *grabeg*?" Valemar asked.

I swallowed, unable to make my jaw work. Valemar drew me to him.

"You're leaving," I said to his chest. Valemar's arms tightened.

"Did Shale tell you this?" Anger laced his voice.

"No. She wouldn't tell me anything. I just sense it." My lips trembled. "And my gut is never wrong. That's why it's rule thirteen."

Valemar laughed. He had been amused when I had told him the rules I lived by as a protocol specialist. He stroked my hair. "Yes, I probably have to leave." He pressed my head against his chest, right above his heart, and held it there a moment. "But let's discuss this once we're more comfortable."

Valemar kissed the top of my head and began to unlace the gown. I just stood there as he pulled the ribbon through the seemingly endless set of holes. He left me in my slip and then pulled his tunic over his head. I stepped out of my shoes while Valemar moved to his dressing room, never lifting my eyes from the spot on the dressing table I had been vacantly staring at since he had confirmed my worst fears. There was nowhere to go. Nowhere that I would be safe.

Valemar returned and lifted my chin, bringing my gaze up to his. "Yes, I am going to have to go," he said, and then I was blinded by the tears that filled my eyes and stuck to my lashes, clouding my vision.

"You shouldn't have to campaign in winter." The words were hardly out of my mouth when the pieces clicked together in my brain as to why this was different, unexpected, why the situation in Aedenfal was so unlike all the history lessons I had pored over and loved. "You don't have a peasant army. You have a standing one."

"Peasant?" Valemar asked, his brow creased with a frown.

"Farmers."

"Why would one have an army of farmers?"

"We don't have moon children on Earth," I said. "So kings that needed armies had to raise one from the general populace."

Valemar snorted. "That's no good. They're not trained."

"It made things interesting," I said dismissively, not wanting to get into a debate.

"It's not a campaign," Valemar said, taking my hands. I looked at them instead of him.

"Then why go?"

Valemar pulled me into his arms. "Because I need to be in Snow Reach."

"In winter?"

"Something strange is happening there."

What is Prince Ander up to? I wondered. But I didn't tell Valemar of my suspicion that the wayward prince was in Aedenfal.

"Remember Master Ean telling you that bird of yours once belonged to Adan, my former steward at Snow Reach?" I nodded. "Well…we now think that Adan was murdered."

I froze. "Ean said they never figured out what killed him."

"We have new reason to suspect that it was poison."

Poison. My stomach clenched, threatening to bring up my dinner. I swallowed frantically.

"Shh." Valemar rubbed my arms. "I know. I know."

When I had gotten my stomach back under control, he continued. "Different from what was done to you and Daria."

"That doesn't make me feel any better," I said, "telling me that there is a more subtle poison out there." Valemar simply sighed. "And what do you hope to find?"

"I need to reinforce the garrison at Snow Reach. Prince Caspin needs to know we're watching. My presence there will tell him that Bánalfar means business."

"And his missing brother?"

Valemar pushed me back a step. A scowl twisted his face.

"You're not the only one who hears things," I said.

"Ander may still be in Darland. He may even be in the Archjarn for all I know."

"That wouldn't be good," I said. A united Cordan and Darland would not bode well for peace.

"At least that deal the Federation did with Raislos should distract the Cordair for a while."

"That's the first good thing you have said about it," I told Valemar.

"It will only be temporary. Just until Raislos decides how to spend that gold he's getting."

I put my arms around Valemar. "I feel like I'll never see you again," I said. "I feel like I'm going to have to do this all alone."

Valemar buried his lips in my hair. I held back new tears. "Come," he said, drawing me to the bed. He lay down and opened his arms. I crawled up with a sob and pressed myself into the shelter of his side. "It will be okay," he said, offering me the same comfort I had offered him when I had told him I would have to leave and he thought he would never see me again.

And it had been okay. This time I was the one who would have to trust that it was the truth.

I awoke the next morning still tucked up beside Valemar. The realization that he would be going had begun to sink into my bones. My fingers gently traced the tattooed livery collar of barat leaves that hung around his neck and draped onto his chest. It was a warrior's mark of protection —the leaves meant to protect their hearts, much as the leaves that wrapped around Valemar's and my forearms were meant to provide swift, sure hands.

The barat leaves were a symbol of Bánalfar and the life-giving trees of Gladama. And much like the heavy gold and enameled chains worn during the Middle Ages on Earth—and still by high officers in the UK— the collars were meant to mark a person's fealty. My husband had pledged his life to his country, and so he had to go to where it was threatened.

Valemar groaned lightly and reached a sleepy hand for me. "Morning, wife," he said, closing his fingers around mine.

"Good morning husband."

Valemar blinked, forcing the last vestiges of sleep from his eyes.

"Now that you've finally told me, will you tell me the rest?" I asked. "All of it. What I am to do. How this is going to work."

"Right now?" A tease laced Valemar's question.

I gave him a shove with my shoulder. "Well not *all* right now. We'd be in bed all day."

Valemar rolled us over, pinning me under him. His fingers fanned my hair out along the pillow. "Tempting." He leaned in and kissed me soundly. "Very tempting."

And suddenly, I didn't want to let him go. I locked my legs around him and wound my fingers into his hair, every inch of me

on fire. Valemar tried to pull back, his eyes wide. I wasn't usually this forward.

"Pregnancy hormones," I said as wetness gathered between my legs. "And all the extra blood flow." I stared at Valemar, savoring the hunger. Valemar stared back at me, his eyes wide.

"Well, what are you waiting for?" I asked. "I'm ready and you'll soon be off to Snow Reach." A sly smile curled my mouth. I wound a lock of his hair around my finger. "Leaving behind a sex-hungry wife." And still he stared. I raised an eyebrow, silently asking him the reason for the delay.

"Really?" he asked.

"I've been told some women develop insatiable appetites."

"Hmm." A smile finally broke through the shock.

"Still waiting," I said.

Valemar leaned down and nuzzled me. "Well, we can't have that," he said, and entered me.

We didn't stay in bed all day. His secret finally revealed, Valemar now included me in most of his plans. After dressing and breaking the fast, we adjourned to Valemar's study. My fingers brushed the map, following the line that led from Aedenfal to the Skargorn mountains and Snow Reach, a week's ride south.

"How many are you taking?" I asked Valemar.

"Twenty. Another forty will join us on the road." A small party would be seen leaving Aedenfal but a larger force would ride into Snow Reach.

"And who are you taking with you?" I asked.

"Heymond," Valemar said.

My heart lurched. Heymond had been the one who had found me wandering on the Fairfada after my escape pod crashed. He

had been the one who had ridden to Vanerife after Daria had been poisoned and I had become catatonic with grief. He had even been the one who first showed me that I could wield a knife and defend myself. My head had known his place would be by Valemar's side but my heart had hoped for the security he would have offered in Valemar's absence.

"Erris," Valemar continued.

"Ah." Nothing like a shadow to look for a shadow.

"The others will be familiar to you as well."

"I guess I should have asked you who you are leaving," I said.

"Orin, of course." As Aedenfal's seneschal, his place would be here, ensuring the town's defense. "Tovan, Segur, and Galwin, among others."

I sat there, trying to weave a picture in my mind of what it would be like. "And Garris will be in charge of running Aedenfal."

Valemar looked up from his list at my tone. "Is there a problem with that?"

I frowned. "Probably not. There's…" I tried to chase after the thread. "I don't know. I get a flicker of caution when I think about it." My fingers twisted one of the folds in my skirt. "I know I'm not Reina and I know I haven't been trained for the responsibility…" I sighed. "I know it wouldn't work…"

"You want to be in charge of your own destiny."

Maybe that was it.

"Meanwhile," Valemar continued. "I'll be worried about your ambassador duties while I'm gone."

"Hopefully there will be nothing," I said.

"And if the Federation asks for another shipment?" Valemar asked.

"I will tell them 'no.' We need to see what Raislos does with this payment." I turned in my seat. "What *has* he done?"

Valemar shuffled through some papers. "It's been more difficult to get intelligence without the heichdar scouts, but they have started work on what we assume is a new armory."

"To make their own weapons and armor?"

"I haven't been able to get Sapir Ilahani to confirm or deny it, but I believe Raislos has reached out to Prince Denhur. Our guess is that Raislos would like to work with R'Kesh to reconstruct the Awrakian armor. He still isn't happy the Shororato took back such a miraculous creation."

My eyebrows rose. "Well good luck with that. I have no idea what goes into the composites that are used." Even though a mass spectrometer could tell you what went into a substance and map its molecular structure, the methods used to recreate the structure were still difficult to uncover and functioned as a trade secret when so much wasn't secret. R'Kesh—or anyone else on Crenfor—wouldn't be able to duplicate the impregnable armor even if someone illegally gave them modern technology. "Do you think R'Kesh would agree to a partnership?"

"Reina has voiced her displeasure and reminded Ilahani that they have contracts with us. But the idea of being able to further enhance their construction techniques…"

"Is tempting," I finished. Just as it was tempting for me to leave Aedenfal and stay with Reina in Valemar's absence. I'd love a chance to play politics in the background where I was more comfortable, all the while watching Reina and learning. But the fact that Valemar hadn't suggested it meant he wanted me here.

Valemar set the papers aside and perched on the edge of his desk.

"What would you have me do while you are gone? Other than grow your child?" I asked with a twist of my lips.

"Stay out of trouble."

"You do realize that trouble usually finds me."

"I am certainly hoping not." He caressed my hand and gave it a squeeze. "I hope you know that I would not leave you unless I thought that allowing things in Snow Reach to stay as they are would grow a cancer that could take hold and spread."

"I do," I said with a sigh. Knowing, rather than suspecting the secret, had drawn off some of its poison. The secret I was keeping brushed my heart.

It would do no good, I argued with myself. It would only create a distraction. Besides, even if my watcher had been Prince Ander, there was no guarantee that he was still in Aedenfal.

"What do you think our wayward prince is up to?" I asked Valemar.

Caution flickered in his eyes. "I'm not sure," he said, which translated as, *I don't want to worry you.*

Seems we both still had secrets.

Valemar spent the rest of the morning acquainting me with the basic workings of Aedenfal. By the time we broke at noon, my head swam and most of the details had fallen away, overloaded by the sheer complexity of it all. I rubbed my hands against my eyes as Valemar cleared off a space on his desk for lunch.

"And Reina does all of this for Vanerife?" I asked wearily.

"No, she could, but she has people in place who do it for her."

"And this is what Orin and Garris do for you here, and Jaros in Torfin, and Colás in Lendurig. Who is the current steward of Snow Reach?" I asked.

"Nevam."

"Right," I said, committing the name to memory. "Nevam. And things run differently in Glábac," I said, naming Bánalfar's final large city.

"The Baraáda are in charge there with the árdim—"

Guild, my chip translated.

"—reporting on the commercial state of affairs to Sciglas, head of the Baraáda."

I pulled the map from the stack of papers. Bánalfar was a vast country. I had seen quite a bit of it but it was still mostly unfamiliar. If something happened to Valemar, I would be the one in charge. A shiver ran down my spine.

"Astrid, what is it?"

The idea was like a snake in the back of my mind—wanting to stay hidden, imminently dangerous—and uncoiled slowly. "What if Ander is trying to draw you away?"

My eyes widened as another piece of information slammed home. It would explain so much. "We worried about the succession before I conceived." My eyes met Valemar's. "We can't have been the only ones. We did think Darland over R'Kesh."

Valemar's face turned grave. His eyes met mine in silent agreement.

"What could be the goal?" I asked.

Valemar gave a heavy sigh. "When we thought we couldn't conceive, I drew up many different scenarios in case I needed to name an heir. If the Darland scenario went through, Caspin would have been named my heir and Ander would have become Darland's ruling prince."

"But Prince Toren married a Darland princess. His blood doesn't sit on the throne."

"Actually, it does. Crown Prince Asmund married his cousin Freyna, Toren's daughter."

I grimaced. Royalty all over Europe had done the same thing back in its heyday for essentially the same reason—strengthening their ties to a throne. "And what would Prince Denhur's claim be?" R'Kesh had a slightly closer claim to Bánalfar's throne.

"There's a sea between R'Kesh and Bánalfar, not a border." Valemar shook his head. "The Alfari wouldn't welcome a R'Keshan king anyway."

"Not while there are heirs of Toren the hero," I said. "Do you trust him? Caspin?"

"I haven't had any reason not to," Valemar said. "Ander, however, is proving to be a different story."

CHAPTER 9

I was glad for the distraction of the Blood Moon fever when it came. Caught up in the rising urge to mate, most of the banqueters that night didn't notice my distress. Valemar and I were among those who left early. I savored the lust that overtook my husband for he didn't notice my crying until after he had climaxed.

"I didn't hurt you?" he asked, quickly shifting off me. He placed a hand on my stomach. I shook my head and tried to smile.

I put my hand over his and pressed, willing the child to kick for the first time. There was nothing.

"Have you felt the child move?" Valemar asked.

"No," I whispered, trying to swallow the grief that raged in every fiber of my body. "You'll miss that."

Valemar bent forward and kissed me. "You'll send me a karawack."

I nodded and wiped away new tears, sniffing as my nose began to run. Valemar gave a gentle frown and added his own efforts as my tears became a stream. I opened my mouth only to breathe, knowing that if I tried to speak, I would only utter sobs.

"Oh, my *grabeg*," Valemar said, and drew me to him.

We held each other the rest of the night, not saying anything, not engaging in further lovemaking. The room slipped from bright crimson to dark as the moon passed it zenith and slowly sank.

Valemar drifted into sleep sometime before dawn. I was glad for it. He had a full day of riding ahead of him. I lay awake and listened to his heartbeat. Rhythmic. Strong. He was a warrior and had a warrior's heart. And a cunning mind. It gave me comfort.

Morning came all too soon. Valemar rose and kissed me and then slipped out of the room to dress elsewhere. Iree laced me into a dark blue gown I chose to match my mood. I stood before the mirror, twisting the muscles of my face until I could fix a mask of calm on it, and then made my way down to the courtyard to see them off.

My knees nearly buckled when Valemar came through the door. His hair had been braided for war, the sides and crown pulled back to keep it out of his eyes. His erect, pointed ears bore gilded steel cuffs to protect them.

Valemar smiled at me and donned the helmet that had been tucked under his arm. It was not Muirbrook that waited for him but one of the regular antlered war darana.

I turned to Heymond. "Keep him safe."

Heymond chuckled. "We've said the same thing to Orin about you."

You are the queen, I said to myself as I turned back around. This leave-taking with Valemar would set the tone in Aedenfal. My Viking ancestors would have cheered the departure of their men. I drew myself up and imagined I was a shield maiden being left behind. But it was an Irish blessing that I found on my tongue.

"May the road rise to meet you," I said to Valemar. "May the wind be always at your back, may the sun shine warm upon your

face, the rains fall soft upon your fields, and, until we meet again, may God hold you in the palm of his hand." Tears welled in my eyes but I willed them to stay.

Valemar kissed my cheek. "I love you," he murmured. Then he mounted up, collected the reins, and, with a whistle, led the others out of the gate. The flagstones rumbled under their hooves.

I stood proudly and watched them go. The blue and green quartered pennants of Bánalfar snapped as they rode by. Their silver armor flashed, adding its own sparkle to the frost that hung on every surface in the cold morning light. I stood, hands clasped in front of me to hide their shaking, until the last darana had disappeared down the road, and then, holding my head high, I turned and walked back into the High to find a good place to mourn.

I retreated to my study. A soothing fire crackled in the grate. I curled up in a chair and watched the flames. My eyes were heavy with tears that refused to fall. Iree brought in tea and departed but I left the pot untouched. I waited for the debilitating onslaught of tears but they didn't come.

The High left me alone for the next several hours. Garris saw to Aedenfal's business and Orin made adjustments to its defense. It was almost as if I had ceased to exist. And maybe I had.

I contemplated that as the flames danced and the tea grew cold. Despite Valemar and Padrid's lessons, I was not necessary to life here. That was partially my fault. I hadn't integrated myself. The other piece lay with the fact that, other than my banishment, I had always gone where Valemar had gone.

And they know you grieve, the voice in my head whispered.

I wiped away the tear that finally fell. It was silly. My husband was perfectly fine, away doing his job. And yet I did grieve.

The fire had burned down to ashy embers and the tea had gone stone cold before I unfolded myself from the chair, my pregnant body demanding that I feed it. I shuffled to the door, my legs cramped from sitting.

"Sandwiches, please. And a new pot of tea," I said to the guard. He nodded and left to go tell the kitchen.

I stirred the embers in the grate and added a new log before taking a seat at my desk. My eyes roamed over the contents— books, files, paper box, pencil box, quill, ink, knife, sealing wax. The Federation tablet sat locked in the bottom drawer. I pulled on the chain that held its key, fishing it up from inside my bodice, and unlocked the drawer. I lifted the thin, book-sized piece of black glass. Its mirror-like surface captured the paraphernalia on my desk in its reflection.

Old life. New.

New technology. Old.

Everything I had on the desk, other than the information, was contained within the tablet. Research. Correspondence.

I ran my finger along the tablet's edge but didn't power it on. It would ask me for things.

I replaced the tablet, twisted the key in the lock, and tucked the chain down my bodice again. There was a soft knock at the door and a servant girl brought in the tray.

"The table is fine," I told her. She offered me a smile and exchanged the old tray for the new. I offered her a smile of my own as she slipped back out and closed the door. My stomach growled as I sat. The smell of the sandwiches made my mouth water. I took a bite and chewed, contemplating.

When all else fails, make a list. Rule seventeen.

I needed to be at dinner tonight. I couldn't hide. I needed to figure out who to seat next to me. I didn't want empty spaces on both sides. I needed someone who could provide a distraction from the emptiness and not remind me of it.

I finished the first sandwich and started in on the second, still debating.

I felt a nudge from the back of my brain and stopped mid-chew. *Garris.* I needed to put Garris at my right.

My jaw began to work again, more slowly—carefully—as I weighed the consequences. Garris always sat in the place at Valemar's left, even when Valemar was absent from Aedenfal. As far as I knew, there was no official seat at high table for the steward of Aedenfal, just one born of tradition. And yet, as queen, I outranked the steward. Even Reina technically fell under my command, which had come as a shock when I'd realized it. I was, again, the highest-ranking person in the city. Garris would have to do as I asked. Moving him might be unconventional but it would be an expression of my authority. Expected even, if it had been Reina ruling over the table and not me.

I washed down the sandwich and left for my dressing room. I had a performance to plan.

Cinched into a dress of Bánalfar green and with the peridot studded crown of intertwined leaves and waves, I waited for the doors to open, appearing as Alfari as was possible. I blew out a breath and shook the tension from my hands. I had hosted dinner on my own only once—when Valemar had ridden out to inspect my escape pod weeks after we were married. A single night, months ago. Tonight was to be the first of many, and the tone of those

evenings would be set by what happened in the next few minutes. No pressure.

The doors swung open, and I watched the two hundred guests rise. I acknowledged their recognition with a tilt of my head and moved to my seat. Garris's expression was one of pleasure rather than annoyance. I counted it a small victory.

"Thank you for joining me," I said to Garris once we'd sat.

"My pleasure, my queen."

"It must be odd for you, sitting somewhere other than your regular place." I lifted the glass of wine a server had just finished pouring.

"I have eaten more meals than I can count on the other side of this table." Garris waved off the wine server and raised his water glass instead. "But then, I did spend years out there." He gestured to the throng in the dining hall. "And the view is not so different from over here."

I raised an eyebrow. "Not a little bit improved?" I asked, fishing for a compliment.

"That goes without saying, my queen."

I drank from my wine while a server placed slices of meat on my plate and another set a bowl of pickled salad next to it. The rest of the tables in the hall were left to fend family-style, but not the king's table.

"It must be quite the task, feeding all these people every night," I said to Garris.

"Do you know how the tradition arose?" he asked.

"A reward for their defense of the High, I've been told."

"Yes, for more than a thousand years." Garris drank from his water glass. "But it's become an obligation after so many years."

"I'd like you to show me around tomorrow, if you have the time. Valemar and Orin have given me tours but I would like to hear from you how it all fits together. You know," I said, leaning closer, "it fills

me with awe, being part of all of this. In my old life, I would have found it rather amazing just to be sitting at one of the communal tables."

"I keep forgetting that you weren't born for this," Garris said.

"I never do," I replied. "I've accepted it, but it's still strange to me. So much responsibility." I turned my attention back to my plate and took up my knife and fork. "How did you become steward of Aedenfal?"

"My father was a cura merchant and supplied kegs to the High. Kelden, the steward at the time, noticed I had a curious mind. I was always asking questions, you see."

I smiled, imagining the boy Garris must have been, tagging along behind the adults and pestering them with his inquiries.

"Well," Garris continued, "Kelden asked my father if I could apprentice, and so I came to live here. I mainly ran errands for Kelden and then Ulrin after him."

"You were raised for the job," I said.

"You could put it that way," Garris said.

No wonder Valemar had retained him after banishing Laera. I wasn't sure who would or could take over after him, but it was not a question I could ask without raising the concern that I meant to replace Garris. It was still something I worried about although I didn't know why.

"I would love to see how it all fits together in the morning," I said.

"As you wish, my queen. Come find me in the morning after you've broken the fast."

Dinner went better—well, easier—than I had feared. The sea of faces had not held judgement, just curiosity. Garris had been pleasant. The empty chair to my left had not created an aching void. It had been a start.

But my bed was a cold, deserted place when I crawled in. Loneliness crept into my heart. I curled the covers in my hands and pressed them to my chest. *As I would have done with Emerson.*

Emerson had been more than my stuffed childhood bear. He had seen me through the loss of Grandma Sarah. He had gone with me when I left for the academy and had been placed in every suitcase I had packed since. Most people put aside their stuffed toys when they reached adulthood, but Emerson had been a little piece of home, and so I had taken him with me.

Until Crenfor. While not technically alien technology, he was indeed alien. And so, I left him on the *Palmas Cove* when I sent it into the sun. My heart still yearned for the comforting pressure his small, fuzzy body had offered. I clambered out of bed.

I opened the door to Valemar's dressing room and walked its length, palm outstretched, brushing the robes and tunics that hung there. The movement of the hangers stirred the air and Valemar's spicy scent lifted from the garments. I buried my nose in one. He had worn it just two days before and, had it been on a mannequin, I could have almost believed it was him.

I slipped the tunic from the hanger and curled it into a ball, pressing it against my chest. Then I padded back to bed, taking the tunic with me, and fell asleep, my nose almost believing that my husband slept beside me.

I got the formal tour in the morning—the store rooms full of flour, the buttery (where wine and other drinks were stored), the larder, the butchery, the vast kitchen where an army of men and women were already at work on the night's meal.

"How long will the stores last?" I asked Garris. Two cooks stood

nearby at opposite ends of a long wooden table, each busy hacking the head off of some kind of creature about the size of a pig. Pots stood just beyond, ready to receive the discarded pieces which would then be boiled for broth.

"Other than the kegs and the cheese, we'll go through most of what you've seen in three days' time," he said.

I gave a low whistle. "The rest of it is stored in the Low?" I asked. "It's winter. There are five months before there will be young plants again."

"There are warehouses about a mile west of here near the Leisna. There's a watergate about a mile west beyond that we use to supply them." A distance that put a buffer between the stores and outside access to them, should someone be tempted to take or destroy them.

"And the taxes needed to pay for all of this?" I asked.

"Aedenfal is the most expensive High to maintain," Garris said. "You would think it would be Vanerife—"

"But they don't entertain on this scale," I said. Reina usually ate alone.

"Vanerife hasn't faced an actual invader in more than two thousand years."

"While Aedenfal was last overrun one hundred fifty years ago."

Garris gave a small shrug. "That is why the tradition continues."

"And do you have an apprentice?" I asked.

Caution shone in Garris's eyes. "Einar is twenty-two. He's learning."

I offered Garris a reassuring smile. "Valemar values your service and so do I. I know the last several months couldn't have been easy for you."

Garris shifted uncomfortably. "I would not see Aedenfal compromised."

The hair on my arms quivered at his choice of words. "Neither would I. I was willing to give my life to protect it."

Garris rested an arm on a stack of torna filled baskets. "I meant no disrespect, my queen."

"I know," I said, forcing comfort into my voice. Warning bells still sounded in the back of my brain. While Garris served Valemar faithfully, I wasn't sure his loyalty extended to me. I was still an outsider in many citizens' eyes, Moon Princess or not. Mother of Bánalfar's heir or not. I had cost Garris his wife, and I knew there would eventually be a price to pay for that.

CHAPTER 10

Aedenfal became a cold, comfortable prison. Snow fell five days after Valemar left. Only about an inch but enough to turn everything into a fairyland until the sun rose high enough to melt most of it away. I put on my heavy winter cloak and walked the ramparts, needing to breathe, needing to be lifted above the politics and the uncertainty.

Despite General Creskin's warning, I did not check my tablet. If the Shororato or Astrun Federation wanted me, they knew where to find me. Receiving daily reports from Orin was the one change in my routine. I needed to ascertain what the Cordair did with their half ton of gold. How much had the scales dipped because of my inability to say no? I found I was hoping the answer was "quite a lot." It would make my decision regarding the trade easier. But things in the Archjarn stayed as murky as everything else.

I had tucked myself away in my study with a cup of hot, spiced wine when a breathless Tovan knocked on my door, his face red from cold.

"You've a visitor," Tovan said, panting as if he had run the whole way. His eyes sparkled.

"Who?"

"Come and see."

My heart leapt, and I quickly put the wine aside. But then reality tamped down my joy. There was no way that my visitor was Valemar. Curious, I followed Tovan down to the courtyard.

A woman in a dark green, hooded cloak stood with her back to me, directing the unloading of the contents of a wagon—casks to the buttery and trunks to be brought inside. She turned.

Brinna.

A sound of joy escaped my lips. I ran down the steps to join her.

"Careful, my queen," she said in her lilting voice as I hugged her. "We don't want you falling."

"I feel like I could fly right now." I loosened my embrace and took her shoulders. So much had happened since she had welcomed me to Torfin back in the summer, eight long months ago. "You don't know how good it is to see you."

"Ach!" she barked to get the attention of a young man who had begun to roll one of the kegs. "Carry, not roll. Don't stir the contents! That's one of Torfin's finest."

Brinna took my hand and hooked an arm around mine. "I have an idea," she said, to me as we turned back toward the steps. "Valemar's karawack message was rather urgent."

"He sent you a message?"

"The note said that he was off to Snow Reach and that 'Astrid despairs to be left alone.' He couldn't bear it. And who was I to defy the wishes of my king or the needs of my queen? I set out the same day."

"You could have warned me."

"I could have…but then you would have been biting your nails and waiting instead of doing what you needed to do here."

We stepped inside and Brinna lowered her hood. She glanced around the small entrance hall as she slipped off her cloak. "Not very welcoming is it?"

"Aedenfal is meant to repel invaders, not welcome visitors," I explained.

"Humpf." Brinna stripped off her gloves. "Throne room?" she asked, pointing down the hall.

"Yes. And banqueting room."

"Thank you, Melia," Brinna said to a girl who came in behind us and took the cloak and gloves from her. Brinna took my arm. "Why don't you show me where you want me and then you can give me a tour."

I smiled, my first genuine one in days. "Tour would be a misnomer," I said. "But I will introduce you to the confusion that is Aedenfal."

I put Brinna down the hall from me. Iree squealed with joy to see her former mistress and was glad as well that Melia had accompanied them. I left them to get settled and caught up, aware that Iree would share all of her observations with Brinna. Technically, it would be a breach of trust, but I didn't mind. I would rather have an informed ally than a servant so discreet that Brinna would have to rely on my perceptions alone as to the state of things in Aedenfal. I had found its tone different from that of other Alfari cities and wondered if Brinna—and Iree—would think it as prejudiced as I did. Even Daria had observed its inhabitants to be more superstitious and off-putting.

I swung by my office for the book I was reading on candle making and retired to a sitting room while I waited for Brinna. Iree brought her in a little while later.

"It is so good to see you. And that bump you're sporting," Brinna said.

"It is good to see you, too. I haven't really had a friend around since…" I trailed off as a lump rose in my throat and silenced the rest of my words.

"Daria," Brinna finished for me. She took a seat across from me. "I know you didn't find them very welcoming here the first time you were here. Has that changed?"

"Quite a few left when Valemar banished Laera," I said. Brinna hummed in disgust and shook her head. "But that could have been because Valemar warned them that war was possibly coming."

"How can I help?" Brinna asked.

I drew in a breath as I thought. "I'm not sure how unusual their attitudes are. For comparison, I have the time I spent with you in Torfin. Glábac is a town of pilgrims." Brinna gave a nod and a wave of her hand in agreement. "Vanerife is a crossroads. They cheered me when I sailed through Lendurig," I finished weakly, running out of examples. "Are the attitudes here the norm? And is it even them? I have never felt safe here but it could be because so much happened to me right before and even after I arrived."

Brinna's eyes widened. "You don't feel safe?"

"Well, I nearly died getting to Crenfor," I said, reminding Brinna of the accident that killed the rest of the crew aboard the *Palmas Cove*. I had nearly died again when the Hormani fired on my escape pod and it had crashed. "And then there was that confrontation with the Cordair. Heymond brought me to Valemar. Hours later I was marrying him so that Raislos couldn't claim me. And…" I held back a shudder. "…Daria finished dressing me for my wedding alone because the other women could barely stand the sight of me."

"Well, you do look an awful lot like the Cordair," Brinna said. "Not that that is an excuse. You are obviously not one of them."

"The women didn't want me here."

"They don't like outsiders," Brinna said.

"I could feel someone watching me on the way to the Cair that first evening." I stared at the floor as it played through my mind. The hairs on my arms lifted at the memory. "Other than the well-wishers lining the streets. You know how you can feel hatred," I said, raising my eyes to Brinna's.

"No," she said. "But I've been told. And you felt it then?"

I hesitated, and Brinna sat forward, her eyes widening. "You've felt it since then? When?"

My hands sought for something to grasp. With nothing close, I interlaced my fingers and pressed them against my chest. "The last time I went to the Cair."

Brinna stared at me. "Which was when?"

"Before Valemar left."

"And you didn't tell him," she said slowly.

I let my hands drop. "Tell him what? Tell him that I am imagining things when he has problems in Snow Reach and trade may continue between the Cordair and the outsiders?"

"What?" Brinna exclaimed.

I waved a dismissive hand. "My outsiders. Whole other story." Brinna sat there a moment, soaking everything in. "Brinna, I don't know whom I can trust. Other than Shale," I added.

"She knows?"

"She does."

"And she didn't tell you anything?" Brinna asked. I raised an eyebrow. "Well, that's typical."

"Can't disturb the threads," I said.

"I am sorry for you, my queen."

"Astrid," I said, correcting her.

"Astrid," Brinna said with a smile.

"I am glad you are here." My nose and eyes pricked. Why couldn't Valemar have told me he had sent for Brinna?

Didn't want to get your hopes up in case it didn't work out.

That was true. I would have been crushed if something had prevented her coming after I had known about it.

"I'm glad I can be of service, m—Astrid," Brinna said. "So I will repeat my question. How can help?"

"I need a second set of eyes. And ears. I need to know how much distrust is left in Aedenfal. I need a shelter from it." I drew a breath. *In for a penny. In for a pound.* "And as long as you're here, let me know how you think Garris is doing as steward." Brinna's eyebrows rose. "He's been fine. Valemar trusts him. But now that Valemar is gone and Laera is banished to Lendurig…"

"You think that might change?" Brinna asked.

"Well, I know he doesn't trust me."

Brinna flopped back in her chair and shook her head. "I had thought Valemar was crazy, putting you through all that training in Torfin."

I blanched at the memory. Valemar had taught me to kill.

Brinna's head continued to move back and forth. "But you seem to be surrounded by plots."

"I enjoyed those weeks with you in Torfin," I said. "I was sad to leave."

Which wasn't exactly true, and we both knew it, but I had missed the easiness that Brinna and Torfin had initially offered.

"And I shall enjoy mine with you. Even if it *is* winter and we'll be surrounded by sour faces." Brinna clapped her hands against the

arms of the chair and sat up. "How about that tour? I have no idea how I got to this room. I don't know that I could find my way back if I had to."

I laughed. "That is the intention. You might be able to get in, but getting out is a whole other venture."

"I'm beginning to see why Pavier carted off the throne the last time the Cordair invaded. It was probably the only thing he could find."

I laughed. I had never been so excited at the prospect of wandering Aedenfal's halls.

I tried to go slow, remembering all too well the feeling that Aedenfal had been laid out like a rabbit warren—corridors that twisted and turned, half staircases that led to yet another turning, rooms that seemed to be jammed in higglety pigglety.

I started in the main entrance hall which had been designed to get people into the High's two public rooms and get them out. The throne room was easy enough to find—enter through the High's main doors and then straight down the hall. The banqueting room lay along the same corridor but to the left, its door less ornately carved and decorated. There were small hallways and staircases that led off the main hall before you reached the throne room but these were not inviting—tight, narrow spaces that gave no clue as to where they would lead.

"So if I can find my way down, I can find my way here?" Brinna asked. Her speech rose and fell with a cadence and light trill that my ear wanted to categorize as Gaelic or Vélla but it wasn't.

"You have an accent," I said, too distracted to confirm her observations. "It reminds me of one on my home world. I know you're not from there but where are you from?"

"A town not far from the border with Tuljerd," Brinna said. "My mother was from Tuljerd. We grow the trees that make the best casks for aging wine. I accompanied my father on a sales trip to Piltuir and happened to meet Jaros." Brinna smiled, her eyes shining. "That was just over three years ago."

"So you're still somewhat of a newlywed."

"Aye. I miss the trees but I have Jaros and the wine to make up for it."

"I've been told the Tulja remember Bánalfar when the Dorchair were here," I said, naming the Cordair ancestors that Valemar's had driven out of Bánalfar.

Brinna nodded. "The Tulja still believe the land is contaminated."

"You don't have that problem," I said.

"Well, my mother doesn't like to come see me. And she won't drink the wine." Brinna shrugged. "In a way, the Tulja live in their own Gladama. The trees and hills there sheltered them at a time when Gladama wasn't safe. They celebrate Antilli's Moon to commemorate the Dorchair being forced to leave, but that—and the trade in trees—is as much interaction as most of them like to have with Bánalfar. I have always gotten the feeling they think it will happen again, and if they stay where they have always stayed, then life won't change too much when it does."

"Your mother must have been a rebel," I said.

"Ah, well, trees grow on both sides of the border, and what started out as a Blood Moon pairing grew into something more when the moon fever wore off and a new fever surfaced."

"Have you ever felt like an oddity in Bánalfar?" I asked. Though still technically blond, Brinna was shorter and darker than most of the Alfari I had met.

"Not really. Sometimes I get curious looks. Things that are different always do." A calculating grin crept up her face, lifting the corners of her mouth. "It will be interesting to see what they make of me at dinner."

"We could have the solar be the next stop on our tour. I have four women in there right now working on my layette." I offered her a mischievous grin of my own.

"How about once I can find my way back to my room?"

I laughed and turned an arm to check a watch that hadn't been there in months. "By that time, you will be dressing for dinner," I said.

"I'll take that challenge." Brinna's eyes flashed. "Care to wager?"

"What?" I asked. Nothing easily came to mind.

"A story," Brinna answered.

Those I did have a great supply of. "Done."

Guests were rare at high table in Aedenfal. Outside guests, that was. Unlike other places I had dined in Bánalfar, they were announced, just like guests had been at formal occasions in the Europe of Earth's past.

It was Brinna who stood first before the doors to the banqueting room, with me, out of sight, a few steps behind her.

"Brinna Fálin, of Torfin," the guard called loudly to the assembled crowd. Murmurs traveled around the room as Brinna entered and then the doors were closed, shutting off the sound.

I stepped forward, waiting while Brinna took her place. When the doors parted, the assembly rose to their feet. I smiled lightly and feigned disinterest in what was going on, all the while noting their reactions. There were a few ruffled feathers. Some looked curiously

at Brinna, but most stood resolutely, as if they, too, were bored by yet another dinner.

I sat. Benches scraped and the room echoed with the sound of so many feet moving.

Brinna accepted a glass of wine and scanned the room with a curious glance. She leaned toward me. "Is this the norm?" she asked, a smile on her lips.

I ran my eyes over the assembly who were now passing platters and talking amongst themselves. A few watched Brinna. "These days, yes."

"And this is better?"

My lips quirked up. "Downright kind."

"Ah." Brinna set her wineglass down and exchanged a pleasant head nod with Garris two seats away on my left, Valemar's empty seat between us. I was not familiar with the man on Garris's left.

"And who would be here if I wasn't?" Brinna asked.

"Padrid, most often, though I've been forcing myself to expand the number of women around me. Usually the women you will meet tomorrow in the solar. There is only one who has really extended any sort of friendship. Our lives are very different but I try."

A strange sensation brushed my lower insides. Had I not been looking for signs a "quickening," I would have just assumed it was nerves. Which it probably was. If one so easily felt gas moving then surely a baby would feel at least as strong. It had not felt like the butterfly wings Amy and others had described it as.

Still, my fingers brushed the bulge of my tummy. Brinna pretended she hadn't seen so as not to draw attention. "The child?" she said to her plate.

"I don't think so. It seemed more imagined than real. And it's probably too early. I'm not even sure when I conceived." I hid my answer between bites of food, knowing we were being watched.

Brinna shifted slightly, scanning the crowd before returning her attention to her plate. "Every dinner is like this?" she asked. I nodded. "Mother and Father," she softly swore.

Dinners in Torfin had varied between just the four of us up to a small group of thirty. Small being relative when compared with two hundred.

"You would expect so many in Glábac," Brinna said. Glábac High was always open to important people making their pilgrimage.

"At least there you are part of the crowd," I said.

"And not the attraction."

"It is different when Valemar is here," I said. "The energy is different. There is an undercurrent of homage, fealty. The king is here, checking on the state of his subjects."

"While you sit in the protective shadow of the king."

Maybe that was it. "Now I am exposed."

Brinna brought her glass up for a sip, her mouth disappearing behind it. "And they do not respect you."

I cut a piece of meat and brought it to my mouth. "So it's not just me?" I asked before I stuck the piece in.

Brinna laughed lightly though it didn't hide the wariness I saw in her eyes. "No. It's not."

CHAPTER 11

We hid behind news and gossip the rest of dinner—how the harvest had gone this year, what I had missed with the pressing of the King's Wine, what was being done with the funds it had raised. We ignored the topic of the Queen's Wine that had been planned before I had been sent to Vanerife and tried to paint the picture of two friends catching up. We almost believed it ourselves.

We retired to my sitting room after dinner, curled up with hot spiced wine in the chairs by the crackling fireplace, and unpacked Brinna's observations.

"This is better?" she asked me. I nodded, and Brinna shook her head. "Mother and Father," she swore, closing her eyes. "They barely look at you. Some stayed facing the tables and didn't even turn when you entered. And Valemar has allowed this?"

"I think he has always known that they would be reluctant," I said. Brinna snorted. "As everyone keeps pointing out to me, I look too much like the Cordair."

"The Cölkans have dark hair," Brinna said.

"And are not well respected from what I understand." Brinna hummed her acquiescence. "Valemar has told them it is treason if they don't support me."

"Which means that those like Laera have only stepped out of the light."

Fear coursed down my limbs, causing them to shake. "Do you think they will try to bring me down?" I asked.

"No," Brinna said with a reassuring glance. "That *would* be treason. But they don't have to like you."

We sat for several minutes, neither speaking, gathering our thoughts. "You are just going to have to go on pretending you don't notice," Brinna said, breaking the silence. "At some point, they are going to have to get used to you."

I finished off my wine. "Then I suggest we both retire to bed. We have the solar to face in the morning."

With a resigned sigh, Brinna drained her cup, and we left the warmth of the study for the cold comfort of our rooms.

"Something cheerful," I said to Iree as she sorted through my gowns.

"The pinwah with the red birds?" Iree pulled out a dress embroidered with bright red paen birds.

"Hmm," I hummed, debating. "It would be a recognition of Torfin's presence here." The reddish-plum of the dress mirrored the color of the fruit used to make Torfin's wine. Paen nested within the large pilva bushes. The tufted birds had been artfully arranged around the boatneck collar and edges of the gown's sleeves.

Laced in, I gathered Brinna from her room to guide her to the solar myself.

"Who will be joining us?" she asked as we made our way through the halls.

"Third right," I said, continuing directions while Brinna silently repeated. "Vienne, middle aged. Her husband is head of the weaving guild. Niah, Vienne's recent daughter-in-law. Niah's father has large herds of anapali on the Fairfada. Féown, wife of Baethan Cherick who is head of the leather crafters' guild. And Cadalin, young wife of the cloth merchant Erhard Aedoch. Cadalin's infant son, Bréick, will be there, as well.

"The staircase with eight steps, not ten," I said, pausing on the bottom tread. "I had to count for a week—half a moon," I amended, hearing the foreign term from my tongue. "They try," I said. "Actually, with Cadalin, acceptance is real. But I don't quite fit."

"I know of Erhard," Brinna said. "He is well respected in Bánalfar."

"I've only met him once," I told her. "We had Cadalin move in here before the Hormani left. She was heavily pregnant and Erhard had grown reluctant to travel with all the unrest. I met him when he came to get Cadalin and Bréick and return them to his house." I had not been surprised to find he was a good decade or more older than Cadalin. The communal tables had made it difficult to pinpoint which of the men was her husband from across the room but, as I had found throughout the galaxy, rich men usually chose younger women as wives.

We left the stone steps of the stairs and continued down a carpeted hall. "Fifth door down," I whispered. The door sat open. The sewing had already begun.

The women rose at our entrance. Heads dipped. "My queen," they murmured.

"May I present Brinna Fálin, wife of Torfin's steward."

"*Grada* Brinna," they said, acknowledging Brinna with the honorific title.

"Ladies," Brinna said, inclining her head.

There was no shuffling of spots. The women had already reserved the best ones by the window for us.

Cadalin handed me a diaper and a threaded needle. Brinna's eyebrows rose. Brinna opened a sewing basket that I recognized as Iree's and drew a piece of blue cloth from it.

"I'm afraid I only know how to hem," I told her.

Brinna looked at my stitches. "Nice and even. Tight fold."

"I spent years folding paper," I explained. "The sewing is a new endeavor."

"The queen can make the most amazing things from paper," Cadalin said brightly. "Frogs—creatures that jump. Cranes—a kind of bird on Ur-eth. Darana, though they do look different. And even little boxes. I'm Cadalin, by the way. Cadalin Aedoch."

"I know of your husband," Brinna replied, her effervescent personality sparkling through. "Nice to make your acquaintance. And who else do we have here?"

The women introduced themselves and Vienne offered Brinna the most genuine smile I had ever seen on her. Brinna turned her attention to the fabric on her lap and began to cut out a small smock or tunic using only her eye to guide her.

"Amazing," I said.

"Years of practice," Brinna said simply.

My hemming was forgotten as she threaded a needle and began to stitch the two pieces together. The seam allowance was tiny. When she came to the end, Brinna opened the seam between her fingers, folded it so that the ends were tucked inside, and began to sew a new seam, creating a pocket that hid the rough edge. "Babies

can't pick at the loose threads this way," she said at my look of astonishment.

"Twice the work," I said.

"Saves trouble in the long run."

The other women didn't comment, leaving me to wonder if they, too, used the strange seam or were feeling shown up by the newcomer.

But Cadalin steered the conversation back into calmer waters, asking Brinna about Torfin, which then led to a telling of what it was like to attend a pressing of the King's Wine. Brinna managed to strike just the right balance between making Valemar look both ridiculous and awe inspiring.

"How long will you be with us, *Grada* Brinna?" Vienne asked.

"As long as the queen will have me," Brinna answered. "I have brought a special reserve of piora for Gellirhird." There were appreciative murmurs all around. "I would like to be here to enjoy it."

"I will have you for as long as Jaros is willing to spare you," I told her gratefully.

"You are the queen," she reminded me. "He will have to spare me if you so wish."

We left the women at lunch time. Brinna and I retired to my sitting room where we could talk more freely.

"What is your assessment of them?" I asked, biting into one of the fruits that had been placed in a bowl on the table. Round and rusty-red in color, the fruit's firm flesh provided the stability necessary for storage through the winter months.

"The sewing circle is certainly more respectful than those at dinner." Brinna arranged some meats and a substance that I always

thought of as "cheese," though I had no idea what it was actually made of, on a slice of bread before continuing. "But whose idea was it for you to work on the diapers?" She held up a hand as I opened my mouth. "I know. You do quite well on them. But you could have just as easily hemmed a smock."

"Laera," I said before Brinna could cut me off.

A stream of decidedly not Alfari words tumbled from Brinna's mouth. Their intensity conveyed their meaning nonetheless. I raised an eyebrow.

"Probably best you didn't understand that," Brinna said. "My mother taught us Tulja but my brother liked to trick me by teaching me phrases that turned out to be more…colorful. It *is* useful now and then." Brinna topped the pile with another slice of bread and fingered the sandwich. "So you owned the insult."

"I could have raged about it. But the best way to remove the sting was to pretend is wasn't an insult at all. Had I not been queen, it would have been a practical suggestion."

"By the Mother, you are a servant queen," Brinna said, a little awed.

"I was never supposed to be a queen. I was only supposed to be useful." It occurred to me then that I had, in fact, been a servant of Agçay Enterprises.

Brinna's focus faded, turning inward as she chewed.

"Where have you gone?" I asked.

The here and now flickered back into Brinna's eyes. "I've been wondering how we could use that to change those infernal dinners." She set aside the sandwich. "Gladama does them but the focus is on community, on being part of the life that surrounds the trees." She tapped her fingers on her lips. "The dinners here are meant to cement the relationship between the king and the people who stand between him—provide a barrier—between him and the Cordair. You need to be among those people. Right now, with Valemar gone, you are a barrier between them and that empty chair."

I paled. When Valemar was here, I was his wife. I was the Moon Princess. With him gone, the casual observer could have mistaken that the high table was now occupied by a Cordair. I closed my eyes, trying to pull up the mental armor I had fashioned as PS Carr, anything to protect me from the truth that began to burn in my stomach.

"All places have their myths, their stories of what is dangerous. It's the way we learn to survive. If it looks like a maskpol," I said, beginning the analogy.

"Beware its teeth and claws," Brinna finished.

"My people had, in their past, a distinction, too, about light things and dark things." I caught my reflection in the mirror and looked away. "From the time I was young, there has been a part of me that wondered if the old tales were true, that my dark hair marks me as an evil one, fit for the shadows. And now here…" I ran out of words. A lump rose from my stomach to fill my throat.

"You face it daily."

That was the thing about prejudice. It often rose from seeds of truth. Never absolute, for absolute truth leaves no room for doubt. And doubt is an insidious little thing that makes you question until you no longer know where reality lies.

In those whisperings, I found a truth. The Cordair were dark and dangerous and so was I. The only time I had ever seen Heymond truly frightened was when he faced the reality of who and what I really was.

"I am like the Cordair," I whispered. "They brought destruction with them to Gladama and even the Archjarn. I, too, have brought destruction to Crenfor."

Brinna opened her mouth to argue but the words faded as she took in the fierceness in my eyes. I held out my left hand and turned it, palm up. "One hand holds the power to tear stone from the earth." My gaze followed my right hand as it rose from my side. "The other—" my fingers tingled as I turned it over "—would stand as a barrier between anything that would threaten the lands of Bánalfar… the trees of Gladama." The tingle in my palm became a pulse.

I looked from hand to hand. The left one was still my own. The potential was still there. The "no" I couldn't give to the Federation, despite Valemar's requests I do so. I might need its power.

I sighed. "I fear they see me for who I am, who I might be." It was all shades of gray, degrees of truth.

"You are speaking of the trade you approved," Brinna said quietly.

"Partially." I let my hands drop. "I am not Alfari. And certainly not one who, for generations, has had to live with Cordair incursions, always on alert for the next attempt. I am different in a place where being different sets off alarm bells." An Earth example came to mind. "I am a solitary suitcase with no minder." Brinna gave me a puzzled glance. "Someone hundreds of years ago discovered you could put a bomb—" Her frown deepened. "Things to make the suitcase explode."

Brinna gasped, her eyes wide. "But why?"

"For the reason you think. To kill." I forced my serious tone to soften. "And you leave that ordinary looking suitcase—" I stopped and lowered my voice, trying to make sure this dangerous, foreign idea was not overheard. "In a market."

Brinna recoiled in horror. "No!"

"Would you not question every suitcase you saw after that?" Brinna trembled from head to toe. I lifted my left hand. "I am

death and destruction." I lifted my right. "I am life and protection. Aedenfal sees my left hand." I brought them both back to my lap and linked my fingers as they began to shake. "And what am I to do about that?"

Despite her best intentions, I saw fear in Brinna's eyes when she looked at me. Something I prayed would pass as her mind processed my information and she watched my future actions and determined again that I was no threat. I insisted that she take some time to herself; that I was fine, I had other things I needed to attend to. I did not tell her that I was going to practice jaldun. In her current state, she didn't need to be thinking of me with blades in my hands.

I gave her a smile as she left and then sat, waiting for her to be well settled somewhere before I went back to my room and changed. I ran my hands over my troublesome belly with a small laugh. I had seen plenty of stomachs like this—pasty-white and protruding—on men. Warm summer days in London were often greeted by men stripping off their shirts to reveal a physique that resembled my current one, though I didn't have the dusting of hair that accompanied theirs.

I cradled my child, reminding myself that I was life and not just darkness. I blew out a slow breath and put on my new modified training outfit—narrow-legged pants that laced up the front, making them expandable. I pulled the tunic over my head and began to braid my hair. I tied it off with a leather thong and stood in front of the mirror.

The warrior queen. The woman Valemar had trained for battle so that I might survive the Cordair and the Hormani. He had encouraged my destructive side.

I thought of the Baraáda—the fearsome warriors who guard the trees of Gladama. *Speak softly but carry a big stick.* U.S. President Teddy Roosevelt had spoken those words in early twentieth century Earth. A time that had been filled with uncertainty. Enemies had loomed. But Roosevelt had thought that the best way to ensure peace was to be willing to fight for it. Predators will leave a bigger predator alone, especially if the bigger one is minding his own business.

I moved to the jaldun practice room to mull that over. With my hands and feet engaged and my ears focused on the hiss the knives made as they cut the air, my mind was free to drift again.

History's greatest peacemakers had often been those willing to fight for it. Frequently labeled as warmongers—until they were needed—they were bustled away again as soon as the threat had passed.

Destruction. Protection.

I was both.

So are the citizens of Aedenfal. They destroyed me in little ways to protect their city.

I went through the movements on pure muscle memory. A single question hung in my mind, awaiting answer—what could I do to add to their defense?

I drifted, lost in the deadly ballet. The answer was out of reach. If I quieted my mind, it would reveal itself. *Speak softly. Carry a big stick.*

My hands slowed as a thread appeared. I was not their king. Valemar was gone and yet I sat at the high table, lording over them. Maybe not in action, but my presence certainly did. An unwanted presence. A dark presence.

I put my knives together and focused on slowing my breathing as I considered the audacious idea that was brewing. I was the

problem. To make them change, I needed to change. I needed to remove myself from the equation without really moving.

It would break tradition.

One side of my mouth quirked up. But then, I wasn't Alfari.

I would give them what they wanted and let them deal with the consequences. I would certainly have to.

I bit my lips, holding back a giggle as I placed the knives back on the rack. I was less successful in holding back the smile that ran from ear to ear.

Be careful what you wish for…

CHAPTER 12

The banqueting room buzzed with low conversation, something the heavy wooden doors that led to it didn't really dampen. I nodded once to Rydan and they opened.

Conversation faded. Every eye turned to me. I stepped forward and stood before the empty table. I had even had the chairs removed. The assembly slowly stood.

I waited while they assessed me, while they wondered what could possibly be going on. Eyes lingered on my dress—Bánalfar green. The crown I wore was of simple gold barat leaves, without the silver waves that represented the Lian Isles. I stood before them as Bánalfar itself.

"People of Aedenfal…for twelve hundred years this hall has welcomed you in thanks for your service. And that will continue. While the high table is empty, yours are not. And that is as it should be for, whether your king is here or not, your service is still needed and appreciated."

I set my jaw. "But your king is not here. You must look to yourselves. I do not rule you. And Garris is your steward, not your king." Looks traveled to the communal table closest to the dais where Garris stood. Heads bent to whisper.

"There are communal dinners at only one other High in this country." The name traveled among the crowd before I spoke it. "Glábac." My gaze roamed the tables. A few heads nodded, remembered smiles on the faces that did. "There they sup as equals.

"You have different ranks, different status, but you are all responsible for this city. It is my intention that while Valemar is away that you dine as they do in Glábac. Tonight is for you. I will not be joining you. You are Alfari and I am an outsider." Soft gasps filled the air. My gaze traveled over the tables, meeting the glances, the hardness in my eyes making sure they understood why I had stepped aside. They had wanted me gone and I was giving it to them. Yet I wasn't going anywhere. I was doing my duty, keeping the tradition, yet crushing it. They had emptied the high table and would sit every night, staring at something that should not be, something that would have horrified their ancestors. Despite their pledge and everything the food still provided for them represented, they had torn apart the very thing they were to protect.

I softened both my voice and eyes that had gone fierce. "This is to be Glábac. Those who visit the city and Gladama would give their lives for it. For generations, your families have given their lives for this city. It is time to remember that."

I bowed my head and made my exit, the crowd still standing in stunned silence. The door boomed as it closed behind me, filling both rooms with a noise like a death knell.

When I had hatched the plan, I had been glad that Valemar was days away. Upsetting the tradition would be another thing for him to be angry about.

Yet, as I made my way up to the small dining room where I would share dinner with Brinna, it was not Valemar's anger that rang in my ears. I smiled.

It was Reina's laughter I heard.

"Well, well, well." Brinna trilled when I entered the private dining room. "Don't you look like Bánalfar."

"And yet, I am an outsider," I said cheerfully as I sat down.

Brinna's expression filled with glee. "You stood before them dressed like that and told them that?"

"Alas," I said with feigned sorrow. "One need only look at my hair to know it is true."

"And so they are to be without you for…how long?"

I took my wine and drank before I answered. "I did more than that. I cleared the high table." Brinna's eyes widened. "I removed all the chairs." Her eyebrows rose. "Garris is now sitting at the communal tables. I told them I was creating Glábac."

Brinna whistled softly. *"Trocá."*

"They didn't want a queen, especially in the absence of the king, and so I provided them with what they desired. I know you didn't like eating in there."

"It was like being on display in a shop window," she said.

"To have left my chair empty would have been acknowledging they had driven me away. And to have sat through those dinners for another moon or more—"

"Would have been torture," Brinna finished.

"Instead, not even the king remains." I took a deep breath as Brinna's eyes took in my costume again. Her mouth curled upward. I had to force the next words from my mouth. "In the place and

custom meant to thank them for their service…"

"You quietly shamed them," Brinna said, her eyes shining with approval.

"If somewhat dramatically," I acknowledged.

"How long are you going to leave it like that?"

"Until Valemar himself orders it to be put right."

"That could be just a few days," Brinna said.

I shrugged. "But I won't return until he does."

Her eyebrows rose. "And if he orders you?"

"I am not Alfari."

"But you are his wife. He is the king."

"I am the Moon Princess and the Astrun Federation ambassador as well as his wife. His people have insulted me repeatedly. He needs to make that right."

As I said the words, I realized that was part of the trouble between us. He had intervened when Laera verbally attacked me in front of him, but he had mostly left me to fend for myself. If I now took matters into my own hands, he could hardly fault me.

"Besides," I added, thinking of Reina's laughter. "The Queen Mother would have surely done more."

"That she would," Brinna said in an awed whisper.

I took up my knife and fork. "So tell me about Tuljerd," I said, and turned the conversation to more cheerful matters.

Brinna and I joined the women in the solar the next morning. The air was thick with tension when we first sat down, the others wondering just how far my retaliation would extend. But I pretended I didn't feel their anxiety and it slowly dissipated. After lunch, I returned to my room and changed into a gown that was hardly more than rags.

Despite my having requested it, Iree was reluctant to hand it over. I could have gotten into it myself as it didn't lace up the back but I still had her help me. I knew she needed me to continue to find her useful.

"It's for jaldun," I said, checking out my reflection in the mirror. "The skirts won't survive the session. I may as well cut a rag into smaller rags."

"Yes, my queen."

"And find me another one, would you?"

Iree's cheeks colored. Such gowns were usually worn the night of a Blood Moon as they were easy to remove.

"Valemar once threatened to teach me to fight clad only in my nightgown." Her eyes grew wide at the scandalous suggestion. "I'm not going to do that," I reassured her. "But I do need to learn just what jaldun will do to my skirts. Actually, find me several that could be cut into ribbons."

What would an attacker do to and with my skirts? I would give myself a couple of days of solo practice and then have Orin find me a sparring partner. He wouldn't be happy about it.

It ended up being a tricky process, moving the jaldun knives without slicing my skirts. I had hardly begun the first kata when the holes started appearing. I slowed down, moving at the speed with which I had first learned them, though far less clumsy.

I experimented with how I held the blades. A few degrees this way, a few millimeters higher, and my skirts were safe. I slowly ran through all of the forms Valemar had taught me. My skirts were basically intact when I stopped due to thirst rather than fatigue. I would attempt to build up speed tomorrow.

I swung by my study before going back to my room and poured myself a glass of water from the decanter on my desk. I flopped into my chair.

The chain around my neck held onto what little sweat I had raised with the exercise, and I drew it out to wipe the moisture away. But once I held the key in my palm, the strange courage I had summoned the day before washed over me. I stuck the key in the lock and turned it, opening the bottom drawer.

Pulling the tablet out, I set it on my desk. I extended a finger and, with a resigned breath, swiped it across the surface. The black glass took on a white glow. I tapped in my password. One message waited for me.

I finished the contents of my water glass and opened the file dated seven days previous. It was from General Creskin, informing me of the timeline of the single trade I had approved—when the Cordair would deliver the ore and when they would receive their payment. There hadn't been any word on exactly what the Cordair had done with the gold because they hadn't received it. Yet.

I counted the dates on my fingers. The exchange should have taken place two days ago.

I typed a short response, thanking the general for keeping me updated and returned the tablet to the drawer. I would have to let Orin know.

I sent word through a guard that I would like to have the seneschal join me in my study when convenient and then returned to my rooms to have Iree help me change. The striking, young lieutenant was waiting for me when I returned.

"That was quick," I said, settling myself behind my desk.

"My queen bids me come and I come," Orin replied.

With his muscular build and casual way of carrying himself Aedenfal's seneschal would have looked at home on any of Earth's beaches, probably with a surfboard in hand, though his hair was far too pretty and kept for such a setting. But his appearance hid his

lethalness, much like a cat's softness camouflaged its claws. Having sparred with Orin, I knew just how deadly he could be with a sword, why he had been put in charge of Aedenfal's defense.

"Your queen bids you to take care of Aedenfal first and me second," I said. "I will let you know if it is anything urgent." Orin acknowledged my command with a tilt of his head. "I wanted to inform you that I have heard from General Creskin. The exchange took place two days ago."

"We saw it."

"Ah." I should have realized the Alfari scouts would have been watching for it. "I know you are keeping Valemar up to date on developments, especially what Raislos will now do with the gold he has received, but please inform me as well. If I am to craft policy, I have to understand what the impact of that trade is."

"Yes, my queen." Orin's voice was devoid of any emotion.

"And I have another request." Orin stood silently at attention. "I have acted on one of Valemar's suggestions and have begun to train in something other than the usual jaldun garb. Since I am generally in skirts, I want to see what difference they make—both for me in wielding the blades as well as the movements of an opponent. I am going to need a sparring partner."

Orin's eyes widened. "Are you sure that's a good idea…in your condition?"

"Valemar once told me that I was more likely to come under attack dressed in my nightgown. I think I'm more likely to come under attack alone and pregnant."

"We would never—"

I held up a hand. "I know. But I can sit around and wait or I can practice and prepare." I gave him a small smile. "Isn't the latter more practical?"

"Then I will trust no one but myself with your training, my queen." Orin's gaze went to my stomach. "It would be my life if anything happened to your child."

"As you wish," I said. "I do not wish to add to your responsibilities but I understand your concern. Give me another day of learning how skirts affect my movements and then we can work around your schedule. We can practice wherever you see fit."

"I will have to let Valemar know," Orin said gravely.

My lips twitched. Yet another thing for my husband to hate. "I am sure if he were here, he would be training me himself. You guard Aedenfal in his absence and therefore me. I will welcome your instruction."

"Anything else, my queen?"

"No. Thank you, Orin." I let the seneschal make his escape.

I watched his retreating form. Valemar would have told me, in no uncertain terms, what my weaknesses were. Heymond would have been as effective, if more subtle, though he had once left me black and blue. I had a feeling Orin would be more cautious, though he was a more deadly sparring partner than anyone else left at Aedenfal. Deadly was what I needed.

Orin looked more than a little nervous when we met in the jaldun room. If he had sent a karawack right after our conversation, it would still be another day before Valemar learned of my plan. Snow Reach lay about four hundred miles to the south, about a three-day flight for a karawack. Today, Valemar would read about how I had changed Aedenfal's dinners. I didn't relish the message I was sure to receive from him in a few days.

"What do you wish me to do?" Orin asked.

"Try and take me," I said simply. "I need to know how these skirts change my movement and how you might plan to use them."

"Very well." His words were hard and clipped. Orin tossed aside the knife that had been in his left hand. It clattered to the floor and slid, scraping across the stones until it came to rest against the wall. "And you will have two knives, my queen?" he asked, staring at the blades I held.

No, I wouldn't. I threw one aside, tossing it toward Orin's discarded blade.

"Now, what do you anticipate?" he asked.

"If you were trying to get me out of the High, what would you do?" I asked.

"You foresee a kidnap attempt?" Orin asked.

"Neither Valemar nor Heymond are here and, nothing against your defense of Aedenfal or me, those are conditions that might make someone think that I am vulnerable. If someone gets past you and your guards, wanting to kill me, I am most likely dead. But if they want to take me, that gives me a chance to fight. A chance for someone from the guard to come to my aid."

Orin nodded. "Very well. Take you." He turned his back and walked away. I peered after him and nearly jumped out of my skin when he spun on his heel and rushed at me. A sudden clench in my belly bent me double. I froze, one hand pressed against the place where my child rested.

Orin gasped and dropped his knife as he rushed to my aid. I put out a hand to halt him. "It's okay." I focused my senses on my abdomen, searching for cramping or other signs of distress. "I just tensed in surprise." My heart thumped against my ribs. I blew out a breath, slowing it as I decided that all was fine, and then straightened. "All right, good to know. Blood rushes to my belly and not just my heart when I'm startled." I pursed my lips and exhaled slowly, blowing off the remaining shock.

When I'd recovered, I gestured for Orin to return to the place where he had been. "Go ahead. Try it again."

Orin retrieved his knife. "Well, I'm not going to try to surprise you."

Instead, we faced each other. Orin took his time sizing me up while I stayed alert, watching for telltale signs as to what he might do next. The knife began to twirl in his hand as he began a slow approach. I backed up, continuing my assessment, until I sensed I was approaching a wall.

"Good, my queen," Orin said when I stopped. "Don't let yourself get boxed in."

Time to flee—that was what Valemar had told me when he had first begun my training, his intent to give me the tools necessary to stay alive. I set myself the goal of getting out the door. Mindful that Orin was watching for clues as well—as would any attacker—I kept my eyes on him while shifting my position, moving like I was trying to get a feel for what he would do.

I had made it about a hundred degrees from my starting point before Orin chuckled. His mouth quirked up into a lopsided smile. "Smart," he said. "But then I'd do this." He lunged, grabbing for the skirts about my knees with one hand while his other brought his blade to my throat. His eyebrows went up with a silent, *Gotcha*.

"I need a practice blade, a dull blade," I told Orin as he released me. "I was afraid of cutting your hand."

"I should have one as well." Orin took a step toward the rack on the left-hand wall.

"No. If you're going to be potentially cutting my skirts, I need them cut. And me afraid of your knife. Is there even a dull one there?" I asked.

There wasn't. Orin called for one to be fetched from the training yard. In the meantime, he put me through a series of exercises. We had sparred before, as part of a group, but Orin wanted to see what I could do.

"Gaining an unfair advantage?" I asked.

"Maybe just a little. I wanted to see how your center of gravity has changed and how you are compensating for it."

"Then you'll be better prepared for what I might do than someone else would."

Orin didn't respond. He continued to watch the way my skirts filled and then emptied as I twisted and swayed.

My steps had slowed and my arms had begun to feel heavy by the time the knife arrived. Orin asked Tovan for water to be brought in, too. "Don't want you getting dehydrated…my queen." He had momentarily forgotten that I wasn't just another trainee.

Orin handed me the blunt knife. "If someone were to slip in, it would be under the cover of darkness. And yes, I realize that we see better in the dark than you do, but there are fewer people around at night and you would most likely be asleep."

"You were trying to tire me out on purpose?" I asked.

"Noise in the hallway would awaken you and alert you that there is a problem. How do you respond?"

"I…" I looked at the knife in my hand. "I need to keep a knife in my room."

Orin crossed his arms. "Good. What's next?"

I ran through the scenario in my head. "Get my knife and stand by the door."

"Show me," Orin said.

There was no door to the jaldun practice room but I flattened myself against the wall by the opening. Orin nodded his approval.

"I'm now going to sneak in."

Over and over we ran it. Unless I waited until Orin was just inside the door and I could get my knife into his back and edge my way out into the hall, my skirts became a tether that was easily grabbed.

"We should do this again at night," I told him. I had finished off most of the water and had begun to pant at every attempt.

"How well do you see in the dark?" Orin asked.

"Not at all really. Humans are not nighttime predators and our moon is white, casting a more lamp-like glow. Our full moon fills the night with dawn."

Orin shook his head. "You truly are at a disadvantage."

I would also need to place a lamp at the bedside so I could light it if I heard anything. I would feel more exposed but being able to see would give me better odds.

CHAPTER 13

The blade of the knife caught the light. Its honed edge gleamed wickedly. I swallowed hard to keep down bile that rose at the thought of actually using it on someone. Careful not to cut the sheets, I slipped it under my mattress.

My hand, half-tucked out of sight, triggered a memory—Valemar's as he snaked it under his pillow on our wedding night. A creak outside the door had caused us both to freeze in the midst of consummating our marriage. My heart hammered as the images in my mind overlapped—both of our hands, wrapped around different weapons, afraid of what could reach us in the safety of our room.

I ripped my pillow from the bed and threw it against the wall. It slipped to the ground in a soft puff. I wanted a *thang* that resonated my anger.

Valemar could have sent me anywhere—Vanerife, Torfin, Glábac. But he had left me here in the heart of danger. Well, not the heart. Snow Reach currently occupied that position.

I threw another pillow then ripped the sheets from the bed. Anything to keep me from throwing the knife at the wall.

And then the fight rushed out, leaving as quickly as it had come. I slid down the wall beside the bed and buried my eyes against my knees. God help me, I actually longed for Vanerife.

I raised my head, sniffing to fight back the tears that were welling. I wanted Reina. Not even the ghost of Daria's death diminished that. I wanted Reina's cruelty, the drive that had enabled her to order the disembowelment of the foolish cook who had—unintentionally—baked the poisoned tarts that had taken Daria's life. The tarts had been meant for me, and it had only been anxiety over the Hormani presence on Crenfor filling my stomach, leaving no room for anything else, that had saved me from eating them as the Hormani trader had intended. Reina's ruthlessness would offer me more protection than her son had left me with.

I rocked my head back and forth against the wall. Here I was, pregnant and learning to thwart my own kidnapping. I squeezed my eyes shut. Was I just seeing monsters where there weren't any?

Brinna doesn't trust them, either, the voice in my head whispered. But were we just two jumpy females seeing shadows where there weren't any?

Three. Shale had seen something, too.

I wrapped my arms around my belly. Valemar had left me with nothing but a child to protect.

Hot tears began to drip down my face. I was torn between hating Valemar, wanting to run, and wanting to eviscerate anyone who looked at me funny. A harsh croak of a laugh broke from my throat. *Blood does tell.*

"So Astrid, daughter of kings, shield maiden," I said, calling up the Viking ancestor I was named for. "What are you going to do?"

I wiped away the tears with the back of my hand. My gaze came to rest on the pile of sheets halfway across the room. My breath

shuddered as the last of the emotion left my body. I pushed myself up, one hand going to my belly as I dealt with the still-odd change in my balance.

This Astrid was going to make the bed.

I curled up on top of the covers when I had finished. The pillow welcomed my weary head, not caring about the violence I had shown it. I sighed and let myself drift. I couldn't run. I couldn't gut them. And I only hated Valemar because I loved him.

I wiped away the moisture collecting along the rim of my eye. I had to stop training. Fearing shadows had only increased my fear. It had to be the pregnancy hormones. Preparing to fight the Hormani had made me strong. But not this. This was creating a heightened frenzy in me. Orin would be relieved.

I rolled over and smoothed the surface of Valemar's pillow, blinking as my eyes began to prick again. God, how I wanted a karawack from him. Had he left me or had he left me in charge? I swallowed, thinking of a thousand things I should have asked him before he had gone.

The fabric was cool under my fingers. My nose bent toward the pillow, searching for his scent, but it was clean, smelling only of the soap used to wash it. I continued to pet the pillow, my hand gently rubbing over the surface as I thought. My brain began a list of tasks that needed to be done.

I needed to check with Garris on the preparations for Gellirhird just nineteen days away. As I was uncertain of what the celebration entailed, I should also meet with Padrid. *Would the high table need to be restored for the festivities?* I hoped Brinna would help me strike a balance between tradition and change.

I pushed at the small creases on the pillowcase with a fingertip. I had created ripples. Having grown up spending summers by the sea, I knew that small ripples could fan out, growing ever larger and swamp the unaware. I prayed that Aedenfal would prove to be a pond and not an ocean.

I arranged for a small chest of drawers to be brought in to use as a nightstand. It roused the curiosity of the servant who had carried it in. Bedside lamps weren't needed by the Alfari as they could see their way to the close stool or garderobe without them. I placed a lamp and matches on the top of it and the knife inside the first drawer.

Brinna and I continued to sew with the women in the solar. It became both our conduit for gossip and our assurance that, despite the changes I had made, all was well.

I received two messages from Valemar in the intervening days. The first demanding *"What in the depths of the ocean and the heights of the heavens?"* was going on in Aedenfal that I had emptied the high table. It had taken me a full day to word a karawack-sized reply that would neither make him rush back nor think that I had acted rashly. The second had been full of concern for the training I had taken up, especially as my reply to the first had not yet reached him.

I could hardly answer "I don't feel safe" or "Sorry, I was overreacting" when the truth lay somewhere in the middle. I hoped the humorous message I had constructed—*You did say I should train in my nightgown. I settled for a dress.*—let him know I was taking his warning seriously. That in itself should give him pause.

Today, I contented myself with a short sewing session before Brinna and I went to the Cair to observe the Resting Moon. It had been more than a month and a half since I had been in the Low,

visiting Master Iru's shop. Four guards accompanied us. Brinna's attempts at light conversation stopped after my first short replies. I was too distracted to keep track of the conversation while I searched for the prickly feeling of being watched as well as taking note of the mood and energy of the people along the streets.

Our crimson veils kept anyone from greeting us—the lace a physical barrier meant to shut out the outside world and center the wearer's thoughts on the Mother and the Father. But I didn't hear any malevolent murmurs or see frowning faces bent in whispered conversation. Those in the Low simply went about their business.

Brinna stood in line to seek the Möd's blessing while I knelt at the side altar. I lit a red candle and added it to the tiers of sand-filled trays already flickering with the prayers of those who had gone before me. Raised Christian as a child on Earth, my journeys through the stars had altered my views, and while I recognized Shale, the Mödatal, as a seer, I did not hold the same faith as the Möd and thought it sacrilegious—to them—for me to act as if I did. I didn't mind being on my knees, praying to the God of my childhood, asking the Mother and Father and the universe to keep my husband and my child—and me—safe.

But my thoughts drifted back to the line of veiled women who came to kneel before the Möd, each one asking, praying, that their Blood Moon couplings fifteen days before would result in a child. Brinna was one in a line of eight to ten that grew and shrank as some moved on and others joined it. I watched Brinna kneel in front of the Möd. He dipped his fingers into a bowl and dripped water onto her. I didn't need to be close to know that it would smell of the sea.

Brinna rose and made her way over. She knelt next to me and added her own candle to the hundred or so burning. "I'm going to

go see the Scanhör," she whispered when she'd finished her prayers. The *knife wielder.*

The Alfari had no wedding rings. Instead, the fleshy pad of the right index finger was sliced open, the butterfly-like scar marking a person as married. Bride and groom pressed their wounds together and offered their mingled blood to Mother Moon and Father Sea. And blood was frequently offered as a sacrifice to enhance one's prayers. I had done it many times myself. First as a show meant to camouflage my true purpose in Vanerife and then more honestly as I began to understand that the bloodletting was a physical acknowledgement that all things bear a cost. To gain one thing, you needed to give up another.

I let Brinna go and turned my thoughts to whether I should visit Shale or not. I often did when I came to the Cair but I didn't usually have a friend with me. And while Shale was a highly respected member of the Cair clergy, one didn't generally seek out the Mödatal. She would only tell you things about the future that didn't affect the future. One frequently got riddles or no answer at all.

Shale had constantly interfered in my life, saving it several times over, showing me things she thought I should know, hiding other things from me. I had hated her at times, loved her at others, and now found her a disconcerting yet necessary part of my life. It had been too long. I rose from the altar when Brinna returned, determined to make my visit.

"We are just going to pop 'round and see Shale for some tea," I said to Brinna, leading the way to the side door. Brinna's eyes were large and round when she raised her veil and settled it over her shoulders as we entered the dormitory section of the Cair. Most Alfari didn't have a day-to-day relationship with their Mödatal.

"Want to see something funny?" I whispered as we rounded the corner. Brinna gave an awed nod. I raised my eyebrows in "watch" and then lifted my hand to Shale's door.

"Enter Astrid," Shale called out before my hand made contact with the wood. "And friend." Brinna's mouth became an O. Shale couldn't resist showing off. I think she knew it threw everyone off balance.

Shale stood before the fire, gazing into the flames. She took a handful of tiny crystals from a bowl on the mantel and tossed them in. The flames turned blue, green, and gold, and a memory of Grandma Sarah doing something similar arose. The past and the present overlapped and, for a moment, I felt my grandmother's presence.

We let Shale continue whatever vision she was seeing in silence. As the colors died out, Shale pushed away from the mantel and turned to us, blinking. She raised a smile. The smile grew as her gaze took in Brinna then traveled to Brinna's abdomen. I crossed my fingers.

"We will be needing some tea." Shale pulled an embroidered cord by the wall and crossed to the sofa. She tucked her feet, bare even now in winter, next to her and gestured for us to sit.

"Welcome, Brinna Fálin," she said.

Brinna bowed her head. "Thank you for receiving me, honored Mödatal."

"You have been busy, Astrid," Shale said to me.

I shrugged. "You know me. Trouble wherever I go." Shale lifted an ironic smile.

"What can I do for you today, my queen?" Shale asked.

"I just fancied a visit." *A bit of normalcy.*

"I can provide that," she said in response to the unspoken part of my sentence. "How are you finding Aedenfal, *Grada* Brinna?"

"Interesting," Brinna answered nervously.

"They don't like change," Shale said. "Especially when the king isn't here." She turned her eyes on me.

I met Shale's gaze. "They should have offered me protection in the absence of my husband but, instead, they let their resentment resurface."

Shale's lips curled up. "And Bánalfar quietly reprimanded them."

"I wouldn't call it quiet," I said.

"It was a quiet action that spoke loudly."

I gave voice to the question that had been lingering in the back of my mind since I had hatched the plan. "Have I made things worse?"

"You have cemented a path. Just as Valemar leaving created difficulties and opportunities for you, you have created difficulties and opportunities for others." Brinna gasped. "Your life here will never be easy, Astrid," Shale said gently.

The spell was broken by a knock announcing the arrival of the tea. Shale poured the first cup and handed it to Brinna. Brinna's eyes widened as she breathed in the aroma. It was a tea most often drunk to increase fertility.

"Thank you," I said, taking the cup Shale offered to me. The woodsy scent hit my nose followed by a wish for honey. For me, it would have balanced the flavor perfectly but the tea was always served unsweetened.

Shale poured her own cup and curled back onto to the sofa. "Ask," she told Brinna, bending her head to take a sip.

Brinna struggled to form her words. I knew well the fear that tore someone between wanting and not wanting to know what the future held. "Will I have a child?" Her words were more thought than air but we all knew what they were.

Shale smiled serenely. "You will."

Brinna gave a tight nod and dashed away tears. I sipped my tea to give her a bit of privacy to recover.

"How about you?" I asked Shale as Brinna took up her tea again. "You have been trying since I met you."

"Soon," Shale answered. "I will have a daughter in the new year."

Maybe birthrates weren't really as bad as I had feared. Of my female acquaintances, that left only the recently wed Niah without children. And Iree. The Blood Moon fever often produced what were called *moon children* who were given over to service if their parents were not married. Every soldier, every member of the Cair, and most servants were moon children. Reina had even had a moon child before she had married Valemar's father. Shale's child would most likely join the Cair, especially if she had red hair. I wondered if she would inherit her mother's abilities as well.

"She won't be mine to raise," Shale reminded me.

"Even if she can see?"

I sensed something snap shut—muscles that tightened, breath that stilled. I had asked a question she wasn't allowed to know the answer to. Shale swallowed. "That will be revealed in time."

CHAPTER 14

Brinna and I spent the afternoon going over plans for Gellirhird with Garris and Padrid. *Bright light in the depths of winter.*

"If it is held on the Blood Moon, how does that actually work?" I asked. Most adults left dinner as soon as the moon rose, drifting away to mate as the fever overtook them. There was a draught that could counteract the pull, but I couldn't see people taking it in order to participate in a festival.

"There is an early dinner, followed by the usual Blood Moon activities," Brinna said with a waggle of her eyebrows. "Gellirhird is celebrated after everyone is thinking a bit more clearly."

Padrid cleared his throat. "The moon is higher, brighter by then, too."

"What is the celebration like here in Aedenfal?" I asked.

Brinna turned her attention to Garris. "People gather in the hall as the moon reaches its zenith," he said.

"Decorations?" I asked.

"The tables will have been set with centerpieces of white and yellow candles interlaced with a vine known as Winter's Candles."

"They have waxy yellow-white blossoms," Brinna added to Garris's description.

"Why all the light if it is held during a full moon?" I asked. The three Alfari bore similar expressions of confusion at my unusual term though it quickly cleared. "I would have thought the color would be red to echo the moon."

"It is the midwinter moon," Padrid said.

My brow furrowed. "But if Gellirhird is about creating light in the darkness then why isn't it held during the Resting Moon when the night would truly be dark."

"The Blood Moon marks the first day of Lardreth." Padrid didn't seem to understand my confusion.

"Never mind me," I said with a wave of my hand. "I had thought it might align with the midwinter celebrations on Earth." Padrid bent toward me, placing his folded hands on the table, and nodded for me to continue. "Many cultures on Earth celebrated the longest night of the year because, with every night that followed, the days grew longer and the nights shorter."

Padrid pursed his lips. "Interesting. Here we give thanks for the brightness of the moon in the cold dark of the midwinter night."

"Red light is harder to duplicate," Brinna said.

"You don't get the color until the embers are ready to sleep," Garris added. "When fires have burned down that far and the candles have gone out, that signals the end of Gellirhird. Even the moon is ready for bed."

I wove the old and new together, searching for a pattern to anchor its meaning. "So, in a way, you are adding to the light of the moon."

"I hadn't thought about it that way, but that is true," Brinna said.

"Okay, people return to tables decorated with lights and greenery. What else?" I asked.

"There are tables set with dishes of midwinter mince and others with moon pies," Garris said.

"Jam tarts," Brinna added for my benefit.

Garris gave her an annoyed glance and continued. "Minstrels and dancing."

"We gather together in unity," Padrid said, his eyes flicking back and forth between the other two Alfari. "Adding our light to the moon's. Together, we light up the midpoint of winter."

"To show the darkness it cannot win," I said, putting my own spin on it.

Padrid chuckled. "I do love the way your mind works. That is not how we think about it, but you are right."

"Kind of like how Glábac unites those that make the pilgrimage to Gladama," I said. Garris's face froze at my comparison. A scowl flashed in the depths of his eyes.

Padrid and Brinna spoke at the same time. "Exactly." "Yes."

"What if we set the food on the dais?" I suggested. "An offering from the High. And this year we have the special reserve of piora from Torfin."

"It usually follows the king," Garris said with an accusing glance at Brinna.

"It was Valemar's suggestion," Brinna said. A hard edge entered her usually lilting voice. "Since he was on campaign, he wanted it to follow the queen."

Garris tilted his head, giving in. It made me wonder what, if anything, Valemar had told him about my care.

"That would free up some room," Padrid said, wading into the fray. He gave a small sigh. "There is nothing like a night at Glábac High." Longing tinged his voice.

My own memories rose, warming my heart. Those evenings in

Glábac had been some of the most contented in my life.

"What arrangements still need to be made?" I asked.

"We have the wine." Garris shot Brinna another annoyed look. "The supplies for the moon pies have been set aside. As have the candles. The Winter's Candles will be gathered the day before."

"Is there an invitation list that is different from the normal dinners?" I asked.

"Same list." Garris's jaw clenched.

My question had made him angry. I searched for a reason why. *First Gellirhird without his wife.*

The thought froze me for a moment. They had been apart for nearly five months with no end in sight to her exile. Their only hope for reunification was Garris resigning. Or a pardon from Valemar. If things in Aedenfal hadn't already been so tense, I would have written to Valemar to suggest it, but the last thing I wanted was an angry Laera in town.

"Is there anything you need from me?" I asked. Brinna shook her head and looked to Garris.

"No, my queen." His eyes were fixed on his desk with such ferocity I wouldn't have been surprised if they drilled holes into his notes.

"Anything else I should know about Gellirhird?" I asked Padrid, trying not to shiver from the tension now rolling off of Garris in waves.

Padrid scratched his chin in thought. "The carols. Someone should probably teach you the dances."

"The sewing circle can teach you the songs," Brinna said. "And we can probably hunt down some young men to practice the dance steps." Her eyes sparkled. "I'm sure Vienne wouldn't mind putting down her needle for that. It *is* for the queen, after all."

Padrid chuckled. And, on that more positive note, I adjourned the meeting.

"What do partners do when they are apart during the Blood Moon?" I asked Brinna at dinner. "Husbands and wives?"

Brinna ran her finger along the base of her wine glass. "It depends. Sometimes they take the draught. Sometimes they find another partner."

"Daria always said it was just sex." For the first time, her name rolled off my tongue without the usual pang that accompanied it.

"It can be more complicated once you are married." A light blush colored Brinna's cheeks. She, too, would be alone on Gellirhird.

"I don't mean to pry," I said.

"No, it is a valid question." Brinna lifted her eyes to mine and I saw her thoughts. Valemar would be alone on Gellirhird, too. I had never asked him what he had done during the Blood Moons that I been in exile in Vanerife.

"Sometimes spouses agree to take the draught. Other times they…expect the night to be like any other Blood Moon. Single people sometimes have moon mates."

"Like Valemar had Zhanet."

"Yes." Brinna gave me a sympathetic smile.

Zhanet had been a thorn in my side when I first arrived. She had sat at her table in the banqueting room watching Valemar and me night after night. After having done my duty consummating my marriage, my skin had crawled at the thought of being touched by a man I hadn't chosen and Valemar hadn't forced me. But Zhanet noticed his desire and frustration and her anger slowly turned to smugness.

When the Blood Moon came, I decided to try to make my ultra-hasty marriage a real one and took Valemar to bed, hoping that my feelings for him would grow, knowing that he would be with Zhanet if I did not. She had vanished from Aedenfal shortly after.

"Both parties recognize that it is just Mother Moon expressing her wish to be with Father Sea," Brinna continued. "They come together once a month and part after the act, where marital sex is something that binds the partners together." Brinna's face flamed.

"So not being together during a Blood Moon strains at those bonds?"

"Many couples acknowledge the incongruence between those two desires. The Blood Moon is primal. Marital sex is more… sacred."

I will shelter you from sun and cold and harm. The final line of the Alfari wedding vows. The entire ceremony represented coming together and protecting each other.

"Then some couples who are apart recognize the instinctual urge and act on the pull?"

"It is difficult either way. If you take the draught, you know what is happening all around you." That had been my experience. "If you don't then, as the fever clears, you are staring into eyes that aren't those you love." Brinna gave me a sad smile.

I wondered if that was true for Alfari males as well. Or if they took the human view of sex as recreation, not something sacred.

I continued to think about it long after dinner. Valemar would be overcome with the urge to mate in fifteen days. Gellirhird was sure to be celebrated in Snow Reach. And even though soldiers took the draught if they were on guard duty, what would a whole battalion do? What was happening at Snow Reach, anyway? I anxiously chewed at my nails as I paced my room.

Once begun, a Blood Moon pairing could not be halted. Valemar had warned me as much when I had finally decided to make my marriage real. The primal urge took over the senses, clearing only after the act was complete. Despite Valemar's marriage vows and protectiveness, I knew that first Blood Moon that if I did not take my then unwanted husband to bed that Valemar's moon lust would be expended on Zhanet. We had only spent two moons apart since.

I poured myself a glass of wine. While some humans had to worry about fetal alcohol syndrome, its cause had lay within the activation of a single recessive gene. Most women were told that moderate consumption was fine and the Alfari had no such concerns. It would be my second of the night but I longed for the relaxation the alcohol would bring. Nerves were probably worse for the baby, raising my blood pressure and releasing stress hormones.

I thought back to the Blood Moon during which we had been afraid of Cordair attack. Twenty minutes of sex and then Valemar left me to join the patrols, the lust gone without a trace. Wasn't it better for a soldier to clear that out of his system and move on? I sipped the wine as I continued pacing.

I was sure Valemar had taken a partner the first moon we had been apart. He had learned that I had lied to him—mainly by omission—just days before and had cast me out. A moon mate would have allowed him to release all kinds of frustration. The second moon, I had been in Vanerife. Shale had shown me a trick with my blood the next day. My mind filled with the sight of Valemar's blood reaching for mine in the bowl, swirling together, refusing to be parted. Something told me he had taken the draught that time.

And what would I want this coming moon? I would bar myself in my room as I had done before, ensuring that no one took my presence as an invitation. And then I would have to emerge and go join the celebration. No post-coital glow for me.

But Gellirhird wasn't about the sex, like most Blood Moons were. The fever dispelled, the focus became the moon and the light—and the community.

My eyes closed. I should have asked Brinna what she was going to do. Padrid would have a partner. He never took the draught. My lips quirked up in a smile. Even when half of Aedenfal had taken it, fearing Cordair attack, Padrid had let nature take its course.

And Garris…he'd had five, soon to be six, moons without Laera. No wonder he had grown resentful.

I set the half-full glass on the table. I wanted my husband strong, not beholden. I lit a candle and made my way to my study. There, I opened my correspondence box and drew out the narrow rectangle that would wrap around a karawack's leg.

Do what you need to do for Gellirhird, I wrote. *I will understand.* And then I added, since I had told him I had been sex crazed, *You will be with me either way.*

CHAPTER 15

My belly showed a definite bump by Gellirhird. I had thought the pooch had been obvious at four months pregnant, but at five—it was like I had stuck a small pillow there.

I had recently had General Creskin send someone to give me a physical. Not knowing when I had conceived had been driving me crazy, along with the lack of prenatal care. There wasn't much Alfari medicine could do for pregnancy, but I had been raised in a culture where everything during gestation was monitored, and so I worried. There was also the practical consideration of needing to know approximately when I would deliver.

A med tech with a scanner showed up the next day. He guessed that, due to the baby's size, I was probably about twenty weeks pregnant. As it was the first interspecies conception of its kind, he really wasn't willing to give me any definite answers other than all the organs seemed to be doing what they should be. I decided to stick to Alfari tradition and be surprised by the sex of my child—something the Federation and Shororato learned as soon as the scan started. I tried to not let that bother me.

Iree finished off the braid that held back the sides of my hair and revealed my ears. I gasped when I viewed my reflection in the full-length mirror. The midnight blue gown scattered with embroidered silver and white stars had transformed me into Nyx—a Greek goddess of such exceptional beauty and power that she was feared by Zeus himself. Not that there was much of either quality about me, especially with the baby bump, but the figure before me was one I had seen before. Painted in stunning detail in a nightclub in Athens, I had stared at the portrait for hours, much to the annoyance of the client who had brought me there.

My fingers reached out and touched the glass. "Something wrong, my queen?" Iree asked.

"Just seeing a ghost, in a way," I answered. My eyes took in the details again. The midnight blue. The iridescent stars. The dark curls hanging past my shoulders.

"Ghost?"

"Spirit from the past." I smiled at Iree's reflection. "I look like the old Earth goddess of the night."

"Oh," she said, though I could tell from the confusion in her eyes that she wasn't making the connection.

My fingers traced my outline on the mirror, much as they had wanted to do that night in Athens. Tonight, the room would be full of Moon Princesses. Part of the reason I had chosen blue rather than red. Mystery. Power. Life. Those were things that Nyx represented.

And then I smiled, for Nyx was also feared. Travelers today are wary of the cold, dark heart of space, even while they admire its beauty. The Alfari would not make the connection but it was one I took into my heart. To me, the Moon Princess had been a lie. I did not come from their moon. But I did come from the darkness of space. I had traveled amongst the stars. I had created life.

Nyx would have walked among the guests tonight, unfearing, knowing that, instead, she was feared. I drew up my tired spine as much as I could and lifted my chin. This was a mantle I could wear.

I slipped into the celebration without fanfare, Brinna by my side.

"I don't know what bothers them more," she said. "The color of your dress or the fact you are showing your ears." I usually wore my hair down to help hide them.

"I thought I should make it abundantly clear that I am not Cordair." Most of the room was attempting to whisper and stare without being obvious.

We picked our way through the crowd to Vienne's table. "Beautiful dress, my queen," Niah said.

"It is everyone else's turn to wear red," I said. "I decided to claim the stars."

Niah's husband, Reez, left to get some piora as Brinna and I took our seats at their table. One of Ean's assistants appeared in the doorway and scanned the room. His eyes alighted on me and he started toward our table. His hand was curled in such a way that I knew it held a karawack message. My heart picked up in tempo.

The mood at our table turned serious even though I marshalled a smile.

"Message from Valemar," he said, handing it over. Attention in the room swung my direction again.

Brinna leaned close. "Do you want to read it here?"

My hand shook. If it was bad news, it was something that should be shared immediately. "Let's have some wine first." A bit of joy to soften any pending disaster.

Reez returned and passed out the goblets. I lifted mine in toast. "To the bright light in the midst of darkness."

The others repeated the words, and we drank. A minstrel took up a song full of hope for winter's ease into spring. I unrolled the message and read.

You are always in my heart.

I bit my lips. Wonderful man.

"Astrid?" Brinna asked.

"He's simply wishing me a joyous Gellirhird." There was a sigh of relief from the table. I lifted my cup again. "And thank you, Valemar, for giving us all a scare." There were huffs as everyone tried to hold back their laughter. I tucked the message into my bodice as I had not thought to put pockets into my gown. It would sit, nestled next to my heart.

The minstrel finished his tune and began another, one of the carols. Thanks to the sewing sessions, I could sing along.

I looked at the smiling faces around the table. Here, I had become accepted. They were proud to see me fitting in. Proud that it was their help that had made me more Alfari. I had been right to clear the high table. Right to let them claim the red while I wore the blue. I had proclaimed myself as different but not above learning.

Reez was the first to claim me for a dance. He was the first but not the last. I finally had to turn down partners when my feet began to swell. I contented myself with watching from the table. The hall was filled with joy. It was everything I had wanted.

I felt a flutter, foreign and alien, a ripple inside my belly. Startled, I pressed my hand to the swell. Just when I began to believe I had imagined it, it came again—a sensation like a butterfly caught in my hands.

I looked back at the revelers and an ache blossomed in my heart. "Your baby is kicking," I whispered. I took a deep breath. The sharp edge of the karawack message pressed against my skin.

You are in my heart, too, I whispered, and flung my love across the miles.

I waited until morning to send Valemar the news. The party broke up hours after I had gone to bed. The candles had not yet burned down to stubs and the embers still held low, yellow flames, but I had begun to yawn as soon as the light in the hall softened.

The castle was quiet when I made my way to my study. I had dressed myself in one of the loose-fitting Blood Moon gowns and asked Tovan not to wake Iree but find someone already stirring in the kitchens to bring me my breakfast.

I missed you last night. The pen scratched against the slip of paper as I wrote out the words. *And I wasn't the only one. Your child kicked to say hello.*

I folded and sealed the paper. I would take it by the karawack nursery later. Ean had told me there was a new clutch of eggs meant for me.

I leaned back in the chair and rubbed my belly, warmed by the success of Gellirhird and the physical confirmation that there was life inside me. Valemar had left for Snow Reach exactly a month ago. I still didn't know what was going on there. At least things were now marginally better in Aedenfal.

Aedenfal.

The determination I had been gathering over the last couple of weeks evaporated with a whoosh. What was there to do now? Four more months of sewing?

I shuddered.

And the new elasticity of my joints left me feeling like a marionette whose strings had been cut. How did women manage to exercise this late in pregnancy? I moaned as I realized that "late" was a relative term. I hadn't even reached my third trimester yet.

Thank God for the karawack eggs, though I didn't know how the young birds would learn to fly with the cold.

I shifted around to look out the window. White flakes drifted past the glass, framed against a dark gray sky. It was the third snow of the season. Aedenfal was definitely more Kentucky than San Francisco or Athens, the closest Earth examples along the same latitude as Aedenfal. While Bánalfar lay in Crenfor's southern hemisphere, I had been able to work out from Padrid's maps the approximate latitudes of Bánalfar's cities and flipped them, hoping to anchor a picture of the geography in my head.

I was still watching the flakes when a knock sounded on the door and an unfamiliar girl brought in the tray. Caution flared around me before I tamped it down. There were many in the High I never had contact with.

"Thank you…" I drifted off, waiting for her to fill in her name.

"Aaya." She gave me a shy smile.

"Thank you, Aaya."

"Anything else, my queen?"

I returned her smile. "No. Thank you."

She slipped out, quietly closing the door behind her. I tucked into my breakfast, still watching the snow. My body tingled with Boxing Day expectations but there was no Christmas here and New Year's was still two months away, timed to begin with the first of spring.

I shivered. Unless you truly spent all your time off planet, your seasonal rhythms and expectations kept tempo with your home

planet. And hemisphere. Katrina had always celebrated Christmas with a cold shrimp salad and beer and had slathered herself in sunscreen so that her nose might at least think she had gone to the beach with the rest of the Aussies even if we were halfway across the galaxy. Based out of Paris, the *Cove's* crew had been mainly human. We celebrated whatever holiday happened to be on our Earth calendar no matter where we found ourselves. We had even picked up some new ones from our non-human companions.

"You, at least, won't be confused by it," I said to my belly. I poked it when there was no response. Having watched the gymnastics that had taken place inside Cadalin before Bréick was born, I knew that there would come a time when I would long for the quiet I now felt. "Fine," I said in defeat.

I sipped my tea and watched the snow fall and waited for the High to come back to life. It did so slowly. Iree came in with a horrified expression on her face and an apology on her lips. I waved it away.

"I am perfectly able to dress myself when there are no laces involved."

"But that's a…" She couldn't even bring herself to say it.

"Blood Moon dress. Yes, I know." I pulled at the extra fabric that hung between my breasts and belly. Blood Moon dresses were designed to be gotten out of in one nice pull over the head. Unlike the constricting laces of the rest of my gowns. "It would be considered a maternity dress on my planet. It's fine."

It was a scandal in Iree's eyes but I triumphed by simply refusing to budge. Iree slunk away to work on other things until I decided to change.

Brinna came in a while later. Her lips twitched with amusement. She snagged an apple-like fruit from the bowl by the window and bit

into it with a loud crunch. "You do realize the problem with walking around in that dress is that it's an invitation to take it off you?" she said when she had swallowed the bite. My cheeks colored. Brinna gave me a lazy smile. "Ach, well now you know."

"What am I to do with myself, Brinna?"

Brinna continued to munch the fruit in her hand. Her eyes gleamed wickedly. "Well, you could walk the halls and see what effect that dress has." I threw a pillow at her. "You truly are a servant queen. Your life does not seem to be complete unless you have some task to undertake."

Her simple truth caught me unawares. But she was right. "I guess that is the way I have always lived my life—school, studying files for the next assignment. Now I have no assignment."

"Then you haven't been paying much attention," she said, waving her fruit-filled hand at my midriff.

"Incubator," I said with a nod. "Now there is a mind-filling task."

"Not to mention bladder-filling."

"Don't," I said, but my bladder perked up at Brinna's words and decided that, yes, it needed to be emptied. I pushed up out of my chair. "Thanks," I told her, my voice full of sarcasm.

"Shout if anyone forgets what day it really is," Brinna called after my retreating form. I flipped my middle finger at her. "Is that what I think it is?" she asked as I headed out the door.

I found her turning her hand every which way when I came back, her fingers curled down to meet her palm. All of them except her middle finger. She held her hand up in the same gesture I'd given her. "This really holds too much promise. This—" She pointed her hand down. "—is the way things usually are." Brinna frowned slightly and switched her middle finger for her ring finger. "There we go. That's more realistic." I bit my lip. It *was* a better representation of the usual dimensions.

"It's an invitation to go do that to yourself," I said, settling myself on the cushions.

"Not as much fun," Brinna observed.

"It's supposed to be an insult."

"Sex on your planet doesn't sound very inviting." Brinna held up her hand again. "Unless you are offering me this."

"It's often accompanied by the suggestion that you do that to your own mother."

Brinna's eyebrows rose. "Oh. Well, that would make a difference."

"*Kwarg* would be about the equivalent."

"Well, that was downright mean of you."

"You gave my bladder ideas," I said in my defense. "And me none at all." Brinna shifted uncomfortably in her seat. "What?"

She bit her lips and stared at the floor. "Do you want me to have Jaros come take a look at how things are running?" Her lip was still clenched in her teeth when she looked up. I paled. If Brinna thought her husband should leave his post in Torfin and inspect Aedenfal, things had to be bad.

Brinna held up a hand as I opened my mouth. "Garris seems to be doing his job well," she said, "but he is not treating you with the respect you deserve. Did he even come talk to you at the celebration last night?"

I opened my mouth to answer but then had to stop and think about it. "No," I admitted. I hadn't missed him with all the other attention I had received.

"His job is to serve you. As steward, he should be seeking your approval in everything he is doing, especially as Valemar is away. Not in meticulous detail, but an overview to reassure you that things are functioning the way they should be."

I ran my thumbnail over my lower lip. "If I send for Jaros, even just as a husband checking in on his wife, Garris will fear that I mean to replace him." Brinna's mouth tightened into a flat line. She would replace the man. But that was not yet a step I was willing to take.

CHAPTER 16

I had stacks of baby clothes piled away in two chests but the sewing circle insisted that we needed more. "They grow so quickly," Cadalin explained as we started in on yet another set.

"If you are not going to embroider, then you can do the hem on this one." Brinna handed over a small blue smock. Waves curled around the front of the neckline, cleverly holding gathers in place. All the stitching had been done except the bottom hem. "Just pretend it's a diaper." The rest of the women had determined I had plenty of those now.

Bréick stirred in his basket and began to fuss. Cadalin plucked him out and put him to her breast where he sucked noisily. "I think he is going through a growth spurt," she said. Bréick looked at his mum and reached for her finger. Once in his grasp, she waved their hands around.

"He won't be in there much longer," Vienne said, surveying his basket. "Has he started rolling over yet?"

"He's trying. Aren't you?" Cadalin bent her head and gazed into Bréick's eyes. He paused in his nursing and gave her a milky smile.

My heart overflowed with longing. Four months seemed a lifetime away before I could hold a little one like that in my arms.

I turned down the edge of the smock and focused on my needle. The intensity of the emotion coursing through me came as a shock. I had wished and prayed that I could give Valemar a child and heir, but the desire had been nothing more than the urge to be useful. I could have been hoping to find yet another item that a client needed. It had never occurred to me that I would be someone's *mother*.

The women talked and I sewed. Bréick was burped and put back in his basket. Cadalin handed him a colorful cloth animal that he frowned at but soon reached for, waving a chubby fist until his hand closed around the toy.

"Finished." I cut the thread and passed the garment to Brinna.

They had started me in on yet another hem when bird master Ean appeared at the solar door. His braid swung toward the floor as he bowed.

"They are hatching, my queen."

"Thank you, Ean. I will be right there."

Still wrestling with the dawning realization that I was actually going to be a parent, and all the responsibility that entailed, my hands began to shake. I wasn't ready and was about to face another birthing.

I wove the needle into the fold and handed the smock to Brinna. The women sensed my distress, offering me awkward smiles as I rose. I tried to lift a reassuring one in response but could feel it twitching.

I paused in the hall and tried to pull myself together. Imprinting on a clutch of karawack as they hatched had always proved to be an emotional experience. Now I was going to be a mum. My arms ached, wanting to hold my own child. I prayed that I wouldn't cry through the whole ritual.

The karawack nursery was warm and dark. I never understood why they housed it in the basement and not in one of the towers where the birds could see the sky. The air in the nursery was filled with the familiar scent of dung and straw. I took my seat on the low stool next to the table that held the hatching nest. The eggs shook, clinking as they knocked together. I ran my fingers over the five speckled shells.

"Hello, little birds. It's time to hatch." Longing washed over me and pulled the first tears from my eyes. A flutter brushed inside my uterus. I placed a hand there. "Your prince or princess would like to meet you as well." The eggs continued to rattle.

I usually sang "Skye Boat Song" to the chicks as they hatched. It was a lullaby my mother had sung to me as a child but today I wanted something different. I wanted it to be my own child that I next sang my mother's song to.

I altered some of the words to "Lavender's Blue" and sang that instead:

Lavender's blue, dilly dilly
Lavender's green
When you are King, dilly dilly
I shall be Queen.

Lavender's green, dilly dilly
Lavender's blue
You must love me, dilly dilly
'cause I love you.

Who told you so, dilly dilly
Who told you so?
'Twas my own heart, dilly dilly
That told me so.

Call up your friends, dilly dilly
Tell them to fly,
Some to the north, dilly dilly
Or wherever I lie.

Tight round your leg, dilly dilly
A message I need.
Bring it to me, dilly dilly
With all of your speed.

The first egg cracked open, soon followed by the chick itself as it gave a mighty shake, tossing off the remnants of the shell. I lifted the bird and brought it close, still singing my song. It squawked. I gently ran a finger over its naked, unseeing head. They were ugly at this stage, in no way resembling the tawny, pigeon-sized, peacock-like birds they would become.

The chick reveled in the attention, pushing against my finger, and tried to croon in its rough voice. It squawked again, loudly, when I put it down to pick up its next brother or sister just out of the egg.

I switched to "Aura Lee" when all five of the eggs had hatched. There were birds in all the verses of the old folk song though I could only remember the first one. My father had studied music at school and had hated that it changed over time from something that everyone could sing to a sole vocalist that no one could mimic. On our summer camping trips, he, my mum, Finn, and I would sit around the fire, belting out tunes that were catchy enough to have been remembered for hundreds of years.

Ean and his assistants had gotten used to not understanding what I sang to my birds. Still, he noted the change when he gathered them up to put under their mother. The eggs were another clutch of

Sari's—the bird that had belonged to Snow Reach's former steward. Sari had imprinted on me when I sang to my first clutch of her eggs. She gave me a trilled greeting of welcome when I stepped forward.

"Your hatching song was different today," Ean remarked as he closed Sari's cage. Five heads poked out from under her wings, searching for me. Sari cooed to them as she settled herself around them before turning her attention back to me.

"I usually sing my mother's cradle song," I explained. My hands folded over the bulge of my dress. "I want it to be my own child I next sing it to."

Ean's look seemed to say what I already knew—*These are your children, too*—but his eyes were also full of understanding. "Most people sing songs they learned from their mothers and fathers."

"I don't know any Alfari songs." The truth of that statement surprised me. "Just the carols I learned for Gellirhird."

"You have a lifetime to learn them," Ean said.

"True." I gave him a smile and left the nursery.

I took the quickest route to the karawy that lay in the upper floor of the tower. There were no direct routes in the High once you left the main hallway and the rooms that lay off it.

"Do you have a message, my queen?" the attendant asked.

I blushed. "Not today. I...I just wanted to be near one of Valemar's birds."

"They are right over there." The attendant gestured to a stack of cages. Eight birds peered at me with interest from the wooden cages. From the other side of the room, one of my birds cooed in greeting. I went over and stroked it before moving to Valemar's. His birds eyed me suspiciously.

"No, I don't have a message for you," I said. Their heads bobbed as their eyes moved from me to the attendant and then back again,

clearly confused. I sighed. They felt Valemar's bond, just like I did but more strongly—I could not find him with mine. Being here with them only increased the ache I felt with his absence. I wondered if my bird had provided Valemar with more comfort when I had gone to call the Shororato and Valemar had kept it with him, knowing the karawack would go into distress if something happened to me. If the bird remained calm, all was fine.

"Thank you," I said to the attendant, and left the karawy.

I wandered aimlessly through the High, eventually finding myself back in my rooms. *Maybe I just need some fresh air*, I thought as I sorted through my closet. But then my eyes focused on the garment in my hand. It was Valemar's, not mine.

I let the tunic drop. The hanger swung back to join the others. My eyes drifted around the closet. A faint scent of spice hung in the air. I curled my arm around my belly. I wanted someplace of my own to nest in, I realized. Where would we put a child?

Images of the future swirled in my mind, fitting together pieces of the High now and from Bréick's first days. The base of every hair tightened, causing my arms to prickle. I edged deeper into Valemar's closet. I didn't want my child here. I didn't want to give birth in Aedenfal, especially not without Valemar.

That is four long months from now, the logical part of my brain said. *He will be back by then.*

But what if he wasn't?

Would he miss the birth of this child he wanted so badly?

"If he was needed elsewhere," I whispered.

I retreated further into the closet. Garments parted behind me, pulling their hangers along the rod until my back came to rest against the wall. The clothing lay across my shoulders, offering an embrace from my absent husband. If I had been anywhere else in the galaxy,

I could have called him and seen his face, or exchanged picture messages with him. But it took a week for someone to transport the birds back to Aedenfal from Snow Reach once they had been used. Two weeks, if you considered the round trip. They were not a resource to use lightly.

I slipped down the wall to the floor. The robes and tunics fell back into place, closing around me and obscuring me from view. A small, sad laugh escaped my throat. *Like a child, hiding in the closet.*

I needed to plan a nursery. But these rooms didn't have the space and I didn't like the idea of my child being housed down the hall. Away from me. Some place I couldn't protect.

Did Aedenfal have a royal nursery? Valemar had spent the vast majority of his childhood in the capital city of Vanerife. He had been the only child of an only child. You had to go back to Valemar's great-great-grandfather before you got any uncles on the family tree. The royal nurseries of Bánalfar had been virtually empty for a considerable amount of time.

The logical part of my brain tried to tell me that it meant I could do what I wanted. But hidden in the back of the closet, the semi-stale air thick around me, I could not escape the feeling of suffocation that Aedenfal imposed me.

The bedroom door opened with a creak. "My queen?" Iree's voice called from far away.

I tried to push myself off the floor but flopped back on my butt when my center of gravity didn't shift like I had expected it to. "Great," I grumbled. I rolled to my hands and knees. "In here, Iree." I had pushed myself up to standing by the time she appeared in the doorway.

"Did you need help with something, my queen?"

"I came in for a coat. I got distracted."

"Would you like me to get it for you?"

"No, thank you." The thoughts of the nursery had overtaken any desire I'd had for the freedom of the ramparts. "I will see you in an hour or so to dress for dinner."

"As you wish." Iree gave me a small head bob and departed.

I stepped out and surveyed the bedroom. There was enough room for a bassinette or cradle, but I had lived with Cadalin during the fog-inducing first few weeks of Bréick's life on the outside and was familiar with an infant's demands. Valemar would get no sleep if we housed our child here, and my status meant there would probably be a nurse assigned to care for the babe. Perhaps even feed it. I added those possibilities to my list of questions.

Either way, that meant a nursery attached to my rooms and space for an actual nurse. I sighed. My old room didn't have such a space, but the apartments I sought would probably be in the same area. Daria would have known. Padrid surely did. He had been here since Valemar was a child.

Feeling much more cheerful, I went in search of Aedenfal's librarian.

I found Padrid in a rather dusty corner of the library pouring over what, at first glance, appeared to be a genealogy. He set a folio on top of it before I got a better look.

"Ah, my queen." Padrid broke into a broad smile. "What can I do for you?"

"Does Aedenfal have a nursery? I know it is still early but…" I gave him a small shrug of apology.

"It hasn't been used in years. Generations, really. Valemar was about three when Enartin started bringing him down here. Reina…"

"Prefers the sunshine," I finished.

"She has been here many times, of course. But the castle is not to her liking."

I could well understand why. However, being without the strong-willed and, frankly, somewhat frightening queen had probably added to the residents' lack of respect. She would not have put up with their attitudes. I was of half a mind to call her in for reinforcement.

"I'm not sure where this one will be born," I said, placing my hands on my belly. "But if Valemar is still away, it may be here." I met Padrid's eyes. "Is there a chance of that, do you think?" I tried to keep my voice matter of fact and not reflect the concern I felt.

Padrid took my hand and patted it. "Early days yet. I know it feels like he has been gone for many moons but these things take time. Especially in winter."

"What is he doing, Padrid?"

Padrid looked down and rearranged his books. I saw the word *Darland* on one before another was placed on top of it. "Ensuring the peace." And, with that, I knew Padrid would give me no more hints.

"Will you show me where the nursery is…was? I want to be doing something other than all this waiting."

Padrid's eyes danced with mirth. "It *is* the season of waiting."

"And it is a month longer than an Earth winter. Not to mention that this—" I pointed at my belly with both index fingers. "— is due in the spring. I bet the farmers are at least preparing for the plow. Sharpening and whatever."

"That they are," Padrid acknowledged.

"Well, help me figure out where to put this spring arrival." I looked at the stack of papers and books that Padrid now had one arm on top of. I would rather be figuring out what was going on with those.

Padrid chuckled and led me out of the library. My instincts had been right and we ended up in the wing that housed the Queen's Room, my first bedroom. He stopped by a door and turned to me, one hand resting on the knob.

"Dönal and his brothers and sisters spent quite a bit of time here, but Dönal never brought Ötten here until he was about ten. He was good with a sword then."

I frowned. Ten was young to be good with a sword. My eyes widened and a hand went to my mouth. The years were longer. "How old are you, Padrid?"

"I am into my fiftieth year."

"And how old is Valemar?"

"Twenty-six."

A laugh that started deep in my solar plexus burst its way out. I counted on my fingers. Their year was a third longer than mine. I was, what? Twenty-two? Twenty-three by their reckoning? "I told Valemar I was twenty-nine."

Padrid gave me an appraising once over. "You look good for twenty-nine."

"Twenty-nine Earth years. Our years are shorter." I covered my mouth with my hand to hide the giggles. My God. No wonder Valemar had been surprised. I had told him I was nearly forty.

And then my hand fell away. One hundred fifty years. A thousand. They were all longer by a third.

"My queen?" Padrid asked, concern lacing his voice.

I brushed it away with a wave of my hand. "It's fine. I simply realized how much more time passes in one of your years." And then a new realization crashed upon me with such force that I closed my eyes against it. A lump formed in my throat. Their years, their time, were the same. Mine wasn't. My life span would be considerably shorter.

But there wasn't time to dwell on that. I could wait until Valemar returned to unpack that new box of implications.

Padrid had got there, too, I found when I opened my eyes. His eyes held the weight of it and calculations were spinning in their depths.

"So, nursery," I said, swallowing down the lump of emotion.

"Baby nursery," Padrid clarified. "There are two children's nurseries on the floor above—one for girls, one for boys." He turned the handle and pushed the door open.

My first impression was dust. The room had turned all shades of gray with it. It had certainly been cleaned in one hundred fifty— two hundred, to me—years, for though there was a thick layer, it wasn't the blanket that would have reflected that much neglect. And the lack of spiderwebs, for Crenfor had no indoor insects similar to them, made it feel cleaner than it was.

I stepped in and looked around, the light from the hall offering the only illumination. Blue and green were visible under all the gray. The walls had been painted with barat trees, encircling the heirs of Bánalfar with their protection. A mural similar to the map Padrid had shown me during our early lessons spanned the space above the mantel of the fireplace. Horned darana in a fighting, rampart stance, connected by their hooves, formed the fire screen. The carpet beneath my feet was soft, even with the sticky layer of dust. I reached down and wove my fingers into the fibers. The silkiness of anapali wool met my touch. All kinds of animals, leaves, and flowers gamboled across the carpet, bright figures that would grab a child's attention when placed on his or her stomach upon it.

I crossed over to the cradle. It was higher than I had expected, about two feet off the floor, but I surmised that was to lift the child above the drafts that would be present closer to the floor. The legs

of the cradle were again rampart darana. A curved, fish-like creature that I recognized from Bánalfar's flag created the rocker. Painted waves and barat leaves scrolled along the sides.

There was also a crib for when the child was old enough to begin sitting up. The leafy scrollwork that formed the slats of the crib showed evidence of having been chewed. One could never have bought something like that on Earth today. It would never pass the stringent safety regulations.

There were wardrobes for clothes and a changing table. Behind a screen was the nurse's bed. I crossed the room and opened the door at the other end. The connecting bedroom was dark and smelled musty with age. Padrid followed me in.

"Ötten's wife, Edinna, never used this room. I believe Richeza did a few times when Enartin was young. If you wish to, we could have it redone."

It was about the same size as my original bedroom down the hall. Besides the lack of spiderwebs, I was surprised to find no evidence of a Crenfor equivalent to mice. Surely something had arisen in the evolutionary chain to take their place.

Like the nursery, the carpet was intact. Nothing had chewed holes to dislodge the fibers and carry them away for its nest. The heavy curtains covering the one tiny, high-placed window showed their age more with their fragility. I held my breath to avoid the ensuing dust cloud and pulled them open. Grime clung to the glass, obscuring the view.

"Right." I rubbed my hand on my skirt to remove the dust. "Definitely needs a good clean." I continued to poke around. "Richeza and Reina used my old room? It's nothing like the ones in Vanerife."

A flush crept over Padrid's cheeks. "Aedenfal hasn't has a queen in fulltime residence since Miray, Dönal's mother."

"And now me." I opened the door to what turned out to be an empty dressing room. The door beyond it opened onto a more primitive bathroom than mine. And that was all the apartment consisted of.

"Right." I turned around again, surveying the space. There was no room here for Valemar. "And where are the king's rooms from here?"

Padrid's face fell. "Down the hall." He opened the door to the corridor. Subtle signs of neglect—dust built up in the edges where the walls met the floor, paint faded and beginning to crack, sconces where wax had dripped and still clung to the ornate cups—spoke to the area's abandonment.

"I suppose I should see it," I said, suppressing a sigh.

Even in the King's Room, the space was dusty from disuse. In the absence of a fulltime family in residence, kings had relocated their apartments to be closer to the High's activity. The Queen's room, my original room, had been moved down the hall, nearer to the central passageways of the High. The former family apartments had been all but abandoned after Prince Carwyn's death at the hands of the Cordair one hundred fifty years ago. Reviving the spaces would be a huge task.

"Thank you, Padrid," I said as I stepped back into the hall. "You have given me a lot to think about."

Three days later, I took the sewing party up to inspect the former royal apartments. I'd had Cadalin leave Bréick with Iree. All the dust wouldn't be good for his lungs. "The nursery is shocking but it is actually in a better state than the rest," I warned them. They still gasped when I opened the door.

"Mother and Father," Vienne swore.

"It's cute," Brinna said. "Under all that neglect."

That's good, I thought. I let them wander in ahead of me.

"A good cleaning," Cadalin said, looking around.

"New linens."

"Check the flue."

"New bed," Vienne said, peering around the nurse's screen. That, she eyed with suspicion.

"I'm just not sure about the rest," I said and turned the handle, opening the door to the Queen's room. Someone sneezed. Vienne stopped just beyond me and muttered incoherently. "I suppose it will work, but I'm not sure I want it to. It's not exactly a space to welcome a king."

"Yes…well, if you were attached to the nursery, he was supposed to leave you alone the first few months," Vienne said.

"Oh," I said, feeling oddly deflated. "I hadn't thought of that. Men on Earth take time off to help out the first few weeks. But Valemar can't do that." My cheeks warmed with embarrassment.

"It must be so different," Cadalin said kindly.

"It is. Even the passage of time." I tilted my head. "I told Valemar I was twenty-nine." Five pairs of eyes looked at me in shock.

"I am thirty-four," Vienne said in astonishment, and then colored.

"I am twenty-nine—well, probably now thirty—in Earth years. Our year is shorter. I'd be somewhere around twenty-two by your reckoning." I crossed to the dressing room door. "This isn't so bad," I said, opening it for them. "It's the bathroom beyond."

They filed past me. Vienne gave a cry of disgust when she reached the bathroom. "I take it you would tear everything out?" I called to her.

"Absolutely," Vienne replied. They filed back out.

I led them into the hall. "I'm not sure what is in these first few rooms." They opened doors to reveal simple chambers consisting of a bed and wardrobe.

"And here's the King's room." They were not impressed with it, either. I closed the door. "Do I do it?" I asked them. "Renovate this whole wing? It hasn't really been done since Dönal's time."

Vienne and Cadalin shared a look, the only mothers in the group. Cadalin nodded.

"You are beginning to nest," Vienne said. "I would do it."

I hesitated. "But I'm not sure I will even give birth here. I don't know what the future holds," I confessed.

Brinna took my hand. "If you leave for Vanerife or somewhere else, you can do it again. You are the queen. You will get to sit with your feet up and approve things and someone else will do the work."

That was true.

Brinna looked at the doors lining the hall, at the slightly grimy carpet beneath our feet. "Besides, it is time someone breathed life back into these apartments. They've been empty far too long." The other women nodded their heads and hummed their agreement.

I drew in a breath. "Then I guess I need to give the order to marshal the cleaners." I just didn't look forward to coordinating with Garris to do it.

Garris was in his office. "My queen, what can I do for you?" He looked up from his books but didn't rise. I wasn't sure whether that was a breach of protocol or not. People usually came to me.

I drew myself up straighter and tried to fill the space. "Since Aedenfal may be my child's first home, I am reopening the family

apartments that have gone unused since Caparen's time. I need cleaners and tradesmen that can refit the rooms with whatever I deem needs replacing—linens, furniture—and the bathroom in the Queen's room needs to be brought up to date."

Garris was nothing but gracious. There was no hint of nervousness or irritation about him. "Of course, my queen."

Inwardly, I relaxed while maintaining my posture. "Thank you, Garris. And thank you for keeping Aedenfal running so smoothly while Valemar is away." I wanted to say more but feared I would inadvertently put my foot in it. I smiled my thanks instead.

"It is my pleasure, my queen." His words were rote.

I inclined my head and left him. Back in my study, I drew out a slip of paper to update Valemar.

Am redoing disused royal apartments. Figured it was necessity since we spend all our time here. You will be down the hall. Apparently, this is to ensure your sleep.

Pain wormed its way out of my heart. I would potentially have him home only to be alone again.

I'd rather you didn't, I finished in tiny letters, squeezing them in, below the last line. My lips quirked up. No, I would much rather he found ways to stay awake.

I blew lightly on the paper, drying the ink, sharing the breath from my lungs and heart. Valemar would never know I had done it but, sometimes, for reasons we still didn't understand, objects retained traces of their use, hints of good or evil that could be felt by someone else. I blew again, covering the slip of paper in love.

The wax I sealed it with was marbled blue and green and soft enough to wrap around a karawack's leg without breaking. Pulling the paper apart to read it left a seam in the wax, and the bead that formed the edge couldn't be melted and resealed without becoming flat. It didn't keep messages from going unread but it did let the receiver know if the message had been compromised.

I took it to the karawack nursery, wanting to sing to my birds before lunch. I sang silly songs to them. Not children's songs but ones that were still funny. Songs about mares eating oats, and flying to the moon, and knowing what to do when you are gambling.

If I had known what was to come, I would have never given the last one my voice.

CHAPTER 17

My first clue that something was wrong was the urgent whispering I could hear as Brinna and I approached the solar. It ended abruptly when I appeared at the door. Vienne, Féown, Niah, and Cadalin all had faces that were flushed and frightened. Brinna halted abruptly in the doorway when she saw them.

"My queen," they all murmured, pointedly not looking at me.

"What has happened?" I asked.

Tears dripped from Vienne's eyes but she did not speak. Niah took her mother-in-law's hand and opened her mouth but nothing came. I looked to Cadalin. Head bowed, she tried to turn her eyes on me but they wouldn't lift. Her lips trembled. A tear rolled down her cheek.

Cadalin brushed it away and took a deep breath. "Laera has returned," she whispered.

"What?" My voiced echoed in the room like a gunshot, though I hadn't shouted. It cut through the air and lay the silence exposed.

Vienne began to whine—in fear, in pain.

"Just tell me what you know." I tried to make my voice gentle and soothe the frightened women.

Again, it was Cadalin who picked up the story. "Lesgé caught up with Vienne last night and said that she had seen Laera staying in the Tellark district." Cadalin swung her gaze over to Vienne who held Niah's hand in a tight grip. I think it was the only thing keeping the older woman from running from the room.

"I take it that it's true," I said softly. Brinna gasped.

"Vienne couldn't believe it but went looking for Laera this morning."

"And found her," I guessed. I had done my best to push all the emotion I could out of my voice. These women had become my allies. I couldn't afford to alienate them.

I took my place on the cushion by the window and removed the smock I was embroidering out of my sewing box. Vienne sniffed and looked up, her brow knit in confusion.

"Thank you for letting me know." I gave the women a gracious smile.

Vienne brushed the tears from her face, her puzzled expression growing.

I would have to take action. Laera was still banished by Valemar's order, as far as I knew. But I needed to give them as much reason as I could to trust me. Being calm when confronted by possible treason, not making them pay for Laera's mistakes, these were things I could do to show them I trusted them.

"On a lighter note," I said, starting in on a border of barat leaves that was to encircle the bottom of the smock I had already hemmed. "It has been brought to my attention that I don't know any Alfari songs other than the ones you taught me for Gellirhird." The women followed my example—opening their sewing baskets and drawing out their work, but my arms still prickled. Something else was out of place.

Bréick.

I looked at Cadalin. "Is Laera the only bad news?" Where was her son?

Cadalin read the panic on my face but not the cause. "My queen?"

"You've not brought Bréick. Is he...?" But I couldn't bring myself to say anything further.

Relief filled Cadalin's face. "No, he's fine. He was just fussy so I gave him to Aaya to keep..." I covered my heart in relief. Cadalin bit her lip. "While we..."

"Sorted things out," I finished for her. I gave her an encouraging smile. "Did you want to go get him?"

Cadalin frowned. "Are you sure?"

I deliberately turned my eyes to my work and began to fill in the leaf I had already outlined. I smiled. "I'm sure." Cadalin set her things down and left to retrieve her son.

"Are there sewing songs?" I asked, pulling the thread tight. I ran my thumb over the satin stitches, marveling at how far I had come. It had not been that long ago that my attempt would have resulted in bloody fingers and a tangle of knots.

"No," Niah said shyly. "Women's work songs tend to be about love."

"Oh!" I exclaimed. "Well, that's something we cannot have enough of. Which one should you start me out with?" Vienne had been staring into her sewing box but now drew a breath and pulled a dark blue smock. A half-finished circle of darana danced around the bottom edge.

"'Under the Innet'?" Niah asked the others.

"That's a good one," Brinna said, and began singing. "Under the innet where the purple nuncha grow, my lover came—" The other women picked up and joined the song. "—a calling, a blanket he

did throw. The sun was brightly shining but the moon was all aglow. What happened to my ribbon, I shall prob'ly never know."

The nerves of earlier were lost in the rest of the lyrics of the slightly naughty song. By the time we broke for lunch, it was as if they had never delivered the disturbing news. Which was just as I had intended.

I tried to keep hold of that lighter feeling when I asked Brinna to start lunch without me in my sitting room. "I wondered when you would go into Queen Mode," she said, and waved a lazy hand. "Never mind me. Do what you need to do." Brinna gave my arm a squeeze and then went one way while I went another.

"I need Orin," I said to a guard I passed in the hall. "My office."

He bowed low. "Very well, my queen."

I checked the contents of my correspondence box while I waited. *Valemar. Jaros. Reina.* I would need to send messages to them all.

"My queen." Orin appeared at my door. I motioned for him to close it.

"Take a seat," I said softly. A furrow appeared on his brow at the unusual request but I needed him close so that I could whisper. I bent across the desk.

"The women I sew with had some news for me this morning." I spoke as softly as I could. "Lesgé Cahnt told Vienne last night that Laera was back in Aedenfal." Orin's eyes widened. "Vienne went looking for her this morning and found her."

Fury filled Orin's face. "And I take it from your reaction that Laera did not have pardon to return."

"No."

I had never seen Aedenfal's seneschal so angry. "I want this done quietly," I told him. I took a deep breath. "I hate to say this, Orin, but Laera would not have dared to return if she didn't think she would find welcome here. Aedenfal is still filled with those who do not trust

me, who do not want me. We can keep pretending otherwise…" But I had no words to finish. Guilt began to replace the anger on Orin's face.

"Take Garris into custody," I continued. "I will send for Jaros to take over until things get sorted out. Garris must have known about his wife." Orin nodded his bitter agreement. "You will need to talk to Vienne. Be kind," I pleaded. "She is breaking her friend's trust."

"She is doing her duty," Orin ground out.

"And if there are other traitors in Aedenfal, I don't want people afraid to turn them in." Orin sighed and gave me a nod. I caught his gaze. The battle line in whatever was going on had just shifted to Aedenfal.

"I should tell you, I have had the feeling I was being watched. Tellark district, actually."

"You should have said something."

"What?" I retorted. "That I *felt* that an unseen someone wished me ill?" And then I confessed the whole of it to him. "I should have told someone that, though I'm not the Mödatal, I sensed that Prince Ander was watching me?" The color drained from Orin's face. I rubbed my forehead. "So the wayward prince has been here."

"We found some evidence of it a couple of months back. Then there were sketchy reports of sightings elsewhere."

"And what is Valemar doing in Snow Reach?"

Orin ran a hand along his chin, debating what to tell me. "Putting pressure on Prince Caspin to call his brother home."

"Ah." Bánalfar's king on his doorstep, backed by an army, would be a persuasive tool. One that wouldn't work as well without the king. Orin and I were on our own.

I leaned my head against the back of my chair. "No matter what, this is going to be a spectacle," I said to the ceiling.

"It is hard to arrest someone in town without drawing attention," Orin told me. "And I don't think Laera is going to come quietly." Everyone in Aedenfal would know about it within twenty minutes of the guards showing up.

"Tell me what to do," I said.

"I can isolate Garris pretty quickly. I'll just post a couple of guards outside his office."

"Inside, too," I said. "We don't want him destroying anything."

"Noted." Orin gave his head a defeated shake, and then hope entered his eyes. "Is Vienne still in the High?"

"Probably not."

Orin grimaced. "Can you send someone 'round for her? Better a servant than a guard if we are trying to keep this quiet."

"I can do that. You can even talk to her here." I hated to put my newfound friendship with her at risk, but I think she and I both knew it would change with the news she had brought this morning. "I will try to reassure Vienne that she is not in any trouble."

"Valemar will reward her."

I sat forward again, resting my arms on the desk, as another problem surfaced. "The communal dinner tonight."

Orin closed his eyes. "Mother and Father."

"Do we cancel?" I asked.

"Yes," Orin said in bitter defeat. "I will call the Laocotan back from the edge of Fairfada. Their numbers in the High will give us an excuse to do that as well as communicate to the Low that something serious is going on."

"Something more than just a disgruntled wife," I said. The High and Low would be a sea of red cloaks once Bánalfar's common army arrived.

"If Laera felt safe enough to return after Valemar's warning, there *is* something serious going on."

I penned notes to Valemar and Jaros and sent for someone to have Vienne return to the High. Brinna ate luncheon without me. I had mine from a tray at my desk while I worked.

I now stared at the blank slip I intended to send to Reina. It was my responsibility to inform her as Valemar wasn't here and wouldn't even hear of it for three days. I just wasn't sure how to word the news.

Valemar's authority flouted in Aedenfal. Have arrested Garris and his wife and sent for Jaros. V has been notified. Advise.

I scribbled down the words and stared at them. Valemar would find out the news only hours before his mother. Surely, he would tell me what to do.

But I would still be on my own. Whatever words of wisdom Reina could send would be welcome. Hell, I wouldn't even mind if she showed up and took over.

I stretched my aching back and rubbed my belly. I only had a couple of weeks left of my second trimester and knew that I could expect to spend the third in increasing discomfort. I wanted to focus on refurbishing the apartments, not rooting out sedition. But if Reina came, actually decided to leave Vanerife in the midst of winter, it would mean that things in Aedenfal were dire. No, it would be best for me to deal with them myself until my due date was closer.

I put a hand on my desk and pushed myself up. After a lap around my office to get the blood flowing through my legs again, I sealed the note to Reina and handed it off to Tovan.

"Last one." Tovan gave me a youthful grin and headed off to the karawy. I ducked down the hall to the garderobe. I peeked in on Brinna on my way back. She stared out the window. A book lay half-forgotten in her hand.

"I have sent for Jaros," I told her.

Brinna beamed and then tried to rearrange her features into something more serious. I raised a puzzled eyebrow. "I think I'm pregnant," she blurted out. "I wasn't going to tell anyone. It is too early to really be sure but…"

I smiled. "Now you get to tell him in person." Her eyes filled with joyful tears.

"Yes," she said in a choked voice. "I know it's terrible timing—"

I cut her off. "No, it's not. It is an answer to many prayers, including mine. Don't let this mess steal that joy." Brinna bit her lips and nodded.

I wanted to stay, to tell her what was going on, but everything was still in motion, nothing settled. "Thank you," I said instead.

She gave me a quizzical look. "For what?"

"For being here," I said. "Right now, it feels like me and Orin against the world."

"But it's not," Brinna said.

"No, it's not," I agreed. "And it is easier to remember that with you here." I gave her another smile and returned to my study with a little piece of happiness to hold onto. Another baby. Maybe the future wasn't so dire.

Vienne was shown into my study about half an hour later. Nervous, she paled even further when Orin came in moments after her. He closed the door behind him and stood against it. With a simple look, he let me know that things with Garris were under control.

I tried to be as gentle with Vienne as I could. "I know you know why you are here." Vienne stared at her lap, blinking back tears, and nodded. "You need to let Orin know which house she is in."

"What is going to happen to her?" Vienne whispered, still afraid to meet my eyes.

I shared a cautious look with Orin. "Ultimately, that will be up to Valemar," I said. "For now, we just need to talk with her."

Vienne was still hesitant to betray her friend and worried the edges of her sleeves, twisting them between her fingers.

"Vienne," I started again, carefully. "Laera being here when Valemar is not here and when he hasn't withdrawn his order to leave is not good for Aedenfal. Surely you realize that."

Vienne blinked as heavy tears began to fall. "I know." The words caught in her throat. Her hands moved, as if she wanted to wipe away the tears but was unable to do so.

Orin shifted impatiently behind her. "Your king needs you," I said, trying again. "He isn't here but you are. He would ask you himself if he could." Vienne paled even further. A shudder racked her hunched frame.

She opened her mouth. "Abker Street," Vienne said, defeated. "House number three." Orin slipped out as unobtrusively as he could.

I poured a glass of wine and handed it to her. Vienne took it from me with shaking hands.

"You know there is unrest in the south," I told her. Vienne stilled. "Problems with Darland. We don't need problems here as well. Today you have kept your oath to help protect Aedenfal. And I do know what it has cost you." Vienne still couldn't look at me. "I just hope you won't look on me any differently. I value your friendship."

Tears began to fall again. Out of habit, I looked for a tissue box but, of course, there wasn't one. When I began to rummage in my pockets, Vienne finally drew out a handkerchief of her own and mopped her face with it.

"Drink," I commanded.

Vienne managed a few sips. "I am so ashamed," she whispered.

"We don't get to choose the actions of others," I said. "Only our own. Even then, it can be hard. You did the right thing. For Aedenfal. For your king. For me." Vienne slowly lifted her eyes. "Thank you." I put as much weight into those words as I could.

Vienne continued to hold the glass rather than drink from it. Her eyes drifted back to her lap. "What is to become of me?"

"You have nothing to fear from me," I said. And then I realized it wasn't me she was afraid of. I closed my eyes with a sigh. *God, I hate this town.* "Do I need to be afraid for you?"

Her silence was my answer. I couldn't shelter her from Aedenfal's resentment. I just prayed that was as far as they would take it.

"I need you, Vienne. I cannot prepare for this baby without you. Move in here or return home. Only you can decide which is best." And still she hesitated.

"If you leave me without allies here, I will have no choice but to have Reina come take control." That got her to look up. Wide eyes, filled with apprehension, stared at me. "Can you stand by me or do I need to set a maskpol loose on Aedenfal?"

Vienne finally drank. Resolve slowly changed her features. Her back had straightened when she set the empty glass on my desk. "I can stand by you, my queen."

"Good." I held back a smirk. Shock and awe. Reina could have written the military strategy. I was beginning to see its uses. Reina's reputation so preceded her that I didn't need anything but the threat of it. "Do you wish to remain? You are more than welcome here."

Vienne bowed her head again. "I humbly thank you for your kind offer, my queen, but I should return to my family. They will be worried for me."

"Of course." Vienne rose on shaking limbs. "I will expect you tomorrow," I told her.

"Until tomorrow, my queen."

Vienne managed to make it to the door without toppling over. I gave her the space to go.

Fidgety, yet needing to plan my next move, I pulled a full-sized sheet of paper from my correspondence box. I folded it into a square, moistened the edge that held the excess, and tore it off. I could have folded *tsuru* quickly, without thinking, but I made my movements deliberate to slow my mind, each fold a prayer that would go into the formation of the sacred crane.

Turn. Fold. Orin was now in charge of Aedenfal.

Turn. Fold. With Garris under arrest, I would need to stand with Orin. *Flip, fold, crease.* Do I meet with Laera?

I had finished folding three of the origami cranes before I had run through all of the different scenarios, calculated their possible outcomes, and had my answer. *Yes.* If she was still as full of vitriol as she had been on the night Valemar had cast her out of Aedenfal, it needed to be brought out into the open and witnessed. I couldn't let hatred like that lurk in the shadows.

I folded my latest crane with less resolve than the first. The whole situation was a horrible, shit-filled mess.

A piece of Earth history reached out from a dusty corner of my mind—a quote from Winston Churchill in Earth's twentieth century: *You have enemies? Good. It means you've stood up for something in your life.*

I pulled the crane's wings, popping out his body. "What do you think, *tsuru?*" I asked the bird, holding it by its tail. "Shall I go face my enemies?"

Orin brought Laera back to his office to question her. She had shrieked in indignation the whole way, alerting everyone in both the Low and the High as to what was going on. Orin's office sat inside the High itself, a midpoint between the courtyard and the dungeons.

"This isn't right!" Laera's shrill voiced bounced off the stones in harsh echoes. "You've got no right to take me!"

Galwin and Inar stood outside Orin's door. They had left their helmets on. Probably to help insulate their ears against the noise.

"Valemar has not given you leave to return, *Grada* Laera." Orin's voice held the weight of someone repeating something for the thousandth time.

"He's left," Laera spat.

"But I haven't." I stepped into the room. Laera's eyes widened before they filled with loathing.

"You should have."

Air rasped through Orin's nose as he gasped at the words and the venom with which Laera delivered them.

"And you should have stayed in Lendurig." I stared her down. Laera finally looked away, muttering.

Orin's eyes widened, catching some of her words. An angry flush blossomed across his cheeks. "Who have you been talking to, *Grada* Laera?" The ice in his voice was in stark contrast to white-hot fury rolling off of him in waves.

"No one," Laera said but the anger in her eyes said otherwise.

"Ander?" I mouthed to Orin. He held my gaze without answering. The fact he wasn't denying it confirmed my fears.

"Do you know why your king left Aedenfal…?" I trailed off, unable to bring myself to use the honorific title as Orin had, even if he had done it to remind Laera of her duty. "He seeks a renegade prince who is stirring up trouble."

Laera turned deep red. "And what if I have? He's right. You are no better than the Cordair. You've blinded the king. You have let others in." Her eyes fixed on my abdomen, hate-filled laser beams directed at the child it held. "You are spawning children that will remove the throne from the Alfari. You're a canker that needs to be cut out."

Orin moved. One moment he had been sitting behind his desk. The next, he was leaning across it, the point of a knife pressed into Laera's throat. Galwin and Inar responded to the hiss of steel and entered the office, swords drawn.

Orin brought his lips inches from Laera's ear and ground out a deadly promise.

"And with that, you forfeit your life."

CHAPTER 18

They put Laera in the dungeon. Normally, the steward would act as judge but a trial would have to wait until Jaros came. I dictated an additional message to him, my hands shaking too much to write it out myself.

The adrenaline coursing through my body flooded my bloodstream and crossed the placenta. My belly filled with flutters and kicks as my child worked off the stress as well. Orin found me pacing his office when he returned from Laera's internment and poured me a glass of wine.

"Have you spoken yet to Garris?" I asked before I drank.

"Not yet."

The wine was sweet and warmed like a bright summer sun. My heart slowed a pace, and a few knots slipped from my shoulders. "I need to be there with you."

"My queen—"

"No. If Garris feels as his wife does then my being there may provoke him into exposing himself as well."

Orin reluctantly gave in. "As you wish. He's in his office."

"Does he know why?"

"No, but he has got to suspect."

I took several more swallows before I followed Orin to Garris's office. Two King's Guard flanked it. Orin opened the door. Garris stood as Orin approached, only to sink back down when I came in. He put the heels of his hands to his eyes.

"I told her not to come."

"How long as she been here, Garris?" I asked. He swallowed several times but didn't speak.

Orin's hand moved to his sword hilt. "*Gradin* Garris, your queen asked you a question."

Garris's lips trembled. "Right before Gellirhird."

I tried to think if he had been at the party. He must have been, for Brinna had noted that he hadn't spoken to me. But he and Laera had celebrated the Blood Moon. I was sure of it. And then he had made an appearance at the festival and left again. I couldn't trust him.

"Oh, dear God." My voice shook.

Orin turned in alarm at my cry. I sank down into a chair and turned disbelieving eyes on Garris. "She wants my child dead and you have been helping me outfit the nursery."

Was it safe? There were all kinds of poisons that could be worked into fabric and wood. I clamped a hand across my mouth as my stomach rolled.

"She's mad," Garris said, turning pasty with fear.

"And yet, you didn't report her." Orin stood in judgement over him.

Garris covered his face with his hands. "She's my wife."

I'd had all I could take. I slowly pushed myself up. "*Sinis* Orin, do as you see fit."

Clammy from the cocktail of pregnancy hormones and stress, I threw up in a garderobe and then headed back to my room. One moment, I wanted to run—anywhere but stay in Aedenfal. The next, I wanted to slit throats. The next, just crawl into bed and cry.

I settled for changing into my training leathers, eager to strip off the confining laces of the gown, and sought the peace and discipline of the jaldun practice room. I had to keep stopping, breaking my form, to run a hand over my face and wipe away tears. Never before had I been confronted by such hatred.

Orin entered the room about half an hour later. He fell to his knees and pressed the blade of his knife against his throat, his head bowed in shame. "I have not protected you like I should have. I don't deserve to live."

"Get up!" I hissed at him. "Would you leave me completely without champion in Aedenfal?"

The point of the knife clinked against the stones as his hand dropped. "How can you trust a champion who does not see what's right before him?"

"The same could be said about Valemar," I said. "It was your king who left me in these conditions, not you." The knife clattered, falling from Orin's hand. "He could have sent me away. Valemar knows how prejudiced the citizens of Aedenfal are."

Orin heaved one breath, then two. "He wanted you close." Orin's voice was husky. "And watching the Shororato."

"Hmph." *Close* was a relative term. And I held little sway over the Shororato.

"They are guilty of treason." Agony tore at Orin's voice. "Treason, here in Aedenfal."

I sighed. "Hate will lead a person to do strange things."

Orin swayed. Every ridge in his throat stood out in detail as he swallowed heavily. He took a deep breath then brought one knee up and folded his arms across it. "The Laocotan patrol the streets tonight. The gates to the Low have been closed. Anyone wishing to leave tomorrow will need to register. The family sheltering Laera have been arrested. They will be questioned in the morning after they have had a chance to think about it."

"I am expecting Vienne and the other women in the morning, as usual."

Orin finally lifted his head. "You think that wise, my queen?"

"To not punish my few supporters?" My eyebrows rose. "To not punish those that turned Laera in? Yes, I think it wise."

I crossed the room and put my knives back on the rack. Orin slowly got to his feet. "You will need to question every tradesman who has worked on the nursery," I told him. "I don't know how it is here but, where I'm from, where I've been, there are poisons that can be worked into materials such as wood and fabric."

"*Nach scoil,*" Orin swore. The words cut the air as they fell from his tongue.

I turned to face him. "After what happened in Vanerife, I'm not willing to take any chances."

"I will see it done, my queen."

"So Ander spoke to Laera in Lendurig?" I asked.

"Sought her out."

"Did Valemar know about Ander's views on me when he left for Snow Reach?" I asked. Laera's words still made my blood run cold.

"No. He would have left you better protected. We only knew that Ander had been seen here in Aedenfal. Without making a formal

visit, which was strange. With the Darland spare poking around in Aedenfal…"

"Something was up," I finished. I ran my hand through my hair, tugging on the strands, until it snagged in my braid. *Urgent* was now a waiting game. Three days for the birds to reach Snow Reach, Torfin, and Vanerife. Six days before we knew their response. Ten days before reinforcements arrived. Communication and travel within the galaxy had spoiled me. I sighed.

"Thank you, Orin. I will be dining with Brinna tonight as usual. Feel free to interrupt to bring me any updates."

"I will keep a guard posted outside your rooms." Orin nodded toward the knife rack. "Might want to keep one of those with you."

I gave him a weary smile. "I already do."

It was ironic, I thought as I walked back to my office. General Creskin would know more about what was happening in Aedenfal than Valemar, Reina, or Jaros. The Shororato were sure to have noticed the movement of the army and the closing off of the city. I needed to notify him as to why.

"Ambassador Carbrev," he said, answering my call on the first tone. "What can I do for you?"

"I just wanted to make you aware that we uncovered a treason plot in Aedenfal. There are those who are not happy I'm here nor that my child isn't fully Alfari."

The general's face hardened. "Have you been threatened?"

"Not directly. Not at this stage, anyway. It is too early to tell if the hate has hatched into concrete plans." The general frowned. "I am too much like the Cordair, General," I explained. "And Federation

plans to continue the chalcopyrite trade are, frankly, putting my life in danger at this point."

"The Cordair don't like you, either," he said.

"I know. They've already tried to kill me."

"I thought that was a Hormani plot."

"The man who supplied the poison was Hormani, but you can't tell me the Cordair didn't know about it."

One side of General Creskin's mouth turned up. "Seems you're damned if you do and damned if you don't."

"Story of my life on Crenfor," I said.

"You could leave," the general offered.

My eyebrows rose. "And go where? I'm dead, remember?"

Though the Shororato had allowed me to remain on Crenfor after violating their *"Do No Contact"* order, meant to protect the planet from off-world influence, they had officially listed me as having perished with the rest of the *Cove*'s crew.

"We could work a way around that. And your child might be safer off-planet, too. I don't need to tell you what frequently happens to the first interspecies offspring." I paled at the memory of the accounts given in the history texts. "I thought the Moon Princess myth protected you in Bánalfar."

"Aedenfal is a city full of prejudice," I told him. "Much of it justified. But our southern neighbor has been stirring up trouble. They would stand to inherit the throne if Valemar dies without issue."

"I don't envy you."

I laughed. "When did you ever?"

A scowl twisted General Creskin's face. "I am serious about that offer to take you off-planet. You are still a Federation citizen."

"I thought I was an outlaw who only missed going to prison because of a miraculous pregnancy."

General Creskin shrugged. "And now you are a Federation ambassador."

"A secret Federation ambassador."

"New identity papers," the general offered. "We could place you anywhere."

I laughed again. "My DNA is on file on at least five planets."

"So we don't place you on any of those."

A new, hidden life in some backwater town on some backwater planet. I couldn't see it. And then my belly fluttered. If I had to, I would do it to save my child.

But Valemar would have to be dead first.

"I will file your offer away for future reference," I said. "Carbrev out." I swiped my finger and disconnected the call.

General Creskin's concern surprised me. I had thought he viewed me simply as a technicality, a presence on the planet that remained only because of a fluke. But he had spent more time studying early contact than I had. A new warning tempo began to beat in the back of my brain and added to the anxiety that simmered in my veins.

A bath and massage later, I felt almost human again when I met Brinna for dinner. Concern filled her face. She moved as if to rise and embrace me, catching herself before she actually did it. I opened my arms. "Oh, come on then."

Brinna sprung from her chair and wrapped her arms around my neck. "How bad is it?" she whispered.

"Bad," I answered, hugging her back. She pulled away to look in my eyes. I bit my lips as they began to tremble.

"Astrid!" Brinna said with a rush of horror.

I tried to swallow down the fear that filled my heart, my bones, and make my lips move. "I am a canker that needs to be cut out," I whispered.

Brinna's arms went slack. "Laera is a dead woman."

"You, too?" I had to smile at my growing number of champions.

But Brinna's face hardened. "No. The penalty for treason is death." She embraced me again and lightly stroked my hair. "Were those Laera's words that you just said to me, that you were a canker that needs to be cut out?"

"Yes."

Brinna shuddered. "Then she has chosen her own death. There is nothing Jaros can do about it."

I pushed back so I could see her face. "What do you mean?"

Brinna was pale with horror. "Plots against the king result in the conspirators getting their assassination plots given back to them. Simple conspiring will result in the king's choice of punishment, but sword will result in sword, head for head…"

Laera would be cut open.

"And Garris?" Brinna asked.

"Not involved supposedly," I said. Brinna made a disbelieving sound of disgust. "But he knew she was here."

Brinna shook her head. "Stupid man. He's dead, too."

We held each other for a moment longer then went over to the sofa by the fire, neither of us even able to contemplate eating.

"Will Valemar return now?" Brinna asked.

"No," I told her. Her eyes grew round. "Prince Ander has left Darland and has been stirring up trouble. He found Laera in Lendurig and convinced her to return. The hate she spewed this afternoon—" I shuddered. "—were things that he had said to her, feeding the

hatred she already bore me." I met Brinna's eyes. "Darland—Ander, anyway—seek the throne of Bánalfar."

"Have they a claim?" Brinna asked.

"Yes, Toren's daughter married her cousin, the crown prince. But the better claim would be—"

"R'Kesh," Brinna answered. I gave her a puzzled glance. "Oh, it's quite the moon tale," she said. "Lareen and Adzil."

I had read the R'Keshan prince's famous work, *The Art of Diplomacy*, while I had been in Vanerife. I knew that Valemar's great-great aunt had married him, but I had just assumed it had been an arranged marriage. "Padrid and Valemar never mentioned anything about it."

"They're men."

"Or Daria," I added.

Brinna shrugged. "It was the romantic story everyone talked of at home in Cüswyn. Dönal's beautiful daughter meeting the handsome and learned prince. A night full of moonlight on the warm sands of the Aelon Sea." She sighed with longing.

I had certainly found the shores of Bánalfar's capital city magical, but maybe Lareen's story was so common it wasn't worth mentioning in Vanerife. In far off, landlocked Cüswyn, it would be an exotic tale.

Brinna's next sigh was a sober one. "Treason. I never would have believed it."

"You said the inhabitants of Aedenfal were different."

"Yes, well..." Brinna threw me a disbelieving look. "They believe themselves to be more Alfari than most Alfari. The only thing standing between the rest of us and the Cordair," she said dramatically. "To let suspicion grow so that it covers the king—"

"Not the king," I said, interrupting her. "Me."

"The *king*," Brinna restated emphatically. "He is bound by his marriage vow to shield you from harm. The two of you are one. Though they seem to forget that," she added with a mutter.

I had forgotten it. The inhabitants of Aedenfal had always treated me differently. But looking at their behavior now through Brinna's eyes, through the vows that Valemar and I had exchanged when we were married…at the time, I had considered the marriage to be a sham and so, it seemed, had many of the citizens of Aedenfal. Why else would they not treat me with the same respect they showed the king? And while I had initially viewed my marriage as a pretense, Valemar never had.

I brushed my thumb against the scar on my index finger. Valemar had thought his vows would be enough to protect me from his own people. He would be crushed.

And then he would be completely without mercy.

As the tension began to leave my body, my blood sugar began to drop. I patted Brinna's hand. "Come, eat. I must. I am eating for two." I cracked a smile. "And hopefully you are, too."

Brinna turned her head and delicately sniffed in the direction of our dinner. I detected the savory scent of bohar stew. "There is always bread and butter," I said. "Or the queen can get you anything else you might desire from the kitchens." I drew Brinna toward the table.

We sat, and I poured each of us a glass of pinwah. Brinna picked up her fork and poked at the chunks of meat and vegetables in gravy.

"Is it true?" she asked. "I suppose it has to be, that the gates of the Low are closed and the Laocotan patrol the streets of Aedenfal tonight?"

I gave in to the tempting smells drifting up from my bowl and ate before I answered. Brinna took a tentative bite.

"It is. On Orin's orders, not mine." I chewed another piece of meat, considering how much I should tell her. "He offered me his life." Brinna's eyes locked onto mine. "On his knees, his knife to his throat. He has taken Garris and Laera's actions as a failure of his own."

"Mother and Father," Brinna softly swore, her eyes wide.

"I expect he will be overly cautious now."

Brinna's hand hung over her bowl, forgotten. "I don't think Aedenfal has seen anything like this since the Cordair marched in a hundred fifty years ago," she said, aghast.

I slowly shook my head. "Valemar warned them. He warned them when he sent Laera away."

"Astrid," Brinna said in a serious tone that lifted the hair on my arms. "If Orin offered you his life, he believes he *has* failed you. If the Laocotan patrol the streets and the gates are locked, then he trusts no one. Orin has proclaimed not only his failure, but the city's. That's a shame they will not soon recover from."

"Fuck." So much for trying to go on as normally as possible.

Brinna's brow knit in puzzlement. "*Kwarg*," I said, giving her the Alfari equivalent.

"Not what you had planned?" she asked.

"No." I turned my attention to my dinner. That, at least, wasn't a disaster. "I had planned to carry on. I told Vienne I wanted her here tomorrow as usual."

"We won't get much sewing done."

I picked at my stew, fishing out my favorite bits. "It will be a start." I speared a soft, steamy piece of torna. "The clothes are safe. Orin is going to interview and review the tradesmen who have been working on the refurbishments."

"You think they might have done something?" Brinna asked, finally beginning to eat.

"A little knowledge is a dangerous thing and I have read too many stories across the galaxy about things being poisoned. Powders worked into fabric, needles that would deliver a deadly scratch. I am now seeing monsters everywhere."

"Well, you did lose Daria to poison. And that does sound like something the Cölkens would do. I would say you were just being cautious."

I stabbed my fork at a chunk of meat. "God, I hate this. No one is going to know anything for three days!"

My fork clattered out of my hand. I pressed my fingers against my eyes. It was too much like being on the *Palmas Cove*, waiting for a response to our distress call, waiting in vain as the ship and my comrades slowly died.

Brinna placed a hand on my arm. "Astrid, you are not alone."

"What do I do? How do I get us out of this mess?"

Brinna gave my arm a squeeze. "You sew. You let Orin do his job. You stay and show Aedenfal that you trust them."

I nodded and brushed at the moisture that had gathered on my lashes. *Shale, I need you.* I sent the thought out into the universe. I knew she would hear it. And I needed the one person in Aedenfal who would let me fall completely apart without fear or judgement. She would hold my hand and guide me into what I needed to do next, be it standing in the shadows or at the forefront. Shale wouldn't let me make things worse.

CHAPTER 19

"My how you have grown," Shale said, taking my arms and inspecting me. She wasn't talking about my belly. When we had first met, nearly eleven months ago, I had hated the sight of her. She had seemed liked some spider in the background, manipulating the threads of my future in ways I didn't like. Now, here I was, sending her silent summons when I needed guidance.

"I'm not that big," I said, deliberately misinterpreting her greeting. I knew it would make her smile.

"That, too." She placed a hand over my child. Her eyes focused on the swell, as if the two of them were having some silent conversation. Which, in all honesty, was a possibility. I rolled my eyes. "Always in such a hurry." She lifted amused eyes to meet mine.

But it didn't take long for my composure to melt. Shale squeezed my hand.

"How was it walking up here?" I asked, drawing her over to the sofa.

"Unsettled," she said in her simple, matter-of-fact way of speaking. "As it should be. They did invite it."

"And now Aedenfal will become a place of death."

"It is not the first time, and it won't be the last."

"Some will say that Valemar invited it."

"Valemar brought them life. They turned it into death."

I shook my head in disbelief. "You are determined to see me as a positive."

Her cat-like smile curled up her face. "I know you are a positive. If you weren't, I would have left you to die."

"What do I do with them, Shale? Not Garris and Laera—" I waved my hand, dismissing them.

"Brinna told you last night what you needed to do."

"How can I show the inhabitants of Aedenfal I trust them with the Laocotan prowling the streets?" My head filled with other questions. *Should I attend the trial when Jaros arrives? Who would Valemar send to help Orin?* I couldn't see Valemar leaving the border now. *How can I act like a queen when I am so afraid?*

"What is the definition of bravery, Astrid?" Shale asked, latching onto my last unvoiced question.

"To do what you are afraid to do," I answered glumly.

"What are you afraid to do?"

"Dinners. The people should be here. And yet…" A horde of disgruntled citizens under my roof was the last thing I wanted.

"So join them. Thank them for doing exactly what they were supposed to do—protect you and their king. The women of Aedenfal did just what they were supposed to do."

I twisted my fingers. I could do that—join Vienne's table, just as I had for Gellirhird.

"It is in you," Shale said. "The ability to be queen. You are the Moon Princess. You have already shown them what you can do. Trust yourself."

I blew out a shaky breath. It had been a long year.

"How does one make a sword?" Shale asked.

"You take a piece of metal and you…" I drifted off. My mind filled with images of heat and hammers.

"You put it into the fire and then you beat it," Shale finished when I didn't. "Leave out either step and the sword will break."

It was true of anything you wanted strong—trees, bromachite, and even people. Adversity made things stronger.

"You are still walking through the fire. You feel like you are being beaten. Had you known you would need to marry, you may have joined your friends on their journey to the sun. Had you known Daria was to die, you would have taken her place." Shale put her hand on my abdomen. "Had you known you were pregnant, you would not have called the Shororato. Had you known there was treason, you would have left Aedenfal and the hate would have festered."

"Is that what you saw?" I asked. "That time I visited you in the Cair? I know you saw something."

"I saw death," Shale said without actually answering my question. "And death is hard to see."

Her gaze fixed on the back of the sofa. Her lowered lids hid her eyes and kept me from reading them. Somehow, I didn't think she meant Laera and Garris but I knew better than to ask. She wouldn't give me information that could change the future.

Shale blinked and looked at me again. She placed a hand on my cheek. "You can do this, Astrid. You will come out of the fire stronger on the other side."

A fractured normalcy settled over the High. Vienne and the others came to sew. Vienne even took over the refurbishment of

the apartments, organizing the tradesmen and ordering them about. Brinna and I continued to lunch together but now ate our dinner at Vienne's table.

My growing belly drew a lot of interest—hands that reached for it only to be withdrawn when the owner remembered that I was the queen. I would draw them back and place them there so the person could feel. This was their future king or queen and a bit of possessiveness that the sharing induced would help protect both me and my child.

The flurry of karawack began to appear at noon on the sixth day—messages for me and Orin and even Brinna. Heymond was riding north to take control of Aedenfal. Jaros was on his way to assume interim stewardship. Reina was ready to ride south if I needed her and had dispatched a carriage in the event that I decided to leave.

Valemar's message to me had been simple—*Stay safe.* Nothing more. I had crumpled it in a fit of anger. No words of love? No thoughts of concern?

No apologies for leaving me here alone, I realized. And no instructions on how to handle the mess. Valemar wanted me in the background while the men dealt with things. I stuck the message, still in its ball, in the back corner of one of my desk drawers, unable to either smooth it out or toss it into the fire.

It snowed the morning of the ninth day. Just a couple of inches. Enough to turn Aedenfal into a fairyland and slow down travel on the roads.

Or so I had thought.

I turned out of my room on my way to dinner and ran smack into Heymond.

"How did you…? How many darana did you…?" Shock jumbled every question that rose to my lips.

Heymond held my arms out to get a better look at me. "Many darana and not nearly enough. I have spent the last six days wishing for a Hormani ship so that I could have been here in moments." The lines on his face currently held more fear than fatigue.

"I'm fine," I said, giving his hands a squeeze. "We're all fine. Well, Garris and Laera not so much."

"You've seen them?" Heymond asked sharply.

"Not since the first interview." I knew they were in the dungeons and that was all I wanted to know. Nothing would have been gained by my seeing them again other than being exposed to more of Laera's vitriol.

"Good," Heymond said. Some of the concern melted from his face.

His eyes came to rest on my abdomen. I took his hand and placed it there. "He or she is kicking now." Heymond's face filled with awe. His expression began to slip when nothing happened. I jabbed my fingers into my belly a couple of times and was rewarded with a rippling protest from inside. Heymond gasped.

"You can write to Valemar and let him know that both of us are fine."

Heymond chuckled, the lines on his face turning to joy. "Today is the nineteenth day of Lardreth."

"So?" I said, missing the connection.

"You first came to us on the nineteenth day of Dérach. Never would I have expected this eleven months ago."

"Me neither," I said. "There is much that I would have never expected when you first put your hand on my arm."

There was another ripple of movement from my belly. Heymond's exhale was a quiet laugh but his energy changed on the inhale. Guilt etched his face, and he slowly removed his hand, as if it was Valemar's that should be there and not his.

"I wouldn't be here if it wasn't for you," I said. "You saved me on the nineteenth of Dérach and now, here you are, riding to my rescue again on the nineteenth of Lardreth."

Heymond's face twisted, filling with pain. "It was the nineteenth of Anform that I arrived in Vanerife."

My eyes filled. A shiver ran down my back. "So you rushed back to ensure that you again arrived on the nineteenth?" I didn't like the coincidence. Maybe making light out of it would take away some of its power.

Heymond chuckled, breaking the tension. "I could leave and come again."

I gave him a gentle shove. "No, you are welcome, my friend." I started down the passageway again, Heymond at my side. "Are you going to dine with us?"

"It is not my place," he said. "Even if you have made changes."

"It wasn't right," I explained. "Me at the high table next to Valemar's empty chair…Garris…the one to his left empty as well. I was an object on display. They resented me. Even Brinna could feel it."

"Hmm." The noise Heymond made was more growl than observation.

"Why don't you at least show me to my place at Vienne's table? This way you can both check out the arrangements and notify Aedenfal that you are back in residence."

"Very well, *mo banorisa*," Heymond said with a chuckle.

I made my entrance through the doors, slower, more purposefully than I usually did. Whispers rippled around the hall as Heymond stepped into view behind me. The captain of the King's Guard was

again among them. Heymond's eyes roamed over the tables, noting their response. Sending a silent warning to some.

He followed in my wake to Vienne's table. *"Grada* Vienne," Heymond said to her. Vienne looked slightly stricken and bowed her head. "Bánalfar thanks you for your service. Valemar has asked me to let you know that you are henceforth to be known as *Shörda* Vienne."

My language chip didn't translate the term but those at the table gasped. Vienne turned pink. "I don't deserve the honor."

"But for you, treason would still be freely roaming Aedenfal. You will receive the income that comes with the title, of course."

"I didn't do it for the money," Vienne said, clearly affronted.

"But you did it without regard to what it could cost you." Heymond's eyes roamed the other tables again. "You have been a friend to the queen when she needed one most. And the king *will* reward you for it."

Heymond bowed to me and left the room, his hand on his sword hilt.

"Shörda, what does that mean?" I asked Brinna. Even she looked slightly awed.

"It is the female equivalent of *Shör,* an honorific given to knights who have proven themselves in battle."

"I don't deserve it," Vienne whispered, still awestruck.

"Valemar apparently believes you do," I said. "It's one thing to stand up to your enemies. It is harder, takes more courage, to stand up to your friends."

"We had known each other since we were girls." Vienne's voice cracked. Tears began to slip down her cheeks.

"And yet, you did the right thing—the hard thing—when you needed to."

I changed the subject. Vienne didn't need to remember that her friend would die while she herself was honored. "I received the fabric samples for the bed covers today. Which would be more soothing do you think? Something in green or blue?"

I kept the rest of our dinner conversation on fripperies and away from Heymond's arrival lest anyone remember that Jaros would arrive on the morrow and the trial would begin.

Tovan appeared outside the door to the nursery. A silent presence meant to convey the message that Jaros had arrived. I nodded once to let him know I understood, and he slipped away again.

We had decided to keep the colorful carpet with its plants and animals. Orin had had one of the tradesmen bring his infant son to crawl on it after it had been cleaned. The idea had initially sickened me but it made sense. If anything had been done to it or the furniture in the room, the tradesman risked the life of his child if he kept silent.

The screen that separated the nurse's bed from the rest of the room had been changed from padded fabric to one of wood painted with a mural of Bánalfar on the room side and a soothing garden on the nurse's side. White and green linens made up the bassinet, crib, and nurse's bed.

My future apartment reverberated with hammering that rang from the bathroom. Bánalfar didn't have indoor plumbing as such but a fireplace and cistern were miraculously being installed, as well as a link to the garderobe in order to carry used bath water away— the most modern technology available.

The two rooms across the hall had once held ladies-in-waiting and their maids. I was still unsure what to do with the "King's

Room." As I chatted with the women about the various merits of the fabric samples and whether it was a good idea to enlarge the tiny, high-placed window in my room—the nursery had none—I decided that Valemar would have to determine where he wanted to be housed. Hell, he might even welcome more mundane news. I smiled, thinking how I could word it—*'I've been told you won't be sleeping with me post-birth as I will be a bohar. Do you wish quarters down the hall?"*

I was sure he was finding the absence of a partner as difficult as I was. My desire for sex had never been higher, and I was getting large enough that intercourse would be difficult, if the sight of my belly didn't put Valemar off. My libido didn't appreciate that he would be housed elsewhere when he did return.

"Something amusing, my queen?" Brinna's eyes held a knowing glint.

"The idea of picking fabric samples," I lied. "I've become terribly domestic in the last eleven months. I didn't even know how to sew when I arrived here."

"We remember," Vienne said. She held up a swatch that was more sky blue than sea. "What do you think? It does add some life to this dingy place." Vienne gave the tiny window a reproachful glare.

"I like it," I said. The color would bring a sense of spring and summer into the room.

"We should see some tapestries next," Brinna said. She, too, stared at the window. "We must be in one of the oldest parts of the High. Windows were tiny when glass was rare. What does that even look down on?" She pulled up a chair and stood on it to get a look.

"Jaros." The word was all breath and took with it the air of domestic bustle. The hammers from the bathroom echoed like a death knell. "The courtyard," Brinna said. Her limbs shook as she clambered down from the chair.

"That is probably why the window is so small and there are none in the nursery." Cadalin's voice was strained but determined to fill the silence that had descended except for the hammering from the bathroom. "Less likely to advertise all those late-night feedings. The High does like to keep its secrets."

Vienne handed me the fabric swatch with trembling hands. "So…this blue it is. I just need to…" She took her skirt in her hands and rushed out of the room. I let her go.

"We can pick this up later," I said to the others.

"Yes, my queen," the girls muttered, bowing their heads, and left.

"Go," I said to Brinna as she hung back. She gave me a thankful smile and darted the other way down the hall, now knowing the High well enough to be able to avoid the others as she rushed to Jaros's side. His time would not be his own once he had unpacked.

I sat down on the edge of the bed, the fabric square still clutched in my lap. The room held none of the joy it was being prepared for. Death stalked Aedenfal, and every shadow was now filled with it.

CHAPTER 20

I hid away in my sitting room the rest of the day, afraid of all the trial would raise. Silent tears that refused all efforts to stop them slid down my cheeks, creating tracks that burned. Iree finally brought me a sleeping potion mid-afternoon that I gladly took. I longed to just wake up and have it all over.

Knowing that Laera would be disemboweled for her wish to have me cut open carried me back to Vanerife after Daria died. Reina had done something similar to the girl who had unintentionally but foolishly poisoned the lian tarts meant for me. I had been catatonic with grief then and hadn't known what had happened to her until after I had returned to Aedenfal. Catatonic with sleep seemed like a good substitute.

Iree covered me with a blanket and left me on the sofa. Tovan stayed outside the door to keep me from being disturbed, and so I slept through the brief trial and semi-private execution that saw the loss of Aedenfal's steward and his wife.

It was dark when I awoke. A candle cast flickering shadows on the wall.

"How is she?" Heymond's whispered voice reached through the gloom.

"Sleeping," Brinna answered in equally hushed tones. She must have come in to keep watch over me.

"Awake," I said. I bit my lips as the tears rose again.

"Oh, my princess." Heymond came and knelt in front of me.

A sob filled my throat and I reached for him. I had always found shelter in his presence. Heymond's muscles were tight with tension. I shoved my pain aside and searched his face.

The air lay thick between him and Brinna. Both held their breath, keeping in some terrible truth.

"Tell me."

Brinna shook her head. Heymond's jaw tightened. His hands began to tremble. I looked back and forth between them. *Careful,* his eyes seemed to say to her, and then he left without another word. My mouth dropped open in surprise.

"Don't," Brinna said when I went to call him back. "It was horrible."

"You were *there?*" I had thought I was past being shocked.

"No." Brinna shivered. "Thank the Mother and Father. But… but Jaros told me." I stayed silent, hoping she would share.

"Laera was not repentant. She didn't just spout treason about you. Valemar…Enartin…" Brinna opened and closed her mouth. I waited for her to find her words. They were a whisper when she finally spoke again. "She believes the line of kings has grown weak."

I gasped. "No!"

"Enartin's treaty. Valemar's marriage to you. The Shororato. The trade."

Damn the Federation. I massaged my brow trying to erase the rising tension. I would have to have another talk with General Creskin.

"There was no question about her guilt," Brinna finished.

And yet, it was too simple. "Are you going to tell me what made it horrible?"

Brinna swallowed and turned her eyes to her lap. "After Jaros passed judgement and declared her sentence…she told the assembly that they could cut her down but others would take her place. She was defiant to the end, spitting on Heymond when he came forward to carry out her sentence."

"Heymond!" Disemboweling was cold and calculated. Not qualities I had come to associate with my protector.

Brinna's eyes widened. She had gone too far with her tale. "Don't tell him I told you."

I scoffed. "The whole High knows and probably most of the Low." His quick exit made more sense to me now.

Come Death and take your evil harvest. You prowl in the hearts of men and in our halls.

It was a Birinyan saying that I had first seen engraved on a marketplace wall on war-torn Eridan. I hadn't thought about it since but it seemed to fit.

"And Garris?" I asked.

"Just wanted his wife," Brinna said with a heavy voice.

"His execution?" I asked, not really wanting to know but it was probably better to have it all at once.

The eyes Brinna lifted to me were full of tears. "Chose to have Heymond snap his neck."

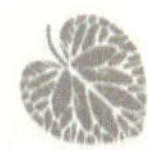

"Why?" I asked. Segur had told me I could find Heymond in Valemar's office. "Why you?" I stared at Heymond's hands. I could almost see the blood on them.

"Someone needed to do it."

I put two glasses on the desk and poured from the decanter I had brought with me. "Piora?" Heymond said with a frown, catching the distinctive scent. Pear mixed with mint was what it reminded me of.

"Torfin's best. You missed Gellirhird and I thought you could use some light in the darkness." I sat and took up my glass. Heymond's hands closed around the stem of his. He stared at the wine. "Why you?" I repeated.

Heymond roughly brought the glass to his mouth and drank. His eyes softened as he swallowed. "Because it was treason." Heymond's jaw ticked, so much like Valemar's. His eyes ceased their attempt to bore a hole in Valemar's desk and met mine. "Because it was you."

My eyes widened. Heymond looked down again. "I know you are Valemar's, but you have felt like my responsibility since I first saw you wandering through Fairfada, brushing the tall grass with your hands as if you didn't think it was real."

"I didn't," I said.

Heymond finally sat back in the chair, taking the wine with him. He gave me half a smile. "I realized that when I came closer and could see your eyes were glazed."

"And then you put your hand on my arm."

"Actually, I spoke to you for quite a while before I did."

I frowned. "You did?"

"Long enough that we nearly had your transport loaded. You didn't seem to hear me."

I searched for the memory. *"Tay! Tay!—Come! Come!"* the chip now translated for me. *"We need to go."*

Until this moment, I'd had no idea what Heymond had said to

me when he took my arm. The chip had needed hours to decode their speech and learn Alfari. "I'd hit my head. Nothing seemed real. Until you put your hand on my arm."

"Even though we had been waiting in the area Shale had told us to, it still took us a while to reach the spot where your craft came down. We had been watching for the Cordair to come investigate the whole time. I finally couldn't risk staying any longer."

"And then they were there," I said, finishing the tale.

"I considered throwing you over my shoulder when you hesitated," Heymond confessed.

"I was afraid you would."

"I would have, too, if you hadn't taken that step toward me."

"You made more sense to my battered brain than they did."

"Good to know." Heymond's lips curled up in a real smile.

I looked down, still needing an answer. "You made sense then but you don't now. You are my protector but what you did to Laera was cold and deliberate. Cruel."

"Not cruel," Heymond said. "If she'd had the opportunity, she would have cut you open and killed your child. She had done to her what she wanted done to you. Valemar wouldn't have hesitated."

"No," I whispered. "He wouldn't have."

"That's what I held onto as it I did it—it could have been you." His gaze dropped to the desk again.

"It still cost you a piece of your soul." I could feel it, much like the blood I sensed on his hands.

"They all do," Heymond said. "Every decision that results in another's death." He drank, washing away more than just the executions. "I can live with myself, though." He returned the now empty glass to the desk. "I would do anything to keep you breathing. Anything."

Heymond drew a folded piece of paper from inside his cloak. I knew it was a letter from Valemar even before I saw the swirl of blue and green wax that sealed it shut.

"Even wait while Valemar wrote this."

"*Astrid.*" The shaky letters and splotchy wax spoke to the rush with which Valemar had written it.

"Doesn't look like you gave him much time," I said.

"I didn't. Once I'd…we'd…realized what was happening here in Aedenfal—" Heymond broke off and poured more wine into his glass. "You seemed to have settled in here. I knew you found it uncomfortable. Valemar confessed to me how much you hated it, but only after you had removed the high table." Heymond drew a slow breath through his nose. "Aedenfal hates that it sits so close to the Cordair. They'd move the city if they could."

"They'd move the Cordair if they could," I noted.

Heymond toasted my observation with his glass and drank. His eyes met mine before focusing on the contents of his glass. "We hadn't realized just how distorted their sight had become." Heymond's nostrils flared and his head moved from side to side. "From that first moment I saw you, I knew you were the Moon Princess. How could they not—?" Wine jumped out of the glass and sloshed the table as Heymond pounded his fist against the wood. "If they couldn't see that, how could we trust them with you? How could we waste any more time?"

I reached out and put my hand on Heymond's arm. "I am fine. I actually have friends here now. Friends who have protected me."

"Not enough," Heymond ground out.

I pulled my hand back. I had never seen Heymond this jumpy.

His eyes followed my hand. He brought the glass to his lips and drank again before speaking. "Go read your letter."

"It can wait." I hated leaving Heymond like this.

"You and Valemar have had nothing between you but three or four lines at a time for a moon and a half."

"If it had really been that urgent, you would have given it to me right away," I protested.

"*When she needs it.* That was what Valemar said when he pressed it into my hands." I glanced down at the slightly crumpled letter with its rushed *Astrid.* "Right now, I need the wine, which I thank you for." Heymond lifted the glass and stared at its light yellow contents. "I did need reminding that there is light in the darkness." His gaze shifted to my belly and Heymond smiled, some of the tension melting away. "And you need to hear from your husband."

I gathered my skirts and crossed to the door.

"Oh, and Astrid…my queen—no going down to dinner tonight. I'll have dinner brought to your private dining room."

"Very well, *Cortan.*" I made sure Heymond's Alfari title was absent of my usual accent, focusing on the word and not the translation. "I place myself under the King's Guard."

Heymond's eyelid twitched. I fought to keep a blush from my cheeks as I recognized something that had been buzzing in the back of my brain. Heymond was in love with me.

"Thank you for rushing to my aid and for bringing me the letter."

Heymond inclined his head. "My life was created to serve."

And, with that, I left him to the piora.

I sat alone by the fire in my dining room. Jaros had been determined to eat with Aedenfal and I didn't want to keep Brinna from him. I had considered bringing back the high table but, with Heymond's command that I remove myself until things settled down, I had decided it could wait. The empty chairs would be too obvious.

I picked at the food, afraid to open Valemar's letter. He had sent Heymond rather than come himself and I couldn't bear to read why. But the swirl of wax kept catching the light, and my hand kept reaching out to touch the paper. I broke the seal.

Heymond is insistent he leave at once but I cannot let him go without first writing this. A karawack message could never convey the grief I feel at having left you there to face this alone. Nor at the burden I inadvertently placed on Orin.

Had I known you felt threatened, I would have left you better protected, my grabeg. I am sure it was Ander you sensed watching you—both on our wedding day and on your way back from the Cair. Laera probably would have remained in Lendurig if not for him. I have told Caspin to recall his brother and have warned him that Ander is a dead man if I find him first. Darland will pay for this.

As for Aedenfal, I told you all those months ago, when you asked me if any of them wanted you dead, that their blood would run in the streets if they tried. Do not mourn them.

Unfortunately, I need to remain here at Snow Reach. I do not want Ander to feel like he may freely come and go, and Caspin needs to see the extent of my wrath, even if that means I miss seeing you bloom with our growing child and his—or her—first kicks of life. I am king first, husband and father second.

All my love,

V

The last letter scrawled across the bottom of the page like a giant check mark. I gently ran my fingers over the lines and traced the space between them, reaching out to my husband. The execution of Laera and Garris would leave me even more isolated than I had been. And Heymond's restrictions chafed. Reina never would have stayed hidden.

I was stuck—neither a queen like Reina nor even like the queen I wanted to be.

Much like you are stuck with the chalcopyrite decision.

And I still couldn't decide. A "yes" could take the spark of treason and turn it into civil war. A "no" and the Cordair could renew their efforts to remove me. I was sure the Shororato had not told Raislos that my presence on the planet was the only thing keeping the trade alive.

I stared at the flames, tracing my lips along the edge of Valemar's letter. The child inside me fluttered, followed by a—

"Ow!"

—sharper kick that surprised me more than it hurt.

They wake up in the evening and tumble around when you want to sleep, Cadalin had warned me.

"What do you think I should do?" I asked my belly. But, having arranged him or herself, the movement in my uterus subsided.

Sew. Nursery. Jaldun.

It was getting harder to flow smoothly through the kata, and I now needed to roll onto my knees to get up from the floor, but Amy had done yoga all the way up until she had delivered. *The midwife says they call it labor for a reason and the better shape you're in, the less tired you will be.* My yoga was rusty. I hadn't done any in months, and I didn't feel like figuring out my new balance in the poses.

Sew. Nursery. Jaldun.

I sighed. My protocol specialist self wanted nothing to do with the treasonous mess. It looked like Queen Astrid was going to be domestic.

Vienne didn't come. The other girls, Brinna, and I sat in the solar, drinking tea and just trying to move beyond the previous day's events. Bréick was awake and sat on Cadalin's lap, grasping her fingers and treating us to drooly smiles that lit up the room. Brinna observed the two of them with a quiet glow.

Watching Bréick provided me with the same satisfaction I had once found reading protocol files. They didn't even sound tempting now.

I let another little piece of my old life slip away. Valemar, Heymond, and Jaros could deal with Ander. Not that long ago, I would have jumped in. For the moment, I just wanted peace.

You're afraid, the little voice whispered from the back of my mind.

I recognized the truth of the words. Everything I had tried had only made things worse.

"What do you want to do with the ladies' rooms?" Cadalin asked me.

"I don't know. I don't need an entourage."

"Ahn-tor-aj?" Cadalin repeated. The other women shared the same furrowed brow.

"Earth word. It means 'the people who surround someone.' They are usually a horde of people who work for an important person and say 'yes' to all of that person's ideas."

"Reina doesn't have an ahn-tor-aj," Brinna said.

"Did Richeza?" I asked them. The girls shrugged and shook their heads apologetically.

"I never met her," Brinna said.

Daria had. Daria had been attached to the household in Vanerife since she'd been small. Daria would have known and would have

told me what to do. I reined in a sigh, feeling yet another hole her loss had created in my life.

"I guess I will just have them cleaned and see if I need them," I said, raising a smile to hide my melancholy. "Though they would need to be people who would tell me 'no.'"

The women giggled. Cadalin smiled shyly. "I think you need to hear 'yes' more than 'no,'" she said. Brinna nodded her agreement.

I shook my head. "It seems I already have an entourage." This time, my smile was real.

Brinna and I lunched together. We hadn't had a chance to speak privately since she had informed me of the trial and its horrific outcome.

"How is Jaros finding Aedenfal? Are things in order?" I added before Brinna thought I meant its temperament.

"Einar, Garris's assistant, has been going over things with him."

"Any idea how long Jaros will need to be here?"

"Probably until Valemar returns," Brinna said. "Thelis can handle Torfin until late spring. Jaros will want to be back by then to inspect the pilva. I would think Valemar would return long before that time," Brinna added when my face fell. My child was expected in early spring. I couldn't imagine Valemar being away for the birth.

"Not until he finds Prince Ander." I stared out the window.

"I'm sure it won't take him more than another two moons before he decides that the forces at Snow Reach can do the same thing without him." Her words didn't bring me any comfort.

"It's all gone wrong, Brinna." I tried to swallow down a rising lump. "Driving away the Hormani was supposed to be the hard part."

"Leaving was supposed to be the hard part," Brinna said. I gaped at her in surprise. "Your confrontation with the Shororato has become legend. We all know the price you were willing to pay, how you expected to be sent to prison for coming to Crenfor but you alerted the Shororato anyway. And now…?"

I pushed myself out of the chair and went to stand at the window. "I have a husband but I don't have a husband. I am a queen—" My throat closed up and I had to push the air through it. "—that no one respects." I pressed a fist against the cold glass. "Everything I touch—the sewing circle, the nursery—" Even the King's Guard. "—it all goes wrong."

"Vienne will come back when she has had a chance to mourn." I nodded an agreement I didn't really feel.

A solitary snowflake drifted past the window. I felt like it— fragile, one breath away from melting. "Something should be easy," I said.

"Pick something," Brinna said.

I slowly shook my head from side to side. Nothing but roadblocks appeared in my thoughts.

"Focus on the nursery," Brinna said.

"I'll be alone there," I said petulantly.

"Move me across the hall," Brinna said. "I will need the practice. I will wait on you while you get used to being a mother."

I turned. "But you have your own responsibilities."

Brinna gave a disbelieving laugh. "And what could be more important than serving my queen?"

"Jaros will hate it."

"Jaros serves the king. And that means he serves you. If you need me, he will adjust."

But I didn't want him—or me—to adjust. Hate, and now blood,

covered both the High and the Low. I leaned my forehead against the glass.

"I really just want to leave."

"So leave." Brinna made it sound so simple.

But it wasn't. "And go where? Torfin? The steward is absent. Vanerife? And pull King's Guard and the Laocotan so far from where they are needed?" My eyes drifted up to the gray clouds that covered the sky, ready to paper the air in white. I had landed in prison and its name was Aedenfal.

I ran my thumb over my wedding mark. The stark white prison cell on Karjiny Five slowly drove you insane. Here, the insanity was on the outside, beating to get in.

Brinna rose and came to stand next to me at the window. "Come and help me pick a room, Astrid." Her hand closed around mine.

The question was—how much of the insanity had already managed to get in?

CHAPTER 21

I sent Brinna to the Cair to pray, tasking her with taking the temperature of the city and seeing Shale. Meanwhile my brain buzzed as my amygdala sorted through all the incoming data, hypervigilant in its threat analysis. The connections the instinctual part of my brain made were rarely wrong, sending out signals to my gut when something was not as it should be.

I played what had happened over and over, searching for patterns. And then a mental file flicked open and provided an analogy that only heightened my anxiety—of being in the middle of a Shakespeare tragedy. Death and intrigue had happened but the stage had not yet been littered with the quantity of bodies that would signal the story's end. With Valemar's admonishment ringing in my ears, I went in search of Heymond.

I found him with Orin.

"It's not over," I said. "I'm no Mödatal. Don't ask me how I know, but I do. I wouldn't even be saying anything now, but Valemar chastised me for not speaking up about feeling like I was being watched."

Heymond exchanged a wary glance with Orin. "Explain," Heymond said.

"Death." That was the best way I could summarize it. "I sense death." Shale's widening eyes filled my memory. "And Shale has seen it. It…surprised her so I don't think it was Laera or Garris."

"She told you this?" Heymond's sharp voice filled the room.

"Yes. She'd had a vision the last time I visited her at the Cair, and when she came to see me, I asked her if Laera's treason was what had frightened her. She told me she had seen death." Heymond and Orin's eyes widened.

"Thank you, my queen," Heymond said. A silent conversation began to run between him and Orin as they stood, arms crossed, staring at each other. And then I recognized the formality of his words. Heymond had just dismissed me.

"Thought you should know," I said limply. I turned and left them to their plans, feeling increasingly shut out of everything.

I sat at my desk with a karawack paper in front of me, unable to decide what to write.

Can I please leave?

I miss you.

I feel trapped.

All of them were true but none of them would be what Valemar wanted to hear. I ran my fingers over the slip, unable to even pick up the pen.

Please come home.

Had my heart been able to write, that would have been the message my fingers would have traced. I picked up the slip of paper with a sigh, placed it back in my correspondence box, and shut the lid.

You will come out of the fire strong on the other side.

I closed my eyes. *Aedenfal*—Fire fall. *The skies used to burn.*

Maybe it was something in the air. Or the very stones.

I got up from my desk and placed my hand flat on the stones that made up one of the four walls in my study. "What do you know?" I asked it. I tensed, half-expecting an answer after my experience in Gladama. I had done this with one of the barat trees. The trees had swayed and whispered until I'd wondered if I simply lacked the ability to understand what they were saying.

The stone was cold and silent but seemed to be waiting. "You, too?" I asked with a sigh.

I fished the key to my desk out of my bodice and unlocked the bottom drawer. I lifted out the tablet and turned it on, willing to even answer Federation correspondence in an effort to distract myself from all the waiting.

Nothing.

I went ahead and sent an update to General Creskin. With nothing left to do, I powered down the tablet and replaced it. As I tucked the key back in its keeping place, the realization of how few keys there were in Aedenfal struck me. Desks were locked, not doors. The only door I knew of that even had a key was the one to the heichdar lab. The gate to the High, the main door, the watergate, and even the throne room could be barred but not locked. I pressed the key against my heart, finding it strange. The inhabitants of the High could try to keep out invaders but became sitting ducks once they were inside.

Makes it harder for them to hold ground should they penetrate, the logical portion of my brain said. Still, my nerves would have been better served by the ability to seal myself away someplace.

To hide away until the danger has passed.

I froze, remembering the fear I had felt on the *Palmas Cove*. And the resulting guilt from having stayed put in my room. "Not this time," I whispered aloud, and then straightened my back. I blew out a breath and inhaled slowly through my nose, gathering my resolve. Then I stepped through the door to my office and went to get my cloak.

My breath steamed before me in the cold air of the ramparts. Even up here, I got the sense of waiting—the quiet anticipation of a shoe about to drop. I leaned on the crenulation and tried to work out what that could be.

Laera and Garris were dead. The household that had sheltered her had been arrested and sentenced to a year in Aedenfal's dungeons before their final fate would be decided. But Ander could not have pinned all his hopes on Laera alone.

And he was still at large.

My hand covered the swell of my womb. I would give Valemar a week and then I would go north to Vanerife. R'Kesh had the better claim to Bánalfar's throne and lay just across the Aelon Sea from Bánalfar's capital city. I would distance myself from the turmoil of the south and work to strengthen the relationship with one of our closest allies.

Besides, I thought as I made my descent, the next Alfari heir needed to be born in a place where he or she would be welcomed.

"She wouldn't see me," Brinna told me upon her return. Her cheeks were flushed with exercise and the cold.

"What?"

"I went to the door of the Cair's dormers and a *vendari* sent me away. 'She doesn't want to see you today, Brinna Fálin,'" Brinna said in a mocking voice.

My mind reeled, going over the scene Brinna painted. "But her door is always open."

"Not today, it isn't." Brinna's displeasure thickened her accent until it was nearly a brogue.

I sat down, stunned. "She's avoiding us." It was the only explanation I could think of.

"Or she has morning sickness." The quick change in attitude told me that Brinna was trying to distract me from the place my mind had gone.

I gave Brinna a sidelong glance. "And what was the mood of Aedenfal?"

Brinna pressed the pad on her left thumb. I knew that motion. She had offered her blood at the Cair. "Tense."

It cemented my earlier decision. "I am leaving Aedenfal in seven days. I am not putting up with this anymore."

Brinna sat. "I can't say I'm surprised. Where will you go?"

"Vanerife. Reina has sent a carriage." I paused as a swell of emotion filled my throat. "I probably should have gone long ago but—" I screwed my eyes tightly shut against the tears I could feel rising. "—I didn't want to add to the distance between me and Valemar." It was the truth, but I had also wanted a chance to prove to I could stand as Queen without him. And maybe I could, but not here.

"Do you want me to come with you?" Brinna asked.

I shook my head and opened my eyes. "No. Jaros needs you right now. And you're still dealing with morning sickness. Travel would be hell for you. I'll have Iree, and maybe Shale will come, too." She did seem to go wherever I did.

"I will miss you," Brinna said.

I laughed. "I haven't left yet."

"No." Brinna raised a mask of a smile. "And you will be back in Torfin for the summer."

Astrid.

My eyes popped open. I held my breath and listened for the voice to speak again. But there was nothing. It had been just a dream.

The low flame on the lamp glowed brightly, a pinpoint of light in the semi-dark room. I slipped my hand under my pillow, reassuring myself that the knife I had moved from the bedside drawer was still there. It was cool, insulated from my body heat by the wool and feathers that filled the pillow. With a slow sigh, I let my eyes drift close.

A soft thump from the hallway hauled them up. I tensed. My ears desperately searched for any hint of sound while my pulse pounded in my throat. I slid off the edge of the bed, away from the door, taking the knife with me. Tovan had probably just brushed against the wall, shifting position as he guarded me through the long, boring night, but I couldn't shake my fear.

Feeling like a ridiculous child hiding from imaginary monsters, I bent my head to peer under the bed and watch the door. *One Mississippi. Two Mississippi.* I'd count to five and then I would get back in bed.

At four, I saw the door move. I stifled a gasp, covering my mouth as I shifted onto my knees, the knife clenched in the grip of my right hand. The door opened a crack. A shadow filled the narrow space. One breath later, the door swung wide.

"As-triiid!" From down the hall, Heymond drew out my name in a booming shout that echoed down the cavernous corridor. His footsteps thundered, growing closer, as the dark figure lunged into my room.

I was trapped between the bed and the wall and unable to rise quickly due to my belly. Despite my knife, I was going to be skewered. The empty bed gave the assassin a moment's pause but I knew the angle of my sheets would give away my location.

Three heartbeats later, he had figured it out and rushed for the bed. The delay allowed Heymond to catch up. He hurtled into the room. The assassin whirled and soon the harsh sound of blades beating against each other filled the room.

But the assassin only cared about keeping Heymond at bay. Their boots drew ever closer to my hiding place.

I raised myself as much as I dared, the knife sweaty in my palm. Heymond's eyes flicked my direction. With the assassin's next sword thrust, Heymond reached out and grabbed the blade, jerking the hooded man toward him. The figure dropped the sword. He grabbed Heymond's arm, keeping Heymond's blade high, and then a knife flashed in the assassin's other hand. I watched in horror as the assassin reached up under Heymond's arm and drove the blade into the flesh at the edge of his breastplate.

Heymond's eyes widened in shock. He grabbed a fistful of the man's cloak and drew him into a deadly embrace. Heymond's knees buckled and still he hung onto the man. There was one tick—not even a heartbeat—where I wondered why Heymond was drawing the man closer and then I understood.

I launched myself onto the assassin and pulled his head back toward me. His eyes widened as they met mine and then filled with surprise as I drew my blade across his throat. Red splashed, covering the three of us with a shower of blood. The assassin's hand went to his neck. With a gagging gurgle, he toppled over and I watched the life drain from yet another pair of blue eyes.

Heymond kicked the body away. "Thank the Mother and the Father." His voice rattled.

Punctured lung. I knew enough from helping Doc in his final days to recognize the sign.

Heymond groaned and tried to scoot away from the growing pool of blood. "Don't move," I said as I dropped to my knees beside him.

Heymond coughed, bringing up blood. "Oh, dear Father," he groaned. His eyes went glassy and his head lolled as he collapsed to the floor. I rolled him onto his side so he wouldn't choke and ran for the hall.

"Guar—" My shout died on my lips. Tovan lay in a pool of red, throat slit. His vacant eyes stared up at me. My jaw trembled but I forced air from my shuddering lungs to call again. Half the household should have been awake after this much racket.

"Guard!" I shouted, as a wave of fear crashed over me. Were they all dead in their beds?

I heard muffled voices from the next corridor and returned to my room. Blood had formed a small puddle beneath Heymond's mouth. I took his hand. "You are not going to leave me, too. You fight, Heymond. I am going to get you help."

Orin and three others rushed into my room. "My queen!" Orin's gaze flicked over me, taking in the blood that stained my nightdress.

"Ferrick. Get Ferrick," I commanded. "And there's a key in my nightstand drawer. It unlocks the bottom drawer of my desk. Bring me my tablet." To hell with interference. The Shororato had done their share. I was going to claim ambassador's privilege and give Heymond every chance. "You are not going to die," I said to him. "I forbid it." My jaw clenched, not wanting to say the words but I forced them out anyway. "Who would put me back together if you left me, too?"

There was the smallest of squeezes from the hand I held in mine. I brought Heymond's hand to my lips and kissed it. "That's right. You keep fighting."

CHAPTER 22

"Repbots and a surgeon."

I was still covered in blood. I figured the shock value would help my request.

"Out of the question," General Creskin said. But his face was ashen and there was no finality to his tone. I pressed my advantage.

"You do realize this blood should be mine. If not for Heymond, it would be."

"It is interference."

"It's giving the Federation ambassador's bodyguard the best chance of survival." Ferrick wasn't sure Heymond would survive. "Four others have already lost their lives tonight. If he dies, my answer will be 'no trade.' If the Federation is willing to interfere with that then they can interfere with this."

A spark of amusement entered General Creskin's eyes and the color began to return to his face. "Very well, Ambassador Carbrev."

"And send a ship. You can put down in the glade north of the High and have the surgeon enter through the watergate."

"Very well. Creskin out." The tablet went dark. I handed it to Alill.

"Put that back in my desk please." I crossed the room and took Heymond's hand again. He was pale and damp with sweat.

"He's gone into shock," Ferrick told me.

We had moved Heymond across the hall. The knife still protruded from under his arm. I knew he had a better chance if we left it in until the surgeon came.

"Someone will be here within half an hour," I informed Ferrick. Galwin drew up a chair for me and I sat.

"This could be a fatal wound, Astrid." Ferrick's voice was full of worry.

"I know." I blinked back tears.

They had removed Heymond's armor and stripped him down to his trousers. The green livery collar and arm bands of tattooed barat leaves were even more brilliant against the pallor of his skin. Red oozed from around the wound and speckled his lips with every rattling breath.

I rested my elbows on the bed and brought our clasped hands to my lips. He could have easily fought off the assassin but had pulled the man close to give me the opportunity to cut his throat.

I brushed away the tears that crept down my cheeks. Valemar had correctly predicted that I would come under attack in my nightgown. But Heymond and Valemar had trained me. They knew what I was capable of. Had it not been for the anapali Valemar had made me practice on, I never would have been able to kill the man. And, even with my weapon, I had been a sitting duck. The assassin could have thrown his knife at me while battling Heymond. Heymond had done the only thing that had ensured my survival.

Time became a blur as I watched the rise and fall of Heymond's chest. His hand grew cold and clammy, despite the blanket Ferrick covered him with. He began to shiver shortly before the Shororato surgeon arrived.

I heard the man's booted footfall down the hall and wiped my tears away. "Hang on, Heymond. Help has arrived."

"Ambassador."

Lekan Arten stood out as alien much more than I did. His bright orange hair, slitted, green eyes, and tan, leopard-like spots visible on his neck had unnerved the Alfari when he'd shown up the month before to do my scan. His foreignness was a shock to those who hadn't seen him the first time.

"Mother and Father," Ferrick swore in a low voice.

Arten put his case down on the small table and stepped forward to examine Heymond. "Good, you left the knife in." He bent over and examined the wound. "Collapsed lung. Shock," he said with a look at Heymond's clammy skin. He stepped back and opened his case, removing an aerosol canister. Arten sprayed down his hands and Heymond's side before donning a mask.

"Ferrick, our healer, can assist you," I said.

Arten looked Ferrick over. "Very well." His attention swung over to me and traveled from my head to my feet. "I am going to assume that's not your blood, Ambassador. You—out," he said, and snapped his fingers at me, pointing to the door.

My eyes, and those of the Alfari, went wide. "I'm staying."

"No, you're not." Arten began setting things from his case on the bed. "You are six-months pregnant. Your heartbeat is rapid. I don't need you fainting over my patient." He gestured again to the door. "Leave. I will send someone for you when we're finished."

I squeezed Heymond's hand and leaned close to whisper in his ear, ignoring Arten's scowl. "Remember, no dying on me. We're not finished, you and me." I placed Heymond's hand at his side.

"Change out of that bloody nightgown," Arten said to me as I walked for the door. "And someone get something hot and soothing into her," he added, continuing to bark orders.

Tovan's body had been moved but a pool of blood remained where he had fallen. I stopped. My hands covered my mouth.

"My queen." Alill took me by the elbow and steered me down the hall. He knocked on Brinna's door.

She opened it, emitting a small scream as she took in my bloodstained appearance.

"None of it's mine," I assured her.

"The alien doctor wants her cleaned up and some tea put in her," Alill told Brinna.

"Of course," Brinna said, drawing me into her room.

"Where is Jaros?" I asked, taking in the empty room.

"With Orin." Brinna surveyed me. "Oh, Astrid." My teeth began to chatter. Brinna pulled the blanket from her bed and wrapped it around me. "Iree and Melia should be here soon." She led me over to a chair.

"When I saw Tovan and no one else had come, I thought the assassin had slit all your throats," I said, choking on the last word.

Brinna rubbed my hand. "None of us were armed. Best to stay out of the way." She smiled. "Where Heymond is, help isn't far behind."

I pulled my hand out of hers and buried my face in my hands. "He's dying." The words rasped in my throat. "He made himself vulnerable." Again, I saw the knife strike. I could no longer hold back the agony of what I had witnessed. "Held the man." My face began to burn. "Knowing I had a knife. Knowing…"

Blood spurted as I ran the blade across the assassin's soft, unprotected neck and covered us in a shower of red. So much easier than the anapali. And much more terrible.

"Oh, Astrid." Brinna gathered me into her arms. She stroked my hair until sounds of activity filled the hall and Iree and Melia entered, followed by four other servants with steaming ewers.

The cascade of water echoed, filling the tiled confines of Brinna's bathroom. I caught the scent of *labras* as Brinna gently got me to my feet and held me up as my legs became too heavy to move. Together she and Iree pulled the nightgown over my head and lowered me into the tub. I pushed away as the warmth of the water licked up my legs and then my thighs. Not heat. I needed cold. Something that matched the frozen piece of my soul. But Brinna and Iree's firm hands forced me all the way in.

"No," I said, protesting.

They exchanged a worried glance. I reached for the edge of the tub, ready to haul myself out.

"Astrid." Brinna took my face in her hands. "Astrid." Slowly, I met her eyes, afraid of what I might find in them. "Heymond needs you. Don't let his efforts be in vain. You've done your best for him. Now you need to do your best for you."

I squeezed my eyes shut. "I can't."

"Yes, you can." Brinna cradled my head with her arm. "You have to." She pried my fingers from the edge of the tub and set my hand on my belly. "Only you can protect this young one now. And Iree and I will protect you. Fall apart. We can catch you."

The whine started at the back of my throat and rose up until it filled the chamber, bouncing off the tiles in harsh echoes. "We've got you," Brinna whispered, and she nodded to Iree. A pitcher dipped at my feet. Warm water poured down my back, ran across my shoulders, and became a river between my breasts.

Iree next dipped a cloth and gently rubbed, lifting away the blood that caked my neck, arms, and hands. Slowly, I let go and let the horror wash over me, sure it would take me with it.

The assassin's last gasp would be mine.

Heymond would give a final exhale and be gone.

The breath that rushed past my lips would float into the room and dissipate.

And me with it.

. . .

. . .

My lungs sucked in another breath. And another. The cloth, rough against my skin, anchored my being. I was not just air. I was skin and pain and…and the flutter that startled me. My child had been silent the entire time but now kicked.

I drew in another breath and settled a hand over him. Or her. Inside me was the future of Bánalfar.

Brinna brushed my hair back and kissed my forehead. I had begun to fight.

They dried me off and put one of Brinna's nightgowns over me.

"Jaros?" I asked when Brinna turned back the covers of her bed.

"Will not be sleeping here tonight. He has work to do."

I climbed in. Brinna pulled the covers up as I laid my head on the pillow. "Sleep, my queen," she said, brushing my damp hair from my face. "A warrior cannot continue to fight without rest."

And, with that, I let myself go.

"I'm just going to check her."

"She needs her sleep!"

The angry whispers woke me. Brinna stood at a crack in the door. Arten's bright orange hair was visible beyond her.

"Let him come in," I called. I needed to know how Heymond was doing.

Brinna glared at Arten and then opened the door so he could enter. Arten bent over me and ran a small scanner over my forehead, wrist, heart, and abdomen.

"No fever. Blood pressure is a little higher than I'd like. Child's heart rate is good."

"And Heymond?" I asked as Arten punched buttons on the device.

"Resting. I mended the damage from the knife. He lost quite a bit of blood. Lung function is restored for now." Arten silenced the question on my tongue with a sharp look. "Yes, I gave him an injection of repbots. He still sustained a lot of damage. He would be on critical care in any clinic. I have analyzed what Ferrick will follow up with and it is likely better for his system than anything I could give him. His DNA is surely more compatible with native cures."

"He'll live?"

"He has a chance," Arten said as he took my wrist. He pressed a small cylinder against my upper arm. It hissed, releasing an injection.

"What's that?" I rubbed at the spot. Pressure, not needles, delivered the serum but the sudden increase in volume always caused my arm to ache.

"A light sedative and something to bring your blood pressure in line."

My eyelids grew heavy again. I fought against it. "I don't want to sleep." I attempted to remove the covers and rise. "Heymond is

critical. Four others have already lost their lives. The assassin could have a partner." Someone had to have let the man in.

Brinna caught my hands and freed the covers from them. "The High is on full alert. No one else is getting in here tonight." She pushed me back against the pillows. "There will be plenty to do tomorrow but only if you aren't falling over from fatigue."

"Elevated blood pressure will put you and your child at risk," Arten added. I folded my arms on top of the blanket, defeated. "That's better."

"No, it's not," I argued. My eyelids drooped, obscuring my vision, and, before I could raise them, I drifted away.

For one brief moment, the comfort of bed and the peace of sleep surrounded me. One inhale before my brain became alert and began its list of what needed to be done. I opened my eyes to find Brinna asleep, bent over, sitting, her torso resting on the bed. She sat up, moaning, when I moved my feet.

"You could have found somewhere to lie down," I said. "Even here. The bed is big enough."

Brinna stretched out her neck and shoulders. "I would never presume without an invitation."

I sat up. "Have you heard any news since we last spoke?"

Brinna shook her head. "I've been here."

I threw the covers off of me. "Then I'm going to get dressed and see what needs to be done."

My bedroom had been scrubbed but a permanent scratch now grooved the floor where Heymond's sword had fallen. The mere sight of it lifted the hairs on my arms. My brain searched for other signs of danger.

"Do you want to wear white, my queen?" Iree asked, going into my closet.

"Why?" I asked, focusing my eyes away from the scarred wood. I joined her in the dressing room. I had no white gown.

"It is what we wear to funerals," she said. "I didn't know if you wanted to attend the burial later this morning."

I had missed Daria's. It seemed wrong to miss Tovan's as well. "I would like to attend, but I will have to check with Orin and see if it's safe." Aedenfal's burial grounds lay north of the city, beyond the Leisna. I had skirted them on my runs but had never walked through the fields and the white flowers that grew there.

"How about we start you with this?" Iree drew out my favorite blue dress. "And I will see if I can track down something white in the meantime."

"I will wear the gold if you can't find a white," I said, torn between wanting to fit in yet feeling uncomfortable at the thought of wearing someone else's dress to such a solemn event. "Every culture has its own mourning color, and gold is one of them."

I stepped into the dress. "Is gold your mourning color?" Iree asked, beginning to do up the laces.

"No," I said. I put my hand on my hip as the dress tightened across my back. "Black is."

"Ah, the darkness of the grave." Iree's hands quickly finished threading the lace through the eyelets and tied it into a bow at the top. I only let her give my hair a quick run-through with the brush before I stepped into a pair of shoes and went to check on Heymond.

Galwin stood guard outside his room. He gave me a solemn nod of acknowledgement as I went in. Heymond lay on the bed, pale and clammy-looking. "My queen," Ferrick's assistant, Perlis, said, rising to his feet.

"How is he?" I took Heymond's hand. There was no strength in it, just the frailty of someone teetering on the edge of life and death.

"Holding his own," Perlis said. "Thanks to your healer. He repaired quite a lot." The awe in his voice spoke to his wonder at Arten's methods.

A white bandage wrapped around Heymond's ribs, covering the incision and wound, but I knew what would be under it—a gash a hand's breadth wide, its edges bound by tissue adhesive, the same bio-serum that held together the damage to the lung and any major vessels.

"No IV," I said, finally putting my finger on what was missing from the room.

"No…?" Perlis asked with a puzzled frown.

"Fluids given into a vein." Many things had changed in medicine over the centuries but a simple needle dripping life-saving hydration directly into a body was not one of them. Here, the concept was utterly foreign. Making it utterly forbidden. "How are you keeping him hydrated?"

"Spooning water into his mouth every hour or so," Perlis answered.

I brushed my fingers along Heymond's damp brow. I feared it wouldn't be enough. But his breathing, at least, was even. Maybe, just maybe, Heymond was one friend whose life wouldn't be snuffed out early.

I squeezed his hand and released it. Hope began to stir along the edges of my heart but I turned from it and Heymond. "Thank you, Perlis."

Hope was a powerful force. Able to lift you from despair.

Only to leave you wide open to be crushed beneath the truth it held at bay. I could not dare to hope that Heymond would live. Only with a hardened heart could I survive another loss.

We laid Tovan and the other three King's Guard to rest that afternoon. Orin had scouts clear the woods from behind the watergate to the burial fields. No one from the Low was allowed to attend. The assassin turned out to be Garris's nephew. He had played in the High as a boy and had thus been able to learn its secrets.

I had suspected it was an Alfari and not a Darlander who had sought my death. No outsider would have been able to navigate the maze of passageways without getting lost. Treason still breathed in Aedenfal.

I dressed in the golden gown. The white Iree had found for me felt foreign in my hands—a mask to put on—and I couldn't pretend, couldn't bring myself to be anything other than honest in my goodbye to the bright young man whose smile had greeted me so many times. And so, I wore the gold. It wasn't as if I could blend in. My dark hair would give me away if the dress didn't.

A group of about forty waited on the far bank while I was rowed across the Leisna; men and women, servants mostly. They—we— were all family to the four fallen King's Guard. As moon children, everyone had been mother and father, sister and brother, to them.

Alill helped pull us out of the boat. As Brinna, Iree, and I took our places in the middle of the procession, the litter bearers began the guards' final journey. Women began to sing. The lament filled the air, its simple phrases like the slow tolling of a death bell:

Gone away,
Oh, gone away.
Our dearest friend
Has left today.

Beneath the moon,
Beneath the sky,
Beneath the sea,
In earth he'll lie.

A white flower
To mark his grave
As earth takes back
What we could not save.

Flesh and bone
Will slowly fade,
And yet his soul
Will still remain

To whisper words
Of love and woe
Until we, too,
Will need to go.

Gone away,
Oh, gone away.
Tovan Ghedra
Has gone away.

The song sent chills running up and down my arms. Grandma Sarah's funeral had been the only real one I had ever attended. We had gathered at the remembrance park, dressed in black but with splashes of color. I had chosen to wear the blue pashmina she'd given me for my fifth birthday. Mum had worn Gran's favorite necklace. Finn—a Sheffield United scarf, Gran's favorite team. The priest had conducted the service for the dead, we'd sung Gran's favorite hymns, and Dad had lowered the vase containing her ashes into the ground.

The funeral I had given the crew of the *Palmas Cove* had been just me on the bridge with a very expensive bottle of wine I had scrounged from Zhou's cabin. I had said a few words about each of them, toasting with a swig from the bottle as I moved from one remembrance to the next.

This was completely different.

Whether it was the song or the steady, deliberate pace—step… pause…step…pause—energy grew, lifting the hairs on my arms.

Each fallen King's Guard had been dressed in their green uniform, hands clasped upon their chests. Their long blond hair blew lightly around them as it caught the breeze. The air filled with a sense of waiting.

The women repeated the song for each man and, by the fourth time through, I knew it well enough to join in.

Slowly, we progressed through the barren trees, past sparse grass and the waxy leaves of evergreen bushes. The burial field, too, had a sense of desolation with the winter. The white flowers that grew on each grave had disappeared. I wondered how they knew where to dig the graves for there were no other markers. No stones to say, "Here lies Tovan. He gave his life in service to the Queen."

Brown slashes marked where they had buried Garris and Laera. Four mounds, about a hundred feet away, showed where the fallen King's Guard would lay. I was glad it wasn't right next to the ones who had had a hand in their deaths.

The Möd turned and faced us as we drew up to the graves. "And so, the cycle is complete. Father and Mother joined to create

life. Body and earth will join in death and begin it anew. In spring *taunaagré* will cover this barren ground; a fragile, white marker that shows the departed are remembered."

The Möd nodded to the men who held the first litter. "Nathid Ghedra," he said as they began to lower it into the grave. "We remember you." The Möd sprinkled sea water onto the body as it made its descent. "The Father remembers you."

He opened a vial. I had been to enough ceremonies in Bánalfar to know what it, too, contained. Bile filled my mouth, and I closed my eyes, not wanting to see blood splattered on the body. "The Mother remembers you."

I kept them closed until I heard the light scrape of earth shifting. The Möd straightened, his fist curled, full of soil. It clattered lightly as he released it, sprinkling it over the body that now lay at the bottom. "Rest now. Your work is done."

Three more times he repeated the words and the ritual. When he had finished the last, the Möd stepped to the side. An older King's Guard named Hynet, just shy of his fortieth birthday, days away from being able to finally take a wife and start a family, reached down and scooped up a handful of soil. "Nathid Ghedra, rest now." The earth trickled into the grave. "Your work is done." Spasms of pain twisted Hynet's mouth. "We remember you," he choked out.

Hynet stepped down to the next pit and began again while another King's Guard took a handful of soil and paid his respects to Nathid.

My eyes were drawn to the brown slashes that marked where Garris and Laera had been buried. Had my would-be assassin done this? Scooped up the ground that would cover his aunt and uncle and whispered, *Your work is done. I remember.*

My fingers twisted the folds of my gown. Who would remember him? Who would take up his cause?

A click in my brain made me look around the burial field again. Laera and Garris's graves. The four that we were currently paying homage to. The assassin would be a fifth, but there was no fifth grave waiting.

And then it was my turn in line. I reached down and scooped up a handful, my fingernails filling with soil. I looked into the grave, thankful that I had not been among the first. Only a few flecks of blood could be seen beneath the crumbles of earth that now covered the body.

"Nathid Ghedra, rest now. Your work is done. We remember you." But as the soil fell from my fingers, it was Daria I remembered. I drew an origami crane out of my pocket. Providing the fallen with the sacred bird to carry their souls to the afterlife had become tradition. "You are not alone," I softly said as I held it pinched between my fingers over the pit. I released them and watched the crane's flight. It came to rest near Nathid's clasped hands. "Thank you for your service."

I moved onto Tovan's grave and repeated the process. Daria was still there at the edge of my awareness, as were the crew of the *Palmas Cove*. I tried to shove them aside and give Tovan the attention he deserved. When I moved onto the third grave, the memories of my fallen friends overwhelmed my few memories of Inar. I went through the motions by rote—scooping and scattering the soil, saying the words, adding the crane—but my mind dwelt on how I had not been able to do this for Daria. That even if I traveled back to Vanerife, she would lie in an unmarked grave. I had lost my chance to give her a proper goodbye.

That snapped me back to the present. I took a handful of soil from the last mound. Gedes lay at the bottom of the pit. My lips pulled tight. He had been just another familiar face at the High—like

the guy who works down the hall from your department. You know he works in Finance but you never really speak to him. I hadn't even known the guard's name was Gedes until the song.

"I'm sorry I didn't know you better," I whispered. I opened my hand and let the soil trickle into the grave. "Gedes Ghedra, rest now. Your work is done. We remember you."

Crumbs of soil stuck to my palm. As I reached up with my other hand to brush it away, I realized I still had a chance to say goodbye to the friend who had died in my place, whose loss had created an ache that still consumed me. I stood by a grave, a prayer already on my lips. I silently offered it up, too late and in the wrong setting, but the closest I would ever come to doing it right.

Daria Ghedra—for I had worked out that all moon children took the last name of Ghedra—*rest now. Your work is done. I remember you.*

I drew the crane from my pocket. "You are not alone." My eyes pricked as tears rose, distorting the images around me. "Thank you for your service."

But I couldn't un-pinch my fingers. My heart wouldn't let the last crane fall. Brinna waited, her hand, full of soil, hovering over the foot of the grave, for me to move on so she could take my place. One breath too long. Two.

Curious eyes began to turn my way, wondering at the delay. *I'm sorry,* I whispered in my mind. *So, so sorry.*

I let the crane fall. It landed in the pit with a soft *thunk* that reverberated through me like an earthquake.

I stepped to the side and joined the others who had already said their goodbyes. My gaze traveled over the field again. Garris and Laera. Nathid and Inar and Gedes and Tovan. Daria. Zhou and Doc and Katrina and so many more. I laced my fingers together to stop their shaking.

Since the moment I had arrived in the Teridun system, Death had stalked me and taken far too many from me that I loved. He might still decide to claim Heymond.

And there was nothing I could do.

"Astrid?" Brinna put an arm around me.

Six—soon to be seven, maybe even eight—graves.

Where would it end?

CHAPTER 23

"Message for you, my queen."

I didn't turn my eyes from Heymond's face. "Thank you, Wyn," I said. I pulled one hand away from Heymond's so that Ean's assistant could drop the roll of paper into it. Heymond's pulse was thready. Even after six days, his life remained a shifting set of scales that hadn't yet decided where the balance fell—to live or to die.

"*A—*"

Just one letter was visible but I knew the hand. I let go of Heymond's so I could unroll and read Valemar's words.

I'm coming.

I bit my lips, but that didn't stop their trembling or the anguished sob that squeaked in my throat. The room became a blur.

"My queen? Are you all right?"

I dashed the back of my hands against my eyelids, protecting Valemar's message. "Yes. I was just surprised." I drew in a bracing breath and raised a smile. "The king is on his way home." I took up Heymond's hand again and squeezed it. "You've still got things to do, my friend." His continued unconsciousness worried me, but General Creskin refused to do anything more. Arten would not be checking up on Heymond. So, I sat and kept watch. And hid away from the turmoil and uncertainty that raged in the Low and bled into the High.

I brushed Heymond's hair from his ashen face. "The king returns and he will want a report. I'm not going to be the one to tell him you were a fool, getting yourself stabbed on purpose in the hope that I could take care of the assassin while you held him."

I sucked in a breath. Had the corner of Heymond's mouth just flickered?

"An anapali is one thing," I continued, trying to make light of the thing that still stalked my dreams. "But really, counting on me being a Viking shield maiden, able to slit the throats of her enemies? That, sir, was a serious risk that I think you need to answer to the king for."

Heymond's eyes began to shift behind his lids. "So enough rest. I would reckon that you have three, maybe four days at the most, before you are going to have to answer to Valemar for what you have done." I bent closer. "And you don't want him to find you lying in bed, do you?"

Heymond's breathing took on a more determined rhythm. He had begun to fight. Finally.

"That's it, my old friend." I pressed his hand to my lips.

Heymond's fingers twitched inside my grip. I placed his hand at his side. It was time for me to withdraw. My presence would only torture him if he was conscious, too weak to do anything.

"I will check on you tomorrow. I expect you to be awake by then," I told him, and I slipped from the room.

Heymond slowly began the process of mending. Two days passed before he finally opened his eyes. Galwin alerted me to the fact, but I took my time, waiting several hours before making my visit.

Pain filled Heymond's expression when he saw me. Perlis rose from his seat by the bed. Heymond turned his gaze to the ceiling.

"I am glad you are finally awake." I crossed the room and stood next to the bed.

"I feel like I should be dead," Heymond said, staring at the ceiling.

"You've been in a coma for ten days." My tongue tied as Heymond continued to avoid looking at me.

"Shall I...? Perlis asked.

"No," Heymond said, stopping the healer as he stepped away. "What can I do for you, my queen?"

My heart tightened at the formality of his words and the irritation that laced them. "I just wanted to see for myself that you were awake." I folded my hands in front of me and wove my fingers together. "Thank you for saving me."

A tear ran out of the corner of Heymond's eye and dripped onto the pillow. His lips trembled. "My life was made to serve."

I clenched my jaw and nodded. Something had broken between us. I prayed that time would mend whatever it was along with Heymond's health.

Tears clouded my eyes. "Thank you for living," I said, and left the room.

Two days later, I sat curled up in a seat by a window in what had once been Orbach Carbrev's council room. It hadn't seen much use

in the five generations since his rule. Noise from the busy courtyard made it difficult to think, but its view had allowed Orbach to observe the comings and goings at the High and would serve me with the same purpose—letting me know the instant that Valemar arrived. Unable to focus on anything other than his return, I had refused Brinna's offer of company.

Hal, as I was currently calling my baby, kept up an enthusiastic set of gymnastics as I waited, until he got the hiccups. I giggled for twenty minutes as my belly twitched with each spasm. Worn out from the activity, Hal finally went to sleep.

"You better be saving your energy," I told him. "Your father hasn't had a chance to meet you. He has waited a long time to feel you move."

The sky was silver-gray, undecided if it wanted to rain, for it was too warm to snow. It was still cold enough that my breath condensed against the glass. The activity in the courtyard was just like any other day, giving no clue that the king was expected or that the moon would be full tonight. Most of the inhabitants of the High planned to take the draught, unwilling to be anything other than fully alert.

I leapt from my chair when the first standard bearer rode through the gates. The twisting turns and staircases became a blur as I raced for the entry hall. Valemar had dismounted and stood talking to Orin when I flung myself out the door. I skidded to a stop, remembering his previous letter. He was king first, husband and father second, and Aedenfal had been torn apart by treason.

But my movement had caught their attention. Valemar's head turned my way, and he froze. I took one step back, unsure if my presence was welcome. His gaze traveled from my face to the bump that swelled at my middle, and he crossed the distance between us in urgent strides.

"Thank the Mother and Father." Valemar wrapped his arms around me and tucked me under his chin. I brought my trembling arms up, hardly believing the strong shoulders I embraced were his.

The air was heavy between us, weighed down with all the events that had occurred since we had last been together. Valemar gently pushed me back. His eyes sought mine. "I need to speak to Orin. I need to find out what has been happening."

I managed a nod. "I will wait for you inside."

Valemar swallowed, torn between duty and desire.

I lifted a smile, knowing full well it wouldn't reach my eyes. "Come find me when you're through," I said, giving him permission to go.

Valemar turned on his heel and strode back to Orin without another look. I don't know if it would have been harder or easier for me if he had. My heart had connected and now unspooled, trailing along the flagstones as he walked away.

I folded my hands, lifted my head, and walked back inside. Somehow, I made it to the staircase and forced my foot up each tread, seeking the privacy and comfort of my room—the Queen's Room—to wait for Valemar.

I had relocated to my original quarters the day after the assassination attempt. Every time I entered the room that Valemar and I had shared, I saw Heymond lying on the floor, a pool of blood blossoming around us as Tovan's unseeing eyes stared at me from the hall. I had feared Daria's ghost in my old rooms, but her memory now kept me company. She had become my guardian angel as I waited—waited for Heymond to live or die, waited for Valemar to return, waited for it to be my turn in this all too real game of chess.

Brinna appeared as I turned a corner. Her smile faltered as she took my expression. "He's back?"

I nodded, wanting to shut her out, my nerves so overloaded that even compassion would be too much to deal with.

"Do you wish me to wait with you?" Her question was common courtesy. Her eyes had lowered, already knowing my answer.

"No, thank you."

I had found it increasingly difficult to be around her in the ten days since the assassin had broken in. It wasn't her fault. She represented normal life and nothing that had happened since we had buried Tovan and the others was normal.

"I'm afraid I wouldn't be much company." I tried to raise an apologetic smile.

"He's with Orin, then?" I nodded. Pity filled Brinna's kind face. "Just let me know if you change your mind."

I nodded again, and Brinna stepped past me, placing a hand on my arm to offer what comfort she could.

I curled up in a chair in my room, the same one I had sat in long ago, waiting for Valemar the night after the Blood Moon when I'd taken him to bed. I had known he would visit me, to see if he would be welcome in my chambers, hoping that I had changed my mind about our marriage. My lips curled up into a smile. I caressed my belly. I'd had a gift for Valemar then, too.

The anxious tension knotting my shoulders lessened. I was no longer alone. Valemar had returned. We could do this together.

Iree appeared with tea and a plate of sweet snacks to tempt me. It had been difficult to eat since the attempt on my life. Nerves filled my stomach and often tried to return whatever I swallowed. I generally managed only enough to keep my blood sugar from plummeting.

Minutes ticked by. Then hours. Light began to fade from the window and a new question raised its head—would Valemar have taken the draught?

I heard the floor squeak outside my room and knew from the footfall that it was him. I brushed away tears that rose, ready to see his pupils dilated, both hoping and dreading that they wouldn't be. The door opened, and Valemar stepped in. I stood.

"You, here, makes the time feel even longer than the two months it has been," he said.

His eyes were clear, not a trace of the coming moon lust.

I gave a small shrug. "Fewer ghosts here." My bottom lip began to tremble. "You were right," I said, choking on the word and, yet, I needed to say it, to make it a joke so that it would have less power over me. "I did come under attack in my nightgown."

Valemar was there in an instant, gathering me into his arms. Even though I could feel his heart beating against my hands, he still didn't seem quite real. "My precious, precious girl," he whispered, leaning his cheek against the top of my head.

"I hated you," I whispered. "I hated you for making me kill the anapali, and yet, if you hadn't—" I shivered. "You saved my life. I don't think I would have been able to do it without the anapali."

Valemar's hands trembled as they combed through the locks of hair that hung down my back. "I should have been wrong." He inhaled. His hands tightened in my hair and his jaw clenched, pressing into the top of my head. "And for it to have been an Alfari."

I reached a hand to his face to smooth away the grief it bore. "I am sorry, my love."

Hal kicked, a sharp jab that struck Valemar where I leaned against him. Valemar's eyes widened in surprise. I took his hand and placed it on my belly. "Your child says 'hello.'"

Hal rolled over and quieted, now that he had made his presence known.

"You're so big," Valemar said, his voice full of wonder. His hands framed my swollen abdomen.

"Hopefully not that big," I said. "I have still three months to go."

Valemar's eyes traveled over me and then met mine. "Let me see you." I turned around and pulled my hair over my shoulder so he could undo the laces. There was no rush as he drew the ribbon through the eyelets. Goosebumps rose on my arms.

At last, the ribbon came free. Valemar let it drop to the ground. His hands ran up my arms and grasped my shoulders. His nose bent to my neck. "How I have missed you," he said, his voice husky.

Valemar's fingers slid under the fabric on my shoulders and eased the gown and slip from them. They caught around my hips, snagging on my belly.

"That's new," Valemar murmured, his lips against my ear. But he left the dress and ran his hands up to cup my breasts. I pressed my head back against his chest as he shifted their weight, feeling the difference with their growth. He stroked my nipples with his thumb. My eyes closed, and I moaned softly. It had been too long since he had caressed me.

Valemar growled lightly with pleasure and snaked his hands down to free the dress. The fabric finally slid to the floor. "Breathtaking," Valemar whispered as his hands traced the melon-like bulge that had developed over the last two months. His fingers pressed, searching for our child hiding inside. Hal stayed quiet.

"He never moves when you want him to," I said softly, not wanting to break the spell.

"He?"

I shrugged. "Or she. I couldn't call our child 'it.'"

Valemar's fingers brushed along the hair that met the lower curve of my belly. "Will he stay quiet if I…?" Valemar's fingers strayed lower. I gasped and bought an arm back to circle around his neck.

"Is that why you took the draught?" I asked breathlessly as Valemar's fingers continued their exploration.

"I wasn't sure what you would welcome." His fingers performed a maneuver that sent tremors shooting through my body, leaving my knees weak. "And I wouldn't have noticed that," he added with a satisfied purr. "So much I wouldn't have noticed."

Valemar gathered me into his arms. "Let's see what else I might have missed," he said, and carried me to the bed.

"I never should have left you alone."

Valemar had spent hours exploring and reclaiming every inch of me. I lay, worn out, tucked up under his arm, using his chest as a pillow. Valemar's fingers traced patterns along my back. They had been teasing, gentle, possessive, and even reverent. Now, I could feel a tremor in them. I lifted my head. Valemar's eyes held grief and disbelief.

"How could you know what would happen here?" I gently said. Valemar swallowed and looked away. "What is it?"

Valemar ran his fingers through my hair. "What kind of king am I?" he whispered.

"What do you mean?" It wasn't me that was troubling him.

"I couldn't tell you the last time that there was treason in Bánalfar." Valemar stared at the ceiling.

"What did Aedenfal do when your father gave the Fairfada back to the Cordair?" I asked.

"Complain."

"And what kind of king was your father?"

Valemar closed his eyes, shutting out my words. There were times he wished Enartin was still king and not him.

I nestled myself against him. "What do you need to do?"

Anger had ruled him earlier. But anger and sadness are two sides of the same coin. Here, with me, Valemar felt safe enough that his pain rose to the surface.

"Send you away."

The words hit me like a slap. Loss began to curl in my heart. "If you must," I said.

"I do not trust them with you." Determination began to creep back into his voice.

"They fear me," I said.

"And they do not fear me enough."

Their blood will run in the streets. His words had chilled me when he had said them all those months ago. Now, after having stepped through so much blood spilled in the High, they sounded like justice.

"So show them that you can not only stand up to the Cordair and foreign princes but to those who would turn against their own people." I raised my head and looked into his eyes. "You are a strong king. As forward thinking as your father. As ruthless as your mother. Protect Aedenfal."

"What have they done to you?" Valemar whispered with a frown.

"Slit Tovan's throat. Nearly ended Heymond's life. Would have ended Heymond's life if not for the Shororato. They think your child an abomination." I swallowed back my own rage. "Our child is not safe if those ideas are left to live."

My words rang in the air. Valemar's eyes widened. "I sound like Reina," I said with a surprised hiccup.

Valemar smiled and tucked a lock of hair behind my ear. "A maskpol protects her cubs."

Any way possible. It was true throughout the galaxy.

And yet, it made me sick, this blood-thirsty side of me. Despite his lethalness, it was a side of himself that Valemar struggled with. What kind of king struck down his own people?

These days, governments could ship their anarchists, treasonists, and others to off-world prisons, to live out their lives without causing problems. Kinder, so the argument went, than the death penalty. But on a world where someone had to labor to feed those who would rape, murder, and betray their fellow citizens—potentially taking food off of their own family's plates—most people would rather drop them down an oubliette and forget them.

What had Aedenfal done to me? Removed some of the veneer of the twenty-fifth century. How many times had I and all the other students of history dismissed medieval Earth punishments as barbaric? From where I now stood, such things seemed practical.

"What do you intend to do?" I asked Valemar.

"Father and Mother." Valemar's oath was soft. He closed his eyes, struggling. "Orin and Jaros have tracked down those who had a hand in sheltering Laera's nephew." My stomach fought against me as pools of blood filled my sight. "Ander, too."

"And their fate?" I asked, afraid of the answer.

"Death, to most of them." Valemar's jaw clenched though his lips trembled. "I warned them. Mother and Father, I did warn them."

I pressed my lips against Valemar's chest, praying my kiss could drive away some of the pain. Then he rolled us over and lost himself in my arms.

CHAPTER 24

I didn't have Valemar see me off. I couldn't bear to feel his touch and then have it slip away. Every curling trace that his fingers had traveled the night before still burned on my skin as I climbed into the carriage Reina had sent for me.

The floor shifted as Brinna mounted the steps and settled herself on the seat across from me. "This is cheery," she said. Her gaze traveled over the golden yellow fabric that lined the interior and gave it a glow like the Vanerife sun.

"It is." I closed my eyes.

The door clicked shut. With a jerk, the carriage began its journey out of the High. I mentally tied a thread around Valemar and let it spool out from my heart with every beat of the daranas' hooves. Hal shifted, turning inside me as if to look back on his father.

Don't worry, little one. I placed a hand on my belly. *He will join us when he can.*

It wasn't until we camped for the night that I realized Shale had come with us. "You do follow me everywhere," I said, joining her at the fire. Her mouth curled into a smile but she didn't answer. And she didn't need to.

Brinna sat down next to us. The night glittered with the fires that warmed the sixty members of the Laocotan that traveled with us. Valemar trusted no one in the vicinity of Aedenfal with me. Brinna and I would sleep in the center of a tight circle of men who had been ordered to let no one approach the camp, and they'd had Shale pick the place to stop for the night.

"What do wine makers do during the winter?" I asked Brinna, hoping her answer would fill the time and my mind.

Shale's smile grew. And then it froze. Her eyes widened.

"Most of the winter is spent doing *corda* and pruning the bushes," Brinna said.

My eyes stayed on Shale's face. Her every muscle was fixed, controlled. She brought her goblet to her mouth, the motion governed and precise, and took a drink. Her eyes never left the fire. *Goddammit.* But she remained sitting. Whatever she had seen that had scared her was not imminent.

"*Corda?*" I asked when the chip didn't translate, my attention on Shale and the goblet she held in her lap.

"It's where we move the wine from cask—" *Racking,* the chip interrupted, now having the context. "—to cask, removing the sediments and filtering the wine."

"Excuse me." Shale stood and walked away from the fire. Brinna stared after her. Shale lifted the flap and ducked insider her tent.

"What was that?" Brinna asked.

I held back an exhale of relief. Shale hadn't sought out Conmel so whatever she had seen wouldn't happen tonight, but it had frightened her enough that she left us.

I lifted a smile to mask my worry and shrugged. "She has never been one for small talk," I explained. Brinna had never traveled with the seer before whereas I had rarely been sent anywhere without her, my red ghost that lurked at the edge of everything.

With the moon nearly full, on the first night of its wane, the red light it cast bathed everything in blood. Shale's vision, my disturbing memories, and the moonlight combined into a cocktail of dread I couldn't shake. Claiming fatigue, it wasn't long before I fled to the cloaked safety of my own tent.

But sleep wouldn't come. Every time I closed my eyes, I found Heymond's locked on mine, filled with the silent command to do what he had sacrificed himself for. I saw the resulting spray of blood as my knife slashed through the artery in the assassin's throat, and witnessed the satisfied smile of Heymond's mouth as he finally relaxed and slipped to the ground. I'd had worse visions, but it wasn't one I wanted to repeat all night or take into my dreams.

Hal paused in his nightly gymnastics as I rose from bed. I lit a candle and carried it over to the small camp table.

"Is everything all right, my queen?" Galwin called from the flap.

"Fine," I called back, my reply hushed. "I just can't sleep."

I pulled my correspondence box towards me and took out a sheet of paper. *Rule seventeen: When all else fails, make a list.* I had intended to write and let my worries bubble up, but my fingers began the folds of origami instead. As I gazed, unseeing, at the side of the tent, my fingers creased and turned the paper. The motion freed my mind, and it began to search for the cause of my sleeplessness.

Assassins.

Hatred.

Uncertainty.

I blinked. The form in my hands came into focus—a crane. Death this time, not hope. My jaw clenched. I fought back the urge to tear the paper to shreds.

But other origami creatures started out as the figure before me. I bent the longest edge into a neck and turned the point into an open mouth. I pleated the tail, half-folded and pleated the wings, and set my now-completed dragon on the scarred wood. Aedenfal—*fire fall.*

For a moment, I let the desire to have the skies burn run through me; a dragon that raced through my veins, searing away the anxiety that plagued me. My mouth curled into a cruel smile as I imagined the city in flames. And then my dragon extinguished the flames.

Asian dragons were found in water and clouds. Unlike their European counterparts, they were symbols of strength, courage, and magic, not destruction.

I folded my hands on the table and rested my chin upon them, coming nose to nose with the dragon. "What should I do?" I whispered to it. Hal stopped his gymnastics as if waiting to hear the answer. I stared at the dragon's eyes.

When in doubt, make a list.

I raised a smile at the twist in my rule and drew out a new sheet. My hand hovered over the paper as the fear that had been gnawing away in the back of my brain took form. My hand shook as I wrote it down.

Was Ander right?

Was I a danger? Aedenfal had been fine until I came, until I stayed.

Hal rolled over, jabbing his feet into my organs. My hand strayed down to cover him. Some Alfari viewed him as an abomination. An alien child who could not be allowed to be king of Bánalfar.

My breath raced out, tightening my chest. How could I keep him safe against that?

You need a guide.

I needed a seer.

"She doesn't want to be disturbed."

Shale had not been in her tent. I finally located Ainsgar, her guard, a short way off from the encampment. A torch glittered in his hands despite the fact that Alfari eyes saw much better in the dark red moonlight than mine did. The flickering torchlight enabled me to make out Shale's red-robed form kneeling in front of a tree. I caught a flash of silver in the dancing light. Shale clutched a knife in one hand, while the other was pressed against the bark of the tree. This was no Cair and yet she had offered Mother Moon her blood.

"What is coming, Shale?" I called. Ainsgar tensed and scanned the shadows.

The Mödatal's head dropped lower. Her fingers dug into the bark. Hal kicked as a new rush of adrenaline entered my bloodstream.

The knife caught the light again as Shale pressed the hand that held it above her other, bracing herself against the tree. She looked as though she could topple over at any moment, crushed by the weight of her vision.

"Do I need to send a karawack to Valemar?" I forced the words from my mouth, afraid of her answer.

Shale gave a tight shake of her head. Her chest rose with her inhale, and then, slowly, she got to her feet. In all the months I had known her, I had never seen her anything but confident. My heartbeat became a frightened bird, trapped within my ribs.

"Go to bed, Astrid. I will help you make your list in the morning. Ainsgar," she said, calling him to her side.

I did as Shale commanded and wove my way back through the tents to crawl beneath the sleeping furs on my bed, but it was a long time before sleep overtook me. I had hoped to be at the end of the mess but now it felt as it if were only the beginning.

Shale lifted the flap of my tent as Brinna and I sat, eating our breakfast. Dark circles framed her eyes, turning their green depths almost black. "Ask," she said, holding the heavy fabric open against the frame.

Brinna scooped up her bowl and ducked under Shale's arm, giving us some privacy. Shale let the flap fall, blocking out the sight of swirling red cloaks as the Laocotan hauled tents onto the backs of waiting darana in the cold morning light.

"Am I the villain as Ander suggests?"

Shale chuckled wearily. "We are all the villain in someone's story. You have often cast me in that role in yours."

"But you're not," I said. "I long ago realized that you're my protector."

"So ask," she said again.

"How do I keep Hal safe?"

Shale smiled. "Hal?"

"That's what I'm calling this one," I said, placing a hand on my belly.

"A servant king."

Brinna's story came flooding back to me—Valemar's ancestor who had not been above pressing wine if that was what it took to help his people. Haldan had created the King's Wine. But King Haldan was not the source of my child's nickname.

"A rowdy prince who turned into a wise king. At least, according to the poets on my world." Shakespeare's Prince Hal had been my inspiration.

"And you think that Haldan wasn't a troublemaker in his youth?"

"I guess he must have been," I said. "That would certainly explain his fondness for wine." I gestured for Shale to take a seat at the table. "Darland seeks to eliminate me."

"Ander," Shale corrected.

"Raislos, too," I continued.

"Not anymore." My eyebrows lifted. Shale smiled. "You hold the key to his dreams."

I filed that piece of information away. "And there is treason in Aedenfal." A cloud passed over Shale's expression. "You see more death."

She laughed. "Now who is the seer?" Shale looked down at the table. "But, no. It is not over."

"So how do I protect my child?" I asked again.

Shale raised her eyes and the answer was written in them, an answer I already knew. I just didn't know how to accomplish it. "Bánalfar will protect your child. It is the heir they have been praying for."

But for Bánalfar to protect my child, I needed to be Queen. I pressed the heels of my hands against my eyes. "I don't know how to do this."

"You do. You are just weary." Shale sighed. The weight of it made me look up. Her mouth twitched—a smile that didn't hold. "Bánalfar will offer support when you need it."

I blinked, tired of waiting, tired of trying all by myself. "I need it now."

"You have it now. The Laocotan ride with you. Even Capalnoc rides with you." My brow furrowed in puzzlement. "I guess with the shades drawn, you didn't notice that the mount Conmel rides is Slánta."

No," I whispered. A lump formed in my throat, choking the words as I asked my next question. "Will I need him?"

"You know I cannot answer that."

"Shale..." But I couldn't make the rest of the words come.

The Mödatal laid her hand on my arm. "You are doing what you need to do. Enartin's words gave you strength for your last task. They will this time, too."

She gave my arm a squeeze and slipped from the tent. I was left alone with the sounds of clattering poles and creaking ropes as the tents were lowered and packed up outside. I gritted my teeth and let the words of Valemar's father wash over me.

Only the hard things are those worth doing.

What was my hard task? I leaned my head against the side of the rocking carriage. *Being queen? Bringing my child into the world?* A sigh escaped my lips. One step forward, two steps back.

"Long night?" Brinna asked.

"Yes," I answered honestly.

"Want to share?"

"Shale is not usually this unsettled," I said. "She is generally overconfident, already knowing what the future holds."

Fear filled Brinna's eyes. "Aedenfal?"

I gave myself a swift mental kick. I had been so focused on myself, I hadn't considered that Brinna might fear for Jaros's safety.

Or Valemar's.

"She would tell us if it was anything definite," I lied. "I asked her if I needed to warn Valemar and she said 'no.'" Brinna slowly exhaled. "But Ander is out there, spreading his poison."

"How can they listen to him?" Brinna asked.

"Enartin gave back the Fairfada. Valemar married me, someone who looks too much like the Cordair. Someone who traded one set of strangers for another." Someone who had put gold into Cordair hands. All our neighbors had to know that by now. "He does have a point."

Brinna scoffed. "And what would Ander do? The Cordair mainly keep to their lands. Would he take the Alfari into the Archjarn and start a war?"

"He has Toren's blood in his veins. Ander would be picking up where Toren left off."

The Alfari prince had chased the Cordair back to the gates of Rock Dorach the last time the Cordair invaded Aedenfal, one hundred fifty years before. Toren would have burned the Cordair stronghold to the ground in retribution for the death of his brother, Carwyn—killed during the battle for Aedenfal—but was stopped by a karawack from his brother, Dönal, the king.

"The Alfari don't want war," Brinna argued. "They want peace. They know that nothing thrives while death walks the land."

"I am death," I said. Brinna's eyes widened. "My crew died. Daria died. Garris and Laera are dead. Heymond nearly died. My own hands wielded the weapon that ended another's life."

"To save others," Brinna protested. "To save your child."

"What kind of world am I leaving him?"

"Him?" Brinna asked.

"Or her," I said.

"A more connected one," Brinna told me. "A world where miracles happen. A mother who knows what it is to travel the stars, who can see Bánalfar's future more clearly than even perhaps his, or her, father." Brinna shook her head. "You are not death. You are the future."

But I wasn't. Hal was. What kind of future would I want for him?

The Cordair problem tempered. A goal that would require me to meet with Raislos and find a way to align some of our interests. Not possible while I was pregnant.

A united Bánalfar. Valemar would bring Aedenfal to heel. And I couldn't see the rest of the Alfari putting up with treason. At some point, they would flush Ander out.

A stronger mother. I had not felt strong since Vanerife. Oh, I had managed to find the resolve to call the Shororato, and I guess that was a strength of sort, but I had done it knowing my heart would shatter when I had to leave. What *would* make me strong again?

A home, whispered the little voice in the back of my brain.

I blinked back the sting that rose. Home on Crenfor had been where Valemar was. And then Vanerife because Daria had been there to support me. Now, I was alone. Again. About to be a guest in Brinna's house.

I flicked through my other options. Vanerife wasn't safe with an assassin on the loose. Daria's death had proved that. Gladama was too full of pilgrims, even with the Baraáda. No, Torfin was the best place to be. I would just have to find a way to make myself useful.

Useful. The Queen's Wine. While it was too late this year to create it, I could use my time in Torfin to learn exactly how the King's Wine supported the Alfari and what I could do to add to the efforts.

Brinna's eyes sparkled and a smile lifted. "What have you decided?"

"Well, we are on our way to Torfin. And Valemar had thought of doing a Queen's Wine this last fall." Brinna's smile faltered. The story Reina had spread as the reason Valemar had sent me to Vanerife was that I had suffered a miscarriage. It wasn't true, but Brinna didn't know that.

"It's fine," I assured Brinna. "I have this one." I placed a hand on my belly. "And there is always this year. I would like to explore how a Queen's Wine could supplement what the King's Wine already does to support Bánalfar."

Brinna's eyes flashed with glee. "I would be more than willing to help my servant queen."

CHAPTER 25

Torfin felt empty without Valemar. He had brought me here the previous summer to escape the scrutiny of Aedenfal, and, for a time, the summer had been one of sunlight, wine, and new friends.

But then Valemar taught me to kill. Death turned his attention to me, filling the eyes of the anapali I slayed with glassy eyes of my dead comrades from the *Palmas Cove*.

This time, I as I looked around, it was not blood I saw, but strength. I had learned the hard but necessary things here, so it was fitting that it was Torfin in which I would build the future.

Brinna sheltered me from inspection, the two of us taking our meal in a private dining room. At some point, I would be ready for it again—dinner and conversation. I had excelled at it for ten years.

Before Aedenfal had stolen it all away.

The next morning, Iree dressed me in my warmest gown and I met Brinna near the back gate of the High. Mist covered the fields, swirling around the bare arms of the pilva bushes. They reminded me of the currants that grew in Grandma Sarah's back garden. Men and women were already at work, plucking blue flowers from the ankle-high plants that covered the ground and tossing them onto tarps.

"What are they harvesting?" I asked Brinna.

"Gorantha," she answered. "The plants begin to appear with the winter rains. The flowers are the first of the season. They will be gone by Luthrach."

"Are they used for dye?" I asked.

"Yes. Torfin's second crop, though the Mother sowed them, not us. A gift to show us that spring will soon be here. The flowers are collected and then sent down river to Haypord. From there they will go to Baildath. That's the town where most of Bánalfar's cloth is woven and dyed."

I watched the men and women squatting among the green leaves and sapphire blue flowers of the gorantha plants, scooping up the blossoms and tossing them onto the tarp, marveling at the effort involved. It was back-breaking work, all to collect something that would be dried, crushed, fermented, strained, and then added to secret recipes to color the cloth. No modern person would want to put in the time necessary.

I followed Brinna, our steps releasing a light citrus fragrance, not unlike the lian tarts I had once been so fond of. Our goal today was to introduce me to the racking process, where wine was transferred from cask to cask.

The heady scent of fermented fruit hit my nose as soon as we entered the thick stone building. As my eyes adjusted to the dimmer light, the activity of the building became apparent. The soft gurgle of falling liquid came from a barrel about halfway down the main corridor. One of the top barrels had been tapped. Wine flowed out of the barrel, down a funnel that was more of a sluice, and into another waiting below. One of the two men working the barrel turned the knob on the tap, shutting off the flow. He took a clear glass and placed it under the spigot. With a twist of his hand, the wine flowed, filling the glass. He handed it to Brinna. She held it up to the small window and swirled it back and forth.

"Corda improves the flavor and clarity. Fine particles sink to the bottom of the cask so when we move the wine from barrel to barrel the impurities are left behind."

"What do you do with the leftover wine?" I asked. The tap stood about four inches from the bottom of the barrel. The process had to leave several liters of wine with each change.

"Feed it to the *vinmuc*," Brinna said. She sniffed the glass and smiled. "Very nice," she said, handing the glass back to the vintner.

"Aren't you going to taste it?" I had enjoyed the flavor of the pilva when I had tried them the previous summer, and pilva pastries were one of Erris's favorite.

Brinna shrugged. "Not until it has been has gone through the process a few times. It won't show its true potential yet.

"Thank you, Obert." Brinna gestured for me to follow her. "Let me show you where the King's Wine is housed."

I followed Brinna past racks containing hundreds of barrels, down to a gated end. The gilded metal gate held a large, ornamental lock. Barat leaves encircled waves that scrolled around the key hole. Twelve barrels sat on the racks beyond the gate.

"How long did it take Valemar to press all that wine?" I asked.

"Five days."

I nodded. "Sometime during Dresam?"

"Yes."

I wondered if Valemar had been here during the Blood Moon. The first moon after my banishment had come just three days later. But the second…

"You said your father traded in the wood that the barrels are made from," I said, changing the subject away from a path that would only lead to heartache. "Are the barrels made here?"

"In Wiggas, far up the Dunna, nearer to Tuljerd. They are shipped down to Piltuir and then carted here."

A swift kick to my bladder pulled my focus away from the racks of wine. "Unfortunately, I am going to need to cut the tour off here." I grimaced and pressed my fingers into my belly in an effort to move Hal away from the organ. "We can come out again tomorrow and pick up where we left off."

A light drizzle fell the next morning but I decided I wanted to venture out anyway. Seven days of being cooped up in the carriage had left me longing for the fresh air of the fields. Besides, the gorantha pickers were out there working, hoods drawn up against a rain that was more a heavy mist.

Brinna and I laughed when we met by the door. Both in soft blue cloaks and nearly the same height, we could have been twins once our hoods were raised.

We walked in the grass along the edge of the road, two King's Guard trailing along behind us, as we made our way down to the field of sulee—the pilva that produced the white wine—about a mile down the road. In between the barren bushes, groups of pickers gathered the precious flowers while they could. A little rain was not a reason to stop the harvest.

I couldn't tell when we left the fields of pinwah and came to the sulee but Brinna could. Segur and Engis took up places near the road as we turned down one of the blue carpeted paths. I bent down and picked one of the blossoms. Shaped like a small, spiky crocus, the

deep blue flower gave off a scent that was more lemon biscuit than lemon fruit.

I held it to my nose and breathed in the aroma. The lemon fragrance reminded me of lian tarts and Daria. And of home, of my family on Earth who thought I'd perished. Hal turned over, and I smiled. I had lots of reasons to be happy, and here, in Torfin, I got to do some welcome research.

I crushed the blossom, rubbing it between my fingers to release the color.

"Ah, I should have warned you," Brinna said. "Your fingers will be blue for a day or two now."

I dropped the flower. The juice soon oxidized into a brilliant shade of sapphire on my fingers, leaving streaks that could have been ink stains.

A lone picker with a tarp slung over his shoulder entered the field and began his task. Segur and Engis moved in closer. Brinna and walked away from him, deeper into the field.

"When will the pilva begin to leaf out?" I asked.

"Not until the end of Luthrach or even into Breán," she said. Which meant the plants were still about two months away from budding.

"So you have this beautiful blue carpet for a month and then another of barren branches before the sticks turn green?" Though the pilva reminded me of currant bushes—straight arms radiating out from the ground—the fruit they produced was walnut-sized and spaced out, more like figs.

The gorantha harvester pulled his tarp further down the path, toward us. An animal, similar to a squirrel but smaller, left the place it had been hiding and hopped down the path, arching its stomach away from the wet foliage.

"*Kaemar*," Brinna said as we watched it go. "They are lucky to have in pilva fields."

"Why is that?" I asked. "Won't it eat the fruit?"

Brinna gave me a dazzling smile. "A few. It prefers insects, and those *would* eat the fruit. Let's see if we can find a nest. They are usually easy to spot this time of year."

We wandered further into the field. Brinna stepped from bush to bush, pushing aside the branches and peering into the bases where the cane-like arms came together.

"Ah! There," she said, bending over and pointing.

I pushed the branches apart to get a better look. The nest appeared to be a ball of leaves and grass tangled together, caught and held by the branches instead of blowing away. But beneath the upper leaves, I could make out a weaving of grasses and a small round hole that served as the doorway.

I was so caught up in my inspection that I didn't pay much attention to the gorantha picker.

Until he grabbed Brinna from behind.

Her startled gasp was silenced by a knife that sliced across her throat in one quick motion. My breath caught somewhere between my lungs and mouth as my eyes met the assailant's. His widened. There was a whiz and a thunk, and the man's eyes widened further. Then he and Brinna toppled over, taking me with them.

The ground slammed against my back and my womb gave an unpleasant tug. My arms were pinned. I closed my eyes and prayed as my chest grew warm and damp. The earth shook as Segur and Engis ran up to us.

"Mother and Father. Mother and Father." Their breathy prayer continued even as they skidded to a stop alongside us.

One body was dragged off of me. "My queen?"

"I'm alive," I managed to get out. "But I hit hard. I'm not sure…" The rest wouldn't come.

Brinna's body was lifted off of me. "I'm just going to stay here," I said. "If someone would go fetch Caenid." I wasn't going to move until Torfin's doctor said it was safe.

I turned my head and opened my eyes. The kaemar's warm, safe nest sat just inches from my face. Brinna had said the kaemar were lucky. But for the rain that still fell, dampening my face as I lay there, the assassin would not have made his mistake. But for the arrow, he would have had time to kill us both.

Iron doors closed over my heart, sheltering it. A warm tear slipped down my cheek. Segur laid his cloak over me as I began to shiver.

I closed my eyes and waited for the healer, offering up a prayer that only two lay dead with me and not three.

Shale was there when I emerged from my bath. I couldn't hate her this time for not warning me of the death of a friend. Her red-rimmed eyes told me she had already paid a price for her silence, and my number of friends was dwindling.

"Caenid says she needs to rest," Iree told her, and tied a robe around me. Torfin's healer had been able to detect Hal's heartbeat and I had not experienced any cramping. He was fairly certain that all would be fine.

Shale nodded. "I'm just going to stay with her."

Hal bumped around, letting me know he was safe. For the time being. "You're not here because…" I drifted off.

"Your child is fine," Shale said, allaying the worst of my fears.

"You can go," I told Iree. Her lips had disappeared, held between her teeth. She nodded and left. She had been Brinna's dresser first.

I stood in the middle of the room, not wanting to lie down but uncertain what else to do. "You don't need to stay," I told Shale. "It's not like Vanerife." I nearly hadn't survived Daria's death.

"I know," Shale said simply. "But I didn't think you should be alone."

I opened my mouth to say I wasn't alone but a sob came out instead. Shale crossed the room in an instant and gathered me into her arms. She eased us to the floor, and I finally gave myself permission to mourn.

"They are moving you to Glábac in the morning," Shale told me as she brushed the hair out of my tear-stained face.

"Brinna's funeral?" I asked.

"No, it won't be safe."

I pushed myself out of her arms. "Then I want to see her now."

"Astrid." Shale's voice was full of warning.

"I know. Yet another face of a dead friend. But you see, I can't have her shocked expression when—" I broke off, blinking back the memory, trying to make it less real. "I can't have that be my last look at her…" My hands rose and covered my mouth. "Oh, my God. Her child…Jaros."

"Astrid." Shale took my hand. "Astrid, don't stay there. Don't dwell on it."

How could I not? But if I did, I would not be able to say my goodbyes. My eyes met Shale's and I gave a nod. She rose and dampened a cloth for me to wash the salt from my face. As I wiped away the tears, she took the gold dress off of its hanger and brought it over.

"I don't know that it will close over my bump." It had been more than twenty days since I had worn it to the King's Guard's funeral… Tovan's funeral…and it had been tight then.

Shale shrugged. "If it is unlaced at the top, it is unlaced at the top."

I dropped the robe and raised my arms. Shale lowered the dress over me and ran the lace through the eyelets. Cool air brushed my back where the garment no longer met due to my added girth, but it eased my heart to be doing this properly. I ran a brush through my hair and slipped on a pair of shoes.

"There is one more thing I need to do before you take me to her," I said to Shale.

I stopped in Jaros's office and took out a sheet of paper. I had to force my fingers, heavy as lead, to work as I made the tear and began to fold it into the sacred crane. I had made way too many of these in the last year.

Brinna had been laid out on one of the tables in the great hall. The other women had already washed and dressed her. A piece of green cloth patterned with barat leaves wound around her throat, hiding the great cut that had ended her life. With her eyes shut, she could have been sleeping.

But her hand was cold when I took it. I pressed my gift into her palm and opened my mouth to sing the lament, but I couldn't make the words come. Brinna wasn't gone. She was right there, holding my hand.

"Thank you," I said, instead. "Thank you for being my friend when no one else would. Thank you for bringing light and laughter into my life. Thank you for being my shield in Aedenfal. And..." I took a deep breath and blinked hard against the rising flood in my eyes.

"Oh, Brinna. He thought you were me. You're only dead because he got us confused." I bent forward and kissed her brow. "I owe you my life," I murmured against her cold skin.

Shale stepped behind me and placed her hands on my shoulders. "Bánalfar will not forget," she said, and I shivered with her words. They were spoken as a prophecy and not an epitaph.

I ran my fingers along Brinna's braid. She had been wearing the same jeweled clasp on its end when I first met her. I placed the plait back against her wrist, against the hand folded over her stomach, risen with a life that would no longer be.

A ragged gasp tore at my throat. "Goodbye, sweet friend." I kissed her brow one last time. The tears I had struggled to contain broke free and ran down my face, wetting hers. I wiped them away and choked back sobs as Shale led me from the room.

CHAPTER 26

"You want me to travel how?" My shocked voice rang through the room.

"It's not safe. We have no idea who the assassin was." Conmel stood, hands on his hips, staring me down. "Alfari. Darlander. We don't know."

"So you want me dressed in that—" I nodded to the pile of armor Segur held in his arms. "And riding Slánta?"

"The armor will protect you against arrows and Slánta will get you to Capalnoc if we are ambushed."

I still couldn't wrap my head around it. "You want a woman who is more than six months pregnant riding a darana?"

"I want both of you to stay alive, and I can't guarantee that if you are in the coach. This will. He will."

I looked at Shale in mute appeal. She simply shrugged. I started in again on Conmel. "Say we are ambushed and Slánta needs to get me to Capalnoc. What do I eat? How do I get back on? I have to pee every hour when I'm simply walking around." Conmel winced at that usually private information. "Riding is going to put even more pressure on my bladder."

"He will be fitted with a pack. And the armor is not heavy. If it was, none of us could fight in it."

I sighed. "You're not going to let this go, are you?"

"Not until we ride through the gates of Glábac."

The armor was not as cumbersome as I had expected. Over the dress that would make my frequent peeing more private, Conmel had furnished me with a leincap—a long, quilted coat—that provided extra protection and kept the riveted mail and solid breastplate from chafing.

"Should you get hit by an arrow, the leincap will help absorb the blow. You will bruise but you will live," Conmel explained when he taught Iree how to dress me in all of it.

The helmet was the heaviest part, to me, anyway. And I had worn enough crowns to know that I would welcome taking it off at the end of the day. The armorer measured the modifications needed to accommodate my belly and promised Conmel that they would be done by the time we left in the morning.

"How am I going to do this?" I asked him again. "I could barely walk after riding to and from the Archjarn. And I didn't have this." I pointed at my belly.

"Slánta will adjust his position to match yours."

I snorted. "I may have ridden him around the courtyard back in Aedenfal with no problem, but there is a lot more of me now. And…" I faltered. "I hit hard against the ground yesterday. What if the extra movement…?"

Conmel paled. "I though Caenid cleared you."

"For walking! But this is riding."

"How much jostling did you feel when you rode Slánta?"

"His gait is smooth. I could have been floating." I pressed my nails into my palms. The physical pain was one I could control and kept me anchored to the here and now.

"That sounds more comfortable than seven days in a jolting carriage."

Conmel and I startled as the door opened. Shale stepped in.

"Capali women ride even in labor," she said. "And Slánta senses your thoughts through the tension and energy your body inevitably gives away. He will know if there is any trouble."

I swallowed heavily. "Will I need him?"

A smile curled her mouth. "Bánalfar will."

We set off the next morning. Dressed in the armor and mounted on Slánta, I felt more like a warrior riding into battle than a pregnant queen fleeing an unsafe city.

Shock filled the faces of the inhabitants of Torfin Low as we rode through the streets. But then jaws clenched and faces turned to look to the east, toward Aedenfal. We met armed men walking eastward as we traveled along the Western road.

"*Mo'shol! Mo'rion!*" they shouted in salute as we passed. Bánalfar was rising up.

"What do they think they can do?" I asked Conmel.

"Put pressure on Aedenfal. Treason has traveled into the heart of Bánalfar and it was Aedenfal that let it in."

"I thought you said you didn't know who the assassin was," I said.

"We don't," Conmel replied, grinding his teeth as he wrestled with his anger. "But they let him in. Darlander. Alfari. It doesn't matter. Ander's poison would not have found a home if Aedenfal's inhabitants weren't so weak."

"No one else has had to live with so much Cordair intrusion," I said.

Conmel grunted. "Lots of others are harassed. They deal with it. Aedenfal hasn't had anything serious happen in a hundred fifty years. No, this is a hatred that has poisoned their hearts and allowed all manner of evil to crawl in." The muscles in Conmel's jaw flared and he looked at me. "I know what you were like riding to and from the Archjarn. I know how dangerous it was for you to call the *tob'iar* yet you did it. You intended to give up your life. And yet, they would take it as if what you did was nothing." Conmel spat.

I shifted my weight, trying to stretch out my protesting thighs. How I was going to spend seven days in this position was beyond me.

Slánta adjusted his posture. I gave his neck a pat. "Sorry, my friend. There is nothing you can do that can make your neck any smaller."

His eyes rolled to meet mine and he gave his mane a shake. Strands caught on his moose-like antlers. I let them hang rather than picking them free, afraid the proud creature might take such an action as an insult.

I gazed back through the branches of Slánta's horns. A sea of razor-sharp antlers and red cloaks surrounded me. Even Shale was dressed in red. Conmel was the only green. The other King's Guard were dots on the edges of the tight circle of Laocotan with me at its center.

Glancing down at the reins in my hands, I tried to focus on something other than the scarlet all around me. My hands tingled and the reins grew sweaty in my palms.

Just like the knife that I had drawn across the assassin's throat.

I closed my eyes as another blade appeared. It drew across Brinna's neck, spilling crimson down her throat.

Slánta nickered, a deep rumble that pulled my eyes back open. I looked around at the army surrounding me, unable to shake the feeling that Ander was right.

I was the villain and blood followed in my wake.

The advantage of having a seer traveling with us was that Shale's voice was able to break through Conmel's paranoia. As he and Galwin had been discussing whether to take over a farmhouse or camp in a field rather than risk finding lodging in the pilgrim-heavy town of Riorgin, Shale broke in and simply stated, "An inn. Your queen will need hot water for a bath."

When Conmel opened his mouth to argue, her piercing stare had dried up his words, unspoken. And while Slánta had been much easier to mount and dismount than I had expected, my thigh muscles were screaming for relief by the time we stopped for the night.

The inn emptied at the sight of the Laocotan streaming in around it. Men dipped their heads to the members of the army and pressed a fist to their chests as they passed by me. Conmel hadn't even needed to ask them to leave.

The empty dining room echoed in the stillness. The innkeeper and his wife hovered by the kitchen door.

"If you need us to go…" she offered. Her wide eyes traveled over my armor.

"No need," I said with a glance at Shale for confirmation. Her green eyes held only fatigue.

The innkeeper's wife put her fist to her heart and bowed. "Just let me know what you require."

"Hot water," Iree said.

Conmel caught the gaze of the Laocotan lieutenant and nodded toward the kitchen door. "Damid will help you prepare the food and assist you with the other duties." A grin began to lift his mouth. "He had lots of practice in the kitchens of Lendurig High before he grew tall enough to pick up a sword." Damid chuckled and followed the woman into the kitchen.

I faced the stairs with trepidation. Last summer, the terror filled eyes, lolling tongues, and final gasps of the anapali I had slaughtered in the name of practice had chipped away at the mental box I'd created to contain the horrors of the *Palmas Cove*—screams, flickering lights, the smell of burning flesh, and far too many white sheets covering the bodies of my friends. Death had been waiting for me at the inn in Riorgin, eager to remind me of everyone he had taken.

I swallowed. This was not the same inn, the same lodgings, but I knew he'd be there, ready to remind me of the harvest I had caused in every town since.

"Would you like me to carry you?" Conmel offered.

I shook my head and heaved myself up the first step. My fingernails dug into the wood to anchor my grip. "Not right now," I said as sweat broke out on my brow with the effort. "I need to stretch out my muscles." But I only made it up four more before I gave in and had him carry me to my room.

I blew out a slow breath when he set me down. My gaze took in the wide double bed that would hold only me. Hal kicked and my hand went to my stomach, still covered by the armor.

Iree began to release me from my metal prison. "Your bath should be ready soon. I packed the oils." There wasn't much she had been able to fit into the bags of the one pack horse I had been allotted. A wagon would have slowed us down. But I gave thanks for her foresight in including the muscle relaxant that my over-stretched muscles needed.

The leincap at last came free. "I'll go check on the water," Iree said, and left me. The door closed with a soft click behind her.

No. The echo of my protest sounded in my head. I forced my lids to stay open so my eyes wouldn't be filled with death. I blinked as the first image rose anyway. Jerra, as Bari and I covered her with her shroud, the harsh light of the *Cove*'s storage bay turning the sheet blindingly white. *No.* I took an involuntary step back. Tovan's lifeless body lying in the hall replaced the image of Jerra.

I turned my gaze away, praying the images would leave my sight. My feet continued their backward journey until I came to rest against the wall. Heat and pain filled my eyes. Valemar had held me the last time that Death had stalked me in Riorgin, and I longed for him to hold me now.

The wall crept past each vertebra as my knees gave way. I blinked and darkness filled my vision. I sucked in a breath and forced my eyes back open and onto the leafy pattern of the wallpaper encircling the room.

Daria. Brinna. So nearly Heymond.

How many more would die because of me?

CHAPTER 27

Giant fingers stretched toward the sky. The green canopy that had clothed the trees back in the summer month of Fásmil had long since departed. With spring still two months away, the trees of Gladama stood like silent sentinels, reaching a thousand feet high. My fingers tightened on the reins, and Slánta's ears perked up.

"Sorry, my friend," I whispered. "It's only ghosts." In Riorgin, I had been haunted by death. In Glábac, it was all that had followed after I confessed to Valemar that I wasn't from the moon and he banished me to Vanerife.

I laid a hand on the curve of metal protecting my belly. The Alfari believed that the trees of Gladama had sheltered the people when they first left Father Sea. For a while, the trees had sheltered me. And if there was anywhere I would be safe in Bánalfar, it would be Glábac and the Glade of Time.

Our arrival in the courtyard was met by two women standing next to the door to the High: an old woman with a white braid and a young woman with hair just a shade lighter than Shale's deep red. Both had a green ribbon woven into their braids, identical to the one that now wound through Shale's. She had abandoned her usual red and donned green, just like the last time she had visited Glábac with me. The city held no Cair. The grove was the cathedral. Here there was no Mother Moon, no Father Sea. Just the trees and their sheltering protection.

A touch of otherworldliness in the women's eyes told me these were no ordinary priestesses. I wound my fingers into Slánta's reins.

"My queen," Shale said. "Allow me to introduce you to Mother Ördu, Tuljerd's Mödatal, and Eskar, my counterpart from Capalnoc."

"Mother. Eskar," I said with a nod. I glanced at Shale, fighting to keep my smile in place when it so wanted to fall. "Strange time to be visiting the grove."

Ördu laughed. "There is never a bad time to visit Gladama."

I bit back the rest of my words. My gut is never wrong and I knew it wasn't a coincidence that they were here. But I couldn't bring myself to argue.

"Astrid?" Shale said.

"Hmm?" I dropped the reins and started to lift my leg over Slánta's massive neck. As soon as I shifted my weight, Slánta knelt, his forelegs folding first, followed by his back. Conmel took my hand, offering his arm for support as I swung my leg over and slid off. The muscles of my face began to ache as I kept my smile in place. *Stupid rule number five.* There is always intrigue, and I was in no mood to deal with it.

I gripped the saddle, drawing strength from the firm leather and the massive animal beneath it before taking Conmel's arm. "Ladies," I said, having no idea what one called a group of seers—A caution?

A prospect? "I am sure I will see you later." Then I mounted the steps, eager to leave the road far behind me.

I sighed as I looked at my reflection in the mirror. The gold and peridot crown carried little weight compared to the helmet I had worn the last seven days. The Queen of Bánalfar stared back at me. It was harder to be her without Valemar by my side. My heart hitched as I thought of the last time I had performed this task, of the magic that had been raised when Valemar and I had gone to the grove to make the offering and pledge to the trees of Gladama. This time, I would be alone.

My fingers crept to my belly where Hal was resting after the gymnastics he had performed during my bath. Valemar and I had both had our prayers answered the last time we made our offerings to the trees. What should I pray for this time?

Conmel accompanied me down to the door in the High that opened onto the grove. I knew the way through the trees well enough, having spent hours within their peaceful sanctuary last summer, but he wasn't going to let me out of his sight.

Nor were the rest of them I discovered when I opened the door. Eight King's Guard waited along with members of the Baraáda—the Tree Guardians, distinguishable by the barat leaves tattooed under each eye like a small green teardrop.

"I am not a tree," I said to Conmel, unhappy about the added security.

"You and the life you carry are sacred," he said. "The plot against you is a plot against the trees."

"Ander doesn't see it that way," I argued. "Quite the opposite, in fact."

Malice entered Conmel's eyes. "He has brought treason and chaos into Bánalfar. He is no better than the Cordair, and we don't know what he will try next. Only the Baraáda can guarantee that the woods are safe. They are familiar with every tree, every blade of grass. They will notice if something is not as it should be."

I pinched my eyes closed and fought back the rising tide of regret. This world had been so much better before I came. But there was no time for sorrow. The offering needed to be made. The pledge needed to be made. And the rest of the pilgrims would not be allowed to return to the grove until I was done.

I opened my eyes and gave Conmel a nod. He followed a discreet distance behind me as the others fanned out and melted into the trees.

The wind whispered through the branches towering high above me. Once more, I felt as if I had stumbled across a forest of Yggdrasil—the great Tree of Life from Norse mythology—for the barat trees dwarfed even the giant sequoia of California on Earth or the poktingi still found in the remote places of Lumpani. Ancient. Mystical. Life-giving.

A basket containing four bottles of wine sat nestled against the roots of the closest tree that ringed the glade. Conmel scanned the open space, hand on his sword, before withdrawing, leaving me alone for the ritual.

"Just pour a little on the roots of one tree and then move your offering to the next." Valemar's words floated back through my memory. I picked up a bottle and clutched it to my chest.

"Do I say anything?"

Valemar's brilliant smile flashed in my mind. *"Only in your heart."*

I uncorked the bottle and walked to the tree on my right. *Thank you for my husband.* I poured a little of the wine on the roots and then stretched out my hand, placing it against the knobby, gray bark. My hand tingled as I waited. Would I feel the vibration, the sensation like a heartbeat pulsing against my hand?

My fingers flexed when the faint sensation traced through them. I lifted my hand, aware that it was probably just the wind, moving the branches, moving the trees, but it added to the eerie impression that the trees were somehow more than alive.

I brushed my fingers against the bark and stepped to the next one. The heady aroma of wine filled my nose as the liquid splashed. I closed my eyes and breathed in memories of summer—of sunshine and Valemar. *Thank you for my child.*

Valemar had prayed for a child when he had brought me here. He had even taken me out into the glade one night and made love to me, his every stroke a desperate plea. And while I hadn't conceived then, I now carried a miraculous answer to prayer. As alien species, our DNA should not have been compatible. But then Hal had happened. And saved my life when I had been willing to pay the price to save the Alfari and the barat trees from a Cordair army armed with alien weapons.

I pressed my hand against the tree before moving to the next. I poured out the measure, hoping something, some words of thanks, would come. I reached out my hand but drew it back. Alone. And not alone. Valemar and I had been alone in the grove. And while he wasn't with me and I was the lone monarch renewing the pledge, I wasn't alone. An army stood hidden in the trees.

I swallowed down the emotions that rose, constricting my throat. An army shouldn't be needed to ensure the safety of Bánalfar's queen. Not in Gladama. The trees were protection, and yet, I had brought instruments of death into it.

I am sorry, I whispered in my head as I turned away.

The next measure splashed like the thunder of hoofbeats as I poured it onto the roots. *Why?* I asked. I clutched the bottle to my chest and moved down to the next tree. *Why am I the cause of so much hate?*

The wine became my blood. So many had lost their lives because of me. But what price had I paid? In the Cair, the faithful offered blood with their prayers. Here, it was wine.

For it is water, not blood, that sustains Yggdrasil. The thought curled through my mind as I crossed the grass to exchange my now-empty bottle for a full one.

In Norse mythology, the three Norns tended Yggdrasil: Urd—the past, Verdani—the present, and Skuld—the future. Every day, they drew water and poured it on the roots to keep the tree healthy while Nidhogg, the dragon, chewed on the roots, trying to pull the world back into chaos.

I had told Reina about dragons when I'd warned her about the technology the Hormani could supply to the Cordair. Now, as I crossed the glade with my new bottle, it was Nidhogg I felt. A dragon chewed on the threads of life in Bánalfar.

I removed the stopper and poured a measure on the tree. I placed my hand against the tree and let the gentle movement wash through me. Life, not death, beat against my palm. Beat within me, as Hal turned, rearranging himself before falling back asleep.

I lifted my hand and crossed to the next tree. "Again, I do not know what to do," I whispered as the wine splashed, heady, rich, and clear.

Show me, I whispered in my heart as I poured the next. And the next. And the next.

By the end, my prayer had become just a plea. *Please.* I pressed my forehead against the bark and watched the last drops gather on

the rim of the overturned bottle until they contained enough weight to fall. *Please protect us from the dragon.*

I rolled the bottle as I brought it up, focused on the last drop and its refusal to be parted from the green glass. My gaze traced the circle of trees that ringed the glade. I'd had such a sense of peace the last time I had performed this task. Grief, too, for I had thought that Valemar's line would end because of me. But the thread of sanctuary had been there.

Now all I sensed was change.

CHAPTER 28

Glábac was unlike any city in Bánalfar and the High was no different. There was no rank, no status. The last time, Valemar and I had sat elbow to elbow with others enjoying the meal. Minstrels received the most regard for they were able to bring the tales and legends to life.

Iree put me into the simple green dress that marked me as a pilgrim, but I hesitated to join the others. The wide, gray eyes of the gorantha picker flashed before me every time I blinked. He had blended in. Until he had ended Brinna's life. I could sit down next to another assassin and none would be the wiser until I was dead.

Hide away and allow fear in? Or trust and allow an assassin in?

…

…

Trust.

I closed my eyes. Trust was the only way one moved forward. It had been the thread that I had held onto after Valemar had banished me.

Trust, Daria had said to me. *You don't know why you're here. And things played out the way they did for a reason.*

Why had things played out the way they had? I pushed the question away. To find the answer, I would have to let down the wall that held back a tidal wave of grief.

I rose from the dressing table. Gladama was a place of shelter. I would have to have faith in its protection.

Shale and the other Mödatals waited for me in the banqueting room. I lifted a shaking smile into place. Other than the seers, I was alone in Gladama. One by one my friends continued to die. With Valemar still in Aedenfal dealing with the network of treason, the influx of Alfari pouring in to pressure the city, a grief-stricken Jaros, and the uncertainty that still reigned in Snow Reach, there was the chance that he would not be able to join me by the end of Breán and would miss the birth of his child.

Friendly smiles met me as I passed through the aisles of tables set with long trestle benches. I nodded my head as I passed and, with some relief, took my place between Shale and Eskar. Mother Ördu sat across from me, a middle-aged man next to her. His braid had been folded and tied tight against the back of his head. A leather thong that cut across his forehead held it in place. I gave him a polite smile.

"My queen," he said with a dip of his head and continued his conversation with the man on his right.

A server placed a platter of meats on the table. A basket of bread soon followed along with bowls of steaming vegetables and soup that would help to dispel the late winter chill which had crept into the hall, even with the crush of people.

"How are the diners chosen?" I asked Shale, taking up a piece of bread to dip in the bowl of soup she ladled and placed in front of me.

"Some pay for the privilege, with the funds going toward purchasing supplies for the meal. Thirty-nine are chosen from the crowds by the árdim to match the thirty-nine trees that ring the glade."

My heart rate increased its tempo. Mother Ördu reached across the table and took my hand. "You are safe, Astrid."

A flash of static passed between our hands and a warning tick flashed in my brain. She wasn't telling the truth.

Mother Ördu's pupils widened as she read my eyes. Her grip increased. "You *are* safe, Astrid."

Shale and Eskar looked at me, concern etched across their faces. Mother Ördu's grip tightened further, biting into my hand. Several heartbeats passed as we stared into each other's eyes.

"Thank you," I whispered, mostly to give her an excuse to let go.

The ancient seer patted my hand. I tucked mine into my lap and rubbed at the places that ached from the pressure of her bony fingers. Shale and Eskar still gazed at me in concern, and I raised a shaky smile into place.

"The Mödatal is correct," the man sitting next to Mother Ördu said, breaking away from his conversation. "Gladama is a place of refuge. You are well away from those who would wish you harm, my queen."

"Aedenfal," the man sitting next to him said in the phlegmy voice of one getting ready to spit. "Treasonous *argrin*." He glared at Shale. "Something you didn't see?"

"She did," I interjected. Plagued by nightmares of the assassin creeping into my room in Aedenfal, the voice that had alerted me spoke over and over again. It sounded so familiar that my brain kept chasing the "why?". When Shale's face appeared, calling my name one night, I hadn't been surprised. "I was given enough warning that I had a chance."

"Your guards can't say the same."

"Would you like to know your future?" Mother Ördu asked in a quiet voice that cut the air like a knife. The man blanched. "It's all there. Your successes…your failures. Your death." Her last word rang in the air.

"Nn…n…no, Mother," the man said and returned to his meal, head bowed, shoulders curled inward.

My heart continued to beat with an erratic thump. I spooned up the meat and vegetables that had once been foreign and were now so familiar and welcomed the heat that slid down my throat. The troubadour perched by the fire began a song. Logs behind him shifted, sending sparks into the air. As they fizzled out, I turned my eyes away from the dark red glow of the coals.

Rage simmered in Gladama. Could death be far behind?

The wagon containing our luggage caught up with us the next afternoon. I stood at the window that looked out on the grove from the solar, watching the pilgrims weave their way through the trees, when Iree brought me the tablet. I hadn't thought to pack it but someone had. The tiny gray message light on the side pulsed softly.

"Thank you," I said with more gratitude than I actually felt. I had no desire to see what General Creskin wanted now. *Yes. No.* It didn't matter. Everything I touched only led to disaster. Iree gave me a sad smile and slipped from the room.

I returned to the view—people dressed in green wending their way along the path that snaked through the tangle of roots, heading toward the glade or back to Glábac, faces etched in awe, joy, or a mixture of the two. But the tablet's flashing light had created a tempo that now beat in my mind.

How much more would I change this world? Treason, death, and hatred had grown with my presence. There was still peace or death to be found in the trees. At that moment, I didn't care which I found.

"Why are the three of you here?"

Shale shifted with my question but her eyes remained on the flames, seeking the answers to questions of her own.

"My place is by your side," she said, finally pulling her gaze away from the fire. Tension swirled in the depths of her eyes when they met mine. My eyebrows lifted.

"And Eskar and Mother Ördu?"

"It is not unusual for the Möda to come to Gladama." Her smile wavered as it crept up her face. "Especially since you have come."

"I know you don't believe that," I said. "You feel it, too." My gaze went to the fire crackling merrily in the grate. "You don't know why, either. That's what you have been looking for."

"You have spent too long surrounded by intrigue," Shale said, and gestured for me to take a seat. I put a hand behind me to help with my balance as I lowered myself onto the couch. "Tea?" Shale asked.

"Yes, please."

She took two cups from the table and filled them from a pot hanging on a hook anchored by the hearth. "Here," she said, handing a cup to me. I caught the trace of dark circles under her eyes and let my questions go, instead breathing in the woodsy aroma that rose from the dark amber depths.

We drank in silence for a while. Shale usually answered my questions before I asked them. The tightness around my heart increased as the quiet lingered.

I turned my eyes to the floor. "You know everyone around me dies," I said when I could stand the silence no longer.

"A shadow still stalks you," Shale said quietly.

I squeezed my eyes shut and tried to swallow the truth. "Then nowhere is safe."

"Not yet." Her achy whisper pulled my eyes back open.

I blinked hard. I didn't know how I would survive another death. I gathered air into my lungs to force the words from my mouth. "I can't lose you, too. I've no—" My voice broke. I set my tea down and tried again. "No one left."

Shale set hers aside and uncurled from her chair. She took my hands. "You and I and your child are in the future, that much I can see. But the rest—" She bit a lip that trembled. "The rest the Mother refuses to show me, no matter how much I try."

My eyes caught a rim of white just inside the fold of her sleeve. A swath of bandage wrapped around her arm. I hid my alarm with a smile. "Then I guess we have some sewing to do."

Shale laughed at the whimper that followed my words. I blinked back the tears that rose, glad that my jest had found the mark even as my heart felt the loss of those who had started Hal's layette.

And there was nothing prepared here, no nursery. "We have rooms to figure out, as well," I added. As hard as it had been to nest in Aedenfal, Glábac felt less permanent, despite the ancient trees. All the pilgrims coming and going created an air of holiday, the crush of a carnival before the emptiness returned.

Shale traced the curve of my jaw and took my chin. "Gladama has sheltered us for millennia. It will shelter you, too."

I nodded an agreement I didn't feel. Only the trees were permanent. Everything else came and went.

Even me.

Glábac had no steward. Sciglas, the captain of the Baraáda, was in charge of the town—the High and the Low. The árdim coordinated trade with all the merchants and innkeepers, functioning like the head of an all-encompassing guild. My previous month in Glábac had been spent in the trees and with Valemar, following his lead. My knowledge of the High and its workings were scant, so I sought out Sciglas to determine where to house the nursery.

His office was located near the barracks by the High's front gate. I knocked on the heavy wooden door and received a curt "Enter" in reply.

Lines etched his forehead, cutting through the barat leaf tattooed on his brow, signifying his rank. Sciglas was of an age where he could have retired from service but had chosen to continue.

"My queen," he said, setting aside the papers that had absorbed his attention. "What may I do for you?"

"Mödatal Shale tells me I may be here awhile so I shall require rooms to outfit for use as a nursery."

Sciglas tilted his head to the side. "I will have to give it some thought. Kings and queens have always come here with their children. We have certainly housed them, but it sounds like you want something more permanent."

"I am a leaf blown on the wind," I said, drawing up a smile to hide the ache in my heart. "I had thought to have been housed elsewhere but this is where I currently find myself."

"Glábac is different from other cities," he warned me. "It is a temporary town. There are no ladies to sit and sew with. They come to spend some time in the grove and glade, connecting themselves to the past and offering thanks before they return to their daily lives, just as you did last summer."

He offered no words of condolence. Sciglas knew I hadn't suffered a miscarriage on my previous visit.

"I have the Möda," I said. His eyebrows rose. "And Iree. I will make do. There is a solar."

"Merchants and craftsmen will need to be sent for. Probably from Torfin. This is a town of pilgrims, not shoppers." The reproach in his voice matched the spark in his eyes.

"It is a town of refuge," I reminded him. "And it is currently called upon to protect Bánalfar's pregnant queen."

Sciglas's fingers tightened around the pen in his grip. "I will let you know later today what I have worked out. People will need to be moved around, their rooms changed. Glábac is crowded this time of year with Altbain and *Chéladt*—First Leaf—approaching. The crush of people will only increase." Frustration strained his voice. "Anything else, my queen?"

I bit back the rebuke I wanted to hurl at him. "Not at the moment," I said, rising from my chair. My head dropped, weary of fighting for the respect Valemar would have instantly been given.

I closed the door to Sciglas's office, tearing myself away from the urge to lean against it. There were too many eyes in the courtyard to witness my distress. I inhaled deeply. The Gellirhird message from Valemar I kept inside my bodice pressed into the skin above my heart. At some point, things would calm down enough in Aedenfal for him to join me.

Or when he finds Ander.

I stumbled. Where was Ander?

Sciglas's frostiness made more sense. I realized it wasn't me that the captain of the Baraáda wasn't happy about. It was what followed me.

CHAPTER 29

I didn't wait for Sciglas. I gathered the three Möda and began an inspection of the High. Many of the rooms were set up for use by visiting dignitaries. "Representatives from all of Bánalfar's neighboring countries come on pilgrimage," Eskar explained.

"Is that why you and Mother Ördu are here?" I asked as I shut the door on yet another room meant for just one person.

"Mother Moon told me I was needed here," Eskar answered.

"And I wanted to celebrate one more *Chéladt*," Mother Ördu said. A wistfulness tinged her voice. Shale gave the older woman a hard look. "There is nothing like being in the presence of the season's first barat leaf as it uncurls and reaches for the warmth of the sun. You can feel life radiating underneath your feet, spreading up from the roots and lifting toward the heavens."

Ördu looked up at the ceiling. Her eyes traced some mental map. "We need to go higher. There is a corner room that looks out on two sides. Richeza used it as a studio for Bánalfar's embroiderers. And Queen Helka had painters from Tuljerd come to capture the trees' embrace that can be felt in the room. We Tulja like proof that the

Cordair are still gone."

We followed the ancient seer up another flight of stairs and down corridors painted with animals arranged around and peering from behind the trunks of smaller-sized trees than the barat that stood just beyond the High's walls. Eskar gave a quick rap on the door and opened it when there was no reply. The room was currently set up as a dining room and study. Dust lay on every surface.

"Not much need for such a room," Mother Ördu said. "But travel and the crush of pilgrims can cause discomfort for some and they seek a space with fewer dining companions."

I crossed to the window that looked out over the grove. From this height, branches forked out from the mammoth trunks and helped to block the view of the crowds wending their way through the roots to the glade.

"If you cleared this lot out," Mother Ördu said with a wave of her hand. "You could put a bed here and a cradle there. A screen over there for the nurse."

I let her words paint a picture in my head and erase the round table with its six chairs, the sideboard, and the writing desk. The window on the other side overlooked the small park that ran between the wall of the Low and the grove, giving the room of the feel of a tree house.

"The other rooms along the hall could be converted for use by Iree and Valemar," Shale said.

"Do you really think he will come?" I asked.

A smile twitched Shale's lips. "Do you really think he would stay away?"

"He would if it meant finding Ander," I said, weary of being alone.

I turned back to the view of the grove. The hair on my arms rose with the sight of the pilgrims moving between the trees. There was no way that Sciglas, the Baraáda, and the King's Guard could truly keep me safe with so many strangers around. But there was nowhere left to go. Daria's and Brinna's deaths had proven that even "safe" towns could still hold dangers.

A sigh escaped my lips, and I turned from the view. "I supposed I should go inform the captain of the Baraáda where I wish to be housed."

Sciglas took my pronouncement with resignation but refused to do anything further until after the holidays, almost a month away. The three Möda and I began sewing in the solar. Mother Ördu's hands were surprisingly nimble for ones so gnarled with age. Unable to shake the fear of being amongst strangers, I stayed inside instead of wandering the grove and took up jaldun again.

The first couple days of practice proved difficult. The hiss of the blade cutting the air matched the hiss of surprise the assassin had uttered in Aedenfal when I had cut his throat. The blade also caught and reflected the light, just like the one in Torfin when it sliced through Brinna's neck. But the weight of the knives filled my hands with strength, reminding me that I was not powerless, and slowly my mind began to relax.

Three days before Altbain, Iree interrupted my practice, rushing in short of breath and flushed.

"You will never believe who is here."

I whirled around, nearly dropping my knives. "Valemar?"

Iree put a steadying hand on her heaving chest. Her expression filled with contrition. "No. Sorry, my queen. Aren Loör has just arrived in the courtyard."

The blades went slack in my hands. Why would Capalnoc's ambassador have come to Glábac?

"If you want to receive him, we should get you changed," Iree said, drawing my attention back to the reason she had come.

I nodded and replaced the weapons. Fifteen minutes later, I entered the dining hall where Aren sat in the middle of the contingent from Capalnoc, all refreshing themselves with tankards of ale.

"Cousin," Aren said, rising at my entrance. He placed a fist on his chest and inclined his head.

"This is a surprise." The rest of the contingent rose in a rumble of feet and protesting benches and repeated Aren's gesture.

"Capalnoc, too, observes Altbain and Chéladt." Aren gestured for me to take a seat on the bench next to him. The other men shifted down to make room for me. I placed my hands on the table for balance as I swung first one leg and then the other over the bench and sat. "Ale?" Aren asked. He hooked an empty tankard with a finger and drew it toward him. "You look flushed."

"Thank you," I said. "I was at jaldun practice when I was told you had arrived."

Aren's blue-gray eyes narrowed. "Not taking your leisure in the trees?"

"The presence of the queen is too much of a bother to the other pilgrims. I made my pledge when I first arrived."

But Aren saw through my half-truth. His mouth thinned.

And then his manner changed completely, something I had done many times to mask what I actually thought. He laughed, his eyes flashing with mirth. "And what will they do when twenty strapping, young horsemen make the journey?"

"Probably start marking out their favorites for a moon mate." Had I not been married, any one of them would have been just my type.

Aren laughed in earnest.

Dinner was much more pleasant that evening. The Möda and I joined the Capalnoc contingent for dinner. Aren's eyes had widened when he took in my companions, but a diplomat's smile lit his face as I approached with the three seers.

"Eskar," Aren said with a nod as the men rearranged themselves so we could sit.

"*Kolrath* Loör," Eskar said. "I'm surprised to find you so far from home."

"And I you." Aren's glance slid to Mother Ördu.

"*Kyvet*, allow me to introduce you to Mother Ördu, Tuljerd's Mödatal," I said, finishing the introductions.

"Glábac is certainly blessed to have the presence of so many Möda at this time."

"We have come for the same reason you have," Mother Ördu said to Aren. His eyes flashed with alarm. "Such an important year deserves to be observed where so much began."

"Then we are blessed, as well, to be here." Aren's smiled widened briefly. He scanned the room, taking in the other guests and noting the positions of both the Baraáda and the King's Guard. He returned several enticing smiles with a saucy wag of his eyebrows. I rolled my eyes and took a slice of bread from the tray in the center of the table. Shale bit her lips but couldn't hide the smile that curled the corners of her mouth.

Aren caught the motion and turned his attention to her. His gaze traced her red braid with its interwoven green ribbon, traveling

from the crown of her head, past her shoulder, between her breasts, to where it disappeared beneath the table.

An ache blossomed in my heart. I smiled to hide it and concentrated on filling my plate with slices of bohar and dishes of both roasted and mashed vegetables. The way that Aren looked at Shale reminded me that Valemar was not here. Reminded me that I would be surrounded by couplings on Altbain but my own bed would be empty. I camouflaged a sigh, turning it into a yawn that I hid with my hand.

"Excuse me," I said from behind it. "My energy waxes and wanes with startling frequency these days." Hal kicked, a sharp jab to my ribs that caused the fabric stretched over my stomach to bounce.

"Father be praised, cousin. You do have a feisty one," Aren said.

I smoothed down the front of my dress. "He likes to make his presence known."

"He?" Aren asked, eyebrows raising.

"Or she."

My heart lurched strangely, squeezing and pulling my insides. I frowned as the twisting continued and the contents of my stomach moved north. Mother Ördu gave me a kind smile but Eskar and Shale looked at me with concern. "It's nothing," I said, swallowing hard. "The child just changed position and left me with less room for my dinner." I stood. The Capali contingent rose, too. "I think I will take my meal in my room. That way I can pick at my food and you can enjoy your dinner and the entertainment without fear of bothering me."

I smiled at the faces that greeted me from the other tables as I made my way out of the banqueting hall, one hand pressed against the swell of my stomach. The discomfort grew with every step. Once through my door, I raced for the close stool and had barely lifted the lid before I heaved, though nothing came up. Resting my head against the padded seat, I gathered the strength to stand, confused by the sudden nausea. Surely sensitivity to smells didn't return in the seventh month.

There was a knock on the door and Shale entered before I could answer.

"You should be downstairs," I said, closing my eyes against another twist in my stomach.

"Tea," Shale said to someone in the hall. She crossed the room and placed a hand on my forehead. "You're not clammy. That's a good sign." Her fingers closed over my wrist. "But your pulse is erratic. Any headache? Shortness of breath?"

I pulled my hand from hers. "I never get a deep breath these days but no headache." Her concern was beginning to frighten me. "You should be enjoying your dinner."

Shale placed her hands under my forearm and assisted me up. She maneuvered me over to the bed and helped me slide onto it. She slipped off my shoes and began to massage my feet. I groaned with pleasure.

"Not too much swelling," she said, easing the knots in my toes and smoothing over my swollen ankles.

"I've been able to do jaldun just fine," I said. "Other than the change in balance."

"Exercise will help keep you strong." Shale smiled but it didn't quite hide her concern.

"Is there something wrong with me?" My hands pressed against my womb. "Is Hal in danger?"

Her fingers slowed and increased their pressure. My heart rate eased and matched their pace. "Probably nothing. You've been doing remarkably well, all things considered. But we'll keep an eye on you."

The history lessons at the academy had covered many aspects of medieval life that had left me thankful those days were far behind us. While today's medicine could save children born as early as fourteen weeks, that had not been the case in centuries past. Mothers had often died, too. Once upon a time, a man had been expected to outlive three wives. Women had taken to the birthing bed praying to be spared. I hadn't given it much thought until Shale's concern.

Shale waved away the servant who entered the room with a plate of food. I covered my mouth and nose to block out the smell of the meat and vegetables that wafted in. "The tea should be here soon," she said.

Galwin knocked on the open door. "How is she?"

"Coping," Shale said, and began work on my other foot. I wiggled the toes on the first one, marveling at how much better it felt.

Galwin frowned. "I'll go fetch the healer."

"Really, there's no need," I said as Galwin turned to go. "Is there?" I asked Shale. Galwin had already disappeared down the hall.

"It never hurts to get you checked out."

"I thought you just did that." It occurred to me that I wasn't sure who would be watching over my labor. Ferrick had kept an eye on Cadalin and then Hartha had come in to help Cadalin with the delivery. But Aedenfal's midwife had stayed behind.

"I am well versed in looking after pregnant women," Shale said. "But we may as well have Ennick give his assessment."

"Really?" I asked. "How many pregnant women have you cared for?"

Shale smiled and covered my legs with the blanket folded on the end of the bed. "As head of the Cair, overseeing the health of the other women falls to me."

"So you'll be with me? For the delivery?"

"Yes, Astrid."

"Is that why the three of you are in Glábac?"

Shale sat down on the edge of the bed. "I know you have realized the significance of the three Möda being here—three ages of Bánalfar coming together to support you and its future."

"But Mother Ördu is from Tuljerd and Eskar is from Capalnoc," I said, trying to shake the notion that the three Norns were indeed in Glábac.

"We all support the same land. This place is important to more than just the Alfari, as are you."

A girl arrived with a tray containing the pot of tea. "Thank you," Shale said, taking it from her. She motioned for the girl to leave us. Shale poured a cup, added a sweetener, and then handed it to me.

I breathed in the woodsy aroma with a sigh. "I've always thought it needed sugar or honey," I said and took a sip.

"I doubt we will get any other sustenance in you tonight. The sugar will provide some energy."

I drank it gratefully. The taste and heat slowed my heart rate and loosened some of the tightness in my chest.

"My queen," Glábac's healer said, appearing in the doorway. "Have we had a scare?"

"Thready heart rate and upset stomach," Shale said, moving back from the bed to give Ennick room.

Ennick took my wrist. "Heart rate seems fine now. Have you felt unwell as of late?"

"Not that it has stood out among all the other stresses I've experienced lately," I said.

The healer's hands hesitated over my stomach. "May I?" he asked, reaching out for the swell. I nodded.

Ennick pressed. The tea in my stomach moved up my esophagus as my organs were displaced. I swallowed hard to keep it down and curled my toes as the pressure on my bladder increased.

"Head is still up," he said, withdrawing his hands. "I think we should put you on modified bed rest for the next couple of days."

"But Altbain is just three days away," I said.

"I don't see why you shouldn't be able to attend," he said, "provided you are feeling well by then. I know you have been avoiding the trees and the crowds and have been practicing jaldun for your exercise, but I would like to get you outside a couple of times a day. The garden next to the High's walls should provide you with access and cover. A fifteen-minute stroll in the morning and afternoon should suffice." Ennick dipped his head. "Just let me know if you need anything else."

Aren joined me the next day for my walk in the garden. "I really don't need a chaperone," I said to him, more testily than I had intended.

"Have I done something?" he asked.

"No," I said, deflating. "It's just…the last time I saw you was in Aedenfal. With Valemar. And…" The ache in my heart silenced the rest of my words.

"Ah."

We strolled along in silence for a while.

"I guess I should thank you," I said. "For Slánta. I did end up riding him."

"The tales of Bánalfar's magnificent armored queen have spread far and wide," Aren replied. "Though I am sorry for the circumstances which required his use."

"Thank you," I said, and tried to put Brinna's loss back into the mental box that held so many others. "Why are you really here?"

"Because Valemar cannot be. And Capalnoc wishes to add its protection to Bánalfar's queen. Ander may be willing to take on one country, hoping to appeal to the fears of its inhabitants, but I doubt he would be willing to incur the wrath of its neighbors."

Despite the assurance Aren offered, his words only added weight. One by one, countries lined up for war.

Because of me.

"Tell me again what the festivities for Altbain include," I said to Shale. My fingers twisted the edge of the blanket, anxious for something to do.

Shale looked up from her embroidery and gave me a smile. "Gifts will be exchanged tomorrow night, tokens of appreciation meant to show new beginnings or the circle of creation."

The ancient Romans and others had done that. Earth's month of January was in recognition of the god Janus—a two-faced god, looking both forward to the future and backward to the past. On Earth, though, it would have been the new moon that would have been observed, a moon about to grow with light. On Crenfor, the full moon heralded the start of things, its light responsible for life to come.

"I don't have anything for anyone," I said.

"It doesn't matter," Shale said, her voice full of compassion. "You carry your gift inside you. We just have to wait a while to receive it in full." She drew something from the basket at her feet. "Why don't you keep your hands busy with this."

Shale handed me a smock I had started weeks ago for Hal. I brushed my fingers against the smooth green stitches that made up

one of the barat leaves circling the neck. My fingers ached, longing to trace the pattern that ran along Valemar's chest. "I wish I had something for Valemar," I said. His absence sat like a stone on my ribcage.

"What did I just tell you?" Shale asked.

"That I already have a gift," I answered glumly.

"Altbain is much more subdued than Gellirhird. We don't need the reassurance that the darkness will end. We have more light during the day. We can feel the sap stirring in the trees and the new life about to burst forth."

"The Alfari can feel it?" I asked.

"Just as we can feel the pull of the moon. It is something in the air that pricks the skin." I sighed heavily. "You can't?" Shale asked, looking up from her hoop.

"No. Though…" I drifted off and gathered my words. "When I'm in the grove, I often get the sense the trees are more than alive. My world once told stories of spirits found in water and in trees. Nyads and dryads they were called. Sometimes, when I'm in the grove, I feel like the trees are talking to each other and listening to me."

Shale smiled but didn't say anything.

"What?" I asked.

"You are becoming more Alfari," she said in answer.

I only prayed that was true.

Despite Shale's assurance that my pregnancy was enough, I wanted some token of appreciation for my friends, especially as I had decided to pass on the Altbain festivities. Unlike Gellirhird, the focus of the holiday was on the creation of life. Despite the gifts

that would be exchanged, the dining hall would be full of people sitting with their chosen moon mates, waiting for the moon to rise and urge them out into the trees. My skin tingled, longing for the touch of my husband, but he was hundreds of miles away.

I sent Shale and Iree into the Low to purchase the gifts. For Iree, I had silver pins to hold up her hair. For Shale, a new set of sewing needles.

"Thank you, my queen," Shale said when she unwrapped them.

"They're for your daughter," I said. "You are helping me with my layette and, when the time comes, I would like to help you with yours." Shale's gaze went to the floor.

A knock sounded on the door. Shale and I looked over to find Aren standing in the doorway. Their gazes met, and an electric current passed between them. I looked away, feeling like an intruder.

"I will see you in the morning, Astrid," Shale said to me, rising. She bent and kissed me on the cheek. "Joyous New Year, my queen."

"Joyous New Year, Shale," I replied.

Shale squeezed my hand and left the room, walking by Aren without a glance.

"I'm sorry you won't be joining us cousin," Aren said.

I fiddled with the blanket covering my lap. "You won't even know I'm missing." I leaned around and pointed at the chest of drawers by the window. "The box over there is for you."

Aren scowled at me as he spied it. His steps were heavy as he crossed the room. I had been torn whether or not it was the right gift for I didn't see how it would represent new beginnings but Shale had convinced me to follow my instincts.

"It's of moonstone," I said, using the Alfari word for obsidian, as Aren removed the lid. He plucked the knife from its cushion.

It was a stunning creation. The volcanic glass had been polished to a high gloss, its black blade so unlike the ones that still haunted my dreams. Caradin wood inset with green stones shaped to resemble barat leaves formed the handle.

"It's for fruit," I told Aren, but the hair on my arms quivered. I prayed the response was just nerves and not a warning.

Aren placed the knife back in the box. "I will think of you when I use it." Aren's eyes met mine. "You are sure you won't be joining us this evening?"

I smoothed the fabric of my gown, molding it to my stomach. "I am sure. Tonight is about starting new and creating life." My fingers brushed against the knobby outline of one of Hal's feet, quiet now, saving his kicking for later. "I've already done that."

"And Valemar is not here," Aren said.

I blinked back the tears that rose, praying the kyvet wouldn't see them fall. "No."

Aren bent and kissed me on the cheek. "Joyous New Year, Astrid."

His touch was like a flame, igniting my cheeks. "Joyous New Year, cousin.," I replied, not meeting his gaze. My ear followed his footsteps as they left the room. The tear slipped down my cheek. Aren wouldn't be alone tonight.

I sucked in a breath and sought my soul for the thread that tied my heart to Valemar. It was only imaginary but provided me with a measure of comfort. I gave it a *twang*, plucking at the invisible cord like the strings of a harp, sending a reverberation down it, hoping that Valemar could sense my love and presence.

Another moon apart. Aedenfal was sure to be filled with people wishing for a very different year. I couldn't see the citizens taking the draught this time.

As for Valemar, I was sure he had taken the draught.

"Joyous New Year, my husband," I whispered. "Come get your gift when you can."

CHAPTER 30

The Möda were the first to notice the change in the trees. Mother Ördu rose one afternoon from her sewing, her eyes unseeing. Eskar and Shale followed a moment later, a smile growing as they turned to face the trees. Within two days, pilgrims paused in their journey to the grove. Hands were placed on the bark and heads gazed up in expectation.

But the running sap made Aren anxious. His agitation was all too evident when he joined me on my daily walks.

"I thought Chéladt was supposed to a time of joy," I said to him when his attention drifted from me to the trees where he cast worried glances.

He smiled but it didn't erase the creases around his eyes. "I must leave after Chéladt. My excuse for being here evaporates with the first leaf that opens."

I threw him a sidelong glance. "I thought you were here for the festivals."

"I am here because I must be."

"And…?" I prompted.

He swallowed. "Because Valemar could not."

Pain curled through my heart. "He asked you to come?"

Aren's smile widened. For a moment, it was real. "No. But after the wife of Torfin's steward was killed, I thought you needed a greater presence around you. You are not the only one the Mother whispers to." He wasn't talking about the three seers.

"And what do you fear, cousin?" I asked.

Aren glanced around and his voice lowered. "You are being followed."

I stumbled. Aren's hand shot out to steady me. His fingers closed around mine.

"How do you know? Who have you told?" I asked.

Aren laughed. "Did you tell Valemar or anyone else about your suspicions in Aedenfal?" My cheeks burned. Aren's voice softened. "But the Möda know this. It's why they have gathered."

We have come for the same reason you have.

Aren sighed. "Their being here is the one consolation I have in leaving."

I cast a glance at the grove, just twenty feet away. Did the trees shelter or did they hide?

We gathered in the grove before dawn. Aren met the Möda and I at the door to the grove. He gave Shale a look that was filled with sad longing. Hers was strangely peaceful.

Aren took my hand and wrapped it around his arm. "I have been told you are basically blind in the dark. Allow me to keep you from tripping over a root."

One of Aren's lieutenants offered Mother Ördu his arm and the rest of the Capali contingent closed ranks around us. Conmel and the other King's Guard took up the rear.

The night was inky black under the trees. The quiet shuffle of feet was the only sound as we headed into the trees. It grew louder as pilgrims from the Low joined the path, but the security of Aren's arm and the tight circle of protectors allowed my heart to fill with joy instead of fear.

The night became filled with song. It began with Mother Ördu, whose clear voice surprised me, coming from one so old. Others soon picked up the tune but the words were old Alfari or some other ancient language, for I didn't understand a word.

The darkness of night began to fade. Shades of gray became dawn. I shifted on my feet, unused to standing, but Ennick had determined that attending Chéladt would be better for my health than watching the crowds from the High and miss the weaving of life and shelter created in the trees.

As the morning's first beam of light broke through the curtain of branches, heads raised to stare high above. I followed their gaze.

Within moments, a faint rustle sounded in the canopy. The sunbeam grew stronger, bathing the trees in its warmth as it reached toward the forest floor. It was probably only the breath of the crowd, but I could have sworn I heard the trees sigh. Two fuzzy, gray pieces that had covered a bud fell away.

The leaf unfolded slowly, its color deepening even as I watched.

"Go rab mait gat as go baitan," the crowd intoned as one. They traded smiles and embraced those around them.

Aren drew me into his arms. "Thank you for your shelter," he said to me.

"Is that what was said?" I asked.

"Yes," he said as he released me.

Shale was the next to claim him. *"Go rab mait gat as go baitan,"* she said.

I shivered and looked away. I was fairly certain the two of them had spent the Blood Moon together but what passed between them now seemed more intimate.

When we had exchanged embraces with everyone standing close, the crowd began to return from where they'd come—pilgrims from the Low to the wider path that met near the High, and those of us from the High toward the door in its towering walls.

A hearty breakfast had been laid out for us. Shale took a seat next to Aren and, from the way their arms touched, took his hand under the table. From the ache that appeared on his face, I was sure I would not be the only one he missed when he left in the morning.

Small yellow-green leaves began to dot the arms of the barat trees in the days after Aren's departure. The breeze picked up the crisp smell of chlorophyll and carried it through the open windows. Mother Ördu announced one morning that I was healthy enough to make the journey to the grove. Chéladt, she insisted, had not harmed me in the least.

Shale set her sewing aside. "You are not needed, my dear," Mother Ördu said to her.

Surprise widened Shale's green eyes. Her brow crinkled as her gaze turned inward. Mother Ördu took her hand. "You are needed here."

"But…" Shale drifted off. Her focus returned, and her eyes searched Mother Ördu's face.

The older woman smiled and squeezed Shale's hand. "Astrid and I are just going for a walk in the woods. Her place is there, where the future is emerging out of the past." Her bony fingers released Shale's hand. "Come," she said to me and placed my hand on her arm. "You have been cooped up in here too long."

I pushed myself out of my chair and shifted my hips, making sure that the bones were truly aligned before I took a step, having stumbled the other day when my hip bone proved to be in a different place than usual.

Mother Ördu cackled. "I have to do that to get mine to loosen up and you have the opposite problem."

"We will certainly be a pair," I said.

We slowly progressed through the High to the door that led onto the grove. I inhaled when it opened, savoring the scent of spring in the air. Birdsong drifted down from the branches, the only sound in the otherwise silent woods. Someone had cleared the trees for us.

Sunlight dappled the path, creating patches of color and shadow. Mother Ördu and I picked our way through the snaking roots of the ancient trees, but the path she chose was not a direct route to the glade. I opened my mouth to ask her about it but she patted my hand.

"The future is here. Can you feel it?" she asked.

"Yes," I said. "Life is pushing its way through the trees, creating the canopy that has sheltered so many for millennia."

"The barat trees have always held out their arms for us." She turned my hand over. My sleeve slid back, exposing the ring of tattooed barat leaves that encircled my arm. "And you have held your arms out for them. You have protected them and now they will protect you."

I stopped still and noticed that the birds had gone silent. "What are you talking about?"

Ördu grasped my hands. "The future starts here, Astrid." She moved, faster than I could believe possible, to my left. I heard a whizzing noise, and a soft *thunk* emanated from Ördu's back. Her eyes closed and peace settled across her face.

The sound came again. Mother Ördu pulled me sharply to the right as an arrow flew by my face and, with a resounding *THUNK*, dug itself deep into the tree behind me. A curse filled the air from the cover of the trees.

"Stay, Astrid," Mother Ördu commanded, tightening her grip. "This is how the future begins."

"With my death?" I croaked out. The seer's iron grasp held me firm.

Her eyes flew open. "With mine."

A hooded figure in green strode out from behind a tree twenty feet away, an arrow knocked in his bow. Adrenaline shot through my body, and my limbs began to shake "Why can't you just die?" a strong, clear voice said from under the hood.

A shout broke through the trees. The assassin pulled back and let his arrow fly. *Thunk.* Mother Ördu pitched forward.

Thunk. Thunk thunk. The rapid succession was quieter, coming from farther away.

The assassin staggered forward, arrows sprouting from his back. His bow snagged on the roots as he inched toward me. "Do you know who I am?" he screamed at the approaching guards and tore off his hood. Long white hair flowed down his back and snagged on the highest arrow sunk into his shoulder. Another arrow sliced through the air and pierced his throat. He clutched at it, and then my eyes were drawn to Mother Ördu. Her hands had gone slack around my wrists and she began to fold toward the ground. My arms went around her, but my knees buckled with the additional weight. I struggled to keep her upright.

"Mother and Father. Mother and Fath—" Conmel's voice cut off as he reached me.

"It is done." Ördu's voice rasped with the words. A breath that was more sigh than anything else followed. The last of her strength ebbed away, pulling her out of my arms and onto the ground.

Conmel looked from her to me. "By the sea and moon…" he said, unable to finish the oath. Conmel raised me up and quickly scanned me, taking in my form and assuring himself that I was fine.

Sciglas strode down from over the small knoll. He grasped the arrow that had buried itself in the bark of the barat tree and yanked it out. His finger ran over the wound. "Not since…" His jaw clenched, unable to finish.

The arrow tightened in his grip. Sciglas stared at the blue and white feathers wound with yellow thread. "Darland," he said with a snarl and snapped the arrow in two.

"Who?" I asked.

Conmel strode over to the body. His jaw tightened. "The clasp on the cloak carries the seal of the royal house of Darland." Conmel stripped off the assassin's left glove and turned the hand. A gold ring glinted on the little finger. "I'm guessing this is the missing Prince Ander."

"He's been hiding in plain sight?" I exclaimed. "How is that possible?"

Sciglas dropped to his knees in front of me and bowed his head. "My life is forfeit. I have not protected the grove. I have failed to spot malintent when it entered the city and, for the first time in a thousand years, the trees have been injured."

I closed my eyes, blocking out the sight. Two people had died but all Sciglas worried about was the tree. Part of me understood, but the rest of me hated him for ignoring the cost in actual lives. The tree would recover. Ördu and Ander would not.

"Conmel, I wish to return to the High," I said.

He stiffened as I dug my fingers into his arm and leaned against it. I inhaled deeply but the air caught in my chest, refusing to release my lungs. Conmel's other hand went under my elbow, keeping me upright as I struggled to breathe.

I forced my feet down the path, away from the scene behind me, blocking out the voices that mingled concern and horror.

"Ander is dead," Conmel said to himself as much as to me.

I could only manage a strangled noise of acknowledgement.

Shale paced between the edge of the grove and the door to the High, arms wrapped around herself. Her face was stained with tears. A hand covered her mouth as we approached. Her eyes asked the question she already knew the answer to. I nodded anyway, confirming Ördu's death for her.

"Thank you, Conmel. I will take her from here." Shale put her arm around me and led me inside.

Once we reached my room, Shale sat me down and removed my shoes. She waved Iree away when she rushed in. "Thank you," I said, grateful that I didn't need to relive the horror again for at least a little while. I was sure that I would need to repeat the story time and again in the coming hours and days.

"It's my fault," Shale said. She clutched my shoes to her chest. "I couldn't see."

"Ördu knew what she was doing." I closed my eyes and prayed that would be the end of it, for at least a little while.

Shale nodded and set the shoes down. She unrolled my stockings and slid them off. "What would you like, my queen?"

I shook my head, uncertain. Sleep? Oblivion? Time to fast forward and things to have been dealt with?

"Let's at least get you off your feet," Shale said when I didn't answer.

I nodded and let her lead me over to the bed. I slid onto it and lay down, pressing a hand against my stomach. At eight months pregnant, there wasn't much room for Hal to turn around anymore but he gave me a reassuring squirm. The breath I'd been holding finally released.

Shale perched on the stool next to the bed and brushed the hair from my face. Her lips twitched as she attempted to smile.

"I'm sorry," I told her.

Shale's hand cupped my face. "Oh, Astrid. It's not your fault."

For the first time in a thousand years, or maybe ever, Glábac was closed and placed in lockdown. Uncertain if Ander had accomplices, Rhygo, Sciglas's replacement, had set up barricades along the road, barring others from entering, and began interviewing every person within the Low. The former captain of the Baraáda had sliced his throat beneath the injured tree, spilling his blood in payment for its damage. I would have thought that enough blood had been spilled that day.

Mother Ördu's body was placed in a coffin and sent back to Tuljerd. Ander's had been taken by the Laocotan and sent to Aedenfal. My heart had sunk when Conmel told me, for the intent was to have Caspin come collect it and give an accounting of his brother to Valemar. My husband would not be here for the birth of our child.

Rhygo, at least, was more tolerant of my presence in Glábac than Sciglas had been.

"If there is anything at all that you need, my queen, the Baraáda are ready to ensure your safety and that of Bánalfar's heir."

"Workmen to finish the nursery," I told him, resigned to the fact that I would give birth here and on my own.

Rhygo placed a fist to his chest and bowed. "I will make sure they are the first to receive clearance." He took two steps backward before he straightened and left the room.

"You won't be alone," Shale said from her seat near the fireplace. Lines now etched her face, aging her almost overnight.

"No." I said, lifting a weary smile. "And neither are you."

Shale gave a wistful hum of agreement. "I am now the oldest Mödatal. It is not a responsibility that I wanted."

I joined her on the wooden settle. The cushion covering the seat kept the heavy piece of furniture from being truly purgatorial. It had been designed for longevity, not comfort. Shale's head rested in the back's winged curve. "What are your responsibilities?" I asked.

"I am now in charge of training the new Möda. They will travel to Bánalfar so that I can oversee the development of their abilities."

"Hmm. So the title of 'Mother' passes to you?" I asked.

"Yes." A sad light filled her eyes. One hand dropped to her belly. *I will have a daughter in the new year.*

It seems the Mother had hidden from Shale just how many she would be responsible for.

CHAPTER 31

Eskar and Shale joined me daily in the solar to sew. After the first crush of realization, the weight of Shale's new responsibilities had settled for nothing truly changed in our daily routine. The Blood Moon came and passed. I focused on my responsibilities to my child and kept my other life locked safely in the bottom drawer of my desk.

I hadn't asked, and no one had shared with me, the other details of Glábac and the High. Valemar would be in Aedenfal, dealing with Prince Caspin, and I would be here with only the two seers and Iree to help me welcome Hal into the world. It was Eskar who first looked up from her sewing, her eyes widening as she lifted her head. Then the corners of Shale's mouth curved up. She put her sewing down.

"Would you like some tea?" she asked, rearranging the quilt around my legs. Ennick had kept me on bed rest, and the lack of activity allowed the chill of the early spring air to sink into my flesh.

"That would be lovely," I said.

Eskar set her sewing aside and gave me a smile. I wondered at the joy that flitted in her eyes as she joined Shale in leaving to track down the tea. I put my own sewing on the table next to me and stared out the window. The leafy canopy of the barat trees had filled in since the Chéloch celebration nearly a month before.

I rubbed my enormous belly and whispered to Hal, "Any day now. You are more than welcome to join me and take your first glimpse of the trees that have sheltered the Alfari as long as time has been." I had come to be at peace with Gladama being the site of Hal's birth. I had even come to accept living a life separate from Valemar. He had, after all, warned me that he was *"King first and father and husband second."*

A soft knock sounded on the door. "Enter," I called.

I turned my head, expecting to see one of the maids with my tea, but a tall, white-blond figure wearing dusty, blue riding gear entered.

Valemar.

A strangled cry erupted from my throat and I pressed a hand against my mouth, not daring to believe that the sight was real. Unable to shift my weight while stretched on the sofa, I could only sit and stare at the figure.

"Mother and Father, you have grown," Valemar softly swore, taking in my form.

I bit my lips and nodded, unable to make any other sound. And then he was there, at my side, dropping to his knees. "By the foam of the sea," he said as his eyes traveled over me. "You don't seem quite real."

"Neither do you," I said, and reached out a hand to touch his face. Warm, smooth skin proved that he was not the illusion I half feared he was.

Valemar's hand wrapped around mine, pressing my fingers against his cheek. His eyes closed and he drew a deep breath. When his brilliant blue eyes opened again, he reached a hesitant hand toward my swollen stomach. "May I?"

I smiled. "You don't even need to ask."

Valemar released me so that both of his hands could travel over the swell, molding my gown and exposing the bulk.

"I've grown a kinwah," I said, for my stomach now looked like I had swallowed the giant pumpkin-like fruit.

"You've grown a child," Valemar said. His fingers gently pushed. Valemar frowned when Hal stayed silent.

"He doesn't do much moving now," I said. "There's not enough room."

"No," Valemar agreed. He leaned closer. "Any day now," he said, speaking to my stomach.

I reached out and brushed my fingers through Valemar's hair. "I can't believe you are here." Aedenfal was a two-week journey to the east.

Valemar's fingers tightened against my stomach before he drew them away. He curled them into cushion, crushing the edge. "I was not about to leave you alone again for another moment." He swallowed hard, biting back anger.

"But Caspin…"

"Can deal with Heymond and Jaros." Valemar gave a bitter laugh. "Caspin had better pray to the Mother that Heymond is well enough to hold Jaros back." I gave Valemar a tearful smile. "Oh, my *grabeg*," he said, and ran a hand along my face.

"I think I've become numb to it all." I had strangely come to expect that everyone I knew would die.

Valemar took my hands. "Show me the nursery."

My brow furrowed as I tried to remember when I last been on my feet.

Valemar frowned. "What is it?"

"I'm only allowed ten minutes of exercise twice a day."

Valemar's eyes widened. "You're not just resting?"

"Ennick is afraid I may have complications from the pregnancy. I've been ordered to rest and keep my blood pressure low."

Valemar gathered me into his arms and stood. "Then I will just need to do the walking for both of us."

He smelled of darana and sweat, and the dust from the road tickled my nose, but I didn't care. "You are really here?" I asked, brushing my lips against his neck. I leaned my head against his shoulder.

"Always."

I showed Valemar the nursery. A green, leafy pattern papered the walls, an echo of the canopy of barat leaves visible from the windows. A thick green carpet covered the dark wooden floors like the moss that grew between the roots in the grove. The screen that hid the nurse's bed had been painted with different fauna found in this region of Bánalfar. A cradle carved from caradin wood sat by the fire. The rocker was the tail of the *bysgog*, the fish-like creature on Bánalfar's flag. Valemar turned us each time I pointed at something, the two of us joined as one in the room that would house our child, and I was thankful that I couldn't walk.

"And through there," I said, pointing at the carved, wooden door that marked the west side of the room, "is my room."

"Your room?" Valemar asked.

"Well, as I wrote to you when I was redoing the family apartments in Aedenfal, I am going to be a bohar for a while and the king needs his sleep."

"You are much mistaken if you think that I am letting you out of my sight any time soon," Valemar said.

I lowered my eyes, afraid I would break if I saw sympathy in Valemar's. "Is that why you haven't bathed yet?" I asked, hoping to distract him. My fingers were now dingy from where they had brushed against his cloak.

Valemar hoisted me higher. "Yes. But if you are going to complain then you will just need to join me."

My heart pounded and blood shot to my groin at the thought of seeing him naked. Running my fingers along his tight muscles…

I held my breath as the spike in blood pressure made me dizzy and then blew it out in a slow stream. "I think it's safer if you leave me on the other side of the door. I'm not supposed to get over excited."

Valemar laughed and rested his chin on my head. His arms tightened around me. "If you are tired of the dust and don't want to join me then you will just have to listen while I bathe."

Valemar gave me a gentle toss, rearranging my weight, and carried me back out into the hall. He called for a guard to move a reclining chair outside his bathroom door and, once I was placed on it, shooed the man out.

A cistern installed behind the tub allowed Valemar to fill it himself. Apparently, he wasn't willing to wait for warmer water. His clothes fell to the floor with a soft *whumpf.* Cloak. Shirt. I closed my eyes and tried to picture anything other than Valemar's perfect chest. One boot. The other boot. His breeches.

"When did you leave?" I called out, not really wanting to know the answer but desperately needing something to distract me from what was on the other side of the half-closed door.

The water splashed as Valemar got into the tub. Then splashed again as he dipped a washcloth. The gentle rasping of cloth against skin drifted through the door before he answered.

"The day after I got the karawack." Valemar's heavy voice echoed in the tiled chamber.

I pulled one hand into the sleeve of my dress and twisted the fabric between my fingers. "I'm sorry it wasn't me who sent the note." I hadn't been able to pick up a pen after Mother Ördu's death. Writing about it would have made me relive the scene. I wasn't sure who had sent the message. Conmel, probably.

The splashing stopped.

"It didn't need to be," Valemar said, but the weight in his voice told me he wished it had been.

"You must have passed the Laocotan on the road," I said, picking up the story and skipping past the difficult part.

"I did. I stopped and inspected the remains just to make sure."

That must have been a grisly sight. Bodies were usually buried within a day of their passing from life to death, not packed up and sent hundreds of miles away. "And it was Ander?"

"Yes. Time…had somewhat altered his appearance but we had met many times before."

"Conmel figured it had to be him as the…" I trailed off as the memory rose.

A splash as Valemar dunked the washcloth overwhelmed the hiss of arrows, reminding me I was in the High and not the grove. I gave my head a shake. "The man had the royal crest of Darland on his cloak clasp and a signet ring."

"It was no imposter or hired assassin," Valemar confirmed.

"And Caspin?"

"Should already be at Aedenfal by now."

There was a *swoosh* as Valemar dipped beneath the water, wetting his hair and rising again, and then a soft snap of bubbles as he lathered his hair. I listened for a moment and then a practice

contraction, more intense than the ones I usually had, gripped my uterus. My fingernails dug into the cushion as I tried to silence a groan.

With a *whoosh* of cascading water, Valemar was out of the bath and through the door.

"Can you put a towel on or something?" I asked through gritted teeth, looking away. I raised a hand to block out the view. "You there like that isn't helping my blood pressure."

"What's wrong?" Valemar asked, dropping to his knees.

"Practice contraction," I said, trying to remember to breathe as Shale had instructed. I pursed my lips and blew a slow breath through them. "Though if these are practice, I don't think I want the real thing."

The contraction passed, and I sighed. The water glistening off Valemar's skin drew my attention. "Okay, seriously. A robe or something. I might just jump you if you don't cover up."

Valemar chuckled. "You'd have to catch me first and I think I can currently outrun you." He returned to the bathroom, giving me a perfect view of his toned and muscled backside.

"So unfair," I muttered.

CHAPTER 32

Valemar finished his bath and exited the bathroom without a towel. He chuckled when I covered my eyes with my hand. "Let me know when you're dressed," I told him.

"Or?"

"I may have to stay this way until I give birth."

He planted a kiss on my cheek. "I can live with that."

"Clothes," I said, swatting him away.

The floor made squelching noises as he walked to the wardrobe. "And wipe down the floor. I am not slipping."

When I'd heard the sounds of fabric sliding over flesh two different times, I lowered my hand. Valemar stood before me in the formal green and gold tunic and trousers of a royal Gladama pilgrim.

"You're going to the grove to make your pledge?" I asked, reluctant to have him out of my sight. Or at least my hearing.

Valemar kissed the top of my head. "I have a lot to be grateful for. You're alive." He placed a hand on my belly. "This one is growing."

Valemar threaded his fingers through mine. "But Bánalfar is still in need of protection. And the barat trees were injured saving your life. I need to give them my thanks and my vow."

I squeezed his hand, thankful that wine would be poured on the roots, washing away—in my mind—the blood. "Then go. You know I'm not going anywhere."

He laughed. "I'll be back as soon as I can."

We had an hour after he returned. He put away the formal garments and put on the plain green tunic and trousers of an ordinary pilgrim. Valemar scooped me up and placed me on the bed so he could sit next to me and cradle me in his arms. We left the hard conversations alone and talked instead about the sewing I had done with Shale and Eskar and why I had chosen the furnishings for the nursery.

When Iree knocked on the door to bring in my evening lamp, Valemar swung his legs off the bed.

"I need to—"

"I know," I said, cutting him off. "I'll be right here when you're done." I drew up my spine and smiled. Too heavily pregnant to do much, I could still serve my people by placing their king in their presence.

Valemar kissed me and left for dinner. I hadn't sat at the communal tables in half a moon. My feet swelled almost instantly if they weren't put up.

I rubbed my aching belly and wiggled my feet. I was done with being pregnant. "You can come out any day," I said to Hal. "I'm perfectly happy with whenever you feel like making an appearance as long as it's soon."

My other role rose up in my brain, and I sighed. My tablet had sat forgotten since my arrival in Glábac. Fear had driven that responsibility from my thoughts. Of course, General Creskin hadn't sent a karawack bugging me to check in, either.

I slid off the bed and waddled over to my desk, feeling like someone had stuck a balloon between my legs. "Any day now," I repeated to Hal.

I drew the key from the chain around my neck and gripped the edge of the desk as I lowered my knees to the floor. Getting down was the easy part. Getting up was always harder. I unlocked the drawer, placed the tablet on the desk, slid the drawer closed again, relocked it, and braced myself for the upward journey. I gripped the seat of the chair and brought one foot up. I pushed off from the chair and slowly rose until I was standing. Sweat broke out on my brow.

"And to think, just seven months ago, I was in the best shape of my life," I muttered to Hal. I gathered up the tablet and made my way to the chaise. Once I had swung my legs on and had rearranged the pillows behind me, I pressed a finger to the button and the tablet glowed to life.

There was just one message from General Creskin, sent on the nineteenth day of Gheistor, eight days after Brinna's death. I looked at the date in shock. Had it really been two months since I had checked for messages?

I hear there has been another attempt on your life. Do you wish me to send someone to Glábac?

I snorted. Of course, he would know where I was. The language chip embedded in my brain was easy to trace. "Stupid chip." I touched the screen and opened up a comm link.

"Well, well. I was beginning to think you had totally abandoned your duties," General Creskin said as his image filled the frame.

"No, just doing my primary one—gestating," I said, and pushed the tablet back so that my belly came into view.

"Any reason your activity has dropped to almost nothing since the attempt on your life last month? Were you injured?" Creskin asked.

I rolled my eyes. They were monitoring my every move. "No but I may have developed…I forget what they call it, some condition with high blood pressure."

"Preeclampsia," the general said with a frown. "It's a serious condition. Do you want me to send Arken?"

"No," I answered, even as my heart fell to the pit of my stomach. "The town is still unsettled. The last…attempt…" I paused, unable to say the word. "Resulted in the death of one of the Möda and damage to one of the sacred trees. A stranger—an alien—seen in Glábac could cause panic."

"So why did you call, Ambassador Carbrev?"

"Valemar arrived today. It made it easier to think of myself as something other than mother-to-be." The weight of my responsibilities began to settle on my shoulders. "Are you willing to share with me what the Cordair have bought with their payment for the chalcopyrite?"

A tick appeared in General Creskin's cheek before he answered. "Weapons. Zagré swords, I believe." My eyelids closed as I sighed. "You were right, Ambassador Carr."

And yet, there was a niggling sense that the situation wasn't finished, that there was something that could make a difference. *Talk to Raislos,* the voice in the back of my mind whispered.

"Continue to monitor," I told the general. "There's not much I can do right now but I don't want to make any final decisions until I've had a chance to do more than just give birth."

362

The general's face turned grave. "I can drop Arken somewhere under the cover of night if you want. Preeclampsia is quite serious and can cause seizures." *Or death.*

His tone conveyed the unspoken words, and the blood drained from my face. "No," I said, remaining firm despite my new concern for my health. "The Alfari see well at night and I don't want to cause panic. I still have Shale with me. She would have warned me or suggested that Arken should come if she thought he would be needed." I clung to that thought and consciously tried to relax and lower my rising blood pressure.

"Very well. And Ambassador," General Creskin said. A gleam entered his eye. "Please don't make us set up a listening post in Glábac. I would like to be notified of the arrival of Bánalfar's heir shortly after his birth."

"His?" I asked. My eyebrows rose.

"Do you want to know?" General Creskin asked.

"Yes…no…" My mouth hung open. "No," I said firmly. If Hal was a daughter and not a son, I would find out soon enough. But the glint in Creskin's eyes confirmed what I had already suspected.

"Carbrev out," I said. "And stop monitoring my movements," I added just as the screen went black.

Valemar returned from dinner shortly after Iree took my tray away. I had already begun to nod with fatigue. He raised me to my feet and pulled the Blood Moon gown I was using as a maternity dress over my head but left me in my slip. Then Valemar gathered me into his arms and carried me to the bed. He lay down next to me, staring into my eyes as I tried to drift to sleep. "Are you going to do this the whole night?" I asked, trying to ignore him all the while I wished he was curled up around me instead.

"You don't seem quite real if I can't see your face," he said.

"Humpf."

Valemar threaded his fingers through mine. My heart swelled. The thing I had wanted most in the world had happened. Valemar was here.

And then a yawn overtook me. "Stupid pregnancy," I muttered when my jaw was mine again.

Valemar kept one hand laced through mine and reached out with the other to rub my belly. "Wonderful pregnancy. Wonderful, miraculous pregnancy."

I nestled deeper into the pillows, truly relaxed for the first time in months. "If you say so."

Valemar kissed my brow, and I drifted away into sleep.

I awoke with the overwhelming urge to pee. A delicious weight encircled my back. Valemar had shifted me into to the middle of the bed and then lay down behind me, wrapping himself around me, one hand resting on the giant swell where Hal lay. I whimpered, unable to find the edge of the bed with my toes.

"What is it?" Valemar asked, sitting up.

"I have to pee, and I'm stuck in the middle of the bed." An elephant shifted easier than I did these days. "Why did you move me?"

Valemar got out of bed and came around to face me. He grasped my feet and gently pulled until I was sitting on the edge of the mattress. I held onto his arms for support as I stood.

"Okay," I said in a voice that rasped with sleep. I waddled off in the direction of the close stool.

Valemar helped me back in when I returned. "I need to be able to get out on my own," I told him. I lay down and fished around for the pillow I stuck between my knees. "I'm up several times a night. They say it's so your body gets used to getting up with the child every couple of hours. I think it's so you are already exhausted by the time the baby comes and don't care what happens."

The corners of Valemar's mouth turned down in the moonlight. "What?" I asked.

He gave his head a gentle shake. "I'm just in awe of all that you can do."

I squeezed his hand. "Do you mind crawling up behind me again? I'll be up several more times tonight but it's nice to have you there beside me."

Valemar kissed me and went around the bed. Soon his warmth and weight settled along my back. "I love you," I whispered as my eyelids drifted closed and sleep began to tug at me.

"I love you, too."

"I'm going to be pregnant forever," I whined to Shale. Three days had passed since Valemar had arrived. He had taken over the running of the High and could frequently be found holed up with Rhygo going over plans for improvements in the Low.

Shale laughed. "There has yet to be a single case of that happening. But your resignation to the state does mean that your pregnancy should be drawing to a close. You have to give up before the baby arrives."

"Don't offer me false hope." I was bored and tired. Nothing interested me. I hated the sight of a sewing needle, the patterns on the wallpaper had begun to bug me, and the barat trees mocked me

by leafing out and growing with no effort at all. The sight of the leaves rippling in the breeze had, at one point, caused me to rip off a shoe and throw it at the window.

"Maybe a change of scenery," Shale said. She put her sewing to the side.

"I don't want any exercise," I complained. "I'm saving my ten minutes for later."

"Let's go show you that everything is ready." Shale held out her hand. I scowled at it before taking it with a sigh.

"Everything's ready but me," I said, continuing to grumble.

Shale placed my hand around her arm and matched my slow, waddling pace. Halfway down the hall, I gave up. "I feel like I have a balloon stuck between my thighs." I turned to head back to the solar.

"Come check the arrangements, Astrid."

I sighed, knowing she would just pester me until she got her way. The nursery sat at the far end of the long hall. Ilana, the night nurse, was looking through the stores in a cabinet when Shale and I entered.

Her face lit up when she saw us. "You look radiant, my queen," she said, sliding the drawer closed. "Everything has been prepared."

I shuffled in and looked around the room. Despite the fact that Glábac had not felt like home when I had first arrived, the sense that this was where my baby was supposed to be born had slowly eased its way into my soul.

I crossed the room and gave the mobile that hung above the cradle a gentle spin. Four rampart, fighting darana pranced their way in a circle above the thin, flat pillow that padded the cradle.

"I have creams for your feet as well as for when you nurse," Ilana said. "They will help relieve the fluid that has built up in your feet and protect your nipples from cracking when you first being feeding baby."

"It all looks ready," I said.

"Just as soon as our prince or princess decides it's time to come out into the world." Ilana smiled.

I lifted a one in return and nodded. Ilana didn't need to know it, but I was probably going to be pregnant forever.

The faint red light of the moon, only four days into its waxing cycle, was just beginning to be chased away by the coming light of dawn when I heaved myself out of bed for the second time that night. Valemar's breathing turned from the slow breaths of slumber to restful alertness before it fell back into rhythm when he recognized it was just me.

I shuffled over to the close stool, rubbing my stomach that was in the grip of yet another practice contraction. Warm fluid began to run down my leg.

"*Kwarg.* Really?" I swore out loud. "I was almost there."

"Astrid?" Valemar asked sleepily, raising his head.

Humiliation warmed my cheeks. "Nothing. I just didn't make it to the stool. Stupid bladder."

Valemar sat up. "Are you sure it's pee?"

His words struck me dumb and my eyes widened as what he was suggesting registered. "I don't know."

Valemar lit the lamp and brought it close. A slow trickle still ran down my leg. "I don't think that's pee, Astrid."

"Fuck me," I swore in astonishment and then clenched my teeth as my stomach tightened again. I had spent days wanting to not be pregnant but as the reality of labor now loomed, I changed my mind.

"Shit. What am I in for?"

At first, labor was rather boring. Contractions tightened my stomach and pinched from time to time but nothing actually seemed to be happening.

"I think we need to send for Shale," Valemar said to me after I had crawled into bed again only to get right back out, bored and uncomfortable.

"No, this could go on for hours," I told him. I grabbed the edge of the table and blew out a breath while the pinching feeling took over my belly again. Shale and Eskar were going to act as midwives and deliver my baby. "I remember something about not truly being in labor unless this is happening every five minutes," I told him when I could speak again. "You can get them when that starts to happen.

I straightened up and rubbed my belly before beginning another slow circuit of the room. "Actually, why don't you go get something to eat. Maybe even check your paperwork. You're going to be busy later."

Valemar's eyebrows had risen like flags when I turned to look at him. "I'm fine here. Go." I shooed him with my hand.

Valemar went to the door and opened it. He leaned out. "Go find the Mödatal," he said to the guard.

"What? No. I'm fine," I insisted.

"Uh huh." Valemar closed the door and watched me circle the room.

"See. Walking it off." And then a stronger contraction stopped me mid-stride. "Fuck! *Kwarg!*" I swore before my breath was taken up with a long, incoherent noise of pain. I puffed when it passed.

"That one was longer," Valemar said unnecessarily.

"Okay, fine. So they're changing. This kid is probably hours away from being born." Then what I had said registered and I swore again.

Valemar came over and pressed his knuckles into my lower back.

"Oh, my God," I said, closing my eyes. "That feels good."

The door opened as Shale knocked on it, entering even as she pushed it wide. "I don't need you yet," I told her. "Go get breakfast. Take this one with you. After he's finished rubbing my back." I put my hands on the table and leaned toward it, giving Valemar's fingers a better surface to work with.

"Fu—shu—" I stammered as another contraction hit. Valemar left his thumbs in place and gently took my hips, creating a soothing pressure against my back as tight pain radiated from my hips to my belly.

"That looks like a productive one," Shale said.

Valemar gently massaged my back as the contraction passed. I pushed away from the table and began another circuit of the room.

"Astrid is right, my king. You should go get some breakfast. This is likely to go on most of the day."

"Do you want anything?" Valemar asked me.

I pictured eggs and toast and then my stomach heaved. I clamped a hand over my mouth and shook my head.

"I'll get a little wine into her. Often mothers just bring back up anything they eat. Too much squeezing going on for the stomach to stay settled."

Valemar brushed the hair from my face. "You are sure you don't want me to stay?" he asked.

"Can't have you falling down from hunger later," I said. Valemar kissed me and slipped from the room.

I eyed the bed and moaned. "I don't want to stand. I don't want to lie down."

"You should try to rest," Shale said. "We need you to save your energy instead of using it all up now."

I nodded and made my way back to the bed. Lying down on my side, I tucked my feet up next to me. My brain wanted the mindlessness of the latest fashion postings from Earth's *La Mode* or Ztemyata's *Fusaga*, but doubted I would be able to access the sites on my tablet since they collected data in order to tailor their advertising. The Shororato were sure to have blocked them. "Where did you grow up?" I asked Shale instead.

"Vanerife," she said, sitting down next to me. "I was attached to the High Cair early. Even when I was very young, my hair was the darkest red."

"What did you do there?"

"Well…" Shale ran her fingers through my hair, combing it out. "I started with tasks a child would do—sweeping, changing out candles, bringing things for the older acolytes."

"When did you discover your gift?"

"When I was about five. I was clearing out the spent candles from the trays of sand and I discovered that I could *see* the person who had placed the candle and what they had prayed for."

"Could you see if their prayers were answered?" I asked.

Shale smiled. "Sometimes."

"That's an amazing gift," I said. "And not so frightening as…" I drifted off, not wanting to say it aloud.

"I think that would be a special gift, too," Shale said.

I clenched my teeth as another contraction started. "Squeeze my hand," Shale said, taking mine. I held hers but didn't need the grip she offered. I blew out a breath when the contraction passed.

Shale went over to the table and poured a glass of wine. "Here," she said, holding it out. "Just a few sips. You need to stay hydrated and the alcohol will help relax you."

"I don't want me or the baby to get drunk."

"You won't. It's just a few sips."

I let the velvety liquid slide down my throat. It warmed my stomach without causing a burn or unsettling it. I swung my legs back over the edge of the bed but Shale stopped me from moving further.

"Rest while you can."

"I can't sleep. Not when my insides are getting squeezed every few minutes."

"Do you want me to check?" I nodded and swung my legs back onto the bed. Shale sat down next to me. I winced as she inserted her hand. "I can get about three fingers in," she said. "You need to be dilated to fist size before it's truly time. Once you've had a bit of a rest, we'll get you up and moving again. Baby's head pressing against the membranes is the best way to get the birth canal to open up."

I gritted my teeth as another wave of pain washed over my belly, turning it to stone. "Breathe through it," Shale said. "And try to let it flow through you and do its work."

"I want to move again," I whimpered when it was over.

This time, Shale let me slide out of bed and walked with me as I made my slow circuit of the room.

The contractions were much closer together when Valemar returned. "How are we doing?" he asked and kissed my sweaty forehead. The sweet odor of *tamin* washed over me. Valemar had followed his meal with the herb so I wouldn't smell whatever he'd had for breakfast.

"I'm going to be pregnant forever," I whimpered and stopped to grip the table as another contraction hit. I blinked back the rising sting in my eyes.

Valemar ran his fingers down my spine while I moaned through the wave of pain that encircled my belly.

"Time to get you down to the grove," Shale announced when the contraction had passed.

"What? No," I protested. Since Mother Ördu's death I had not been able to shake the feeling of danger lurking in the grove. The trees were fine, safe, when I looked at them from a distance, but my back tingled uncomfortably every time I thought of being among them.

Shale took my face in her hands. "You child deserves to be born with all the protection of Gladama around it. Don't you want your child's first breath to be of the sacred air and its first glimpse to be of the sheltering trees?"

No, I thought. *I want his or her first sight to be me.* "I can't walk that far."

"You've been walking around this room for several hours. You can make it all the way into the trees," Shale said. I whimpered again but leaned on her hands as she began to guide me from the room. "You," she said to Valemar over her shoulder, "go find Eskar and have her join us. Then you can find somewhere to wait."

"What?" I asked, coming to a sudden standstill. "Valemar isn't coming with us?"

"Men get in the way," Shale said. She threw Valemar a pointed look. "They try to fix things that can't be fixed and become more trouble than the laboring mother."

"But I can't do this without him," I wailed. I looked at Valemar. My eyes pleaded to not be left to face this alone.

Shale sighed. "If you can support her and not try to fix this then you are welcome to join us for as long as Astrid wishes. This is her labor and she gets whatever she wants."

Valemar nodded. "I can do that."

"Just so you know, mothers change their minds constantly."

Valemar nodded his acceptance again and the three of us slowly made our way toward the door that led out to the grove.

CHAPTER 33

"The corridors keep getting longer," I said, unclenching my teeth. I pushed off of the wall I had braced myself against during the latest contraction.

"I could carry you," Valemar offered.

"No," Shale said as I began to entertain the tantalizing offer. "Walking will help the child come more quickly."

I whimpered and began shuffling again. Every step was difficult with the baby's head in the way. "Are you sure he's not already crowning? It's hard to walk."

Shale placed a hand on my abdomen and traced the baby's position. "Head down, just like we want, and engaged in the canal but not quite ready yet."

Slowly we shuffled toward the blessed door to the grove. Tears spilled down my face. Once we were through the door, I was going to lie down and give birth right there.

I gripped Valemar's hands as another band of pain doubled me over. "You can do this," he said as I struggled to breathe. "If you were able to get on the Hormani ship and send the message, you can do this."

"Apparently Heymond never told you that he carried me the last part of the way," I told him when I was again able to catch my breath. "I'm fine with history repeating itself."

Valemar looked at Shale who shrugged in resignation. He swept me up.

"Thank the Mother and the Father," I said as I nestled my head into his shoulder.

Eskar trotted alongside us, a basket slung over one arm and her hands full of linens. Shale motioned for Valemar to put me down when we came to the edge of the trees. "She can walk in circles again once we get to wherever we're going," he said, refusing to part with me. My limbs began to shake as pain gripped my belly again.

Valemar stopped. My fingers dug into his upper back, but he never complained as I hung on and tried to ride out the especially fierce contraction. "I can't do this," I whispered as the pain began to recede and the steel band loosened around my belly.

"Yes, you can," he said, placing his forehead against mine.

I didn't answer. Shale motioned with her head for Valemar to follow. I closed my eyes and allowed the silence of the woods to wash over me.

My eyes opened and I lifted my head. Silence.

"Where is everyone?" I asked. Though pilgrims left Bánalfar's king and queen to make their offering in peace, I had spent much of my time the previous summer curled up against the trunks with just a single guard a discreet distance away while other travelers wended through the trees, visiting the glade.

"In town, giving the grove to Bánalfar's heir," Eskar answered.

I let the soft rustling of the leaves and the quiet birdsong from the top of the canopy drift over me.

"Put me down," I said to Valemar as the next contraction started, before it stole my breath. I dropped to my hands and knees as soon as my feet touched the earth and cried out, overwhelmed with an urge to remove the pain by any means possible.

"That looks like a push," Shale said. I vaguely became aware that was just what I was doing.

Eskar spread out a sheet. I rolled onto it when the contraction loosened its grip. "I'm too tired. I can't do this." My words were little more than breath.

Valemar placed his back against the tree and drew me to him.

"Your body is going to go ahead and do this for you," Shale said. "Your job is to help it along."

"I can't."

Valemar placed his lips alongside my ear. "Yes, you can. You can do anything."

Eskar looped one of my feet through a leather strap and ran it behind Valemar, placing it around his hips. She placed my other foot through a second loop and then adjusted its fit with a buckle. "We usually like to have mothers push against a footboard or sit in a stool so they can put their full weight into baby being born, but this should help since you are out here."

Her hands quickly moved out of the way as I put the contraption to use as another contraction surged over me.

"Breathe," Shale reminded me as I clenched my teeth against the pain.

"I…fucking…can't," I panted when I was finally able to draw breath again.

Time became a wash of pain and tears as wave after wave overtook me and carried my body away.

"One more, Astrid," Shale's voice said from far away.

"I…can't," I whispered through lips that didn't want to move.

Valemar reached around the mound of my stomach and put his hand between my legs. "She's right here. I can feel her. Don't you want to meet her, too?"

Her? Pain gripped my belly again and I imagined pushing, too weak to do anything else. I felt movement then heard a gush of water, and the pain blessedly stopped.

"Don't babies usually cry?" Valemar asked, panic rising in his voice.

"Give your son a second," Shale said, and hung him by his feet. Eskar wrapped him in a towel and rubbed while Shale flicked his heel sharply. There was a tiny gasp and then the woods filled with wailing. Valemar exhaled in relief.

Shale tied a string around the umbilical cord and cut it with a knife. She handed the small, amazingly bloody bundle to me.

"Hello, little one," I said. My son's head made contact with my chest and the crying stopped. With short, raspy breaths, he opened his eyes to look at me. "Your daddy is here, too."

"He will want to eat soon, but give him a minute to get used to being on the outside." Shale gently massaged my stomach. "You're not quite done."

"Son," Valemar said, awed. "I always thought you carried a daughter."

"Disappointed?" I asked.

Valemar shook his head. "A little scared, maybe. I thought I could practice on a daughter before a son came along. I couldn't make a mess of raising a daughter, but a son…"

I leaned my head back to look in his eyes. "You don't need practice. You're going to make a great father."

With one last clench, the afterbirth came free, and my body was mine again. Eskar wrapped the placenta in a cloth and slipped away.

My son snuffled around my chest, sensing that food was near. "Is this what you're looking for?" I asked, and put him to my breast. He squeaked in frustration, still rooting but not latching on.

"It can take them a minute to get the idea," Shale said. "Keep trying."

I put a finger under his chin and gently closed his mouth. He sucked in for another wail and then his eyes popped open. There was a sudden pinch, like I had just caught my nipple in a drawer, and Hal began nursing happily.

"Ow," I said, gritting my teeth once again.

"You'll get used to it," Eskar said, returning. "Ilana has some cream that will help keep you from getting too cracked."

Young as she was, hardly older than Erris, I realized that Eskar must have already had a moon child.

Valemar reached down and stroked the wet, chestnut gold hair that crowned our son's head. "He's a miracle," Valemar said, his voice full of awe.

"We'll let your son get a meal in and then Valemar can carry you back to the High," Shale said to me. She cleaned up around us, putting the knife and string back into the basket, taking a trowel from Eskar and adding it too. With my son engaged in feeding, Shale slipped the nubby towel from around him and wrapped him in a swaddling blanket.

"What are we going to call him?" I asked Valemar.

"I thought you were already calling him 'Hal.'"

I shrugged. "I needed something to call the child."

"I thought my servant queen was calling her child after Bánalfar's servant king."

"That was more after the stories of a roguish prince on Earth," I explained. Though troublesome Prince Hal had grown up to be the King Henry who had led the miraculous defeat of the French at the battle of Agincourt.

And gentlemen in England now a-bed, shall think themselves accurs'd they were not here. I had loved Henry V's Saint Crispin's Day speech. I leaned forward and nuzzled my son's head. "We could call him Haldan," I said. *A piece of Bánalfar. A piece of me.*

"Any other names you'd like?" Valemar asked.

I lifted my head and fought to find my voice again. "Something to honor Heymond. Hal and I wouldn't be here without him," I managed. "And something to remember my brother, Finn."

Loss washed over my heart as I thought of Finn. I eased a finger into Hal's grip, biting my lips as his fingers closed around mine. For a moment, it was Finn's hand that was clasped with mine and we were racing down the endless stretches of sand on Mum's favorite Norfolk beach.

"Haldan Finmond," Valemar said. He stroked the tiny hand wrapped around my finger.

"Finmond," I whispered. I closed my eyes and flung my heart out into the universe. Maybe one day Finn would feel the love and honor I sent him and not just my loss.

CHAPTER 34

Valemar and I stayed in Glábac, marveling at this life we had created. Though my sleep was constantly disrupted by Haldan's demands, I got more rest than most mothers thanks to Ilana's assistance. As I settled into being a mother, my thoughts turned from what it would be like to be a mum to questioning what kind of future I would leave my child.

Recommendation…

I had the power to decide it.

The Baraáda's investigations had determined that Ander had disguised himself as a barrel merchant from a town near the southern border. His bow had been a walking stick restrung once he'd reached the cover of the woods. The arrows had been secreted inside a carving meant to be an offering. According to a karawack he'd sent to Caspin shortly after arriving in Glábac, his attempt on my life had been blessed by the Mother, and he had believed the barat trees would shelter him, for he sought the end of their greatest threat—me.

When Valemar and Rhygo were satisfied that Ander had no more supporters in the area, Valemar made plans to leave for Aedenfal.

The city was still coping with stain of treason and the influx of Alfari intent on making it secure. Caspin's presence when he turned up to collect his brother's body had nearly caused riots in the streets of Aedenfal, and only the Laocotan had been able to break up the crowds.

"Go to Vanerife," Valemar told me. I was too nervous to return to Aedenfal, especially with the city in an uproar. "I know it will be hard for you but Reina can provide shelter and security."

However, the knowledge of the weapons flowing into Cordair lands ate at me. Even if I told the Federation "no more trade," Raislos might still decide the time had come to arm Cordan. Getting him to stop the trade, however, was a possibility if I gave him the right incentive.

And so, on the nineteenth of Dérach, one year—one Crenfor year—from when I had first set foot on the planet, I left my son in Lendurig and mounted a borrowed darana. Conmel was not happy.

"Valemar knows of this plan?" Conmel asked as I turned my mount's head toward the road. I had been evasive when I made the arrangements this morning.

"The karawack is on its way."

Conmel narrowed his eyes. I gave him no choice but to follow as I pressed my heels into my darana and coaxed it into a trot. He couldn't very well take me prisoner.

Four days later, I paced around the small dining room in Aedenfal used to host foreign dignitaries. My red skirts swished around me as I walked. After staring at the clothes that Iree had packed from my chest in Lendurig, I had decided to dress as the Moon Princess and not wear the blue or green that would have marked me as Bánalfar's queen.

The small round table held an assortment of beverages but I doubted that Raislos would join me in any of them. A short knocked echoed, and I turned and faced the door.

I hadn't seen Raislos since our confrontation months ago, the day after I had arrived on Crenfor when he had come to claim me as his property, but his expression held the same look of contempt.

His eyes traveled over the gown and then back up to my head, noting the lack of a crown. "Ambassador."

I gestured toward the table. "Please, take a seat." Raislos crossed his arms and remained where he was. I went ahead and sat.

"Your note was rather cryptic," he said.

I held back a sigh and began the script that I had worked on in my head for weeks after Hal was born. The thoughts had been brewing longer, ever since General Creskin had informed me of the trade deal. "Notes have the tendency to fall into the wrong hands."

"And whose hands do you wish to avoid?" he asked. Anger laced his voice.

"The Shororato."

Raislos snorted.

"Do you trust them?" I asked.

"They are paying customers. All I care about is what their gold can buy."

"Such as the Zagré steel."

Raislos's sardonic smile showed his teeth. "Watchful, aren't you?"

"Oh, that information I got from the Shororato themselves." The smile slipped from Raislos's face. His arms fell to his sides. "You are being cheated," I said.

Raislos stared at me a moment and then tipped his head back and laughed. "How? Do you think a miner cannot recognize true gold when he sees it?"

"Their gold is real. But not as valuable as the ore they trade for."

Raislos froze. "That's not possible," he whispered.

"The *bronvier*—" as I learned the Cordair called the chalcopyrite, "—is the most precious substance I've ever come across in all my years of traveling the stars. Diamonds are not as valuable as that ore."

He shook my words away as if they were an annoying insect. "Pah."

I shrugged. "Fine. Go ahead and trade it. Rob your descendants of the riches that they could have had. Someone else can provide Crenfor with the fuel to travel the stars when the time comes." I stood. "That was all I wanted, to provide you with that information."

I waited until Raislos started for the door. "I do have one suggestion. You could ask to trade for technology instead of gold."

Raislos turned. His eyes narrowed. "I know that trade in technology is forbidden. Your Shororato took back the armor the Hormani had given us."

"You wish to return to Bánalfar not just because your ancestors once lived here but because they used up the natural resources that the Archjarn once held," I said. "There is technology that would help the hills sprout trees once again. You could be the man who turned the Iron Hills green."

I could see the ideas begin to take root in Raislos's eyes but I also knew I needed to give him time to mull things over. "Think on it. I am more than willing to talk later if you wish."

A sneer half-curled his lip. "Yes, you must be in a hurry to return to your son in Lendurig."

The hair on the back of my neck stood up, shooting prickles down my spine until even my feet tingled. I marshalled a smile to hide my concern. "As a new mother, any time away from my child is difficult, but I thought it worth the absence to see if we could begin to build some trust."

Raislos's jaw clenched. He spun on his heel. The door banged against the wall as he threw it open, and Raislos marched from the room.

"Apparently not," I said to the empty room. But I had conducted enough negotiations over the years to know that my words would continue to ferment. Raislos would wonder if he was truly being cheated. The possibility of an Archjarn cloaked again in trees would stir in his mind.

The startled guard peered into the room. "Are you well, my queen?"

"Yes," I said, bringing a smile to my face. Tomorrow I would start the journey back to the Red Valley and the city where my son waited for me, leaving Aedenfal and the Cordair far behind.